FALLOW'S FINAL DUTY

CARL FAZIO

ISBN 978-1-952481-69-7

Library of Congress Information available upon request.

Printed in the United States of America

Within the hidden confines of Peter Fallow's poetic heart dwells this
unsung song:

My Final Duty
In the end, everything must go
Except for my tortured soul.
Upon my death, take my eyes and see
Harvest my heart and let yours beat
Have my carcass, whatever you need
But before I die, this I pledge indeed
I must destroy one of the greedy
So you remain free.

This novel is dedicated to the brave men and women who fought wars under the American flag to protect our sacred freedom and also to free others from their dictators. Their heroisms and sacrifices were given in the faith that their civilian leadership would protect and defend the United States Constitution with the same fidelity.

The characters in the novel who loved and served their country felt some of our nation's leaders have betrayed its constitutional oath and have set this nation on an intractable path of destruction.

INTRODUCTION

Protecting and defending the United States Constitution is an ongoing battle, which can only be won by an army of caring citizens who fight the war against greedy corporations and corrupt politicians right here in the Unites States. Millions of United States armed military cannot protect us when the enemies of our rights are here in our own Congress.

In fact, the greedy corporations are helpless without the willingness of our elected officials to accept their bribe money. In the miserable, dishonest exchanges between the two entities, it is the objectives of corporations to increase profits. They do what they must to place their interests in favorable positions. They hire lobbyists. Elected officials are supposed to protect the interests of the people. However, the people's representatives are deceitful and greedy, selling out their commitment of the people. Corporations, on the other hand, improve the conditions of only their shareholders.

When a soldier deserts his unit on the battlefield, he can be shot by a firing squad. Why aren't our elected officials held to the same standards? Why aren't congressmen who desert the people by selling out to the enemy also shot by a firing squad?

FOREWORD

The sole person American citizens historically most trust is their
president, regardless of any party affiliation. President George Bush,
with his cowboy demeanor and bold-faced lying to the people, broke
that trust by targeting Iraq as a sponsor of the terrorist attack on the
Trade Center's Twin Towers on September 1, 2001—all the while
knowing full well that wasn't true. Where was the outrage? Why
wasn't he brought to trial in a world court?

The reasons he provided to the American people for the invasion
of Iraq were later shown to be based upon untruths. Armed with
tailor-made intelligence designed to mislead the United Nations,
Congress, and the American people, he invaded the sovereign nation
of Iraq. A war that was started five years ago now may last longer
than World War II.

As of writing this, 4,000 American military personnel were killed
in that action. This misguided war cost American taxpayers $12
billion dollars a month, or $144 billion annually. That doesn't
include the $40 billion for the flawed intelligence. Thank you very
much. The betrayal and extravagance of this war is denying revenues
for the real needs of the American people: to defend its borders,

repair failing bridges, road, fix social security, and provide quality medical care for the growing millions of medically underinsured and the uncovered 45 million Americans. For all of these billions of dollars, what do we have? We have thousands of dead soldiers, thousands wounded for life, and thousands more dead Iraqis. The biggest result is we have a world community, which once looked to us for moral leadership, now hating us.

Based upon our knowledge that the Iraq war was falsely contrived, again, why isn't the President being charged with war crimes? Article one section eight of the constitution gives the power to declare war to Congress. So then, why aren't members of the Congressional leadership being impeached for the failure to obey and defend the constitution? They took an oath to obey and defend the constitution when they took office, didn't they?

While searching for the opprobrium concerning the abject hatred and division of the American people and their pernicious distrust of the administration, House, Senate, and judicial branches of our government, it's rather obvious when you look at the lobbying statistics. In the 1960s there were around 60 registered lobbyists in Washington, D.C. Today there are more than 5,000. There are nearly 10 lobbyists to every elected official. That fact alone explains the overwhelming congressmen have for the lobbyists' big corporate money and the growing irrelevance for the average American citizen. When you factor in the growing complicity and distrust of the corporate press, you'll further begin to realize that the first amendment of the constitution is in serious jeopardy. And without a free press, we are not a free nation.

The American people are hopelessly divided over issues such as abortion, gun control, unfair trade agreements, the Iraq war, and economy. All of these issues are met with an open and complacent political indifference. Our elected officials are conspicuously ignoring the middle class, and, without an open free press investigating and reporting the truth, the public doesn't stand a chance. Add a corporate press to the sold-out column and kiss the first amendment goodbye.

Hatred between Republicans and Democrats is creating a laceration between the parties that can no longer be sutured. Widespread despair over illegal immigration and a lack of governmental will to enforce our border laws have widened the people's mistrust. Most citizens understand that corporations own and control Congress to the extent that government of the people, by the people, for the people no longer exists. The people have become irrelevant. So much is broken, and we generally place blame upon corporate greed and political corruption, but we fail to see its personal greed as well, which prevents people from taking any proactive positions against governmental wrongdoings. The definition of a corporation is, "an artificial entity which has the same rights as a natural being." Therefore, you can't have an artificial existence held for its actions; however, all officers of the corporation are human beings who seek the legal shelter of a corporation. They are greedy and shouldn't be protected from criminal liability. Their personal greed subverts the implied intent of corporations.

With a corporate friendly government ignoring the collective interest of the people and the greater good of our democracy, the United States is being destroyed by the oath-takers. We have evolved into a society of greedy, territorial people who don't want to get involved in anything beyond their own comfort levels. "I got mine, so fuck you."

The question becomes this: Are we sure that the United States is rebellion proof and revolution impossible? Because we are a young, powerful, foolish nation bullying our people with corrupt indifferences, does this increase the possibilities of rebellion? For that reason, the following fictitious story is about a group of patriotic senior citizens who decided to dedicate their final days/years in a plot to permanently remove corrupt legislators from office. This story points out that our older, weaker senior citizens can become the most serious, powerful revolutionary catalysts to fear. Yes, it's true. The young with their whole lives ahead of them accepted death. Why not take out a perceived national enemy of the people while exiting? These patriotic men who would receive no medals for bravery or valor would become honored in their graves if honor were restored to the government.

 —Carl Fazio 2005

OUR FINAL DUTY

It's 2023. The population of the United States exceeds 300,000,000 with 299,990,000 of the citizens living in abject poverty. The army, navy, marines, and air force have all been deserted. Our piers and airports are abandoned. The commander in chief no longer has a military to command. The American flag, torn and tattered, flaps lifelessly against rusting staffs.

Our government, beleaguered in wars with the Arab nations, spent all of the United States treasury and depleted social security and Medicare trust funds fighting wars it couldn't win—leaving the treasury broke. While the Arab nations are now doing well supplying crude oil to China, most of the people in America live in unheated, substandard housing. Millions are homeless. Many are chronically sick, hungry, and so weak they lack the strength to cry.

The population of illegal Hispanics, paying no taxes in Texas, overwhelmed the budgets of education and healthcare to the extent that productive property owners could no longer sustain those government service programs.

With the continued growth of legal and illegal immigrants, the service institutions of government were forced to close their doors.

Following service institutionalized losses in Texas, massive emigration of the American born citizens took place, which resulted in a new ethnic majority. The new Hispanic majority seceded from the United States, and today the flag of Texas was replaced with the flag of Mexico.

Death from starvation is so widespread that crews with beat-up old push carts pick up dead bodies from streets and doorways and deliver them to disposal pits for mass cremation. Many of the bodies are of babies, children, and elderly, who were too weak to fight off starvation and disease. Skeletal people with depressed, sunken eyes wear soiled masks in an attempt to block the odor of death.

During the past decade, nothing was manufactured in the United States, not even military war materials, which were for the most part purchased from our potential enemies. Remnants of idle industrial buildings rise upon the dark horizon like ugly festered skin eruptions in a morbid state of decay.

Cities and boroughs everywhere are bankrupt. All public services are closed. Streets are rutted and potholed. Streetlights no longer light the night. The only light in all the darkness comes from scattered homeless campfires. Public water systems are closed, and raw sewage has returned to the streets.

In the interest of accelerating globalization and competitively participate in the world markets, America lost most of its manufacturing industries. During the past three decades, all manufacturing of goods was outsourced for lower wages. In the wake of outsourcing, meaningful employment was lost, and citizens were without incomes to pay taxes, purchase goods, or buy services.

Because living conditions are now better in Mexico—which now includes the former state of Texas—poor Americans are unable to immigrate into Mexico, because Mexico is strictly protecting its borders and enforcing its illegal immigration policies at the point of a gun. They have no objection to shooting Americans who attempt illegal entrance into their country.

China and Japan foreclosed their financial holding in the United

States. The cashing of all their bonds caused financial ruin for the U.S. government and its private institutions. Fast food restaurants, shopping malls, banks, hospitals, colleges, and government offices all closed. County governments are broke and unable to pay sheriffs to confiscate homes for unpaid taxes. Sheriffs are compensated by commissions from sales and fines, however they aren't able to resell foreclosed properties for the same reasons the original owners couldn't pay their mortgage and taxes.

Federal and state prisons, no longer being funded, were forced to fold, but most prisoners chose to stay in the prisons, bewildered by a reverse culture shock. Their cells felt safer than the chaos in the streets.

America's democracy and its capitalistic dream of a free global economy traded off the United States manufacturing jobs for the new age economy. Congress evolved into an auction house for corrupt corporate lobbyists selling out the American people. The theory was that the United States would become the world's leading marketing nation and its people the consumer of world produced goods. The sell-out phase for global marketing was so frenetic with grade to the extent that the reality of the concept was completely ignored. A simple fact was repressed: How can a nation of unemployed citizens maintain purchase power to consume those goods or services? How can unemployed citizens provide a tax base for its governmental institutions? And how can they feed the insatiable appetite of its military industrial complex?

The former United States of America is a wasteland in such a deplorable state of disunity and decay that it isn't even worthy of invasion. The only remaining assets were the sun rising in the morning and the moon and stars that still lit the skies over America.

The only exceptions to this sad state are the 10,000 American executive shareholders holding offshore bank accounts and the political crooks who led America to this abject state of misery, who now live elsewhere on the planet with their profits. They live in homes protected by barred windows and full-time security.

America is a bankrupt nation reduced to tragic poverty, sickness, and lawless misery. It's a nation destroyed by greed, not weapons of mass distraction. No mushroom cloud ever appeared. Could this have been avoided?

Peter Fallow and Joe Richards thought so. In 2003, this is what happened. Were they patriots, terrorists, or common criminals? You decide.

CHAPTER ONE

On Friday, September 11, 2005, Senator Smith, Republican of the great state of Nevada, was having his first bite of filet de sole when he began bleeding from his nose and mouth. His head crashed into his dinner plate, resulting in blood and tiny pieces skull draining from his head onto the fine china. The brain tissue, bone fragments, and blood comingled with his food.

Senator Smith was serving the last year of his third term in the Senate. At 69, he was planning to retire. He was 52 when he won the office in a very close race. Although he wasn't very popular in his own community, he had major financial backing from the Republican party, and he enjoyed the benefits of their deep pocket corporations. District newspapers were filled with pro-Smith political ads, usually showing photos of him with his family—the Republicans and their family value thing.

Rumors said that his wife, Sarah, wanted a divorce. TV segments were actually nauseating to the people who knew who he really was and that corrupt money had bought the office.

Locals hated Smith because of a large trucking depot he owned and his support for NAFTA. Imagine, the Teamsters union supported him. It was no secret he preferred hiring illegal immigrants to work the loading docks. Locals couldn't get those jobs because it was cheaper to hire illegals for less pay and no benefits. Local workers hated to hear from his office, "American workers don't want these jobs." It was such an insult to hard-working Americans.

Felony crimes were on the rise in Smith's district. The older generation remembered the town as peaceful and quiet, a place where anyone could go anywhere without fear of being attacked. You could leave the keys in your car and your home unlocked without the fear of burglaries. That all changed with illegal immigration and the lowering of wage standards, and everyone knew Smith was responsible.

Senator Smith didn't live in the community. He lived in a spacious ranch house outside Reno, where he employed low-wage, illegal, domestic help and had around-the-clock security.

It was no surprise to anyone that Senator Smith was a huge supporter of the President's proposed worker amnesty program, and he vigorously opposed any Senate bill that would tighten border security. Nevada's gaming commissioners were under his influence. Because his party controlled the administration and held majority in both Houses, he was solidly in position to remain in office.

Smith's decision to retire angered the administration, which jealously guarded every member of its party who held power. His retirement placed them at risk of losing control of his district as well as another seat in the Senate. The administration and RNC operatives constantly visited him, urging him to run again.

Nevertheless, the people in Smith's district would spit at his image and give him the passing finger. By him not running for re-election, he was turning on the party people who funded his campaign, got him elected, and put him in power—just as he betrayed the people in his district. It proves the old saying: Some people will fuck their own mother. Smith won't be missed by anyone.

It took several moments for the other patrons in the restaurant to realize Smith had been shot in the back of the head. The ambient environmental noises and the excitement going on in the room served the assassin well.

"He's been shot. Dear God, the man was shot." screamed one horrified old woman, who jumped to her feet, holding both of her hands to her cheeks.

As she continued to scream, another man reached over and slapped her across the face. The shocked woman stopped screaming.

"Good. Now shut the fuck up." said the man, softly and deliberately. "He was just a greedy politician."

"I saw an old man exiting the restaurant about the same time the Senator was shot," said someone in the crowd. "He was moving rather slowly. He didn't look back, as if he knew what had just happened."

"Good," the man who had slapped the old woman said. "I hope he gets away."

The Senator was later pronounced dead by the medical examiner, who was preparing the crime scene investigation. As in any homicide, a lead detective was soon on the scene.

It was a fabulous September evening. The city lights had been on just a short while when Detective Michael Walters backed his car out of his driveway and into traffic.

Yes. Oh yes, God is in his heaven. Right, right. Mike thought. *What I wouldn't do for a week of uninterrupted peace.*

As Mike sped toward the crime scene, he opened the driver's side window and placed the red police light on the roof to motivate any nuisance motorist out of the way. He breathed in the late summer air and felt exhilarated. He was on his way; he was needed. It was nighttime, and he felt very much alive. He always enjoyed this part of a pursuit. The practice of using the flashing light (often abused by egotistical police), served his purpose.

As Mike continued on, several more homicide call codes came in.

"I'm already responding to a homicide," he radioed back to HQ. "Call the others."

At age 52, Mike was a ruggedly handsome man blessed with a

six-foot tall, muscular, European-like body. His piercing, blue eyes were devastating to anyone he encountered, particularly the opposite sex.

Yet, despite Mike's great masculine looks, he was a calm mild-mannered person who never took advantage of people or of his position. In fact, he was a very modest, unintimidating man. He entered law enforcement at the age of 25 and currently has 27 years with the Washington, DC police department in the homicide division. He is regarded by his colleagues as a man's man and an ace investigator. If you were an infantry solider under fire, he's the kind of man you would want in your foxhole covering your back.

Mike got divorced 10 years ago, following seven grueling years of marriage. His divorce was caused by the usual problems plaguing his career law enforcement officers: neglecting his wife and too many nights away from home. His wife had grown weary and impatient of feeling second to the department. Mike's dedication and devotion to the job brought an irreconcilable end to their marriage. He tried explaining his plans for their future, but she became unreachable.

Because there were no children in the marriage, she felt she had no reason to place her physical and emotional needs on hold until he was able to retire. Mike also tired of her attacks on his career and reached a point where he visualized her out of his life. He always planned on retiring at 55, when his 30 years of service would provide him with a comfortable pension.

As a detective, he became a nocturnal creature whose loneliness caught up to him in the daytime. He felt that retirement would change all that, affording him the time to find a soul mate and enjoy the good life. He had a recurring vision of a goddess—a blurred vision without clarity. She was beautiful, and he hoped she was out there somewhere, waiting to rescue him from his loneliness.

At the moment, Mike's dedication to his department and career afforded him little opportunity for distractions, especially with the opposite sex. He knew he didn't want to be responsible for destroying another relationship or marriage, nor did he have the time to commit to another person.

Mike arrived at and secured the crime scene. Donning latex gloves, he asked, "Did you get all the photos?"

He gently lifted the Senator's head off the plate and into an upward position.

"The bullet entered the base of the Senator's head and exited just below his Adam's apple. It looks like a clean hit, doc." Mike said.

Holding back a smile, Mike looked rather amusedly at Dan Crook, the medical examiner. "Do you think he had any enemies?"

"Would about half the citizens of the county answer that?" Dan replied.

Mike signaled for the other detectives and uniformed officers in the restaurant to come over to him and asked, "Do you have any statements from witnesses?"

"Yes, sir. Every witness has been checked out," said a uniform.

"Okay," Mike said. "As usual, gentlemen, nothing is touched or moved until I approve. Is that clear?"

The others nodded, and Mike went back to work. He completed his crime scene inspection and told Dan, "Get back to me when you've completed the autopsy."

Prior to leaving, he instructed the officers to secure the scene and check with him before allowing anyone access, including the FBI.

Back at the station, Mike reviewed the report he had just finished writing: Friday, September 11, 2005. At 7:20 pm, Senator Smith of Nevada was shot dead.

An office telephone rang, sounding much louder than usual. *Amazing,* he thought, *even the phone sounds panicked.* He picked it up and gave his usual greeting. "Lo. Mike here, what's up?"

"The President is holding a press conference in an hour. Turn on your TV," Ben exclaimed. "The networks are in a frenzy."

Mike flipped on the television to see the President's face appear, pale and lined with stress. He relayed with condemnation the assassination of seven United States senators, all of whom had been killed at approximately the same time. The President described it as a massacre. The victims included Senator Smith of Nevada, hit while eating in a DC restaurant; Senator Goldberg, Republican of Florida, murdered while entering his apartment in the quiet section of the District of Colombia; Senator Terrence Riggs, Democrat of California, shot in the head while walking from the Capitol building toward his car; Senator Marty Collins, Republican of Wyoming, downed by a gunman in his DC hotel parking lot; Senator Richards, Republican of Michigan; Senator Loretta Sails, Democrat of New Jersey; and Senator Tommy Walters, Republican of Ohio—the latter three assassinated while meeting with a church group in Virginia.

As stern as the President could appear, he said, "I call upon the nation to lower all flags to half-staff. I vow to protect the rest of the Senate while flushing out the cause of this blood bath. This may very well be a plot to destabilize our nation enacted by foreign invaders. As such, I'm summoning all staff chiefs of the military into active status and ordering all cabinet members to report to the White House immediately."

His speech went on for 15 minutes and ended without taking questions from the press. Still, they asked anyway.

"Where was our intelligence, Mr. President?" members of the press shouted, accusation in their voices as he departed without answering.

Vice President Donald Chently made a brief announcement and requested that all US Senators avoid open public meetings, especially, any situations where groups of members gathered—such as where scheduled public events were to take place. "Temporarily, the Senate is suspending meeting until suitable, secure location can be arranged," Chently said.

"What caused this?" shouted the press. "What is going on?"

Not having any solid information to share with the media, the VP ignored the questions and made a hurried exit. He wiped the sweat from his bald head and thought to himself, *Those motherfuckers.*

Simple-minded bastards. How dare they think they could get away with this?

The networks went wild with speculations, ranging from single acts of terrorism to an internal rebellion somewhat like the peasants uprising in 13th century Europe—a rebellion that sprung up out of nowhere, yet was surprisingly well organized.

"Seven US Senators assassinated at the same time. What's wrong?" asked Kurt Maggio of MSNBC's evening show *Dirty Pool.* "What's broken? America. Will we ever be the same?"

Every imaginable political pundit was being interviewed on the competing networks.

CNN interrupted with breaking news: "A bulletin just in. An unidentified hooded man spoke on camera to a reporter, making an official statement from an organization he identified as Take Back America, a group who has been secretly recruiting political activists throughout the US."

The feed cut to the man.

"Our mission is to return the government back to the people from whom it was stolen." he explained. "Corruption is no longer a rare thing in our government. The majority of elected officials governing America are totally controlled by corporate lobbyists. We shamefully live in a country where honesty is punished, and dishonesty is lauded. It may already be too late, but we are committed to cutting the head off the venomous snake of corruption. In this nation today, with its sold-out governmental institutions, the people no longer have a voice. Their petitions are shrugged off by fake smiled politicians as they throw them into the wastebaskets."

With a stern, poignant resolve, he stated, "Today's assassinations are just the beginning. Irrevocable plans are now in effect that will take out seven known corrupt US Congressmen each and every day until the President resigns. US Senators and Congressmen are no longer for sale to Wall Street, pharmaceutical, petroleum, and war manufacturing entities nor all of the Jesus freaks and insurance corporations controlling our country. Greedy corporations in

America must get the message that they're out of business. The people will no longer tolerate the purchase of their Congress. Those power-crazed lunatics must not stand above the well being of our nation and its citizens—people without medical coverage, neglected homeless, hungry, chronically ill, unemployed, under employed, and all over-taxed.

"We have reached a deplorable level of Congressional misrepresentation in our country wherein the people are considered irrelevant. The election rate for incumbents is somewhere around 98 percent. Today, government by the people, for the people, and of the people is an illusion. In these United States of America, civic and political organizations re meeting in every square foot of our sovereignty, all perfunctorily pledging allegiance to our flag. Is it still applicable to pledge to one nation under God, with liberty and justice for all or would it be more accurate to pledge "one nation under corporate control with limitless profits for the greedy and fuck the needy. Wouldn't that be a more correct pledge during these times?

"Take Back America, TBA, has an alternative solution for getting those bastards out of office. We are well organized and unafraid of the consequence of death. You cannot stop us, but you can join us. If you demand that all elected officials give their bribe money back to greedy corporations, maybe it will bring back representation of the people and for the people. We call upon all citizens to purge the elected traitors from the hallowed halls of Congress. The general public has nothing to fear. They are not the targets we're going after."

The TV screens all went blank as the TBA man's feed was cut.

CHAPTER TWO

A platoon of Marine Special Forces surrounded the President as he entered the White House. An entire company of marines completely surrounded the grounds with armed riflemen tactically spaced on the roof.

Jets flew in squad formation throughout the DC skies, all jet pilots having been summoned to active duty at Dover Air Base. All pilots were in operation gear, ready to roll.

All roads within a half mile of the White House in every direction were sealed off. Only vital staff, chiefs, and cabinet-level members were allowed passage, and even they were required a military escort through the restricted zone.

Order to defend to the death against any intruders were issued. One caveat was that all efforts to capture intruders were to be employed prior to shooting to kill. The FBI felt that interrogating an intruder could possibly yield valuable information about the organization behind the assassinations.

The Secret Service whisked the First Lady to an undisclosed, secure location outside the District of Columbia. A highly professional female officer was assigned to watch over the First Lady as she slept. Because the President and First Lady had no children and all in-laws were deceased, there were no extended family members to protect.

At the District of Columbia police headquarters, Mike entered a room where the entire police complement of his district were gathered. Commissioner John Craig was presiding when he spotted Mike in the rear of the room.

"Mike, what information do you have on the bullet from Senator Smith?" Commissioner Craig asked. "Where are we with forensics?"

"Forget the fucking forensics in this case," Mike replied. "Did you hear the news? Seven, I'm telling you seven US Senators were assassinated, some right here in DC at the same time. Are we looking for a murderer or a lone assassin? I don't think so. We should start looking for an organized group with a large-scale plan to overthrow Congress. No routine murder investigation will solve this case. Commissioner, I suggest we start profiling the assassinated Senators to try to find out why they were selected as targets."

"Okay, I'll assign a team to you, Mike," the commissioner said. "But I want results fast. We don't know how far or fast this thing will spread. I want you to work closely with the FBI."

"Commissioner, I've always felt the same way about them that you do. Imagine the most sophisticated body of our nation denying in the existence of organized crime in America until that meeting in Appalachia. And don't forget the single bullet theory in the Kennedy assassination."

Commissioner Craig swiftly dismissed the group and called Mike to his office, walking past phones ringing off their hooks.

"Okay, Mike, give it to me straight," the commissioner said. "What the fuck is going on here?"

"My gut feeling is that this has been in the works for years. It was too well organized for any spontaneous eruption of anger or recent political opponents of an issue to have had this effect."

"Now look, Mike, I'll give you all the help and support you need, but I need your absolute loyalty to me. What I mean by that is that everything comes to me first. I don't want to be caught by the press with developments I know nothing about. If this organization makes another hit, our entire government could fall."

"Boss," Mike said, "you have my word."

"One more thing. I know I told you to work closely with the FBI, but I don't want you to *trust* them. Bring it to me first. I'm still not convinced they weren't involved with the Kennedy and King assassinations."

CHAPTER THREE

TWO YEARS EARLIER: AUGUST 30, 2003

Deep in the northeast coal fields of Pennsylvania, the sun was fading slowly on the western horizon. The city streetlights gradually turned, creating shadows between the tall, vacant buildings, softening the appearance of aging streets in the former business district of Hazleton, Pennsylvania.

The former bustling coal town was in its final stages of death. One could argue metaphorically the stages of a community's death are the same as an individual's. Nevertheless, homegrown poets and artists have the ineffable duty of rekindling the wonderful memories in the hearts of those former residents. The current residents of Hazleton meet in corner bars, living in denial and discussing their daily boilermakers.

The main streets are replete with empty department store buildings due to several decades of shopping mall developments. The once wealthy family that owned anchor retail stores and feeder retail business, which comprised the traditional commerce for the city unable to compete, had retired and closed their doors. Like dominoes falling, they would never open again. A once proud, bustling city commerce had come to an end. The proprietors and their commerce simply vanished. Except for some residual commuter and pedestrian traffic, nothing was moving in this town.

The declining signs of life pervaded the city. Sadly, very few city fathers could see that the city was actually dead. Nor could any of them predict the economic circumstances that would lead to the city's demise. Without any hope of resuscitation, traffic lights wait with long intervals at each intersection for people and motorists.

It was obvious to Peter Fallow that the past several decades of city leadership had missed the redevelopment boat. Without any doubt, many mini acts of political corruption contributed to its demise. And to some extent, just a plain lack of vision for the future was responsible.

Hazleton was famous for nothing special during its two centuries of existence except, perhaps, for its reputation of hard-working immigrants who made up the work force to labor in the coalmines and harvest anthracite coal, creating a new class of wealthy coal barons.

As darkness fell upon the tired old city, a crowd of former Masons gathered in the basement of the former Capital Theatre building. Although they had Masonic life in common, their gathering wasn't of a Masonic purpose, so no Masonic dialogue or symbols were allowed. The gathering was in the spirit of a constitutional right to free assembly.

A tall, rakish, gray-haired gentleman stood at the podium and broke the silence. In a slow, controlled voice and tone, he said, "All of you were invited here tonight because of some common qualities we possess. We are all citizens of this great nation. We are elderly and nearing infirmity. We do not have long to live. We are patriotic veterans who once served our great country. We have grandchildren who will inherit what is left of the nation we leave behind. We have accepted our inevitable fate of death, and we will have no fear of dying. We love our country for what it used to be and could be again, and if we could serve once again before we die, we would. And finally, my brothers, your selection is solidly based upon your reputation as men who lived in principles of a Masonic life. Your trust is well established and beyond question.

"Brothers," he continued, "if you care, and I know you do, and believe in the precepts I have thus far laid out and you want to hear more, I invite you to walk through that door behind me and be seated. If you feel uninspired at this time, I ask you to leave and forget this entire session. As former Masons, I rely upon your teachings and the oath of loyal acceptance and secrecy. You may now proceed into the next room or leave, as you wish."

Pete keenly observed from behind the podium as five of the invited guests got up and departed from the room. He paused for a long moment to reflect upon the long road, which had led him to this resolve. It began to feel like all of his thoughts were converging into a single thought, *veritas*—Latin for "truth." He wasn't thinking about truth in its general social applications, but rather self-truth. He drifted back to an old, reoccurring image of himself as a child sucking in the morning sunshine and feeling good about life. He felt the presence of God and the power of country. The feeling pleased him as he sensed a validation of an ineffable destiny, a spiritual commitment and assignment that was bestowed upon him was about to begin.

Now all governmental lies, betraying us, and getting us into an undeclared war with a sovereign nation led us to a serious mistrust of our elected officials in Washington, Peter thought. *A phony war with daily doses of misleading slogans fed to good honest Americans, such as, "support the troops." And further distract us with more phony pitches to reform Social Security. Hoping we're not intelligent enough to understand that the trust fund money was being squandered on the war. The hypocrites on the right and left who claim Jesus would be registered in their party will learn that Jesus wasn't a hypocrite or a liar. Tonight, I will initiate the process to deliver America back to the people. My choice of living a life as a Democrat, of loyalty to a party, and believing in social justice has been in a life with a sustained broken heart. All the years of despair, disappointment, and deception were without remedy. Freedom and equal opportunity were just slogans. When I was at functions and political rallies, I felt surrounded by insincerity and corruption. Pledging allegiance and saluting the flag became routine, empty acts of hypocrisy.*

Peter broke his meditation and shook himself back to the present task before him. He knew that once he walked through the door to address the waiting group, there could be no turning back. That door would open to a better future for the citizens of America, one where citizens could once again sing the "Star-Spangled Banner" with genuine pride.

Peter stood at the podium for the longest moment of his life, surveying the remaining guests. He estimated about 16 guests remained. The room was dimly lit, the silence intimidating, and every heart was surely pounding. Somehow, they all knew their final purpose was about to be revealed. Their duty and desire to right the wrongs of their government were now upon them. Peter, as he so often did, found himself thinking about the Boston Tea Party and the secret lodge meeting that preceded the event. He wondered, *What were they thinking as they planned their mission? Did they understand their deed would mark the beginning of freedom from tyranny?*

"Well, brothers, here we are," Peter said, quietly, with poised dignity.

The room went deadly silent. An electrifying moment filled the hearts and souls of every man present. It was both terrifying and exciting at the same time. A heightened sense of being entered every heart in the room.

Peter took a deep breath. "Gentlemen, since you and I fought in the wars defending our nation's freedom, the growing greed and corruption in our government have broken its promise to an open, honest representation for the people. With that realization, it becomes obvious that serving our country hasn't ended with our final duty as patriotic Americans. Each of you will now receive an oath, which will complete your purpose here in this great nation. Please raise your dominant hand and repeat after me."

He paused briefly, allowing them to absorb his words. "I, state your name, do hereby solemnly swear to sacrifice, with knowledge of my impending death, to the higher purpose of returning back to its people. I understand that America has been sold by the Congress of these United States to corporate interests, and we the people have lost freedom and democracy. I will accept the assignment to assassinate one corrupt elected official without question. In the event that I am captured, I will accept any measured punishment without revealing any part of this plot. I will accept a verdict of life or death with dignity, and as a patriot that sentence will become an honor conferred upon me in recognition of our high moral cause. I understand that this is a sacred mission, and it is my final duty to serve my country. God bless our cause to preserve our great nation."

A chorus of voices echoed back the words.

Peter went on to explain the oath they had just received, state their strategy, and reveal their tactics.

"Our entire project will be guided by the following plan," he started. "Phase one will require absolute secrecy of participants and of details by oath. Phase two will include the acquisition of necessary tools. Phase three will have the required training, and phase four will be the execution of assignments."

A moment passed, and Peter continued, "Gentleman, this meeting marks the beginning of the end of a corrupt America. Your contribution of your death to its cause is commendable beyond human understanding. I will honor you now so that you may have some time to share in the glory of your departure from life with the knowledge that you have fulfilled your destiny. You must come to realize the power of your life and what it means to those in your world to learn someday that you sacrificed your life for their freedom. In as much as you have accepted your oath and pledged loyalty to our cause, much work needs to be done by me and the leadership to establish a national network of assassin cells. You are blessed with a final purpose, go now and wait for your call."

The remaining men slowly filed out of the room.

Flipping off the light switch and closing the door behind him,

Peter entered the nocturnal street of the tired city and walked proudly toward Broad and Church streets. While standing at the corner, he realized the full impact of what he had just accomplished. He recalled the faces in the room and was pleased with the agreeable expressions of the new geriatric patriotic hit squad. He would contact his old friend Joe Richards immediately and begin the hard work of setting up a national meeting of leaders.

Tomorrow, he thought, *yes tomorrow. Braced by an army of men who have accepted their fate, I will greet the day with new energy and fight the war on corruption.*

Peter was a retired self-employed truck driver, who was about to turn 73 on the day after Christmas. Strangely, he didn't like Christmas. It reminded him too much of the poverty of his youth. In his opinion, Christmas was much more economic than spiritual. A faithful man, he resented the growing gap between God and man that had been forged by the dollar bill.

Everyone told Pete how good he looked, but he knew what was on the inside of his youthful appearance. Eight years ago, during his retirement physical, he learned about his high blood pressure. Last year, a stress test had revealed two nearly blocked arteries. The cardiologist stinted both arteries and informed him that bypass surgery wasn't too far off.

As Pete walked, he reflected on his childhood. His parent's landlord, a Tyrolean immigrant, told him a story once.

"In the olda country, I had-a this-a priest, and-a every Sunday he would-a preach without the need for money. When-a I comma to this country and whata you-a know the priest comma here, too. Now I go to the church and have-a the same priest as in the old-a country. Now every Sunday he ask-a for more and more money. I ask-a the priest after mass, 'Hey fatta, how a come God in the old-a country has a belly like a sardine and in a this country, God has a belly like a whale?'"

Pete understood what the long haul meant. During his 40 years on the road, he spent many hours chatting with other truckers on the

CB. Most conversations were political with solid opinions exchanged featuring growing anger over the sellout of Congress. Fair taxation, or lack thereof, was often discussed as well as their mutual desire for a straight, flat income tax. It was obvious that every working citizen paying a simple flat tax would eliminate all the corporate loopholes in the current system. The corruption of unfair taxation falls upon all levels of government.

Separation of church and state was another hot issue. Most of the truckers felt that God couldn't possibly be registered as a right-wing Republican fanatic, resulting in heated discussions. They felt God would walk into the polling place on the shoulders of all honorable votes without prejudice.

Pete recognized his status of an opinion leader, and he took it in stride. He was a smart man with a degree in the arts, though he'd never been able to settle on a professional field. He didn't care to be bossed by anyone, nor did he like to boss anyone else. As a young man, he despised bullies. His resentment of them evolved into a belief that abusive elected officials were bullies of the highest, worst caliber.

It was nearly midnight when Pete got Joe on the phone.

"Pete," Joe answered, "how the hell are you?"

Pete's mind was overwhelmed, and he flatly blurted out, "Storm clouds are gathering." The phrase was code for the plan, and it was all he could manage to say.

Joe was quiet for long moment before he said, "Thank God. I've waited years to hear those words."

"Joe, will you meet me in Los Angeles Monday night at 6 pm, two weeks from tonight? You know the place."

"Say no more."

"Just say you understand and will be there."

Without hesitation, Joe said, "I understand. See you then."

Thirty-five years ago, when Joe and Peter were entering their thirties, they owned rigs, had similar political philosophies, and shared the status of veteran. They understood dedication, hard work, and loyalty, but they also had a low tolerance for betrayal—and that's exactly what they felt Congress and the administration had done to the people of the United States.

The two men also bonded over their time in the Korean Conflict.

Conflict, Pete thought, hell, they didn't even call it a war. They referred to it as a "police action." A "fight but don't win" situation. If that isn't a betrayal to those who died believing they were fighting a war for freedom and democracy, I don't know what is. I can say with certainty that the Korean War (or conflict, as they say) marked the beginning of a corrupt America. General Douglas Macarthur was fired by President Truman for wanting to confront the real enemies in China and Moscow head on.

Ironically, both Peter and Joe were active Masons. As Masons, they studied American history and would often discuss revolutions such as the Boston Tea Party.

Their distrust of elected officials started when President John Kennedy was assassinated and with the wide-spread belief that the government had their hands in it. Too many unanswered questions remained. Martin Luther King Jr., a non-violent advocate for civil rights, was also assassinated suspiciously. Had his assassination been aided or plotted by the FBI? Vietnam, another phony political war, resulted in the death of more than 50,000 American military personnel. Nixon's Watergate happened, Reagan's Iran-Contra, and Bush's Iraq War. It was exactly that, too. *His* war.

On September 13, 2003, Peter landed in Los Angeles on time. Joe met him at the airport, holding up a sign with his name on it. They embraced, slapped each other's backs, and laughed about how they'd both changed since their last meeting.

Joe's hair had turned gray and was thinning, and cancer had robbed him of the once muscular body he proudly displayed. His piercing blue eyes had dimmed, with broken blood vessels dominating the whites of his eyes.

"You look great," Pete said, upon breaking apart from their embrace.

"Cut the shit," Joe balked. "You and I both know the truth."

They laughed.

"Okay, okay," Pete said, "we have a lot to talk about, so let's get out of here and get down to business."

Joe had lost his driver's license due to his illness, so they left the airport by taxicab. Joe instructed the cabbie to take them to an address in the business district of LA.

"Pete, let's get this thing going fast," Joe said as the cab wound its way through the streets. "I don't have long to go."

"I know, Joe," Pete said, "We will."

The cab pulled alongside the curb in front of an old gymnasium.

Well, this makes sense, Pete thought. *This is the place where he worked out during his youthful years.*

The old friends disembarked from the cab and walked into the gym. Inside, Joe guided Pete through the weights and workout sections, up a staircase, and into a grimy hall on the second floor. The hall once housed a boxing ring where young hopefuls trained. The whole place reeked of old, dry sweat.

We're living dead men criticizing the present because it doesn't have the qualities of the past, Pete thought. He tried rearranging that thought over in his mind, not quite understanding its meaning or accuracy. Then he looked at Joe, who appeared to be taking his own walk down memory lane. Pete he noticed a podium in the far corner of the room, standing resolutely, like it was awaiting a speaker.

Even that podium has life and duty, Pete thought.

Several feet away, an old, dusty banquet table seemed to be saying, "Me, too. I want people."

Oh, Lord Jesus, Pete thought, *you are the father of poetic sensitivity who has assigned purpose to the inanimate and animate as well. I hear you loud and clear.*

To Pete, the thrill of being proactive was more life-giving than oxygen and more orgasmic than sex. All those emotions and experiences were nothing compared to the feeling in his chest.

What life was worth living that ended without its meaning or purpose completed? Pete mused. *We will enter into eternity with "mission approved and complete" tagged on our souls.*

"Will this do for a meeting place?" Joe asked, breaking Pete's meditation.

"Absolutely," Pete said, "This will do just fine."

"Okay, great. I have access to a tap-proof phone, and nobody should bother us while we work."

"Do you have a list of trusted contacts?"

"Yes. They are dependable and can be trusted. All of them are Masons with a belief in its history. They all read *Born in Blood*."

"*Born in Blood?*" Pete repeated. "Never heard of it."

"It's a book that helps to pinpoint the origin of our Masonic institution," Joe explained. "It identifies the Knights Templar as its possible origin."

"I'll have to check it out when I have time."

The pair sat on a couple of badly maintained chairs and stretched their arms over their heads. Joe's laughter ended the tension of their long day. An aura of peace shrouded their space.

Time often softens and changes people, replacing their youthful philosophies with wisdom. Cautiously, both men were anxious to validate the theories they shared many years ago about honesty and commitment. Would they still be the same?

Joe and Pete spoke for several hours. They concluded that they were still solid in their commitment to return America back to a citizen-based government. Both of them liked the folksy style governor Jessie Ventura had given to the state of Minnesota — an "in your face" style to the phony, politically correct.

Joe lived alone. Although he was involved with a lot of women, he never found the time to marry. He worked hard and saved money, enough to buy an upscale home in the suburban area of LA. He lived rather well for a truck driver.

Joe insisted Pete stay with him this visit, and Pete knew there was no debating: That was that.

After all, Pete thought, *truck drivers are just as important members of our society as any damn politician. Why shouldn't they live just as comfortably?*

Joe hailed a cab to take them to his home. Once settled in, Pete sipped a scotch in the study room while Joe had seltzer water with a slice of lime. Pete reflected that it felt good to be with Joe once more in this rapidly fading life. They discussed more politics and religion. Joe was a freethinker all his life.

"I am deeply spiritual," Joe said when the topic turned to religion. "I love the mysterious aspects of creation, and I mean all of creation, including every star in every galaxy in the universe—not just the birth of an illegitimate child in Bethlehem more than 2,000 years ago. The oxygen we consume for life consumes us in death. I love life, and I love the God of Gods who created it. If that's what a freethinker or an atheist is, then I guess I'm one."

"I appreciate your views, Joe, you know I always did," Pete said.

"My baptism and confirmation as a Catholic were conferred upon me as a child, and as a child I had no say in the matter. I lived my life as a causal Catholic. That is to say, I received the sacraments as required by the church. They call Catholics like me 'C and E Catholics,' the Christmas and Easter types. But you know, Joe, I've been thinking a lot about the role religion plays in life, and I see how nations and men are manipulated by the church and theocratic governments. Both entities use religion to control the masses. In the name of religions through the centuries, millions of people have been slaughtered in the name of God. I look at the communist nations, and I understand that there is no place for God. Then I look at our democratic nations, and I see the ongoing fight to separate church from state, and I conclude there is no place for God in either form of government. Therefore, the only right and practical place for God is in our hearts. Since science has failed to prove the exclusivity of any religious origin, faith then becomes the key to all religious value in any single life. If you believe and have faith in that belief, then that's all that's necessary to validate your faith."

"Joe, could I have a refill?" Pete asked.

Laughingly, Joe replied, "You haven't changed a bit."

"Pete, do you remember when we were kids sitting in the field, talking about the stars and the wonders of the universe? You looked at me, and I never forgot what you said. You felt that only the elderly should fight wars because it didn't make sense to send kids and young men off to be killed in battle. Why not kill off the people who already lived a full life instead of those who are just beginning life and who are to become the future? It's breathtaking to recall that story. In some ways, I can still almost smell our youth."

"Joe, I felt that many times through the years," Pete said. "I think it's called nostalgia. You know what we are about to do here ironically may be a fulfillment of that philosophy. Think of it as the ultimate salvation of our beloved nation restored to its people by a small army of terminally ill seniors. We won't be young fanatics strapping dynamite on our bodies and killing innocent civilians to please Allah so we can receive seven virgins in heaven. Because of what we will do, the Americans of the future will receive the benefits of an uncorrupt and freer nation."

"Pete, I haven't felt this alive in decades."

"Wouldn't it be funny if we succeed and then suddenly are miraculously cured of our infirmities?"

"See you in the morning." Joe said as he retired to his room for a good night's sleep.

CHAPTER FOUR

SENATE REACTIONS

Senators everywhere scrambled for information on the assassinations of their colleagues. While in flight from Iraq to DC, Senator Robert Santo, Republican of Pennsylvania, on a secure phone line was frantically suggesting that those Senators all voted like him for the open border bill to Senator Anthony Sparker, also a Republican of Pennsylvania, "Tony, do you think it's because we refused to fund money and place our military on the southern borders?"

"I don't think we can face Pennsylvanians on this issue and delay action to prevent the influx of illegal immigrants."

"I am beginning to have complaints from mayors across the state," replied Senator Sparker

"I told you fucking guys over and over again that ignoring the erosion of decent jobs for our constituents would eventually lead to an uprising," Senator Santo said. "And I'm afraid it's beginning to happen. The manufacturers and contractors aren't the ones being assassinated, are they? You're right, Tony, what can we do to turn this around?"

"Well, I suggest we take a long look at who our contributors are and if in fact we have received monies from those lobbyists, then we should start correcting the record. We must attempt to distance ourselves from their influence if possible. I don't know what else to tell you, Bob."

"Good luck, I know it's a secure line, but in view of recent events, I don't have faith in much of anything. Hang up, Bob, and I'll see you at the location. Bye."

Senator Santo hung up the phone and turned his thoughts toward the war in Iraq. *What a Goddamn mess that prick in the White House got our party and this country into. He fucked all of us. He listened to that bloated, bastard Chently and his cronies, who could only think of one way to resolve our issues with Saddam: War, using terrorism as an appeal and lying to the people about having conclusive evidence that Saddam had weapons of mass destruction that would lead to a mushroom cloud over our nation. It was an absolute lie. Telling us that we would fight terrorism in Iraq or in our own streets was an extortion to gain approval for going to war with Iraq. At the same time, refusing to recognize our porous borders as a fundamental defense against terrorism was an even bigger mistake that every common citizen understood. Now we look like fools, and the chickens are coming home to roost. God willing, I'm going to put an end to this party loyalty shit of following the President just for the sake of keeping our party in power. It is absolute bullshit. We better start thinking country first.*

Senator Santo cranked the back of his seat as far back as it would go and settled in with the sound and rhythms of the flight. He always liked flying and felt as though the heavens were close and he was being cradled by the clouds. Laughing to himself, he thought, *There goes my hopes of running for President. Although I was on a fast track to the White House yesterday, today I'm on a fast run to distance myself from corporate corruption. As soon as I get to the office, I will review all my fund-raising records and see just how encumbered I am attached with the administration's corporate obligations. Thank God I'm not on a corporate jet.*

Being a Catholic, Santo blessed himself and asked God to help him through this situation. He admitted that he was scared.

The pilot announced, "This is your captain. We are one hour from New York's Kennedy Airport. Please watch for the seatbelt sign to appear at the front of the passenger section. Thank you for flying American."

CHAPTER FIVE

I t was 7 am in Los Angeles when Joe appeared in Pete's bedroom with an orange juice in one hand and a new toothbrush in the other.

"Everything else you will need is in the bathroom, down the hall on your left. See you in the kitchen when you're through grooming. It will be my pleasure to cook your breakfast. Anything you like I have, except scrapple that is."

Joe loved to feed his friends, but it had been a long time since he entertained anyone in his home. Cancer and chemo robbed him of the vigor he once had in abundance.

It's strange, he thought. *Once you're afflicted, everyone you know greets you with concern. And you start to resent it because what they're thinking is, 'I'm glad it's you and not me.' After a while, you get used to their insincerity. It seems they then gradually start avoiding you to repress feelings about the reality of their own inevitable death. Maybe they feel it's contagious. You become a person to avoid.*

Joe felt it was great having Pete with him once again. Their visit wouldn't be about his cancer or about pity. Today they would start to use all their brainpower to establish a network of key assassins to change the nation.

Pete came into the kitchen with a towel around his neck. His gray hair still wet, his hair appeared darker, making Pete look more youthful. He was smiling as he announced, "Two up and cremate the bacon. If you have whole wheat bread, toast it dark. And another one of those cold orange juices, please."

"Damn, Pete, it comes back to me now how you always got a rise out of the truck stop waitresses with that cremation order," Joe said.

During breakfast, the old friends discussed who would be their initial contacts for recruitment.

"Particularly," Pete said, "the most important operative we'll need is the one who will identify the list and order of targets. The person I have in mind is an avid follower of House and Senate bills and knows the voting records of each member of Congress. Do you remember Bill Rodgers from Ohio?"

"Yes," Joe replied, "It's all coming back to me how he took great pride in letting us know the significance of what was at stake."

"Okay, he's our first contact after breakfast. I suggest that we conduct our business at the office we agreed upon last night. We don't want any traces to our homes."

"You're right."

At 5 a.m. on the morning of Thursday, September 17, 2005, daylight was just hinting of its arrival in the east when a Greyhound bus stopped in front of a bus stop. George Stanton waited to hear the nostalgic sound of the bus door's air release, having always loved the sound bus doors make when opening. It took him back through his years of travel and the excitement of discovering new places.

This wasn't George's first trip to Tennessee. He had visited Memphis several times during his marketing career. At 76, he moved slowly toward the door of the bus to make his exit. Once safely on the sidewalk, he waited for the driver to unlock the belly hatch and get his luggage. Among the waiting passengers, he was as common as any elderly traveler would be. With his bags in hand, he entered the bus terminal and found a place to rest until full daybreak.

George rehearsed his plan over and over until his heart started to palpitate. No doubt about it, he was frightened, but not to the extent that he would change his mind and abort the mission. He thought about the past few retired years. He remembered his wife and how much they loved one another. He didn't feel he could talk to anyone about her because no one has time for old romantics. Lately he found himself crying at night when alone in the dark with his memories.

Watching old black-and-white movies was particularly emotional for him. He well understood that he was suffering from acute grief depression. Yet, somehow, he also knew his lonely tears were a justification for missing her so much, and he wouldn't give them up for any cure.

George pulled his one grandchild's photo out of his wallet. That immediately restored his desire to give that generation back the America he once knew—this once great country, which was gradually corrupted and stolen from the people through the years. Yes. Oh yes, he would do it. And those who knew him would understand and be proud.

At 9 am, George placed his bags in a locker, locked the door, and held the key. George looked at the key for a long moment before putting it into his pocket. He was informed that Congressman Buckles would be going to his district office for his morning audiences with his constituents. His plans were to go to his office and ask to see the congressman about a Medicare problem. Once in with the congressman, the mission George had accepted was to kill him by any means possible. He chose a 22-caliber pistol with a silencer. A well-placed bullet in the forehead should do it.

George laughed to himself as he thought about the one bullet. It would be dedicated to his stance on supporting the rising prices at the pumps. He might fire a second bullet as payback for Buckles's helping to support legislation enabling corporations to roll back pensions.

At exactly 9:55 am, George entered the congressman's office, and the secretary led him into the office in the rear of the room.

The congressman stood to shake his hand saying, "It's good to meet you Mr... ah, yeah, Mr..."

George helped by saying, "Stanton, George, Mr. Congressman. George Stanton."

As the congressman sat, he was distracted just long enough for George to get out his weapon and shoot him in the head as planned. With blood gushing from his forehead, Congressman Buckles stared at George in dazed disbelief then fell forward onto his desk. He was no doubt dead by the time his head hit the desk, so there was no need for a second bullet.

George was amazed at how calm he had suddenly become. The gunshot was muffled and didn't draw any immediate attention. Calmly, he walked out of the office, past the secretary, said thank you, and then exited onto the street where he heard a loud scream. Reflexively, he rushed down the street clutching his chest to control a sudden, horrible pain. Unable to breathe, George fell to the sidewalk. The last thing he heard in his life was someone screaming, "Call 911."

CNN BROKE FIRST WITH THE NEWS, "FOUR MEMBERS OF Congress were assassinated today in their district offices."

CNN was interrupted by a message from the White House.

"The President pledges to catch the persons or sponsor nation responsible for these recent attacks on our Senators and Congressmen," said the spokesman for the White House. "In view of the vastness of these assassinations, I am maintaining a high state of alert and closing all international airports until further notice. The President is also requesting anyone with information about these assassinations to come forward. He further reminds Americans of their civic and patriotic duty to assist their government and elected leaders in capturing those involved in this new form of terrorism."

CNN was back on the screen. "Well, there you have it from the White House," correspondent Bernie Shade said. "Our man Daniel Ritz is in Tennessee standing by to give us what he knows about the assassination of Congressman Edward Buckles. Dan, what can you tell us?"

"Bernie, behind me the congressman's office has been surrounded by police barriers to keep people away from the crime scene. Up the street you can see another cordoned-off area around the covered body of the potential assassin. The name is either unknown or they simply won't release it yet. What we know so far is that an elderly man entered the congressman's office requesting to see the congressman about healthcare related issues. The secretary allowed the man in to visit the congressman, and after a short time he departed the office, passing her by rather hurriedly. She was suspicious about the quick ending of the session and went in to inquire if everything was okay. That's when she observed the congressman's red bloody head on the desk."

"Dan, what can you tell us of the congressman?" Bernie continued. "What could have made him a target for assassination?"

"We'll have to research his record and recent activities to find that out, Bernie."

At that Bernie faced the camera. "Now, for details about the other assassinated congressmen. Early this morning New Jersey's Republican Congressman Todd Sherman was killed by a single shot to the heart hit while entering his office in Wrightstown. The area of his district office was replete with law enforcement teams from every imaginable department, yet no one saw the assassin or assassins. Obviously, it was a well-coordinated plan, which succeeded.

"Also this morning, Georgia Democratic Congressman Harold Dicks arrived at his office by his valet driver. While he was exiting the vehicle, a cracking noise, according to his driver, was heard, and the Congressman slumped to the ground with one hand still inside the passenger side floor of the vehicle. It was later determined he died from a single gunshot to his right temple. No capture of any assassin or any other details are available at this time.

"The fourth member of Congress assassinated today was a Democrat from Ohio. Carl Majors openly and arrogantly supported NAFTA and was pushing a bill to open up trade agreements with more South American nations. Plant closings in his district, with worker displacements and job losses, caused him a steady loss in popularity. He was hit in the same manner but didn't die quickly. He lived for an hour before expiring. Again, no details or identity of an assassin or assassins are available."

Bernie Shade finished reporting the identities of the assassinated congressmen and observed, "We are a divided nation at war with ourselves. Seven senators and four congressmen were murdered within three days. With the President's poll standings at an all-time low of 27 percent and Congress with a sustained poll standing by the American people at 25 percent, and falling, is there any wonder that we have come to this?"

In a sign-off editorial, Bernie said, "Can this 215-year-old great nation, with its cherished constitutional republic, continue to survive with a conspicuous disregard of its people? Is revolution becoming less theory and more reality?"

Outside the newsroom window, the skyline appeared static. It wasn't dark or bright, it simply was still. Bernie pondered the lack of calm or panic as a sign that nothing would change. Or, was it wishful thinking?

A cryptic message on a piece of crumbled paper came into the CNN office and was handed to Bernie. He looked at it for a brief moment, then looking deadly into the camera, he stated the contents of the note.

"A member of TBA will gladly speak to the American people, but these are the conditions: One, it will not be in your station. Two, you must dispatch a major member of your news staff to a secure location designated by us. Three, you will not ask questions and four, the session will be terminated if we observe your man/woman being followed. And finally, for you Mr. President, you must come to understand that we will not be deterred. We don't fear death. In many ways, you and Congress killed us by murdering our souls and the spirit of our American government of the people for the people and by the people years ago. CNN, please indicate your acceptance of these terms by stating 'okay' on the air."

Bernie looked off-stage and got a sign of agreement from his managers.

"Your terms are agreeable," he said. "We await your direction."

In a meeting with the Cabinet, the President pounded his fist on the table.

"Everyone in this room" he boomed, "and I mean everyone, I'm holding responsible for this mess. Since last Friday, I've been waiting for answers from all of you, and you've given me nothing. Nothing. Well, nothing except for another round of assassinations. God damn it, what a mess. Every fucking one of you, I'm walking out that door, and I'll be back in one hour. When I return, I want answers. No damn bullshit."

"Mr. President, the good news is that only four Congressmen were hit instead of the seven promised," the Secretary of State said.

"What's that supposed to mean? Should I feel grateful?"

"It simply means they had an organizational dysfunction. That's what it means."

"I see your point, but please for the sake of God don't repeat that to the media. I'll see all of you in an hour."

All members of congress were notified and ordered by their leadership to avoid any public meetings, particularly routine appointments in their district offices. The leaders promised that when the safety of our congressmen reaches a higher level, normal activities will resume.

Congressman Fairchild of Virginia objected and responded to the order stating, "We already look bad and have a poor standing with the people. This will make us look yellow, guilty, and afraid to face our constituents."

Congressman Michael Logan, a Democrat of Florida, said, "I agree with Fairchild. If we have nothing to hide, we have nothing to fear. Obviously, most of you senior House members do have a lot to fear because you've been hiding a lot from your constituents. And now your chickens are coming home for the roost. Not ours."

Logan was a first-term member of Congress and Fairchild was serving his second term. The leadership's directive held up solidly by both parties. No other congressmen were willing to talk with the media

MSNBC, CNN, FOX, and virtually every network manager contacted the administration and members of the Senate and House, begging them to come on live TV to discuss the assassinations. There were no takers.

The White House related that it would broadcast to the American people directly from the new war room when it has information to report. All significant staff of CNN was instructed to man their positions 24-7 until further notice. Bernie was in session with the station manager while they awaited instructions from the TBA.

"Steve, I know this type of news makes network stars, but this way doesn't make me happy." Bernie explained to Steven Perlman,

"Bernie, come off of it. Humility doesn't suit you. It's time for balls, and I know you got 'em."

"Steve, you were just out of high school when I made my bones with CNN. If it wasn't for your grandfather's influence, you'd be in the copy room delivering coffee and donuts. Enough of your office bullshit. How far are you willing to go with TBA's requests?"

"Just like them, Bernie, 'to the death'."

"Go for it. Yours or mine, Steve?"

The phones were ringing throughout the newsroom. The other networks wanted any tidbit of information on the meeting proposed by the organization.

Bernie was on the line speaking with Kurt Maggio of MSNBC. "Kurt, we'll release everything we have on this story as soon as proper. It will go out to the public and all media simultaneously. Did you manage to get anyone from Congress or the administration to appear on your show?"

"No Bernie, no luck at all. They're going to the trenches."

"Okay, Kurt, stay well."

Soft music was playing in the background as Bernie kicked back into his chair. His legs crossed with his feet up on the desk, he looked at his shoe and admired his wingtips. He thought about his life and Steve's arrogance.

"No damn way," he said to himself, "I made it on merit and that's it, merit."

He continued enjoying the music and decided to set in for the long haul. His eyes were getting too heavy to head home now.

Other than Steve maybe, Bernie was well liked by his CNN colleagues. And he liked them.

CHAPTER SIX

Mike was in the police station adding the new assassinations to his report. When he completed the updates, he entered Commissioner Craig's office and sat down.

"John, I don't know whether to shit or go blind, but I'll tell you one thing, I'm not overwhelmed with passion by their loss."

"Mike, please just give me what you have."

"Okay here are the facts: 11 elected officials were murdered. According to the TBA's promise, more should have been assassinated, and the shortfall indicates they had an organizational failure. An observer of the Smith hit stated that he "saw an elderly person exiting the scene." Couple that with the fact that Buckles's assassin had a coronary during his flight, and he was elderly. Is that a coincidence? I doubt it. I haven't had any interaction with the FBI. I suspect they are avoiding our jurisdiction, or they're completely lost. John, I think it's important for us to get the autopsy report of that dead assassin."

"I agree, Mike. I'll make arrangements for you to go to Memphis."

"Thanks, John."

. . .

"BERNIE. BERNIE. WAKE UP, THE TBA IS IN WITH INSTRUCTIONS."

Bernie rubbed his eyes open and looked up at Steve, who was shaking an envelope at him.

"Okay, Steve, let me read see it."

The envelope was sealed with tape, and the writing on the outside said, "To be opened only by Bernie."

Jesus. They want me and only me to meet their guy in a small village outside of Annapolis, Maryland, Bernie thought as he speed-read the letter. *I'm to be alone and without cameras. I could have a recorder to tape our conversation. I must not announce our meeting to anyone. And the time for the meeting is 10 am tomorrow. I will be contacted this evening with sequential directions that I must follow.*

Bernie handed the letter to Steve, explaining, "Steve, I will honor the TBA's requests. Doubtlessly, they could have selected another network to communicate their plans. So, let's not betray their confidence in getting this thing done. I don't want you to even hint at this on the next broadcast. Tell me right now you will respect my wishes on this matter."

"Okay, Bernie, you got it. Trust me."

Waiting was a vicious thing for a busy group of journalists. The station office was in desperate need of a good cleaning. Stale paper coffee cups and open pizza and donut boxes were strewn about. It smelled like an unaired room after 30 people had a bean-and-hot-dog party.

Bernie settled back into his chair and started the waiting process all over again. He thought about how he would question the man he would be meeting.

Question my ass. Bernie thought. *It's more like I will be given specific information and not allowed to question or editorialize anything. Whatever. Our job is to report the news—not make it. Shit I keep saying that, and it's beginning to sound like bullshit rhetoric.*

Marjorie Allen, Bernie's secretary, came in to sit with him for comfort as she often did, but he was never sure if it was for his or her benefit. She asked Bernie if he was nervous.

"Well, Marjorie Allen," with two first names as he always liked to kid with her, "You bet your butt I'm nervous. But you know what? I always felt we were in for a revolution. And I, too, am for change in our country. But I didn't want this kind of bloodshed. However, when you consider the slippery political slope this government has been on during the past 40 years, I'll ask you, is there any other way to restore our principles of democracy?"

"Do you want the short answer?"

"There is no short answer, only hope that our great nation of democracy and freedom will be here for our children and grandchildren. Stay awhile, Marge, I need the company."

"That's why I'm here, Bernie."

While Bernie and the staff were waiting for further TBA instructions, a fresh bulletin came in announcing that Congressman David Roberts, Democrat from the 12th district in Dayton, Ohio, was found dead in the basement of his home. Bernie was back on the air.

"Let's go to our man Sheldon in Dayton," Bernie announced. "Sheldon, what information do you have on the congressman's death?"

"So far, all we know is that his wife, Laura, found the dead congressman in their basement," Sheldon said. "He appeared to have hanged himself. But so far that hasn't been confirmed."

"Sheldon, please stand by for a follow up on developments," Bernie said to the camera. "Well, viewers, there you have it, Congressman Roberts found dead in the basement of his home by his wife, Laura. If confirmation comes that he was hanged, the question will be: Did he hang himself or was he hanged by someone else to give the appearance of suicide? In the meantime, links to the recent assassinations of 11 U.S. Senators are being investigated. What in the name of reason is going on?"

After stopping just a beat after that rhetorical question, Bernie continued, "Our correspondent in Washington, Hal Richards, is standing by with this report. Go ahead, Hal."

"Not much information is coming out of the White House at this time," Hal said. "Much is being speculated about Robert's Congressional record. Reportedly he accepted in excess of $200,000 from a lobbyist two years ago. Investigations are focusing upon any quid pro quo that may have resulted from that money. These questions will require answers: Was there a quid pro quo? What was it for? How many others were involved? Who supplied the money? There are many questions and few answers for us at this moment. I'm Hal Richards, reporting the news from Washington, D.C."

"Thank you, Hal," Bernie said. "We anxiously await your next report."

Over the next few days, editorials in all major newspapers screamed for investigations into the assassinations. A related story in a major newspaper revealed the names of all Senators and House members of both parties who were donating money they had received from lobbyists to their favorite charities. The implication was that by donating the lobbyist money, they thought they could cleanse themselves of the corruption the money implies. The article continued on to question whether or not the connection between the receiving lobbyist money actually leads to favorable votes for or against certain House or Senate Bills. This, of course, would determine the extent of and the intent of any corruption.

Media reports from Europe offered the consensus that, "We aren't surprised. A corrupt America has been obvious to Europeans for a long time. Americans are simply naïve. However, we have no doubt that the American public will rise to their traditional strength and correct whatever is wrong. They will do so with great introspective style, which will last for several years before returning to their insatiable appetite for greed."

Soon there were calls from both sides of the aisle for investigations into campaign finance rules. But many felt they are only lukewarm, conspicuously phony and lack commitment. Only lobbying without money, gifts, or favor should be allowed under the law, and with a ceiling limiting candidates for public office to spending a maximum amount of their own monies should also be established. This method would protect the rights of all the people and or groups to address their representatives and preserve the integrity of our constitution. All airwaves should be available with equal time for all the candidates for public office. (Not desirable for TV, radio, or newspapers of course) This would establish an opportunity for any underfunded candidates to compete with the extremely wealthy candidates who virtually buy the high offices of the land. What would it mean for America is this, "instead of candidates competing for special interest money, they would be forced to compete with ideas for the well-being of our beloved nation?"

What would Washington be like in an atmosphere free of any influence money? How would lawmakers respond to national needs without the special interests seeking their votes? Would lawmakers finally be able to vote on the merits of an issue? Would war products manufacturers really have to compete on a level playing field for contracts? Would pharmaceuticals be forced to supply their products in America at the same prices they supply to other nations? Would insurance companies be forced to pay claims without routine denials? These questions will be answered with the new generation of lawmakers in America. One can only envision and dream of what a clean uncorrupted legislature will bring to America.

One outraged caller on C-SPAN characterized, "These donation returns are somewhat like a policeman who accepts a bribe during a motor vehicle stop from an offender then allows the offender to continue on without issuing a citation. Should a policeman who later returns the bribe money be considered clean?"

CHAPTER SEVEN

Mike entered the morgue in Memphis, Tennessee. He spoke with the head of forensics, Linda Marshall, MD, a gorgeous, leggy woman with fiery red hair. Mike felt clumsy and stupid when he realized that he was staring at her and forgot why he was there.

"Detective, would you care to follow me and view the body of Mr. George Stanton?"

Oh, shit, Mike thought.

"Forgive me, doctor," he said. "Of course, lead the way."

Mike kept thinking, as he followed her through the corridors into the pathology room, *Goddamn, what I wouldn't do for a night in bed with her.*

From behind where he deliberately lagged slightly more than good manners called for, Mike admired her full length of reddish hair. Her ass seemed to be chiseled out of granite, with curves that cascaded to the back of her legs and met her calves in a delicious way. He visualized his tongue all over her legs and butt. He felt boyish and timid in her presence. He imagined fucking her from the rear, with drops of his semen rolling down the back of her legs.

If there's a God, she's gay, and I'll be free from the agony of wanting her body, Mike thought, laughingly.

Dr. Marshal turned and asked, "Are you okay, Detective?"

Standing alongside the table in the morgue, she pointed to the open thorax and particularly his heart. She stoically held the heart in her gloved hand and related, "Do you see how enlarged it is? Two of his coronary arteries received bypasses and three others have stents."

She replaced the heart back into the open chest cavity and directed Mike to his head. The skull had been removed. She called Mike's attention to several small plaques and tangles, explaining that the man had the onset of Alzheimer's disease. She then pointed to a small pea-shaped mass with small tentacles.

"This," she said, "is an incubating astrocytoma. Detective, this man succumbed to a coronary occlusion, more commonly known as a massive heart attack. However, it isn't likely that he could've lived more than a month even if he didn't subject himself to any recent added stress. I'll file a completed autopsy report, which will be available for officers of the court. I hope I have been helpful to you."

"Indeed you have, doctor. Thank you very much."

Mike thought to himself, *What could I do to keep this thing going with her?*

He thought he detected a hint of interest from her and wondered if she might be willing to have lunch with him, but he needed it to be issue related. If she suspected that he was physically attracted to her, she may coolly reject him.

Give it up Mike, you're asking for trouble you can't handle, he thought. *Yeah, yeah.*

Then he felt a rush in his penis that he hadn't felt in a long time, and he blurted out in a jerky voice, "Care for some lunch, doctor? Ah, strictly business that is. I would like to discuss this man's pre-mortem condition with you in a more pleasant environment."

"Of course, detective," Linda replied, coolly. "What other reason could there be for us to have lunch together? I'm not in the habit of having lunch with every detective who comes here for pathology reports."

Mike felt his anxiety subside. Her acceptance of his lunch invitation was a validation to his manhood. His unsteady unevenly pitched voice returned to normal. She didn't reject him. His confidence was back, and that made his day.

They walked together to a luncheonette two blocks from the hospital, which catered to hospital workers who had the typical one-half hour lunches. The place had a reputation for fast food with atypical quality.

Mike pulled out the chair for Linda to be seated. She thanked him as she sat down in the chair. Once again Mike was aroused by her solid feminine curves. She was one of the most attractive women he had ever met. He became aware that she'd noticed him staring, so he averted his gaze.

A waitress appeared and greeted the doctor with routine cordiality. She then introduced her guest as "Mike the detective from Washington, D.C."

Mike grinned and thought, *This won't be the easiest thing I've ever done in my life. But she's worth the effort.*

They both ordered diet sodas and the Tuesday lunch special on the menu. As Linda leaned backward in an attempt to remove her lab smock, Mike rushed to assist her. He got a topside view of her hair and the pleasant residual smell of her shampoo. God, he was hopelessly attracted to her since he was able to make physical contact with her by helping her with her smock. He liked it and knew he would be back in Memphis.

CHAPTER EIGHT

M ike arrived back in the District of Columbia earlier than he expected, the airport time was 9:20 am. He called Commissioner Craig and requested a meeting with him and the team, proudly following through as he promised in the beginning of the investigation.

John agreed and said, "I'll set up a meeting for 11:00 am. I hope you have something for us, Mike."

It was exactly 11:00 am when Mike entered the office where the commissioner and three junior detectives, two men and a woman, were waiting.

Mike took a pensive moment to look at each member of the team. He then moved an easel to the front of the room and wrote in large letters across the top, *NO FEAR OF DEATH.*

"Gentlemen and lady, that's what I suspect we're up against." Mike said. "The facts in this case so far are few but simple: Eleven US lawmakers were assassinated and one died in a suspicious suicide. In the Senator Smith case, the only witness in the restaurant stated that he observed an elderly man departing the room slowly and not looking back. I believe he didn't have to look back because he knew what had just happened because he had just *caused* it to happen.

"In the Smith case, we know the assassin was an elderly man named George Stanton. Were both Senators assassinated by elderly men? We know George Stanton did not have long to live. Could both assassins have been in the advanced stages of chronic illness? No clues about who assassinated the other lawmakers are currently available.

Mike pointed to the words he had written on the easel and said, "With what precious little we have to go on, I will tell you what's in my gut. I call your attention to that message on the chart, NO FEAR OF DEATH. That's what I think we're up against: elderly citizens who are going to die soon and have nothing to lose by becoming hit men. They no doubt feel their mission is patriotic and are willing to accept the consequence of their actions as duty to their God and country."

"For God's sake, Mike, do you realize what you're implying?" asked the commissioner. "Do you really believe that sick, old, maybe even senile conspirators are taking out elected officials?"

"History is replete with men whose principles are so intense that death is its own reward," Mike replied. "The Japanese had their kamikaze suicide bombers who dove their planes into enemy ships. Islamic fanatics have been sending young suicide bombers into civilian and military venues exploding themselves and killing the innocent for years. These people are willing to die instantly for their beliefs, often believing that it's God's will.

"I think that the assassins we're looking for have a sort of suicide pact." Mike concluded.

"Well, Mike, how do you think we should proceed?" asked the commissioner.

"I would like one member of this team to research Stanton and dig up everything they can about him, such as where he went to school, his religious affiliations, and any public or political institutions he belonged to, a general data base workup. I want another team member to do a workup on Congressman Buckles. The last team member and I will research and profile the other assassinated lawmakers."

"I agree, Mike."

Mike then gave the three team members their assignments and wished them luck. He went to his desk and sat down, placing his legs up on the side of the desk, thinking about writing his report of the autopsy summarizing everything he had just shared with the commissioner and his team.

His thoughts drifted to Linda. He just couldn't help wanting to run straight back to Memphis. And he then wondered if it was too soon to call her.

I wonder if she was impressed with me or thought I was clumsy and stupid, Mike looked at the phone and thought to himself. *I could use the company phone claiming it is part of my work detail.*

He grabbed the phone with the determination of a seasoned professional and dialed her number. "May I please speak with Dr. Marshall? Tell her it's Mike from the D.C. police department."

As he waited for her to pick up on the other line, he felt the anxiety building in his throat.

"Yes, detective," the same voice returned to the line. "Dr. Marshall is in conference presently and instructed me to have you call back tomorrow."

"Thank you."

Mike hung up and started the usual rationalization. *No way does she think of me romantically. It's me and me alone entertaining any physical attractions. Pull yourself together; she's just a cold fish and not interested in you anyway. That's it. I will treat her as an acquaintance in the same way she does me. Strictly business.*

Oh shit, I have no further business with her. I guess I won't have any need to call her tomorrow. Yeah, right, I'll be counting the hours. I need this lady in my life.

While Mike was staring into space, Commissioner Craig tapped him on the shoulders.

"Mike, are you okay?" the commissioner asked. "I hope this investigation isn't getting you down. Do you need a break?"

"No, John, I'm just a little tired from the travel—nothing a good night's sleep won't cure."

"Okay, Mike, and get yourself something to eat in the process," the commissioner urged. "You'll need all the energy you can get before this thing is over."

CHAPTER NINE

Bernie followed his instructions to the letter. Alone, he sat in an old diner in a small town several miles outside of Baltimore. As instructed, he wasn't wearing a suit, which might signal any locals that he was someone important. Instead, he wore a blue sweater, jeans, and sneakers. There were no cameras or any video equipment present.

Bernie was approached by a short, morbidly obese waitress whose uniform was badly soiled with yesterday's food stains and in need of desperate laundering.

"What would ya like, hon?" she asked.

"Just coffee for now, thank you."

As Mike sipped his coffee, another woman approached him.

"Are you here to meet somebody?" she asked.

"Why, yes, I am. Why do you ask?"

"Mister, if you will follow me, I'll help you locate your guest."

Bernie followed the lady through the kitchen and into a sort of pantry or entryway, where he was stopped and blindfolded. A man then instructed him to be patient.

"We can't afford taking any chances with you—or anyone in the media," the man said.

The man led Bernie down a flight of steps and through what he felt like was a tunnel. They walked for several hundred feet or so. Bernie stopped counting because he wanted to hone his senses on the surroundings. Suddenly he felt the fresh outside air entering his nostrils.

"Put him in the car," another man's voice commanded, and Bernie felt himself being shoved into the backseat. He heard the doors slam, and they drove off.

The driver never spoke, and it seemed to Bernie he was traveling in too many deliberate turns. About 15 minutes later, they came to a stop. Bernie was pulled out of the car then led into another building, down more steps, through a corridor, and into a room. Bernie was part-pushed, part-guided into a chair.

"Sit and wait," the driver said.

Before the man left the room, he removed Bernie's blindfold from behind so Bernie wouldn't see his face.

The room was obviously in a basement with solid structures. Bernie thought that he was in the lower level of an expensive home. The chair he was sitting in was very comfortable, and the material was of fine-quality leather. All the furnishings in the room were quality pieces, too. Along one wall was a series of built-in bookcases, filled with books. Bernie took a little comfort in the thought that at least he would be dealing with someone who would be well informed. There was another chair a few feet away from Bernie. As he waited the soft music coming through a speaker system helped him to relax.

"Are you comfortable?" inquired a man who entered the room. The man wore a one-piece, hooded jump suit, which concealed his entire body and covered his ankles. His shoes were completely covered with masking tape, and he wore a hat on top of the hood.

Holy shit, thought Bernie, *these people aren't taking any risks about their identity at all.*

"Why yes, yes, I am. Thank you, ah Mr. . . .?"

"Nice try, Bernard," said the man as he sat on the chair near Bernie. "Just forget the names, and we'll get on with the reason you're here. To answer what logically would be your first question, yes, we are responsible for the assassinations of the lawmakers. You may report to the nation that you have met with a representative of TBA, and we are admitting to the responsibility as I have stated. You must emphasize that no private citizens will be harmed.

"Our mission is to redirect our national leadership back to a government that respects the rights of the people recognized under our sacred Constitution," the man in the hood continued. "Specifically, we want the Congress of the United States of America to be taken off the auction table. You may now ask me any political question you need to—but nothing regarding our identity."

"Fair enough." Bernie said. "First, how shall I refer to you today and during my broadcasts?"

"As 'the man.' Just simply the man."

"Sir, I guess the first thing the public will want to know is why your organization is doing this."

"Let's begin with the concept of truth. How about government by the people, for the people, and with an informed citizenry? The framers of our Constitution developed it with participation of the citizenry and that was only possible by having an informed citizenry. Thomas Jefferson said something to the effect of "an informed citizenry is the key to the success of democracy." What then do we have today?

"What we have is an administration bought by big business, dedicated to sustaining itself in office and remaining in power. It's an administration that has lied to its people over and over again and has deceived us into fighting a war we never should have entered. Thousands of young men and women died fighting for a deliberately orchestrated phony war. And then the administration deceived us about the cost of the war—in money, injuries, and bodies.

"They told us the war would pay for itself when the oil production resumed," the man said. "The fact is: Before the war, oil production was two and a half million barrels a day, today it's one and a half million barrels a day. Yet Americans are paying twice as much for gas at the pumps along with shameful costs for heating their homes.

"Consider an administration that adds insult to injury by enacting a Patriot Act to frighten citizens into believing that the terrorists will get us in our homes and towns if we don't allow them to spy on its own people. We are a Constitutional nation with laws protecting our people from unlawful searches and seizure. We are a free people with redress of government, as far as I'm concerned if we allow this lying administration to proceed unchecked by the courts, then we have already lost to terrorism. What we fear most are the terrorists elected as our national leaders.

"Consider an administration, while spending billions on a phony war, ignores 43 million American who are without healthcare and children and elderly who go to bed every night hungry. Bernie, throw in lying to us about the deficit and mortgaging the future of our children. Our children won't be able to pay the bills.

"Medicare D, want to talk about that? What's that all about? Pharmaceutical companies basically who wrote the plans, which are now in a state of chaos. Add the fact that the member of Congress who pushed the bill has left office and is now working for the pharmaceutical company. The program is definitely not senior friendly. Here again, Congress betrayed the people and sold out to big business, and the special interests involved with pharmaceutical and insurance companies.

"Do you think we're told the truth?" the man in the hood continued. "The administration treats the public like children who are incapable of thinking. And therefore, they say they need to do the thinking for us. And they are getting away with it. Because they have the majority control in both legislative bodies, the House and Senate are representing only the party line. They spend most of their time running for re-election and raising campaign monies. In short, Congress no longer represents the people. Now, because right now the nation's administrative and legislative branches are under the control of one party, they have controlling appointment powers over the judicial branch and therefore the Supreme Court. Bernie, would you be willing to ask the average citizen this one question without your own edification: Do you trust this government? I'm willing to bet the answer would be an overwhelming no."

"I must ask you this basic question," interrupted Bernie. "Is your organization affiliated with Al Qaeda or the Taliban?"

"No. We are 100 percent Constitutional Americans with the primary interest of returning representative government back to our people."

"Are you or any members of your organization also members of any militias, racial hate groups, or Nazi movements?"

"No. Indeed, we are opposed to those organizations who in themselves are special interest movements. We do, however, respect their right to enjoy our first amendment. Again, we are seeking to give back true representation and freedom to our people. We are on a mission to get rid of the corrupt politicians whose greed for money and lust of power eclipse our freedom and are ruining our children's future.

"The saddest thing of all about the corruption and decay of political integrity in our nation is that it is being aided and abetted by the medias. Yes, Bernie, the media of which you are part. The media who are supposed to be the public watchdogs are corrupted by corporate greed as well because the TV networks and major newspapers have all fallen into the hands of corporate America. All you do now is pitch programming for ratings. You feed 10-second sound bites to the public. And then the talking heads interpret for the people what they have just heard. Like the government, the media believes that people aren't capable of thinking for themselves. You too, are culpable in helping the corruption of corporate America to prosper. Where are the investigative reports about price gouging at the pumps and in the pharmacies? Why aren't you shoving the facts down their greedy throats? When will the press become patriotic?"

"Fair enough, I get it." Bernie exclaimed, finally able to get a word in edgewise. "Do you think what you're doing will bring about the changes you want?"

"The only thing that matches the accumulation of power and greed is the shedding of the swine's blood. No change throughout the history of nations during the centuries has simply happened because the greedy felt guilty and decided to share their wealth. Bloody wars were fought. They were part of all revolutions. Yes, it will bring about the change we seek. I believe it's already begun. Many lawmakers are returning corruption money and denying any intent on their part of a quid pro quo. We feel it is our duty to remove these thugs from office. I also know that if people in the media like you say "enough is enough" and stop spoon-feeding lies to the public, it will happen much sooner. And with a lot less bloodshed. Once people know the truth, change will be inevitable."

"How long will you continue with these assassinations?"

"For as long as it takes, Bernie." the man answered. "When these self-serving career politicians come to understand that their lives and public careers are truly in jeopardy, they may suddenly spout wings and fly away."

"What do you have to gain personally? Are you the leader?"

"Our lives are essentially meaningless if we ignore wrongdoing and sit quietly by doing nothing. Our members have chosen to take action. We have dedicated ourselves to correcting the course our evil leadership has set our nation upon. What I have to gain personally is the self-satisfaction that I have done something to help our nation regain respect for our Constitution and personal freedom. I have fought in a war to protect our nation, but that fight didn't end when I came home. As a civilian, my patriotic duty continues. I am a voter and sentry of our rights. As a matter of fact, that is the answer each of our members would share with you, if asked. Am I the leader? No, I am not. However, I have been chosen for this detail because of my availability and knowledge."

"May I have a glass of water?" Bernie asked.

"Certainly, Bernie. We can do better than that. We could break for a little food to go with that water. And by the way, we can do better than water."

"Thanks, water will be fine." Bernie said. "But, yes, some food would be appreciated."

"I'll be back in an hour," the man said, then left the room, presumably to order the food and water for Bernie.

An hour later, the food and water arrived, and Bernie dined alone. As he slowly devoured his BLT, he thought about the way the interview was going and wondered if he was learning everything he was supposed to. Was he asking the right questions? What other questions should he be asking?

Shortly after Bernie finished eating, the man re-entered the room and sat across from Bernie. Bernie thought to himself that he was somehow being observed.

"Thank you very much; the sandwich was delicious," Bernie said

"You're very welcome."

"May I go now and relieve myself, sir?"

"Yes of course, over there behind that bookcase wall, you'll find a rest room."

"Thank you."

After Bernie returned, the interview resumed.

"Sir, does this place belong to you?" Bernie asked.

"Good try, Bernie. Now you and I both know that if I agreed that it was, and then you'd be able to place me within an hour of your base, wouldn't you?"

Bernie laughed along with the man. Bernie sensed that the interview was near its end, and he desperately searched his brain for that one concluding question.

"I have one final question for you, sir."

"What is your question?"

"Is there any room for a compromise solution, and are you or an agent of your membership willing to meet in a public forum to debate the issues you have presented?"

"The time for open debate is over," the man replied. "Words out of the mouths of politicians and the media talking heads are an insult to the average American citizen. We are willing to die for their removal, and they know who they are. As we said previously, no civilian citizen is in any danger. In fact, any citizen may help end this problem by standing up to lawmakers and demanding change in their fund-raising schemes. Now if you have no further questions, I will arrange for your return."

"Thank you for this interview," Bernie said. "Is it possible for us to have a follow-up interview in the near future?"

"That is entirely possible. When the situation requires, you will be notified. Thank you, Bernie."

Bernie's return to the pickup point was uneventful. They followed the same procedure in reverse. He drove slowly back to CNN headquarters, rehashing the interview as he drove. Balancing between reporting the news to the public without injecting his own feelings was going to be a challenge. His personal views were emerging with a great deal of ambivalence. He thought, *On one hand, these assassinations were tragic and should evoke public outrage. On the other hand, it makes sense that major changes, which are admittedly needed within our elected officials, can only be realized by drastic means. And no doubt about it, these are drastic means.*

Bernie continued to ponder this. *Is this a form of vigilantism? Should a responsible government and a public condone what's happening? Should the people and the press become a booster club for the cause?* He knew that he would need a pre-broadcast conference with a few history professors and Steve. Too much was at stake. Bernie thought this had to be well thought out before airtime. As he rolled along, he decided to run his tape recorders to make sure there were no electronic failures with the equipment. He did anticipate the possibility during preparation and had two tape recorders running simultaneously. Thank God both pieces of equipment functioned well.

Bernie thought to himself *this would be a good time to light up a cigarette and relax,* but he wasn't a smoker. He thought about how insignificant his need to relax was in contrast to the magnitude of this event. He pulled into his reserved parking spot and took a deep breath.

Bernie was leaning toward becoming a fan of the assassins. However, for the sake of protocol, he would have to appear objective. What the hell, he could do it. After all he'd done it many times through the years without detection. He rationalized that his colleagues in the business must also do it. How the hell could they not do it? It isn't possible to be stoically involved in all the worldly issues and not have opinions. He agreed with his reasoning and entered the building.

CHAPTER TEN

—————————

Pete and Joe had spent several days making telephone calls to all the William Rodgers they could find in listed in Dayton, Ohio. Finally, they located someone who told them that the William Rodgers they were looking for was living in a senior group home known as Serenity Acres. The person put them on hold while looking up the number of Serenity Acres.

It was September 21, 2003, when Joe and Pete rolled up in front of Serenity Acres in a rental car. The grounds and building were beautiful.

I wouldn't mind living in a place like this myself, Pete thought as they walked up the pathway to the entrance.

The receptionist was a pretty, little red head who looked like she was working her way through college.

"How can I help you?" she greeted them, cheerfully.

"Do you have a Mr. Rodgers residing here?"

"Oh yes, Mr. Rodgers is in room 14. It's on the second floor. Who may I ask is calling on Mr. Rodgers?"

"Tell him two of his oldest pals, Pete and Joe."

She placed a call to the charge nurse on the second floor and asked if Mr. Rodgers could be brought to the visiting area to visit with some old friends.

The charge nurse happily said, "I'll bring him right down."

"Gentlemen," the receptionist announced, "Mr. Rodgers will be down shortly. If you go over to the visiting area, it's over there beyond that glass door. Follow the hallway down to the canteen and it's just beyond there. Enjoy your visit."

Pete and Joe sat in the guest room, anxiously awaiting the arrival of their old pal Bill. About 20 minutes passed when he finally arrived in a wheelchair, Pete and Joe looked at one another, their eyes expressed much surprise. An escort nurse announced his presence as she stroked Bills hair back off his forehead. Bill was leaning toward his right side, and he held the wrist of his right arm with his left hand. He had a smile on his face as he ignored Joe's invitation for a handshake.

Pete broke in by saying, "Hello, Bill. Gee, it's great to see you."

Bill moaned, "Yeah, yeah, Mike. Yeah, yeah, Mike." He just kept on smiling.

It was clear to Pete and Joe that their old pal who didn't recognize them was suffering from some sort of brain disease. They stayed with Bill for 20 minutes and tried to help restore his memory of their friendship—without success. Frustrated, they called for the nurse and said they had finished their visit. When she arrived, they noticed that Bill had had a urinary accident, and they shared that with the nurse. They waved goodbye to Bill, who was still smiling as the nurse rolled him away.

"We really need to kick this project up a notch," Pete said to Joe, under his breath.

Outside, while walking to the parking lot, they looked back at the institution and made a reverent comment to their old friend.

Pete said, "Bye, old pal, enjoy whatever is left of your ability to dream."

Pete drove Joe home. In Joe's living room, they rehashed their experience with Bill Rodgers.

"We need to revise our tactics," Joe reminded Pete. "We need a new person to help coordinate targets."

Pete nodded in agreement. "You know Joe, I have now come to realize that only the young can dream of a tomorrow. But it will take old people like us who are living those tomorrows we once dreamed of to help the dreams of our youth to be realized."

They looked at one another and shook hands.

"When I get back home, Joe, we'll search for a new coordinator."

"Okay, back to the drawing board," Joe replied.

It was a beautiful day in LA.

Joe woke Pete up and said, "Okay, my boy, it's time to rise and shine. We have a lot of work to get done and not much time to do it."

"What time is it?"

"It's 8:30 am and absolutely beautiful," Joe replied. "The sun is shining. Let's hit the bacon and eggs."

"Okay, be with you in a minute."

Joe already had breakfast on the table when Pete sat down. "Pete, I was up most of the night thinking about replacing Rodgers. It came to me that we really don't need a coordinator in the way that we were originally thinking. Why don't we start contacting and organizing as many of our old likeminded friends as we can?"

"I think you're right. But we must be careful how we approach these guys. Then will each of them organize their own network of geriatric assassins?"

"That's right, Pete. Let's start a list on paper, but then we'll research them on the Internet. We can't assume these guys are still living, and if they are living that they are capable of carrying out the act of a principled assassin, meaning they still have the same feelings about our government screwing everyone as they did during our more viable years. Rodgers taught us that fact."

"Jesus, we have a lot to consider, don't we?"

"Yes, but we'll stay positive and keep on moving."

"Okay, I agree. Pete, how should we assemble these guys for orientation?"

"We must factor in the economics and logistics of their participation," Pete answered. "If they don't have the means or ability to travel, we may have to pool our resources. If they are willing to act, we should be willing to help them in any way we can."

Three days later, Joe and Pete had completed their list of potential members, having worked day and night to finalize their list. Now the real work of making contacts would begin. They identified 22 old friends who they believed were fair possibilities. The 22 were divided evenly between Joe and Pete to make the initial contacts. It was 4 pm, and they decided to break for dinner and start calling later that evening.

The Powder Keg, a pub where Joe liked to go once in a while, was packed. But he was lucky enough to find a table in the rear of the dining room. Joe always liked the place because it had good food and easy listening music.

"This is a great looking place," Pete said. "I could get used to it quickly."

"Glad you like it, Pete. I'm hoping we can have a little fun before going back to work."

"Hey, Joe. Good to see yah. How the hell are you, and who's your friend?" inquired a big, brawny waiter.

"Not too bad, and you, Larry? This is my old pal Pete. We're looking for a few drinks and something to eat, can you handle it?"

"Can we handle it? You know you're in the right place. I'll have the waitress get your orders. The first drink is on me."

Two large cold mugs of beer and bourbon chasers were placed on the table, "Compliments of the house," she stated while placing her pencil on the order pad. "Our special tonight is a 16-ounce Strip Steak prepared to your liking."

Pete and Joe looked at one another and Joe asked, "Do you think we could handle something that big?" They both laughed, and the waitress assured them that two big guys like them could handle them easily.

"Well, I don't know about you, Joe, but I'm game," Pete said. "Bring it on. I'll have mine Pittsburgh blackened."

"What the hell is that, Pete?"

"It's seasoned and seared on both sides with high heat so the juices are locked in."

"Mother of God, that sounds delicious. I'll have mine the same way as his," Joe said to the waitress.

To their surprise both of them cleaned up the steaks, leaving nothing for doggy bags. Pete downed his beer and the bourbon while eating and was feeling a little buzz. Joe, still sipping on his drinks, called the waitress for another round of drinks.

"Tell Larry to have his usual on me," he added.

Pete looked at Joe for a long savoring moment, then asked him if he was comfortable with what they were undertaking.

"God damn, Pete, you know that I am. Why the hell are you asking me now?"

"I know you are, Joe, but I guess in many ways this may be the last time you and I will have to just sit, relax, and share our thoughts with one another. Maybe I'm being a little nostalgic, thinking about how we used to have long conversations about life and politics. I missed them through the years. And I guess I'm also hoping that we aren't just compensating in some psychological way for the years in between when we were out of touch."

"No, Pete. I understand what you're saying, and I also miss those times when we had a few drinks and shared our thoughts. As for the seriousness of our mission, I am more determined than ever to see it through. We are doing something that will create a temporary shock to the nation. But when all the smoke clears and the positive changes emerge, historians will discover the purity of our motives. I am ready and still able, and because of that I want to get it on. More than everything else that motivates us, it's the prospect of ending a time when our people sit back and never complain. Instead, we've taken action. I'm for any action that gets the corrupt sons of bitches out of office and returns honesty to government. And if that's naive, so be it. But I simply don't give a shit. It's worth giving my life for, well, what's left of it."

Pete reached over and placed his hand on the back of Joe's neck and pulled him close—until their eyes were several inches away from each other.

"Joe, you old bastard, I love yah. I never had a brother or anyone other than you to share the big and little things of life with. If ever I needed to count on someone, I always knew it was you. Now before we finish our drinks and get back to business at the ranch, I have one more question for you. Is there any Scotch left at the house?"

"Plenty. Let's get going."

"Okay, Joe, we're out of here."

They split the tab and left a generous tip for the waitress. Larry yelled to them as they were leaving, "Hey Joe, don't be a stranger. I need the money for a new roof."

Pete and Joe vowed to Larry that it wouldn't be too long.

"The steaks were great." he added.

That night they worked until 2 am. The contacts were all made. Of the 22 names on the list, they managed to have positive results with 12. They spent the rest of the week setting up a meeting with all of the prospects and through the general goals presentation recruited every one of them as members.

In October, they concluded the organizational part of the strategy and allowed each member to establish his own team. When they had their individual teams in place, the members were instructed to contact Pete and Joe, who soon became known to the group as "the fathers."

Within one month, all cell leaders responded with positive results. All would await signals to initiate the plans. Pete and Joe established their own mini-cells, so they now had a combined total of 14 revolutionary cells. The states now represented by the organization were: Alabama, Florida, Massachusetts, Nevada, Texas,

Missouri, Oregon, Wyoming, Utah, Mississippi, New York, New Jersey, Pennsylvania, and California. The mix between red and blue states was just about right, Pete and Joe thought, and they both were satisfied with the logistics of their plan and felt any expansion of states would increase the risk of exposure and betrayal. That then was it; they were on their way toward the final phases and execution.

On October 25, 2003, Pete decided to wind up his mission in LA. He and Joe had their final parting moment in the airport.

"Joe, if I have a tear in my eye, you'll understand that I know I'll never see you again." Pete said. "You have been my family and my friend, and as far as I'm concerned if you have either in life, you had the essence of life. If there is a life in the hereafter, it will be worth dying for to get there."

"Goodbye, old pal, and good luck."

As Pete walked toward the security screening, Joe yelled to him a choking voice, "See yah up there, Pete."

Joe wiped the tears from his eyes and walked back to the taxi stand. He thought to himself, *I love that guy*.

CHAPTER ELEVEN

September 21, 2005, Bernie was live on CNN with results of his interview with the TBA representative. He opened by stating the facts leading up to his interview and the conditional limitations he was bound with in accepting the clandestine interview.

"In order to honor the meeting requirements, this station and I have agreed to the conditions. I will now air the taped conversation I had with the TBA representative. The tape, which is about one hour long, will be aired uninterrupted by commercial or edification. Following the tape, there will be no attempts to explain the intent of the participants. At this time, neither this station nor I will attempt to answer questions. A program exclusively dedicated to caller comments will be scheduled for a later date. The complete unedited tape will begin right after this commercial announcement."

As the tape ran, Bernie went into conference with his staff and station managers. Presently all felt that their approach to the airing of the tape without edification was absolutely the appropriate approach, particularly with the safety of so many at stake.

The question now becomes, thought Bernie, *how to bring about a balance of news reporting and achieve the nagging thing of conscience and duty to the station and the people.* He knew that would be the thing that would ultimately require his and his decision alone. He was still troubled by the dynamics of conscience and duty.

While Bernie explained all of that to everyone in the room, he observed Steve's demeanor. It was evident that Steve didn't give a fuck about conscience. He wanted the station to have all of the advantages of the breaking news. That's all he cared about. The others were mixed but soft in their opinions because they didn't want to cross Bernie or Steve. The bottom line was that Bernie would decide his program content. However, everyone was on board with the upcoming question program being free of host interpretation. Theirs would be the only network with that program format.

Bernie later spoke with Tom Russell, host of the popular Sunday morning show, *Address the Nation.* Russell said he was working with contacts in the House and Senate to appear live this coming Sunday. He felt certain that he would get someone, but wasn't sure at this time who it would be.

Bernie also spoke with Kurt Maggio, host of MSNBC's evening show *Dirty Pool.* Maggio was begging lawmakers and key administration officials to come on his show. He was confident he could get a member of the former administration to come on the air with him and summarize what was happening. He had plenty of newspaper and magazine editors readily agree to come on his shows and share their opinions, but he needed experts.

Bernie shared that it would be better active-duty generals give their assessments, not lawmakers. Bernie, however, felt strongly that the military shouldn't be involved in the situation. The TBA representative stated during both interviews that no citizen would be in danger. He was concerned the military would approach this situation as an act of terrorism.

"No, Kurt," Bernie explained. "This might be domestic terrorism, but only the elected lawmakers and administration are the declared targets. Jesus. This has all the ingredients of domestic terrorism and a revolution combined."

Kurt thanked Bernie for his help and thoughts.

"Good luck, Kurt."

"Good luck to you, too, Bernie."

Bernie heard from the other popular news show hosts as well. They all shared the same general feelings.

"It's coffee time," Bernie shouted loudly enough for Marjorie to hear. He knew she would bring him a fresh cup of coffee. It wasn't just the coffee he wanted, but also her company because she had just the right temperament to keep him focused. Though they had a past too. Years ago, when they first met at the station, their mutual attraction resulted in them sleeping together and enjoying sensual exploratory sex. To avoid risking their careers and public criticism, they agreed to stop their sexual relationship. But they did continue being friends.

Marjorie stood in front of Bernie with the steam moving up from the coffee. He could smell the hazelnut aroma. She also held a plate bearing a large, sumptuous-looking cream donut.

"Please have a seat, Marge. Thank you for the coffee," Bernie said, thinking, *This is the life I like. All is well for the moment.*

He kicked back and closed his eyes. Marge was used to it, so she waited till he fell asleep before going back to her desk.

Thank God for Bernie, she thought, as she started to pull up the story on the computer.

CHAPTER TWELVE

Thomas Russell, host of NBC's Sunday morning show *Address the Nation*, was facing his guest, Senator Laura Lowell of New York. Thomas introduced his guest and announced that she would be on the show for the entire hour.

"Welcome to our show," Thomas addressed Senator Lowell. "And, may I say, particularly during these dangerous times for elected officials, welcome."

"Thank you for inviting me here today," Senator Lowell said agreeably. "I'll try to earn my pay."

"Senator, as you are aware, the nation's lawmakers have been somewhat underground since Friday, September 11th, when seven United States Senators were assassinated. And on September 17th, just six days later, four members of Congress were also assassinated. A total of 11 U.S. lawmakers. How has that affected you personally?"

"Well, first of all, let me express my sympathies to the families who suffered these losses, and also to our nation as a whole, which is in a state of national mourning. To all of you, I mourn with you. Personally, I will remain actively engaged with my constituents as a United States Senator. As for the Senators being underground for their own safety, and for the safety of the nation, the Vice President has scheduled Senate activities to be held in undisclosed locations until further notice. I hope that will not last too long, because we are an open government."

"As you know, Senator, following the deadly attacks on our lawmakers, a hooded representative of Take Back America appeared on CNN, taking responsibility for the assassinations. He proclaimed that the US Congress is bought and paid for by corporate America, and that our lawmakers no longer represent the people. Is this true? Is Congress bought and paid for?"

"It is indeed." Senator Lowell exclaimed. "Special interests conspicuously control some members on both sides of the aisle in both the House and Senate. I agree with the perceptions of the general public—who aren't too close to the trees to see the whole forest. Consider the exposures in recent years showing the public how war products and defense contracts were awarded to the Carlisle Group, Enron, and Halliburton Corporations, without open bidding. Couple that with the results corporate lobbyists are having in healthcare legislation. All this creates a credibility problem for the both Congress and the administration. Yes, I do believe the people are being under-represented by their elected officials, while corporate America is given special treatment."

"Senator, are *you* bought and paid for by corporate interest?"

"My financial records are clean and open for any inspection the public may require. I have accepted corporate quid pro quo monies, and I will not in the future. I advocate in the best interest of the nation and people."

"Senator, TBA explained that their irrevocable plans to assassinate lawmakers is well organized and will continue until the President resigns and all Congressmen return their corporate bribe monies. Do you think the President will resign? Will any Congressional bribe money be returned?"

"It would not be in our best interest of our nation for our President to resign under this type of threat. Instead, I feel strongly that our President should call for a blue ribbon independent investigation immediately. If in fact he has benefitted from funding that influenced his leadership, he should contritely admit any culpability. I believe this could start a healing process by demonstrating top-down examples.

"As for individual legislators, they must start returning any special interest monies that compromised their representation in Congress," the Senator continued. "If the administration and Congress are to regain the trust and confidence of the people, this cleansing action must be taken. Now I'd like to make a public appeal to TBA: Stop the bloodshed and allow those of us who aren't corrupt to pursue the changes in government you seek."

"Senator, should this cleansing process include giving up gifts, meals, and air travel perks provided for by corporate jets?"

"Yes, I believe all of these practices must be reformed," the Senator said. "More transparency is needed in any reform measure that is presented for legislation. These issues obviously negatively affect the public's perception of our lawmakers. No elected official should be in Switzerland playing gold, wining, and dining on a corporation's dime. Nothing of that nature should occur, period."

"Are there any exceptions?" Thomas asked.

"No, I don't think so. If any elected official desires a golfing vacation in Switzerland, then he or she should pay for it out of their own finances—not corporation money or campaign funds."

"Well, Senator, what about gifts and meals? What is the solution for that?"

"Sometimes elected officials are requested to be guest speakers at organizational meetings, such as the Lions club and the YMCA. As you know very often meals are served at these events. It's common to present guest speakers with token gifts, such as hats, t-shirts, and plaques. The acceptance of these meals and token gifts is okay. In fact, it would be ungracious to reject the token gestures of these organizations.

"Along the same lines, when a lawmaker visits with foreign leaders, the refusal of symbolic gifts may be considered an insult and bad for foreign relations. I don't believe the general public is offended by accepting this type of gift. But we need to mandate for change and eliminate the influence corporate money has on elected officials. I will work hard with my colleagues to pass reform legislation."

"Is it fair to say to your constituents that you haven't inappropriately accepted free meals or gifts as a reason for your vote?"

"Yes, it is fair to say that," Senator Lowell asserted. "I do have an impressive collection of hats from all the New York ball clubs, including Little League. When I travel abroad, I do it on commercial airlines."

"Let's look at another matter concerning people across the United States over the past two years: the rising costs of gas and heating fuel. What is causing that? What is our government doing about it?"

"I understand the concerns of our people, particularly those of lower and middle incomes who are among the hardest working people in our nation. Secondly, our elderly on fixed incomes are often faced with the budgetary conflict choosing between food, fuel, or medicines. All of us in government must join together and change our dependency on the oil we have grown to devour. Thankfully hearings have finally begun, but it isn't good enough just to reveal the causes of these increases. We must explore new sources of energy to reduce our dependency on foreign oil. I am convinced that the end results will tell us that the quick increases in fuel pricing were largely based on greed for quarterly profits. As we all now know the petroleum corporations are posting their largest margins of profit in their history. How can this be accepted by the public as refining incapacity problems, increased demand, low supply, depleting resources, and market competition? Their record posted profits destroy those claims.

"Continuing on the subject of oil supply, Tom, I feel that our growing reliance upon oil from the Arab nations is clouding our policies and leadership position in the world community. It's turning us into hypocrites despised by the world. We proclaimed that a country rich in oil has weapons of mass destruction, and for that reason we invaded their country, destroyed their infrastructures, captured their leader, and set up an occupation. When all post invasion evidence showed no evidence for the pre-attack claims, the whole world knew it was about oil.

"This administration's foreign policy of aggression is incongruous with our democratic principles of peace, freedom, and human dignity. I maintain that a full throttle research and development initiative for alternative sources of cleaner energy is the answer."

"Senator, the TBA spokesperson stated that because members of Congress are for sale, the people have become irrelevant," Thomas said. "Are they correct?"

"Many members of both houses are not corrupted by the system, and your broad stroking could unjustly implicate the entire body. I sympathize with the anger and mood of the people, but I call upon the public to evaluate that claim on an individual basis. I agree that our image has been damaged by the acceptance of quid pro quo monies, but that being said I can tell you that some of us do get it.

"Mr. Russell, I'd like to extend an invitation to TBA to meet in a forum of their choice to discuss their issues. However, that invitation must not be construed as a promise of amnesty. They have committed felonies, which will require prosecution. Any consideration for amnesty or forgiveness would be the jurisdiction of our President."

"Senator, time is running out for this program, so I want to give you the opportunity to share with America your plans for the future. Do they include a run for the presidency?"

"I am grateful to you for giving me this opportunity," Senator Lowell said, smiling. "To answer the first part, I want to let my constituents know that I will continue to work hard to make America the best it can be. I will work toward campaign finance reform, health care for all citizens, better employment opportunities, and world peace. My hope is that our citizens and the world can sleep each night without the fear of terrorist attacks. As for the presidency, I have no plans to seek that office. The people of New York have elected me to the United States Senate, and I am devoted to completing my full term."

"Senator, one final question. Do you think you are one of TBA's targets?"

"I'm confident that the issues forwarded by their spokesperson are not things of which I am guilty. I have presented myself with openness, and hope my constituents have faith in my representation."

"Senator Lowell, thank you for being on our show today. Will you promise to come back? Up next is the local news, I'm Tom Russell see you next week on NBC's *Address the Nation*."

CHAPTER THIRTEEN

Monday morning, September 23, President Brazil met with his Cabinet at 6:30 am.

"Gentlemen. Again, I must tell you that I am disappointed with the informational results provided to me to date. TBA is causing a great deal of embarrassment on the congressional institution of these United States. It is despicable. Meanwhile, all our airports are shut down. Our Senate and Congress are forced to meet in alternate, secure locations, and the White House is militarily secured. The American people and the world community are demanding answers. Mr. Secretary of Defense, what can you tell us that we don't already know?"

"Mr. President, with all due respect, my expertise falls within international relations. However, I assure you that I am greatly concerned with these assassinations. The concerns have spread to other nations, which are beginning to question our true powers. I will, of course, cooperate with any assignment you wish, but I believe this is a matter for the FBI and CIA under the auspices of Homeland Defense."

The Homeland Defense Secretary, Wilson Chambers, signaled the President for the floor.

"Mr. Chambers, what can you tell us about the assassinations?" the President asked. "Was the hanging death of Congressman Roberts linked to the assassinations?"

"So far the FBI is reporting that all indications are that the organization is domestic—without foreign aid or involvement. That does not mean that we have ignored the possibility of any foreign involvement, therefore the CIA remains proactively engaged. Most of the investigation is being conducted by detective Mike Walters from the DC police headquarters. His investigation points to a theory of a patriotic suicide pact of organized elders. Our officers are sharing the findings as they develop in a cooperative spirit. The investigation into the hanging death of Congressman Roberts so far shows no links to him as a target. However, he might have feared he was a potential target, and so suicide is definitely a possibility. That investigation is ongoing as well."

"Thank goodness some agencies are working in a spirit of cooperation, Mr. Chambers," President Brazil said. "Do you have any idea what it will take to end this nightmare?"

"Several things are in play," Wilson said. "As you know, their representative called for your resignation. I believe that's out of the question."

"What else?"

"Well, some feel perhaps you or a delegate should arrange for a meeting with their leadership."

"That also is out of the question," the President said, indignantly.

"Mr. President, it might not be a sign of weakness. Ultimately, it could be a sign of strength in this matter. If you send an envoy to explore their strengths and weaknesses, wouldn't that be a sign of strong leadership?"

"I'll give that possibility some thought, but for the moment it's out."

"Okay, may I organize a briefing for you from the CIA, FBI,

Detective Walters, and me, as soon as possible? I believe that would be a priority order, sir."

"Yes, thank you," the President replied. "Upon adjournment of this Cabinet meeting I will make this official announcement. All airports will remain closed, and I am ordering strict surveillance on all interstate travel. At 10:30, I will address the nation, including those mandates and an appeal to the TBA to come forward and end to their rebellion. This meeting is adjourned. General Metcalf, meet me in the Oval Office in 10."

General Arnold Metcalf, Chairman of the Joint Chiefs of Staff, was a Machiavellian political general who dutifully served one master, right or wrong. President Brazil had wasted no time appointing him to the coveted Cabinet position of CJCS.

"General. First of all, am I a target?" the President began their meeting. "What is the status of the White House defense? Are we adequately secured?"

"We are, Mr. President. It would be impossible for any hostile force to get through our defense. This institution is safe. As for your first question, are you a target? That, sir, is impossible to know—particularly since we know precious little about the organization behind this operation. I would, however, assume that you are a target."

"General, I'm no fool. Quite frankly, I'm worried. I'm not ready to buy into the theory that this is a domestic organization with a vowed mission of death to take back America. Of course, that is *remotely* possible, but it's too damn romantic for me. What I need to know from you is: Are our military chiefs prepared to interdict any foreign invasion that may be linked to these assassinations? Are they ready to defend our nation and allies?"

"Yes, Mr. President. I met with all of the generals commanding the branches of our military. They are equipped and ready to deploy at a moment's notice. I will meet with them tomorrow and every day until this crisis ends. We are ready."

"General, at the outside possibility that this *could* end up being a domestic organization, what could you contribute toward an investigation and resolution?"

"Mr. President, certainly were there any ties to the military involving active members of the service, contractors, or civilian employees, I assume we would have jurisdictional authority to investigate. To that extent, Mr. President, we both know the Constitutional limitations regarding the military's interference into civilian affairs."

"Certainly, General. I wouldn't order or condone any interference of the military into civilian affairs. On the other hand, I readily accept anything the military can do under the Uniform Code of Military Justice. However, your preparedness to take the bull by the horns if and when any links to our military is discovered is comforting to me. Thank you, General Metcalf. I appreciate your loyalty and service to our country."

CHAPTER FOURTEEN

At 6:30 pm on September 23, a line of mourners waited for several blocks to view US Congressman Todd Sherman, a Republican of Wrightstown, New Jersey, who had been assassinated on September 17. It was one of those beautiful early fall evenings with a slowly setting warm sun that creates nostalgia in everyone's heart who loves autumn. A mourner's moment of life too beautiful to let go and a reminder someone else is dead—not you.

Nathan's Funeral Home was located in an upscale section of Wrightstown, one of the Burlington County Boroughs in New Jersey. Because of the limited seating capacity, once the mourners were inside the viewing area, it was necessary to keep moving through the home and exit immediately. As they paraded through, they were observed by members of the FBI and plain clothed New Jersey State Police.

A Roman Catholic priest came forward, sprinkling holy water over the crowd and finally upon the body and coffin of the late Congressman. Bishop O'Reilly assisted by the Reverend Father Leonard, performed a mass of the sacrament of death. Upon completion of the service, the bishop offered the condolences of the Roman Catholic Church to the widow.

It was 8 pm when Governor Sarah Whitaker appeared at the podium. The church was eerily quiet, except for some muffled sobs throughout the room. She stood at the podium gently drying her eyes with a tissue supplied by the funeral director.

In a tone just two degrees above a whisper she spoke, "I am deeply honored to have been a personal friend of Congressman Todd Sherman, long before I became governor and he became congressman. I wish to express my whole-hearted sympathies to his family, relatives, friends, and colleagues. Todd was a devoted husband, caring father, loyal friend. He loved Wrightstown, his church and fellow worshippers, and most of all, our nation, which he served so well. We who are survived by him have the best possible memories of a man who did everything in his power to make this a better world for all of us. New Jersey will remember him well. As our beloved Todd passes into the hands of God, I will share with you one of his pastimes loves—poetry. His favorite poet was Omar Khayyam and his favorite poem from *Rubaiyat*. Allow me to read for you two of Todd's favorite verses:

XXXII

There was a Veil past which I could not see
Some little Talk awhile of thee and me
There seemed—and then no
more of Thee or Me

LXXI

The Moving Finger writes and having writ,
Moves on; nor all your Piety nor Wit
Shall lure it back to cancel one half a line,
Nor all your Tears wash out a Word of it.

"Todd, now in the hands of God, a key to heaven will not be

needed as the door will be opened and the veil will be lifted to give you eternal peace. Go now, my friend, and find God's peace."

Governor Whitaker stepped away from the podium and embraced the crying widow.

"Thank you, so much for that beautiful tribute to my husband. Todd would have loved hearing you offer those special verses," Mrs. Sherman said with a sob.

The funeral director announced, "The funeral procession will begin at 9 am tomorrow. Anyone who wishes to pay their final respects may do so between 8:30 and 9 am. Following the last service in the cemetery chapel, the family will be inviting you to join them in a breakfast. The details will be announced in the morning."

Earlier that morning, 73-year-old Donald Wadsworth was interviewed by the manager of Madison's Complete Catering Service, the only catering company in Wrightstown. However, Donald wasn't Donald. He was interviewing as Marie Lemon. As Marie, he explained to the manager that he needed part-time work to pay for home heating fuel this coming winter.

"Do you have any experience as a waitress?" the manager asked.

"I worked most of my life as a waitress in Atlantic City restaurants, mostly part- time during the holidays to help supplement the child support I received from my ex-husband.

"The only positions I currently have available are for servers to handle occasional catered breakfasts and banquets. The breakfasts typically are after baptisms, funerals, and the occasional bowling teams who work night shifts and bowl in the morning. I can offer you about one job a week at the flat rate of $70. If that's okay for you, you can start tomorrow. We are catering a funeral breakfast."

"Yes, that would be fine." Donald exclaimed happily. "Once a week at $70 dollars gives me $280 dollars a month. It'll be perfect."

"Okay, Marie, go to the office to fill out some paperwork. Then check with Sally over in the hall. She'll fix you up with uniforms. By the way, sometimes we have generous tips, which we split evenly with all the servers."

Marie shook hands with the manager then went over to the office and filled out the necessary paperwork before she met Sally, who oriented her and provided her with a new uniform.

Later that evening, Donald sat in his first-floor apartment near McGuire Air Force Base. He thought about his plan to assassinate any Congressman or Senator attending the funeral breakfast. It would be a sure bet that some elected officials would attend. As Marie an elderly woman, he would appear harmless and inconspicuous when serving food at the tables. Once he identified a target, he would see to it that either the food or beverage the target was to consume would be poisoned. He now needed to contact his designate for the toxic agent.

Donald called his contact, who arranged to meet him with the material and instructions that day.

Satisfied with the success of getting the waitress job, Donald kicked back and thought about his life. He was a short man who always felt self-conscious about his height. It was difficult for him to get girls to take him seriously. He compensated for his structural shortcomings by becoming a professional photographer. With Donald's very pleasant nature and soft features, he was endearing to some women. He was a masterful photographer, skilled at making people look more attractive in photos than in reality, so his work attracted some very wealthy clients.

Eventually Donald had managed to marry a very attractive lady who was 10 years younger. They lived in an upscale home with their two daughters near Trenton. Donald always felt inferior to his beautiful wife, which she knew and used to her advantage. After 12 years of marriage, they divorced. Donald never recovered and despite his many affairs with different types of women, he could never again attract the pretty girls he coveted. Of the ones he dated, a few were obese and mean-natured, who obviously only wanted his money. In short, he wound up a very brilliant accomplished, lonely old man.

Even after Donald finally accepted their divorce, he developed a paranoia that everywhere he went, his beautiful wife was watching. He felt that he was still seeking her approval—like a son seeks approval from his mother. He pestered his friends for updates on his ex-wife. In time, his friends began to see his situation as pathetic. They began avoiding him because they didn't want to feed into his obsession.

Donald swore into TBA believing it would be the one thing he could do to redeem himself with his God and hopefully his family. A mild stroke last year made him realize that he was vulnerable to a fatal heart attack or disabling strokes, and he understood the rest of his life must be more meaningful. He was a patriotic little man who slanted toward the left. He felt even smaller against his perception of a conspiratorial government who oppressed its people. He had hatred for the Republican Party who he felt despised the arts and artistic people like him.

When this would all be over, Donald vowed it would show the people how tall he really is. And they would all love him. He would become famous like his idol Frank Sinatra. He imagined that people would come to his funeral someday and remember him reverently. They would love and respect him at last.

The noise of a military transport plane making a final approach to the airstrip interrupted Donald's increasingly grandiose thoughts.

THE MORNING OF THE FUNERAL, DONALD STOOD WITH THE other servers in the catering company kitchen. Donald laughed and socialized with the other staff.

In Donald's pocket, he had two clear capsules, which were given to him at his meeting with the TBA contact. He was briefed with photos of several congressmen who would most likely be present for the breakfast. It would be his duty to place the capsules into a food or dark beverage of any two congressmen.

Some of the mourners were beginning to arrive at the catering hall. They were muddling about from conversation to conversation, careful to observe the protocol required for these events. The ladies' restroom doors were constantly opening and closing to accommodate those whole full bladders were near the leg crossing stage of a urinary crisis. The men, for whatever reason, appeared calmer than the ladies while socializing in this environment.

The hall was filled with round tables, which each seated 10 and were covered with white tablecloths and matching napkins. There were 25 tables set up to accommodate the 250 guests expected to attend the breakfast. The widow and her family would be seated at a central location. Once all of the mourners arrived, Bishop O'Reilly offered grace, and the serving began.

Donald was responsible for serving a table located two tables away from the main table, which was close to the rear exit of the hall. Seated at his table were Congressman Marcus Hinkle, Republican of Pennsylvania; Senator Steven Deeb, Republican of Michigan; and Congressman George Mitchell, Democrat of Pennsylvania. Also seated at the table were the top aides of the elected officials and the mayor of some New Jersey city.

The breakfast was going well. Solemn tones of conversation gradually morphed into jokes and occasional laughter. Signs of healing were already setting in. The main courses were all served. And now the moment of precise action was required of Donald. Without hesitation, as he carried the tray of food from the kitchen, he balanced it on one hip and deftly emptied one capsule into the desserts of Congressman Hinkle and Mitchell. He then placed the tainted food in front of the targets and the benign food in front of the others. Everyone at the table began to heartily eat, and Donald made an excuse to go outside for a cigarette. His car parked in the nearby lot allowed him to make an easy, unobserved exit.

Donald was well on his way to his apartment when he heard ambulances screaming toward the catering hall. Once safely in his apartment, he sat glued to the TV, waiting for the news breaks to start.

Donald's heart started to pound as he waited for any news of the event. Why now? He didn't experience any preactivity anxiety. He calmed himself with the reminder of their mission: the ending of a corrupt Congress.

Congressmen Hinkle and Mitchell were rushed to the hospital emergency room with abdominal cramping and frothing at their mouths. Both were pronounced dead soon after arrival. Both bodies were sent to the morgue for autopsies.

CHAPTER FIFTEEN

Local security, aided by the FBI, ordered the entire catering complex and its staff to be quarantined. Nobody was allowed to enter or exit the premises until they had been questioned.

Soon the news spread among the guests that both congressmen were dead.

The New Jersey state police and FBI began a thorough investigation of the deaths. Over the next week, they deposed all employees, vendors, and management staff. One by one everyone was cleared of any involvement.

The only person not deposed was Marie Lemon, who had disappeared without a trace that morning. She has been placed on the bulletins alert with an artist sketch and posted in post offices of America. The police were confident she was the perpetrator.

During the next two weeks, the media wildly speculated the incidents being linked to the national TBA plot. There were no shortages of criticism for the President and the Senate regarding their cocoon behavior since the beginning of the assassinations.

One New York paper headline screamed, "The Weasels Are in Their Holes."

The article read, "Come out, come out, wherever you are. It's time to face the American public and explain what's going on. A continuation of this cowardly conduct will not be tolerated much longer by the people. In fact, if members are so frightened, then perhaps it's time to resign and allow new members to start America on the path of recovery."

In Washington, the President and his Cabinet received daily FBI briefings. In an effort to minimize panic, the President limited his press conferences. His general statement was, "We are investigating the TBA and are close to obtaining their identities. Meanwhile, all precautions are being taken to protect our elected officials from harm."

House and Senate leaderships expressed their outrage at the President. Their general consensus was: *The President's family is protected by the Secret Service. And he's not even the target. We are the targets, yet we are not receiving personal protection.*

CHAPTER SIXTEEN

On the evening of September 27, the sun was setting slowly and beautifully in the west. Donald stood on his balcony overlooking a nearby park, which was dignified by a beautiful mixture of oaks and other trees. He mumbled the lyrics of his favorite song, *Autumn Leaves.*

Donald's eyes moistened, and he knew he was about to be overwhelmed by the memories of his life and his lots. The oaks, birch, and maples were signaling the beginning of fall. Donald loved fall; it was his favorite season. Soon the colors of fall would paint the trees. He thought of the season and how it represented the beauty of death. All things, by design of nature, die to make room for the new birth of spring.

That's well and good, Donald thought. *Some things live too long, others not long enough.*

Then Donald thought of the words the Roman emperor asked Jesus, "Who are you?" To which Jesus replied, "I am, I am, that but you are not."

Who am I? Why am I? Donald thought.

Donald diagnosed himself as an incurable romantic with an insatiable need to be validated by declarations of love from the opposite sex. He was quick to tell you over a drink that he was sexually addicted to beautiful women. He intensely disliked fat women, who he thought of as lazy pigs. If he judged women to be physically unattractive, he would direct them to other photographers. But he accepted the truth that gorgeous women didn't take short men seriously. They always seemed to regard his declarations of passion as comedic, thinking of him as the funny little guy who wears platform shoes.

Donald's thoughts turned to the love of his life, and he knew he was about to die without the ultimate gratification of being hugged and kissed by his beautiful Ruth.

The breathlessness of the view filled Donald with a sudden terror, as he suddenly feared that what he had done might be vastly misunderstood. What if Ruth and his daughters believed that he was nothing more than a common murderer and anti-American terrorist? Might he achieve the opposite effect from the adulation and respect he desperately coveted all of his life?

What if I'm wrong? Donald began to panic. *What is the organization was wrong? What if we all are caught and were executed? Our oath of secrecy and death will be meaningless without being perceived as glorious patriots.*

Donald's super ego refused to except that, and he fixated on the thought that he'd be heralded as a hero in the end. But then that thought caused its own anxiety. Donald was not able to accept delayed gratification. He was never good at waiting.

The only way to resolve this, he thought, *is if I am dead. If I am dead, I can't be tortured into confessing or making any statements contrary to the glorious goals of the TBA.*

When the sun went down, Donald sat on his comfortable, brown, leather lounge chair, turned on his favorite Frank Sinatra CD, poured a large scotch on the rocks, and started to drink himself into a mood. When feeling a pleasant buzz, he wrote, *To whom it may concern, I am not a terrorist. I am part of revolutionary organization that loves America. God bless America.*

The music and the scotch were intoxicating. Donald felt pleasantly euphoric and thought, *This is how I want to end, on a beautiful day in this beautiful season with background music by Frank and sipping the world's best scotch.*

As Donald emptied the bottle of Dewar's, his eyes filled up with tears. He knew it was the end. He turned up the music and shouted, "God, I'm with you now."

Donald placed a 9 mm into his mouth and blew his brains out. Marie Lemon would never be found.

A few minutes later, when the police stormed into the room, Frank Sinatra's music was still playing, *"Luck be a lady tonight."*

CHAPTER SEVENTEEN

It was 10 am on September 28 when Mike was escorted by a very large, unsmiling Secret Service agent into a room where President Brazil was waiting. Seated on his right was the head of the FBI, George Prendergast, and on his left the controversial head of the CIA, Maximillian Bird. Mike felt as though he was summoned to appear before a tribunal. As Mike entered the room, all three stood and reached over to shake Mike's hand. Mike sat directly across from the President, who greeted him warmly, effectively relieving his heart palpitations.

The President spoke first, stating, "Mr. Walters, from the information I have received to date, it appears that you have been and remain to be the most active law enforcement officer investigating these assassinations."

"With all due respect, Mr. President, that comes as a surprise to me. I thought the FBI and the CIA were working equally as hard as me. Given the national and international implications, it would be expected—especially considering their elite staffs and resources. It just surprises me to hear that I'm leading the charge."

"Mr. Walters, please understand that the FBA and CIA have

been actively engaged. However, I hear you've put together an interesting theory about the organization, and to date our federal agencies haven't."

Prendergast interjected, "Mike, may I call you Mike?"

"By all means, please do."

"Okay, Mike. Because of the lower ranking status of a city detective vis-à-vis the intrepid nature of facing an FBI agent, you have some advantages that we think could help accelerate this case. I don't mean to offend you with that analogy, the simple truth is that we all have to be realistic about duty and leave personality at home."

"Well, Mr. Prendergast, I am more than willing to serve our nation in this matter in any way that gives us all the results we're seeking. Of course, I'm not offended, and it does make sense. But what exactly are you proposing? Is it that I become some kind of ersatz FBI agent? I hope you understand, my investigation will continue with or without this added auspice. Regarding the FBI, I have no problem sharing developments with you on an ongoing basis. And, I expect the same reciprocal commitment from you."

"Mike, to crystallize our idea, let's assume that you continue your investigation just as you have been. But if we perceive something of a non-jurisdictional nature, could we count on you to do some non-jurisdictional probing?"

"Sir, I would be open to anything that helps bring these assassins to justice. As for working with you and other federal agencies, I don't see that as a problem. Although, that would be subject to complete disclosure to me what my involvement would be."

Maximilian spoke up at this point, stating, "Mike, the CIA will have very little open status with all this. Our part will be concentrated on international connections if they exist. Do you understand that our people operate undercover? At times, it is necessary to secretly employ people outside the law to help achieve our goals. You and others in this room don't want to know of these things, and you won't be accountable for participating in our plots."

"How will you channel your agency's international discoveries to our mainstream investigation, Max? May I call you Max?"

Laughingly, Max responded and said, "Be my guest. To answer your question, if the CIA develops relative information, that information will reach you. That's all you need to know. You'll understand when it does."

"Gentlemen, I think our understanding of each of the entities you represent is clear to all present," interjected President Brazil. "Can we agree on that?"

Everyone nodded in agreement.

"Is it agreed that we can proceed with the capacity in which you will cooperate together?"

Again, all agreed.

"At this time Mike, would you present to us your findings and theories concerning TBA?"

"Certainly."

"Mr. President, gentlemen, I will be happy to share with you all that I know and what I believe we are facing. First, I will give you the chronological findings of facts, and all of the clues and clinical determinations that led to my theories regarding the organization we're up against."

Mike stood and gestured to the white board behind him. "May I use this?" he asked."

"Anything you need, Mike."

"During any investigation, I like be thorough and be sure to get my ducks in order."

"By all means, I welcome the opportunity to listen to someone who can enlighten me with a theory that makes some sense of this fucking mess," the President said. "What a goddamn political quagmire. Please proceed."

Mike nodded. Just as he had in the DC office, he wrote on the white board, "NO FEAR OF DEATH."

"Gentlemen, as you are well aware, 13 lawmakers were assassinated in September. If you include the hanging, it's 14.

"The two poisonings in New Jersey are being investigated by the FBI. The leading suspect is an elderly waitress who hasn't been located. The previous suspects were male. Does her suspected involvement mean TBA also has female members?

The FBI continues the search for this missing waitress, who gave her employer the name 'Marie Lemon.'"

Prendergast nodded in agreement.

"Jurisdictionally, I had no part in that investigation. But, we are looking for a female named Marie Lemon, and so we should at least consider the possibility that she used a fake name."

"Well, the manager said that she produced the proper documents to establish her identity."

"Fair enough, But please allow me to make the next several points. Fake documents and disguises and/or cross-dressing. Aren't those possibilities as well? With all due respect, I suggest broadening the scope of your investigation a bit. The organization we are facing seems to be a group of unsophisticated but devoted people who have all the advantages of surprise tactics. They know where they're going and when. And if I'm right that they are all elderly with significant health problems, they have no fear of death," Mike said, pointing to the white board.

"Here we are, the most powerful nation on this planet with unlimited resources, and we're helpless against a bunch of nut cases? Is that your theory, Mr. Walters?" the President asked, annoyed.

"No, sir. I merely present the data and expect that with all these resources and brainpower, a tentative analysis of the organization will develop and point us in the right direction."

Mike moved closer to the white board and listed the casualty breakdown:

- Democrats—seven
- Republicans—seven
- Ohio—three
- Nevada—one

- California—one
- Wyoming—one
- New Jersey—two
- Pennsylvania—two
- Florida—one
- Michigan—one
- Georgia—one
- Tennessee—one

"Since we have seven 7 Democrats and 7 Republicans equally assassinated, obviously it's not a grievance against a single party."

Prendergast interjected, "Right, they're non-discriminating assassins."

No one laughed.

"Continuing on with the breakdown of states, it's not exactly a pattern without clusters. However, the Southeast was hit the hardest. In the West, both California and Nevada suffered only two losses."

"So far, that's it."

"That's correct, Mr. President, and that summarizes the data, gentlemen," Mike said. "And we have three elderly suspects.

"Now for motivation," Mike continued. "We don't have to look beyond the statement made by the TBA representative. They feel that Congress has sold out the American people. I believe they have organized into a pact to resolve this corruption by sacrificing the remainder of their days fighting for what they feel must be done to change things for America. The question is, do they have open recruitment, which would open the possibility of infiltration. But that would be especially difficult considering we have no target suspect to start the process.

"Now, Mr. President, I know that refusing to meet with any TBA representative is a sound resolve. What, sir, is your position on sending an envoy to a meeting, someone with the power to represent the nation's policies?"

"I couldn't rule that possibility out without a complete evaluation of the circumstances under which it would be presented. Under the right circumstances, I would consider a surrogate."

"George and Max, what are your thoughts?"

"Jesus Christ, you're absolutely right. No damn negotiations involving the President. The FBI supports your policy."

"May I point out to you all, these are domestic terrorists," Max said. "The official US policy is that we don't negotiate with terrorists."

"As solid as we may be on that point, I rather doubt that they regard themselves as terrorists," Mike said. "More likely, they see themselves as patriots."

"Well, Mike, I certainly want to thank you for all your time and effort in this matter and especially for coming here today and sharing your thoughts with us," the President said. "You have added some new dimension to this crisis."

The President cast an accusatory glance at Max and George.

"Mr. President, it's been a pleasure for me to be here today and help in any way I could," Mike said

"Would you be willing to add federal status to your resume?"

"What are you proposing, Mr. President?"

"Since you are thoroughly acquainted with all the facts surrounding the investigation, I am willing to grant you a commission appointing you as a special federal investigator in this case."

"I'm honored to have the offer and especially your confidence, sir, but I'm tenured with the DC police department and frankly looking forward to retirement."

"I don't see that as a problem," the President continued. "I could arrange for you to remain on staff at the DC police department while you would be on special assignment to the federal government and have the federal commissioner status as well. You would receive the benefits of both levels of government."

"If I accept, who would I be reporting to?"

"You would be accountable to me and me alone. I would arrange the access protocol. I would ask, however, that you share all discoveries with the FBI, but they would have no rank over you. I'm asking you to accept this offer in the national security interest. Since you are actively investigating these assassinations, it would give you a legitimate national jurisdiction and that should appeal to you as an investigator."

Mike looked long and hard at the men in the room. He was having a momentary state of paralysis. "Mr. President, I'm going to say yes. But in accepting your generous offer, I must let you know that I have concerns that I feel need to be addressed. For one, would my commission be announced to the press?"

"Why, would you want that?"

"Well, I would want my status known because if it were not known to the public that I was commissioned, if something goes wrong during the course of this investigation, I wouldn't be sacrificed by some ultimate solution. I feel that openness of my commission would help with gaining the access to all forensic institutions."

"Okay, Mike. I will arrange the press release, and by the way, I agree with your thoughts about the openness. Let's break for lunch. I have a few things to work on, which should last until 2 pm. Let's get together for a press conference at three. George and Max will also be part of the announcement. I believe it will show that we are working together to do the people's work."

"Sir, I do have one human resource request."

"Okay, let's hear it."

"During my investigation, I attended the autopsy of Congressman Buckles in Memphis Tennessee, and I was thoroughly impressed with the pathologist, Dr. Linda Marshall. I would like to have her on my team, perhaps also with some temporary form of duty."

"I will have George check her out for a security clearance. If she presents no security risk, and if she agrees, it will be approved. Now if that's all, I would like to get on with clearing up some loose ends before our 3 o'clock press conference."

Mike stood and shook hands with the men. "I'll see you at three."

CHAPTER EIGHTEEN

For the press conference, President Brazil sat directly at the podium with Maximilian Bird and George Prendergast to his right and Michael Walters to his left.

"Good afternoon members of the press. I called this conference today to inform the public of a decision I made this morning to name Michael Walters, detective of the DC police department, to serve as a federal investigative commissioner to head up the ongoing investigation into the assassinations of our US lawmakers. His status as a detective with the DC Police Department will remain consecutively constant. In all participation beyond his DC jurisdictions, he will report directly to me and work reciprocally with FBI chief George Prendergast. At this time, I am pleased to present Mike Walters."

"I arrived here this morning with the sole intent of sharing my knowledge concerning the assassinations of our lawmakers this month. I had no expectation of anything else beyond sharing information and ideas with the President. Upon conclusion of the briefing, President Brazil conditionally offered me this federal position as an ad-hoc commissioner for this case. He made me an offer I couldn't refuse, and of course I accepted. Mr. President, for the good of our nation and your confidence in me, I am honored to accept this challenge."

A reporter from the *Washington Time* asked the first question, "Mr. Walters, what qualifications do you have for this position?"

"I've served with the District of Columbia Police Department for 27 years, currently as an elite detective. During my career, I have been involved in many homicide investigations exposing me to the forensic science of all types of murders. Armed with all my experience, will I succeed? I don't know, but I will do my best."

Every member of the press had their hand raised.

The President acknowledged a female reporter.

"Mr. President, what effect will this have on the chief of the FBI, Mr. Prendergast? Is he being replaced by Mr. Walters?"

"Not at all. Mr. Prendergast will remain the chief law enforcement officer of America. Again, Mr. Walters's federal commission is for this special assignment only. When he completes the assignment, his position will end. I may also point out again that Mr. Walters will remain on staff with the District of Columbia Police Department. Mr. Walters and Mr. Prendergast will work together."

A *Washington Tribune* reporter got the next question in.

"Mr. Walters, do you have any suspects?"

"We have some leads. I will be following up on a theory I developed. When I have solid evidence authenticated by our Justice Department, I will have comments for the media."

"Will you have any support staff working with you during this period?" the reporter followed-up.

"Yes, however the staff haven't been determined nor cleared by security. Until that happens, no identities will be revealed."

The press secretary took over the podium and announced that the conference had ended. He thanked everyone for their attendance and cooperation. Reporters were shouting questions at the backs of the departing men, but all the president would do is turn his head and wave to the crowd.

Inside the White House, the President shook hands with the three men and thanked them for their service to the country.

"I'll do my best," Mike said sincerely.

The next day, Mike arrived at the office early. He had a lot of catching up to do. His desk was full of memos he needed to read. First of all, he had to brief John Craig about his new dual functions. He was certain, knowing John, that he would be a little jaundiced over the matter. But he would help John understand that his loyalties were still with the department. He could do it; it would be a piece of cake.

At 9 am, Mike met with John in his office.

John closed the door and went into a tirade.

"How the fuck would you like it if you heard about one of your lead detectives accepting a special position from the federal government? I don't hear it from you. No, I heard it from some prick in the White House. You know Mike, we go way back. We were so close. Why didn't you tell me you were going after this federal job? What is it? The money? The prestige? Jesus, you could've been upfront with me."

"Now if you're through ranting, you can give those bulging veins in your neck and mouth a break. I'll tell you what happened."

"Go ahead tell me how you gave me the shaft. Go right ahead, Mike."

"God dammit, John. You understood that I was going to the White House to brief the President at his request. It wasn't something I thought of my own. Think about it—detective Mike Walters calls the President of the United States and informs him that he wants to meet with him to discuss the assassinations. President Brazil says,

"Come right on down. Just like that. The President opens his busy day schedule of running the nation to allow Michael Walters of the DC police to direct his meetings. Get real, John."

"Are you telling me that you had no idea the President wanted you to head up a special investigation?"

"That's exactly right. Now if you're ready to hear the details about what happened, I'll be happy to share."

"I'm listening."

"To begin with, I had no idea about any job offering or special assignment or commission when I went to the White House. And neither did the President. I briefed him exactly as I did during our conference here with our staff. It wasn't until the President heard my summary remarks about the assassins being compromised of a group of infirm, elderly citizens that he offered me the proposal. I had lots of time thinking over the reason that the President wanted me to do this. It's political. If he directed the FBI to investigate senior citizens, it would be a political disaster for his party and this reelection cycle. The reality is my federal commission is for this investigation only. And it doesn't change my position in our department. If you understand me at all, you know I won't allow this to divide us. And I agree, we do go way back."

"Shit, Mike, it upset me. I didn't want to believe you perpetrated the damn thing."

"So now that you understand how it happened, I can only tell you what I told them and what I told you during our briefing. Nothing has changed since. As a matter fact, things are too quiet. John, between us, I don't know how I'm going to proceed. It was routine for me here in the department, but with this new commitment I don't know if I can justify their confidence in me. The pressure has increased, and I hope I can handle it. All I want is to do three more years and retire. I want to enjoy some of that so-called good life. Oh well, what the fuck, I better get started."

When Mike stood to exit the room, John walked around the desk.

"I'm happy for you Mike. I'll help you in any way I can. Good luck."

CHAPTER NINETEEN

Mike returned to his desk and tried to read his memos, but he kept reviewing his meetings with the President and John in his head. Did he do the right thing? Was his theory of a group of elderly patriots coming out of left field? Who the hell did he think he was, briefing the president of the United States on such a wild theory?

I wasn't scared before, but I am now, he thought.

Looking at a paper in his hand for the first time, he started to read. It said, "The body of Donald Wadsworth was located in an apartment building near Wrightstown, New Jersey. The elderly man had apparently committed suicide. You may be interested in seeing if he was connected to the New Jersey assassinations. Regards, Hank."

Hank Craigle was the third member of the investigative team assigned to the case by John. It was his job to start looking into the assassinated lawmakers. Mike quickly emailed Hank, *I know you're assigned to investigate involvements of the assassinated congressmen, but I'm extremely interested in the suicide of the Jersey man. Keep digging into the life of Donald Wadsworth. Great work. Keep it up.*

Refreshed with this new information and the possible links to the killings, Mike pulled up all the reports regarding the two lawmakers poisoning during the funeral breakfast of Todd Sherman in Wrightstown, New Jersey. Impulsively, he yelled to the staff secretary, "Mary."

Mary returned his demanding yell, "What is it you want, your honor?"

"Cut the shit, Mary," Mike yelled. "Get me everything you have on the Jersey funeral breakfast poisoning, please."

Several minutes later, Mary arrived with copies of the police reports along with newspaper clippings.

"Here they are, your eminence," she joked, dropping them in front of him. She was cute, and Mike liked her, but not in a physical way. He regarded her as if she were one of the guys.

Mike felt great, and he was motivated to get into the thing he liked best: sleuthing out the facts. *I'm back*, he thought.

"Mary, get back here."

"Now what does his honor want?"

"Get Hank on the phone."

Seconds later, his phone rang, and it was Hank calling from Wrightstown.

"What's up, Mike?"

"Listen, I want you to get over to the local morgue. If they haven't disposed of the body, put a hold on it. If necessary, I'll get a federal warrant. When you have that accomplished, go to his apartment and make sure the suicide scene is secured. Do not allow the local authorities to return the apartment over to the landlord, family, or anyone else. This is a vitally important. We have no idea what locals know about this man. When you talk with them, tell them that it's a federal matter involving taxes or something innocuous. Let me know ASAP what you achieved. I'm going to wrap up a few loose ends here, and then I'm coming up to Wrightstown."

Mike put the phone back on the hook, but before he removed his hand from the receiver, it rang again.

"Hello, Mike Walters? I am Patricia Mazur, human resource

manager for the federal administration. I'm calling to inform you that Dr. Linda Marshall has been cleared for security and approved for temporary employment as your project assistant."

"That's wonderful. I assume she can be brought on board immediately?"

"That will depend upon her acceptance of the offer. I just ran the background checks as requested by the President. To date, she hasn't been involved in the process, and I'm sure she knows nothing about the proposal."

"Well, what do you suggest?"

"I suggest that someone contact her and gain her acceptance."

"Patricia, I am very new with the federal civil service system. For that reason, I'd prefer to have someone with high-level status in the administration make the pitch to her. Her participation is very important to our need. I don't want to screw it up."

"Okay, I see what you mean, Mr. Walters. I'll consult with the right people and get you through this delicate situation. I'll get back to you sometime today."

"Okay, I'll be in and out of the office today so I'll give you my cell number. Keep trying until you reach me. Thank you for helping me with this matter. I really appreciate it."

It was 1:45 pm when Hank got back to Mike with the results of his Wrightstown checks.

"Mike, Donald Wadsworth shot himself in the head sometime in the early evening of September 27th. That was only two days ago, so they still have him on ice. I don't believe they did the post yet, so I managed to put a tentative hold on his body. You will need to get here to assert your federal authority. They aren't too impressed by me. As for the Wadsworth apartment, the police are willing to keep it sealed until you have a chance to inspect the area. But they're also requesting a federal warrant upon your arrival. They're not being cynical; it's more a matter of due process and following protocol."

"Thanks, Hank. I need you to stay up there and set up a command station. But don't make any long-term commitments. Let's say for only two days, and we'll pay one day at a time. I hope to have things clear here today and be in Wrightstown tomorrow morning. If I get the warrants early enough, I'll leave tonight."

"When and where will I meet you, Mike?"

"When I leave, I'll call you on your cell, and we can agree to a meeting point. By then, you should have us booked into a command center. I will leave the selection of accommodations up to you. You know our needs. See you soon. By the way, you're doing a great job."

"Okay, Mike. I'm on it."

CHAPTER TWENTY

The next morning, Mike left home at 5 am and headed to Wrightstown. He got lucky the day before and yesterday by acquiring the federal warrants he needed. Also, the contacts were made with Linda, and she accepted the appointment—on the condition that it would be temporary and wouldn't affect her position in Memphis.

Mike was feeling rather upbeat on his drive to Wrightstown. One of the first things he needed to do was convince Linda to join him in New Jersey. It was a must. He rationalized that his physical attraction to her wasn't the reason. She would be needed to interpret the autopsy results, he told himself. Desperately, he suppressed his ultimate desire to make love to Linda.

I will insist that she assist with the autopsy, he thought. *That will prove her value to this investigation and camouflage my personal interest in her.*

Mike continued driving, going through towns without even realizing it. His mind was spinning with ideas, procedures, and possible results. If ever he needed validation, it was now. Now was the time to make his bones. If he played it out successfully, the assassinations mystery would be solved, and he would have proved his worth. Then, Linda would be his. His mind had quickly shifted back to her already. Then together they would live happily ever after in retirement.

It was nearly 8 am when Mike passed a sign proclaiming, "Welcome to Wrightstown." He found a Turkey Hill and pulled in for gas and to use the men's restroom. When he was finished, he called Hank on his cell. "Hank."

"What's up, Mike?"

"I just got into Wrightstown. I'm at the Turkey Hill. Can you direct me to our location?"

"Mike, it would be a lot easier if I just met you there and led you. Get yourself a coffee and wait. I'll be there in about 10 minutes."

"Okay, Hank. See you soon."

Mike bought a coffee and a local paper. He moved his car over to the less busy side of the lot and started to read. A headline said, "President Brazil Appoints New Special Federal Agent. The article went on to say, "New Agent Walters will have complete autonomy along with the national jurisdiction he needs to bring the assassins to justice. The President has complete faith in Agent Walters, but he insists there will be no status loss with his FBI chief, George Prendergast. Both Prendergast and Walters will share mutual consultations, and neither will answer to the other. Rather, both will report to the President directly."

Mike's reading was interrupted by a car horn. It was Hank trying to get his attention. He waved for Mike to follow, and Mike obliged. It was much easier to follow him than trying to navigate on his own.

The place Hank arranged was perfect. It was a second-floor apartment atop a laundromat on a secondary road about a quarter mile from any hustle and bustle of the town. The apartment was in good shape with all the accommodations they needed and three bedrooms and two baths.

"Hank, who did you have to blow to get this place?"

Hank laughed and said, "I have my contacts, Mike. By the way, the fridge is full."

"Thanks for everything, Hank. I'm going to take a shower. When I'm finished, I'll brief you."

"Do you want me to whip up some French toast or eggs while you're in the shower?"

"Great idea. Does coffee go along with that offer?"

"Absolutely. What a guy. Gets some federal recognition and suddenly I'm his lackey. Anything else, your majesty?"

"Yes, you can kiss my royal ass." Mike said, laughing.

At one point, Hank turned on the hot water in the kitchen. Mike let out a rush of curse words before the hot water returned to his shower, feeling a rush of happiness to be on this mission with his old friend.

After Mike had dried off and put on a fresh set of clothes, he joined Hank in the kitchen. Hank had his breakfast waiting for him at the table, as well as a hot cup of coffee.

"Hank, aside from your usual bullshit, I really do appreciate your hard work and dedication," Mike said. "This thing that's facing our nation is causing a lot of concern for the survival of democracy. It's not unrealistic to think in those bleak terms. If we don't stop these assassinations soon, it could force our elected officials into a legislative process wherein they could justify secret meetings by the threat to their safety. We are living in troubled times. Our nation is badly divided over church-and-state rights. Politicians exploit the spiritual needs of a confused society. They use abortion as a moral issue, dividing those who believe it's a woman's right to choose versus an archaic women's biblical duty to bear human fruit. Our government is sticking its ugly nose unto issues that shouldn't be their issues. What it boils down to is: We are a nation without credible leadership. People are angry and confused, and they are tired of being talked down to and lied to. I think a revolution is coming."

"Mike, it's only been 19 days since this started. Do you really think that could happen in America today?"

"Absolutely. What makes you think we're revolution-proof? You must admit there has been a lot of corruption in this country during the past 50 years—especially in the past 10."

"You're not wrong, but maybe I'm more optimistic than you."

"Let's forget the political forecast and get down to tactics. You have the apartment under police restriction and the morgue reserved. The warrants are taken care of on my end. Let's call Linda Marshall and assess our next move."

Mike dialed the number. A man with a kind, high-pitched voice picked up. "Doctor is on the other line," he said. "Will you hold?"

"Yes, but it's urgent. Tell her it's Commissioner Mike Walters."

After a few minutes of elevator music, Linda answered. "Hi, Mike. Sorry to keep you waiting so long."

"No problem at all. I'll be brief, doctor. I need you to come to Wrightstown, New Jersey, as fast as you can. There's an elderly male suicide victim who may or may not be linked to the congressional assassinations. The corpse is ready for an autopsy, and I would prefer your judgment."

"Well, *Commissioner*," she teased, "I don't know if I should curse you or thank you for the recommendation to our President. But the truth is, I'm flattered and frightened at the same time. Nevertheless, I accepted the offer. I'll do whatever I can to aid you in this investigation."

"I'll take that as a thank you," he joked back. "How soon can you get here?"

"Well, if I manage to clear out a couple of backlogs, I can leave today."

"Great. Use your federal status, contact the White House, and see if they can get you a priority flight into Fort Dix. I will arrange for you to get picked up there."

"Detective, you better be right about all this. I admit I feel a little intimidated. I keep thinking that it's my duty to serve our country, and I guess fate dictates that's a duty we share."

"Let me know the details of your departure and arrival as soon as you can. Your assistant can book you a hotel room, of course, or we have a three-bedroom command post set up here. You are welcome to stay here if you'd like."

Linda laughed, and Mike thought about how good it was to hear that. She took things a lot better than he expected. He half expected her to lash out at him for getting her involved without prior discussion.

After the call, he informed Hank about Linda.

"So, she's a pathologist, but what makes her any different than anyone else in that field?" Hank asked. "Oh, no, you have that look on your face. Your interest in this doctor isn't purely science, is it?"

"Guilty," Mike confessed, "but that being said, the investigation comes first. Linda is incredibly knowledgeable and experienced. Please treat her with the respect she's entitled to as a professional."

"Of course," Hank said.

"While we're waiting for her arrival, see about getting a delay on that autopsy. Use whatever stall tactics you must. Federal intervention, what have you. Also, make tentative arrangements for all of us to examine the apartment and suicide scene.

Hank went to work, and Mike found himself thinking about how his friend deserved a promotion. He was reliable, dependable, and a good friend to him.

CHAPTER TWENTY-ONE

It was 6:30 am on September 30th when Linda landed. The flight had been smooth and enjoyable, and she had plenty of time to process the events of past few days as well as what loomed ahead. Her career was reaching heights she never could have imagined. Working with the White House? Who would've thought?

Yet, her personal life felt empty. While in medical school, she'd steered clear of relationships and focused solely on establishing herself in pathology. She'd dated every once in a while but found no one met her standards. Now, at 48, she'd lowered her standards only slightly. No one was perfect, herself included, but she refused to settle, though now she craved more in her life than just a thriving career.

Part of her was curious about the political realm, but her interest in government affairs was mild at best. Perhaps being thrust into it would change her mind. She felt pulled right into the middle of the political world and assassination scandal—and by that Mike guy.

Detective, commissioner, mysterious, attractive, these were all ways she could describe him. Interest aside, she resolved to focus on the task at hand. Soon she'd be headed back to Memphis, though she didn't know whether the thought was comforting or upsetting.

As Linda entered the terminal, a man waved to get her attention. She approached him cautiously.

"I'm Detective Hank Craigle," he said, shaking her hand, "Mike sent me to escort you to our command center."

"Nice to meet you, Detective Craigle."

"Oh, please, call me Hank."

During their ride to the control center, Linda decided that she liked Hank. He was sweet and made her feel comfortable.

"How long have you been with the police department?" she asked.

Twenty years, but it seems like it was just yesterday when I got out of the academy. I was 25 and full of piss and vinegar. The last quarter century has changed that to blood and tears. Kidding, of course. It's been a good ride. I never get bored."

"My profession has its own degree of excitement, but I don't know if people outside of the field would agree," Linda said.

As they pulled up to the apartment building, Linda took a few steadying breaths. She hadn't felt this nervous in a long while. After a moment, she was ready.

CHAPTER TWENTY-TWO

Mike greeted Linda enthusiastically, letting her know how important her role was to the investigation. He pointed out that although the suicide death of Donald Wadsworth was without evidence connecting him to the assassinations of elected officials, he was operating on a hunch.

"His age could be a significant factor, which could link him to the organization that's responsible for the assassinations." Mike explained. "That's where you come into the picture. The autopsy must be performed with the utmost integrity and conducted under the auspices of local and federal authority. Since it's going on 8 pm, I'll spring for dinner. We'll get back early and get an early start tomorrow morning."

"Count me in." Hank said. "What about you, Linda?"

"Count me in, too. While you guys are grooming for dinner, I'll get in touch with the local pathologist and arrange for the autopsy to take place tomorrow morning. Is that okay with you, Mike?"

"By all means, get right on it. The earlier the better, unless you have a different time preference. Do you?"

"No, early is good."

"Okay, we all agree to get right on it as early as possible. If we complete the post in a reasonable amount of time, we can make a site visit to the apartment and take it from there."

October 2nd, Mike, Linda, and Hank entered the morgue and introduced themselves to the local pathologist, Hans Steiner, MD.

"I welcome all of you to participate with me in this procedure," he said, "however, before we proceed, I must see your warrants and official identifications."

Mike produced the warrants, and Hans had his assistant make copies.

"Thank you very much for cooperating, as you know we'll most likely all be in court one day. I'm a stickler for verification."

Prior to initiating the autopsy, the doctors and witnesses were provided with the proper gowns and masks required by institutional policy.

Linda spoke into the recorder, "Dr. Steiner, as you perhaps noted, the warrant gives me the authorization to conduct an examination of the body, and although I have no objection to a joint examination, I will assume a lead role in this procedure. Do you understand?"

"It is understood, and I am comfortable with this arrangement, particularly since you will have the primary responsibility for the finding in the forensic report," Hans said.

"Noted," Linda replied. "But please feel free to enter your own observations as we proceed."

"It's all about an investigation, not about territorialism," Mike injected. "Now may we do the people's work, please?"

Dr. Marshall entered the routine data into the recorder. "It's October 2, 2005, 6:23 am, I'm in the Wrightstown, New Jersey, Memorial Hospital Morgue and about to conduct an official federally warranted autopsy on the body of Donald Wadsworth, a Caucasian male with records showing his age at 74.

"The soma type of Mr. Wadsworth was of a short mesomorph

man who measured 63 inches in length; he was well toned and with good skin integrity. Other than the gunshot wound to his head, he had a few minor scars: a one-inch scar on his right forearm and a small jiggered scar on his right lower rib area. Dr. Hans Steiner, who is the chief pathologist here at Wrightstown Memorial, will also participate in this autopsy. Also in observation of this procedure are Michael Walters, Special Investigative Commissioner in charge of this investigation, and his assistant, Detective Henry Craigle. For the record, I will remove the top of his cranium in a skull-cap form and remove the parenchyma for a detailed examination."

It's amazing to watch this beautiful woman work, Mike thought, realizing the irony of what she was actually doing.

Linda continued to announce into the recorder everything she did procedurally as well as her clinical findings. With each entry, she would call upon Steiner for comment. He found no areas of disagreement so far. Linda removed Donald's brain, placed it on a scale, and noted the weight.

"Note, material evidence shows a gunshot initiated into the buccal cavity, which exploded upward into the frontal lobe and exited through the frontal plane of the skull, causing his death. Dr. Steiner, do you agree that there is a significant degree of brain atrophy here? Perhaps advanced beyond his 74 years?"

"Yes, Dr. Marshall. It suggests to me that he was misrepresenting his age. His brain is more like the brain of someone in their eighties."

"I agree." said Dr. Marshall, entering that finding into the recorder. "No plaques or tangles are present, suggesting Alzheimer's disease was not a factor. Evidence does, however, show that he had some micro-arterial stenosis. Based upon some parenchyma damage, he did suffer at least two slight strokes."

Upon completing the examination of his head, Linda cut open his chest and methodically removed each organ with the same businesslike manner. She entered her findings for the record.

It was 2:50 pm when they concluded the autopsy. The official cause of death was attributed to a single self-inflicted gunshot wound to the frontal area of the brain. All other vital organs showed age-appropriate degeneration, within normal ranges and of capacity except for the brain mass, which had evidence of slight strokes. That would become the official diagnosis on the certificate of death along with the content of the official report.

It was nearly 4 pm when the group completed all the protocol required by the host hospital, local, state, and federal governments prior to their leaving the institution. They all agreed to get a late lunch somewhere en route to Donald Wadsworth's apartment to give them some time to summarize the autopsy results before they made the site visit.

As they entered a diner, Mike looked for a table or booth where they could talk without being overheard. Hank quickly took a seat with his back to the wall, giving him a command view of everyone in the restaurant. It was a habit, but he rationalized that it was a good one. Mike gestured for Linda to sit on the inside across from Hank, and he sat alongside the doctor.

"Well, doctor, is there anything other than what was officially noted in the report?"

"Officially, no. The post findings are common, with the exception of the damage to his oral cavity and brain mass from the gunshot. The rest of his anatomy and vital organs were in fair condition. I believe that whereas his age may support your theory in part, I can't make a determination that he was in an infirm state of health."

"Thank you doctor. I guess that would exclude any terminal condition leading him to make himself into a martyred patriot. Okay, that would be the physical aspects but not necessarily the psychological composite. Maybe we should look into that aspect of this man's history?" Mike paused. "I hope that we'll get some direction when we examine his home."

Being in the company of Linda drove Mike bonkers. He was so distracted by her nearness that keeping an analytical focus on the case was difficult. He wondered how long he could pretend to be businesslike before he made some stupid romantic overture that would likely turn her off. Her passion and knowledge in her field made him even more attracted to her. She was beautiful, but she was incredibly intelligent and kind. While he maintained his outward composure, he couldn't help but imagine what it would be like to kiss her.

CHAPTER TWENTY-THREE

It was 7 pm when they had finished supper and entered Donald Wadsworth's apartment.

Hank looked to Mike and asked, "What exactly are we looking for?"

"I don't exactly know," Mike answered. "I'll know it when I see it. I suggest we start looking for items that could link him to others and hopefully to the organization."

"I hope both of you understand that I'm a pathologist and realize I'm out of my area of expertise in this situation." Linda said.

"Fair enough," said Mike. "I have an idea. Pretend that this apartment is a corpse and examine it from head to toe."

"Very funny," Linda replied. "Then to extend the metaphor I'll be searching for a cause of death, correct?"

"Correct."

Hank found a photo album in the bedroom.

"Hey, Mike, come in here. Look at this album."

The three of them started looking at the photos and discovered the entire series were of black-and-white photos taken in the fifties. It showed Donald in his twenties in what appeared to be an amusement park. One photo of him was with an older woman, which could have been his mother or an aunt, in front of a Hershey sign. "Were they in Hershey Park, in Hershey, Pennsylvania? Were they originally from Pennsylvania?" Mike wondered aloud.

"Over here, Mike, maybe this will help." Linda pointed to a group photo hanging on the wall above a desk.

"My God, Linda. I think you might have hit the jackpot."

The photo was of 21 Masons, who looked like they just received their Scottish rite, 32nd degree. Donald, being a short man, was in the center of the front row. But the most valuable thing about the photo was the labeled date, May 21, 1974, and location, the Adamsburg, Pennsylvania, Consistory.

"My guess is that we have struck pay dirt with the photos, but I want us to keep searching. The more we find, the easier it will be to develop any possible links of our subject to the organization that's responsible."

Aside from the obvious evidence of his profession as a photographer, including awards from the National Photographers Association, there was a gallery of Frank Sinatra memorabilia, which looked almost like a shrine.

Mike felt that they now had a good direction from which to launch his federal investigation. The next step would be a trip to Adamsburg.

The three returned to their command post and soon retired for the night.

Mike was an early riser, thus he was up at 5 am the next day. Though he wasn't well rested, having tossed and turned all night. Going from one subject to the next in his dreams, he reviewed the results of the autopsy, then the apartment search, and then his attraction to Dr. Marshall. When he would reach satisfaction of his reviews, he would repeat the process over and over and over again throughout the night.

Mike was used to having control of situations, but his hunger to love Dr. Marshall was something he had no control over. Yet she was unaware of his feelings. Or was she? What the hell was he going to do about it? Because he had manufactured a need for her to be on the investigation team, the challenges for him now were to justify that decision, stay focused on the goal, hide his feelings, and achieve an ultimate investigatory success.

God help me. Mike thought. *Now that's a novel thought, a very common empty cliché that so many people utter in times of emotional stress. But what if I really do want God to help me? Why should he? God certainly would know if I'm honestly worthy of having Linda as a love partner in my life—or not? Well maybe I should do the right thing by God and make my request for guidance in the proper venue. I'll go to church.*

It was 6:30 am when Hank joined Mike in the kitchen.

"How long have you been up, Mike?"

"Since about five."

"Have coffee yet?"

"No, not yet."

"Hank, look, I've got something of a personal nature to take care of. Would you mind hanging around here and taking care of breakfast for yourself and Linda when she wakes?"

"No, of course not. What's up?"

"It's not something I want to talk about right now, but I promise I'll tell you when I feel up to it. It's 6:45. If I leave now, I should be back in about an hour."

"Okay, Mike. If there's anything I can do for you, I'm here. I think you know that."

"Thank you, Hank. You're a great friend, and I appreciate your understanding."

CHAPTER TWENTY-FOUR

On his way into Wrightstown, Mike had spotted a Roman Catholic church. Saints Peter and Paul was a beautiful, modern church located on the right side of the highway. The church was set back a good distance from the highway and had a large, beautifully landscaped parking area.

As Mike admired the fall-colored mums interspersed between the bushes, he felt his eyes moisten with the thoughts of autumn's beauty. All created by God—the God he was now going to ask for some emotional help.

Mike parked his car and walked into the church. Although it had been several years since he had been to a service, he felt comfortable entering the sanctuary. He realized how empty his life really had been without the spiritual lift he used to receive going to mass on Sundays. The feeling, after receiving the sacraments and being cleansed of sin, was unlike any other peace.

Everything was familiar to Mike as he sat in a pew and fumbled his way through an extemporaneous prayer. A priest entered the alter area, and from the pew, Mike could see that the priest was waiting for him to make some kind of request for assistance. Mike motioned to the priest to come to him.

As the priest walked toward Mike, he extended his hand in a sign of welcome. "Can I be of any assistance to you, my son?"

"Yes, father. I would like to have your counsel and perhaps make a confession."

The priest motioned for Mike to follow him to a room off the alter area and gestured for him to take a seat. "I'm Father Doman. How may I help?"

"Father, I'm a federal commissioner, investigating a very serious assault on our elected government officials, but that's not the problem. I made a tactical error by getting a women involved as my assistant."

"Why is this a problem, my son?"

"Because, Father, I have a romantic interest in her."

"It's not wrong for anyone to be romantically interested in a member of the opposite sex."

"It's a little more complicated than that, Father. She doesn't know of my interest in her, and she believes that I got her involved in the investigation solely on the basis of her professional skills."

"I still don't understand how this troubles you," the priest continued. "Has she expressed discomfort to you?"

"No. Nothing has happened. Father, I feel I'm being dishonest in our professional relationship because my motives go beyond the borders of this investigation. I'm afraid that if I continue letting her believe my interests in her are purely professional, the longer it goes on, the worse it will become to get us on a corrective course. I don't want to lose her. Should I tell her the truth?"

"With all that you have shared with me about this woman and your feelings for her, you haven't mentioned anything about either of you being married. Are either of you married?"

"I was divorced 10 years ago."

"You know the Catholic church prohibits divorce, but I'm also a realist. Kicking dead horses isn't part of my nature. I see where you're conflicted, and I'm going to help guide you through the emotional tangles. First, what is it that you want to happen?"

"Father, I want it to be a few weeks ago, when I didn't know this woman. I was unencumbered, free from needing her or anyone else. Now, well, now I'm tortured."

"Here it is, my son. You need to remove the veil of secrecy you created between the two of you. You can only achieve that by being open and honest. Consider the consequences of continuing along in the same way as you are now. You're an emotional wreck. What would you be like in another month?" Worst-case scenario, you come clean with her, and she becomes angry and walks away from you. Time will heal her momentary upset, and you'll have an opportunity to gain her respect later when she realizes that you were honest. If you have any chance of having a solid relationship with this woman, it will only be through honesty. Tell her the truth as quickly as possible. What are your thoughts?"

"I have been sitting in this church feeling the spiritual impact that's been vacant in my life for quite some time, and it feels good. I realize that my faith in God has never left me. And Father, I understand more than ever the need for me to be truthful. Thank you so much. I will handle this and place my trust in God for the eventual fate of this relationship."

"Good luck, my son."

It was 8:20 am when Mike entered the apartment. Hank and Linda were having breakfast. The smell of eggs, bacon, and toast permeated the apartment.

Mike was uneasy. He wanted to waste no time following through with Linda, but he needed to be alone with her, and it would be a challenge getting her away from Hank.

"Dr. Marshall, I need us to go back to the hospital lab and review something in your report. Could we do that now?"

Shit, thought Mike, *already I'm being untruthful.*

"Hank, will you make the arrangements for our trip to Adamsburg, Pennsylvania?"

"No problem, boss."

Mike and Linda headed in the general direction of the hospital. Mike was growing more anxious by the second as he felt his heart palpitating in his throat. He spotted a coffee shop and suggested that they have a fresh hit of caffeine. She agreed. As they sat waiting for the coffee to arrive, Mike took a deep breath and made his opening statement,

"Linda, I have a confession to make. It won't be easy for me, so I'm hoping that you would hold off any comments until I'm finished."

Linda's eyes sharpened to a laser-like focus. "What's going on here, Mike?"

"In as much as I deeply respect your professionalism, you need to know that I had ulterior motives for requesting your assistance. When I first laid eyes on you in Memphis, I was so attracted to you that I could barely focus on my purpose. The last thing I expected was to be dealing with a female pathologist, particularly one as attractive as you. I couldn't take my eyes off of you long enough to concentrate on what we were doing. I didn't want to leave Memphis because I wanted to explore a relationship with you. But that was out of the question;I had to leave. But even after I returned to DC, I had a very difficult time focusing. When the President offered me this commission, I saw a way to combine my personal interest in you with the investigation. It's important for me to be completely honest with you."

"Well, Mike, I don't know whether to be shocked, insulted, or flattered. I felt your clumsiness and stares, but I dismissed them as passing interest. I initially felt honored to be considered as a professional pathologist by our government, but now that feeling has been tainted. I have to admit I feel flattered by your interest. I'm also impressed by the intensity of your feelings. Though, you should've handled them differently. On the other hand, if you had, I wouldn't have seen the depth of your suffering and feelings for me. For that I am touched. However, for the moment I am stunned, so now please let's go back to the command post so I can arrange my return to Memphis. I need time to think about all this. For the benefit of this investigation, I won't make any decisive statements now. I will leave you with a patchwork of explanations for the President. I am as much of a patriot as you, and I want this investigation to succeed."

"Linda, I'm truly sorry that I got you involved mostly for my own selfish reasons, but for the record I want you to know that you were extremely helpful to me in Memphis and again here in New Jersey. I deeply regret the way I handled this."

While returning to the apartment, they avoided looking at one another. The drive felt endless.

Upon returning, Mike announced, "Hank. Please book Dr. Marshall on the first available flight back to Memphis. Her work here is complete."

Hank glanced at Mike and then at Linda. Both had looks of disappointment on their faces, and he knew better than to ask any questions.

"I'll get right on it, boss."

Mike went into the bathroom and stared into the mirror, analyzing the wrinkles around his eyes and sides of his mouth. He thought about how stupid he had been, and how he didn't deserve a woman like Linda. Why the hell would she want with an over-the-hill, wrinkle-faced, gumshoe like him anyway? The question went unanswered in his mind, and he decided to deal with his emotions concerning Linda later, when this was all over. For now, he needed to concentrate on the investigation.

CHAPTER TWENTY-FIVE

O n October 4, all the major networks carried the following
Presidential announcement.

"Good morning, my fellow Americans. The investigation into assassinations that have shocked our nation is moving along and gaining significant ground. As of noon today, the US Congress will return to their normal schedule and resume public business in public openness. We are confident that the risks will be no greater than would exist under normal business operation. I am, however, extending the heightened Capitol and White House security indefinitely."

CHAPTER TWENTY-SIX

On October 5, at 3 pm, Peter Fallow and Joe Richards met at the Avoca Airport in Scranton, Pennsylvania. When Joe entered baggage claim, Peter could see that his health was failing. Although Joe had his usual broad smile on his face, he was limping slightly and had a slight drag to his left leg.

Joe noticed Peter looking rather oddly at him, and so he made an effort to conceal his impairment by distracting his gaze. He opened his arms for a quick embrace, saying, "Hey, old pal, it's great to see you again."

The old friends embraced tightly. Peter felt his eyes moisten and burn, but he didn't want Joe to notice his emotion, so he held the embrace a little longer until he felt composed.

They turned and walked side by side to exit the airport. While walking, Peter wondered if his collaborative friend's limp might be due to a stroke. After listening to him talk, Peter concluded that Joe may have developed a walking impairment, but his speech was clear, and he appeared to be lucid.

Thank you, God, Peter thought.

Sensitive to the obvious, Peter said, "You look great, Joe. So much has happened. I can't wait to review everything with you, but I would prefer waiting until we get to my place first. Is that okay, Joe?"

"No problem, Pete. Do we have far to go?"

"We'll be there in 45 minutes."

They rode in silence through the airport grounds until they started onto the interstate when Joe said, "By the way, you look great, too."

They both laughed and shared bullshit and giggles the rest of the way to Hazleton, Pennsylvania.

The trees were beginning to change colors, providing a magnificent view as they ascended the mountains and looked down into Cunningham and Drums valleys, which formed the western valleys of Hazleton.

"Feast your eyes, Pete. At our age, this could be the last time we see these most precious wonders of God's creation."

"I agree, Joe, but I'll tell you this: Everything God created is beautiful. I repeat everything, but a few greedy men who have made it ugly."

"If only we could have been frozen in those first moments we shared of our youth," Peter continued. "The first experience of everything is the best experience of all—the first time we witnessed the leaves turning color in the autumn, the newness of spring, and the warmth of summer, those were the significant experiences that define life. When our eyes were opened to the wondrous sight of rivers and streams basking in a hot summer sun with colorful trees and flowers of the rivers banks cradling their flow. What we saw was real, what we smelled was clean, and what we touched we loved. I declare our first kiss of a girl should've been our last. From then on every kiss was an imitation that paled in comparison."

Joe laughed and Peter joined him.

"We love God," Peter continued. "We celebrate Him and then we rebuke him with questions of why. We use the why's to shelter our greedy need to relive those first experiences of love for life, which then after are never the same as that first experience. We become desperate and more self-indulgent in our quest to have that first kiss of life again. We become educated and socialized into a homogenous society. We gather wealth and many things along the way, and we fight wars to defend and protect ourselves from the one thing we never saw in the beginning—giving. When God gave us that first wonderful experience of life, we lost sight of the fact that He gave it to us. The secret we never learned is that we must also give. Please forgive me, Joe, I didn't mean to lecture on and on about God and the universe. You know how I am."

"My dear friend, Pete, you don't realize that it's these times when we're together and share the simple things about life is what makes our friendship good. If I could have anything frozen in time, Pete, it would be this very moment with us sharing our feelings about the perspective of change autumn is bringing to our attention."

"This too, Peter. God is giving it to us while on this trip for the first time. What shall we give to God, Pete?"

Peter looked over at Joe and caught his eyes. They held a stare for a moment. Peter took his right hand off the wheel and reached over to shake Joe's hand using the Masonic grip.

Once inside Peter's house in the Hazleton heights, Peter wasted no time getting to the point with Joe.

"Okay, Joe, we both know the extent of what has gone down since we made our plans in 2003. My first question I guess is, from your perspective is everything going according to expectation? And secondly, but perhaps more importantly, what has happened to you? I mean it's obvious to me that something has affected your walking."

"Well let me answer the second question first," Joe replied. "I had a slight stroke last year, just before Christmas. The doctor said in all probability I had strokes in the past and will continue to have them in the future. I went through all the diagnostic scans and vascular tests and was told that I was okay, whatever the hell that meant. But the doctor cautioned me that I may have another stroke in the future that could be more involved and leave me paralyzed. For now, my good friend, I am fine and in control of all my faculties. Except for my left leg being a little uncooperative, I'm fine."

"Well, what about the prostate cancer, Joe?"

"Thank God I haven't had any more problems with that."

"Jesus, Joe. Why the hell didn't you at least drop me a postcard or something. Maybe I could've helped in some way?"

"Pete, I didn't want to alarm and cause you any worry. Besides, when it first happened, I wasn't able to contact anyone. I was sort of out of it, and by the time I was aware of what was wrong, I was okay and able to take care of myself. Now please let's not dwell on my health any longer. To answer your other question, following my initial contacts with the operatives in the west coast, they all came on board with the cause, accepted the duty, and received the oath. After that I pretty much left the recruiting and plans of action up to each of the operatives because I thought any micromanaging might disturb them. I hope you agree with me that that would be extremely unwise.

"As for the extent of what has happened to date, I'm disappointed that our original declaration of seven assassinations a day hasn't been achieved," Joe continued. "However, a total of 13 corrupt politicians dead is progress—enough so that the other sons of bitches are franticly hiding their stolen treasures and sleeping with the lights on. So, I guess my answer to your question is no, everything is not to my expectations. But I am pleased that things are happening that will impact our corrupt, sold-out Congress."

"Yesterday the President announced a decision to order Congress back into open scheduling," Pete said. "That signals to me that they're feeling more secure. Perhaps, with that hotshot commissioner he appointed, they've identified our organization. What do you think, Joe?"

"Well, first of all, it was a smart move on the President's part. It was unwise to have Congress meeting secretly in the first place. It made them appear cowardly at a time when they should've been showing courage. So yes, that was a good move. Do I think they identified us? No, I don't think so. I don't know all the players, you don't know all the players, and the players don't know us. I'm sure Commissioner Mike Walters is no further along than when he first got involved."

"Okay, Joe, I feel the same as you. I think we should take advantage of the President's declaration of openness and allow for a period of normalization. Let's give them a sense of security for about a month, and then we'll start another round of hits. Can you contact the leaders you installed to see if this is possible? Also, please find out what slowed them down and what they need to see the mission through. Can you do that?"

"I think so. I'll take every precaution, but I think I can make the contacts."

"Okay, other than that, I this period of slow-down could be to our advantage. If we use our heads, it could actually work out better intervals of hits instead of sustained, unrelenting assassinations."

"The only downside is our health, Pete. Will we have the time to see it through the prolonged system of intervals?"

"That, Joe, is what we don't know. But for that reason, coupled with your recent history of strokes, we're going to cut this visit short."

"Tomorrow we will see about getting you back to Los Angeles on the first available flight. You must make those contacts as soon as possible."

"I know it important to get back and do what must be done, and I'm ready for that, but tonight let's please share perhaps our final night of friendship enjoying a few drinks and some good old fashion bullshit."

They laughed and shook hands again.

"I have just the place for us to go tonight," Peter said.

Peter lived in the Heights section of the city, which was located in the southeast section of Hazleton—a section of the city where many Italian immigrants settled to work the coal mine and railroad. "We're going to a place that serves the best damn Italian meatballs and sausage in the entire region. A man hasn't lived until he tasted Tony's Italian food."

CHAPTER TWENTY-SEVEN

Mike closed out the rental for the Wrightstown control center, and he and Hank hit the proverbial road for Adamsburg, Pennsylvania. Hank drove west along interstate 80 while Mike called John in Washington, DC.

"How's your progress?" John asked, without preamble.

"Well, Hank and I are heading to Adamsburg, Pennsylvania, to follow up with a possible connection of the late Mr. Wadsworth who may be a vital link in our investigation," Mike replied.

"What's your probability?"

"Well, John, it's pretty speculative. I've secured some materials that might establish a basis for the assassins' goals. If I'm right, the material will become concrete evidence for our prosecution."

Hank interrupted, "Mike, will you notify the institution in advance of our arrival?"

"Excuse me John, Hank and I need to talk about our approach to the people we'll be interviewing in Adamsburg." Mike said. "Depending upon where everything leads us today, which could go well into the evening, I'll give you a report sometime tomorrow."

"Okay, Mike, I'll be waiting to hear from you. Good luck."

Mike hung up the phone, then addressed Hank, "For our purposes, Hank, it would be more advantageous to appear without notice. Why give them any opportunity to prepare for our inquiry?"

Mike placed another call to the President's Chief of Staff to relate the same ambiguous report, just enough to establish that he was being proactive.

Mike felt a surge of satisfaction. He was beginning to feel validated as an investigator. *Damn straight*, he thought, *a man must be honest and true to his own convictions.*

Hank quizzically glanced at Mike.

"What's with the look?" Mike said, annoyed. "Jesus Christ, Hank, watch the fucking road."

The driver of a car in the passing lane blasted his horn and gave Hank the finger as he was almost forced off the road by Hank's distracted driving.

"Hey, Mike, can I ask how your mission went yesterday, when you left me alone with Linda? Come on, Mike, spill."

"Look, Hank, you are certainly one of the most trusted friends a man could be fortunate enough to have, and you're entitled to at least have an understanding of the circle you're involved with. I'm terribly attracted to Linda, so much so that she was monopolizing my thoughts. It became clear to me that if I didn't correct it, I could jeopardize this investigation. Imagine a lovesick detective investigating the most serious terror facing our nation today, a man unable to concentrate on anything but the woman who is torturing his mind.

"You said she *was* dominating your thoughts. She isn't any more?" Hank laughed with the question crossing Mikes face. "I knew it, Mike. First let me say that I'm glad you shared that with me. But I'm happier that you admitted this to yourself and did something about it. Think of how bad this could've become if you continued lying to yourself about her role in this investigation?"

Well, Hank, in my defense, she was introduced into the investigation because of a legitimate autopsy I was assigned to attend in

Memphis. But you're correct, and I thank God I discovered my impropriety as soon as I did."

"What the hell did you say to her to get her off the investigation?"

"I told her the truth. I was as honest as I could be with her about my feeling and selfish motivations. I think she understood, but she was hurt by my deception, I know that much for sure. I am truly sorry that I acted so stupidly, and I apologize to you for involving you in a stupid situation."

"Forget about it, Mike. You're only human. Although I must admit, for a while I wondered why you never showed any interest in the dating scene."

"That's easy, I inherited the poor marriage syndrome that often plagues cops with too many nights away from home and too little attention to the duties of a husband."

It was nearly 12:30 pm when they passed an interstate sign saying Adamsburg, 10 miles.

"First, let's locate the consistory first, and then we'll get some lunch while we review our approach," Peter said. "Depending upon results, we'll take it from there and go wherever necessary."

Hank rolled off the interstate and followed the signs on route 11 into the business district of Adamsburg. The town reminded Mike the days before shopping malls. It was nostalgically intoxicating looking at all of the specialty stores as they made their way through the traffic lights on the main street.

Suddenly they had arrived. The Consistory was in sight on the right corner of an almost town square. The majestic red stone building was enhanced by age, and it stood proudly in historic glory and dignity. Just looking at it made Mike feel more American and patriotic. Mike took a deep breath, his purpose renewed.

The men decided to skip lunch because it was nearly 1 pm. As they entered the building, Mike felt intimidated by the powerful effect this building had on him. He felt some historic inspiration—especially looking at a large painting of George Washington.

They were soon greeted in the lobby by a gentleman who introduced himself as Jerome Daniels, Consistory manager. "May I be of some help to you gentlemen," he inquired. "What lodge do you belong to?"

"None," replied Mike and Hank in chorus, presenting their badges.

"I'm Mike Walters, a federal commissioner on a special assignment for the President," Mike explained. "My colleague Hank is assisting. Do you mind answering a few questions, sir?"

"Based on our society's rules and policies, there are many things I am not allowed to divulge to non-Masonic members. However, questions of a general nature would be permissible," Jerome said.

"Mr. Daniels, please take a look at this group photo of a Scottish rite graduation class dated May 21, 1971. Can you identify the 21 Masons in this photo?"

"I'm afraid I cannot do that," Jerome said. "It's against our policy to identify any of our members."

"Let me emphasize that this request is being made as part of an official investigation by the federal government," Mike said, his irritation rising.

"Fortunately, Commissioner Walters, an American citizen of this institution is protected by the US Constitution."

"I don't have any reason to believe that by you giving me the identification of these members, you would be compromising the honorable tradition of this institution," Mike said.

"I'm very sorry, gentleman, but that is my position in this matter. Without a warrant, I cannot give you this information. If you have nothing further, I would like to get back to work."

"Fair enough, thank you for your time, Mr. Daniels. It's been a pleasure meeting you."

As Mike and Hank got back into the car, Mike explained they needed to go to a federal judge in Scranton, Pennsylvania, to acquire a warrant.

"How far is that from here, Mike?"

"My guess is about an hour or so. It's the closest federal district from here."

Mike pulled the address up on his GPS and found that by continuing north on route 11, they would go directly into Scranton, Pennsylvania.

"The identification of the members on that photo is critical to this investigation, Hank."

"Yes, Mike, but what do we give the judge as probable cause? The crux of your pursuit is based upon theory. Nothing here is concrete enough to establish probable cause."

"You're right, I know it. I must convince the judge there's a connection between Congressman Samuel Buckles's assassination in Tennessee and the assassinator George Stanton's age and autopsy results. Also, we must connect Donald Wadsworth's suicide with the poisonings of the congressman in New Jersey."

"I think that the possibility of Wadsworth's suicide having been caused by extreme guilt over his involvement in the deaths of those congressmen could persuade the judge to grant at least a limited warrant."

"Well, let's hope that the judge isn't a Mason," Hank quipped

They laughed together and were silent for the rest of the trip to Scranton.

It was 2:15 pm when they entered the federal building in Scranton. Inside the Federal Court Building, they were directed to the Honorable Floyd Brill, a federal district judge. The judge was a friendly, balding old gentleman with Irish written all over his badly wrinkled face. Mike presented all of the information about himself and the special investigation he was conducting. Mike reasoned with the judge that the expansion of his jurisdiction was indicated by the serious national safety threats our nation faced.

"As the lead investigator, all of my instincts tell me that I must know the identities of the men in this photo," Mike said. "We cannot move this investigation forward without those identities. This photo is the only significant trail developing since these assassinations begun."

"With all due respect, Commissioner Walters, as you know, we are a nation of laws. That's what distinguishes our country from others in the world. Now the reasons you lay out for the acquisition of a warrant does intuitively make sense; however, the probable cause requirement is rather anemic.

"In the interest of national security, I will provide you with a warrant only to obtain the names of the people appearing on the photo from the consistory," the judge said, reasoning to himself that it could be argued that by the very nature of taking part in a group photo is acknowledge you could be identified at some future point in time.

"Gentlemen, I think the requirements of the law will be met and as such we can live with it," the judge concluded. "If you obtain material evidence requiring additional warrants, please come to me for them without delay. In a court of law, delays or obvious attempts to circumvent the law won't be tolerated. Protocol, follow due process. I don't want any of us to be bit in the ass when we prosecute. Here is your warrant. Good luck."

"I want to tell you not to worry, your honor, but I know you will anyway.

"I guess I'll worry enough for all of us"

"Thank you very much, your honor. We'll do our best to justify your contribution in helping to uncover this organization of assassins."

Exiting the federal building at an enthusiastic pace Mike proclaimed, "Yeah. Right on."

Hank reached up, and they slapped hands in jubilation.

"Hank, I think we earned something to eat. Do you want to stop somewhere here in Scranton or somewhere along the way back to the consistory?"

"If it's okay with your stomach, I'd just as soon wait until were out of the city," Mike said.

"Good enough, I can wait, too."

It was 3:10 pm when they stopped on route 11 for a late lunch. Mike explained that since they still had enough time to get back to the Consistory before the end of the business day, it would be wise to eat something fast.

"I'm betting that the business manager has a 5 pm quit."

CHAPTER TWENTY-EIGHT

While Mike and Hank drove back to the consistory, they listened to an ABC news report.

"A new survey polled 1,000 voters," the commentator explained. "A whopping 81 percent of the subjects said they agreed that Congress was for sale to corporate interests. And an alarming 89 percent related that they believe the American people were lied to about the need to invade Iraq. The survey also found that the people polled believe the 'real threat' to our national security is being ignored due to the needs of big business to hire illegal immigrants for cheap labor. The group of 1000 were also outraged about the rising cost of energy."

"Sounds like the anti-establishment element is at work here, Mike," Hank said. "I'm going to try hard not to pay attention to what people are saying. It's important that we stay focused on the investigation. I know it sounds self-serving, but I hope that this trip leads us into a solid connection to the responsible organization."

"I'll tell you one thing, Hank, if it doesn't, we're back to square one."

It was 4:30 when they re-entered the consistory in Adamsburg. Luckily Mr. Daniels was still at his desk.

"Well gentlemen, I see you're back," he said.

"Yes, we are, Mr. Daniels," Mike said. "Only this time we have a federal warrant for the names of the people in this photo."

"May I please see the warrant?"

Mike handed the paper to Jerome, who gave the warrant a cursory review and acknowledged its validity, stating, "You do know, Commissioner, that this is for the names of the members appearing on the consistory class photo and that nothing beyond that information will be provided."

"Yes, that was the only information we were looking for earlier today."

"Gentlemen, since this photo was taken in the seventies, I'll have to check our archives. That will take some time. Could you come back tomorrow morning?"

Mike shook his head indicating an emphatic NO. Jerome was visibly annoyed because he was now going to put in some overtime. Hank winked at Mike, showing his "I don't give a shit" attitude.

"Please make yourselves comfortable out in the lobby," Jerome said, gesturing back to the lobby they just walked through. "I'll come to you when I have the information that the warrant requests."

"Thank you, we'll be fine. Go on and do whatever you must,"

Mike and Hank sat in the lobby, which was pleasantly decorated with historic photos and documents. CNN news was on in the lobby television.

Hank leaned over and whispered in Mikes ear, "Fuck the little bastard, this is probably the first work he's done in a month." Then Hank excused himself to go across the street where he had spotted an ice cream parlor.

"Would you like me to bring something back?" he asked Mike.

"No, thanks, I'm just going to kick back and relax."

Mike sighed and thought of Linda.

CHAPTER TWENTY-NINE

The next morning, in Roanoke, Virginia, Henry Lister sat in a doctor's office, waiting for the nurse to announce, "You're next." Henry was scheduled for 9:30 am, which was to be the doctor's second appointment.

"Mister Lister, you may go right in and take the second cubicle on the left, the doctor will be right with you."

Well, actually what happened next was a nurse came in, took his blood pressure, and asked him a lot of questions before finally saying, "The doctor will be you with shortly."

While waiting, Henry thought about the past 10 years. Since his early retirement 10 years ago, he spent a lot of time in doctor's offices and was getting used to waiting. He resented it, but he accepted it.

As a self-employed electrician, Henry had made a lot of money, and he was able to retire comfortably at the age of 67. He planned to do a lot of small craft boating in the Virginia Beach area, enjoying the rest of his life near the ocean and in the sun. Henry had no problem adjusting to the retirement of his dreams during those first several years of retirement. He went from the occasional use of his boat while working to daily recreational adventure on the waters. But he was only three years into his retirement when he lost his first mate, Joan.

Joanie, as he fondly called her during their 40 years of marriage, had a massive stroke and wound up in a long-term care facility. Few things are more devastating than the need to provide personal care to the one you love. Joanie had been the glue that held their family together, the strength of the family who provided the stability of the proverbial Home Sweet Home. The couple's only daughter lived across the country in California. Henry had cared for his wife at home as long as possible, but after a long, grueling month he accepted suggestions from visiting nurses to move her to a nursing home.

Henry tearfully acquiesced. It was extremely painful for him to watch his life's mate being removed from their home, which they built together and lived in all their loving years, knowing never to return. Sadly, it would never be the same.

Henry moved Joanie to the most reputable facility he could find. He visited her faithfully every day, until her death one year later.

Following Joanie's death, Henry tried getting back to his boating but it was never the same. His boat, the *Sweet Joan*, reminded him of how much he missed her and how empty his life and the boat now seemed.

These things have no meaning anymore without my Joan being here to share them with me, Henry thought. *They're just things—dead as she is and as dead as I am without her.*

Henry wiped the mist from his eyes as the doctor entered the cubicle.

"Henry, are you ok?" the doctor asked kindly.

"Just reminiscing," Henry replied. "Who the hell ever said, you can't live in the past? Let me tell you, doc, that's the only way I can live now that my wife is gone. I have tons of photographs that we took throughout our years, and I spend a lot of time looking at them. When I die, I want them buried with me. Nobody else will need or want them anyway."

The doctor nodded sadly, then said, "Henry, I have news. The results from your tests showed the tumor has enlarged and metastasized throughout your body. The chemo and radiation, which slowed the process before, haven't worked for us this time around."

Henry absorbed this news and asked, "How long do I have?"

"I have no exact time to tell you. However, I estimate that you have three, maybe six months to live."

"What will it be like?"

"Over the next few months, you'll lose a lot of weight. During the later months, you'll become weak and spend most of your time in a chair or in bed. The final phase will be painful, but we'll prescribe a morphine drip for you to administer according to your own level of tolerance. This could be done in your own home or at hospice."

"If at all possible, staying at home would be preferable."

"We can arrange for a local hospice to assist you through the final ordeal,"

"I don't think that will be necessary."

"Well, I think you should at least talk to the people from a hospice; they can be very comforting for you at this time. I'm sorry to be the bearer of such bad news."

"Doctor, I've been preparing for this ever since I was first diagnosed," Henry said. "Also, my life without Joan has been lonely and empty. No disrespect to all of those who tried to help me forget and get on with my life, but joining her in eternal sleep sounds pretty good to me about now. I appreciate whatever chemical relief that you could make available for my end. However, I have other ideas for a painless exit. I thank you and your nurses for the fine compassionate care you have shown me this past year. You've all been great; thank you very much."

"Henry, please give those people an opportunity to help you through this. I don't care for the way you announced, 'other plans for a pain free exit.' That's not the way to make your exit. Please listen to me. It's not a good time to be alone. See those people and contact your daughter."

Back home, Henry wrote a long letter to his daughter in California explaining his terminal condition. He let her to know that he was proud of her and loved her very much. He gave her a detailed account of his holdings and that she could find all his financial documents in a bank box in Roanoke. He didn't want to have her flying home to be with him during his terminal state; she would only be in his way. So, when he completed the letter, he sealed it and gave it to his attorney with instructions that it be delivered at the time of his death.

On October 3rd, Henry called the number on the slip of paper he had been carrying in his wallet since 2003. He left a short coded message, "I am ready to make the final sacrifice."

Henry hung up the phone and decided to take his usual midday nap. He fell asleep, holding his wife's photo in his hand.

On October 4th, Henry looked out the window, thinking how wonderful it is to wake and see the morning sun. *To live and take its warmth for granted is one thing, but to be alive with all its warmth in your heart is quite another.*

Henry shook off the feeling that he didn't have too many more sunrises to enjoy. In fact, if all went according to his plan this would be the last day of his life.

Henry could not allow any distractions, so he went about his routine of grooming, ate a light breakfast, and straightened up his bedroom. He always prided himself in being neat. He always believed his mother would haunt him if he embarrassed her with a filthy home. So, he would leave behind a neat, clean, orderly home.

It was 7 am when he rolled onto route 81, headed north onto route 66, and from there would go south to Richmond, Virginia. In Richmond, he'd sleuth out Congressman Luther Nobles and that would be that—the end for the both of them: the end of Nobles's reign of corruption and the fulfillment of my Henry's duty.

Congressman Nobles was a "blue dog" Democrats who earned his seat by acting like a Republican. He paid a lot more attention to the needs of big business than he did to his middle-class, hard-working constituents. He was identified as a back stabber by those who contributed money and worked hard for his election. It became apparent to his supporters that his hand was extended to both sides. With many Richmond husbands and wives working two jobs, yet earning less and less and unable to meet the needs of their families, having a Congressman favor an amnesty program for illegal immigrants was a betrayal of the American worker.

Henry was on the road for an hour and a half and still on 81 when it started to rain. He turned on the windshield wipers and was soon caught up in their rhythmic sound. To Henry, it sounded like they were saying, "I'm coming home. I'm coming Joan. I'll soon be with you."

It was 10 am when Henry parked his car in a crowded downtown parking lot located near Congressman Nobles's district office. Henry took special care to park neatly between the yellow lines. He wrote a note requesting that his money from the future sale of car be donated to the American Cancer Association and American Heart Association. He thanked them in his letter and signed goodbye.

As Henry crossed the street to the administrative building, he could smell the humidity of the air coming evaporating off the cement sidewalk. He was overwhelmed with nostalgia. *Amazing,* he thought, *how peculiar a feeling when smelling the air could remind one of so many places and things.* With a deep breath he pondered this day. *Is it possible today could be one of the most peaceful days of my life? It's like a climax to a life of waiting for the ultimate unity of faith. If all goes well, I will reunite with my Joanie and give the American people a gift of hope at the same time.*

The city sidewalks were bustling with people going to and from activities in all directions. *They have purpose and their own things going on. I guess that is all that really matters.*

Henry was so lost in his musings that he suddenly realized he was in front of Congressman Nobles's district office. The large plate glass window had impressive large gold print lettering "U.S. Congress District Office" arched across the top. The entrance door was slightly angled and recessed. Henry entered through the door and into the narrow hallway, which had postings on both sides of the hallway. One pink paper posting caught his immediate attention: Town Hall Meeting, 8 pm October 4, 2005, American Legion Post 835.

Henry thought the angels were already on his side. *This is perfect.*

He looked at his watch; it was now 11:12 am. The challenge he now faced was how to stay busy for the next eight hours. He felt that he could inconspicuously spend the afternoon hours in the public library, leave just before 6 pm, and then use up an hour sitting in a church, which would be perfect for making his spiritual peace just before the end.

Henry walked the few blocks to the public library, where he found a book by Colonel Robert Engersoll, a great orator and philosopher during the early years of the nineteenth century. As he paged through the chapters, he came upon a chapter entitled "Love" and was moved by the words, "Love is the only bough on life's dark cloud; the kindler of every fire on every hearth, the morning and the evening star. It shines upon the babe and sheds its radiance upon the quiet tomb."

Henry loved the meaning and felt the depth of that chapter and thought, *If I were willing to go on living without my love, I would memorize every line. But without her, I will settle for the love we shared together and let the quiet radiance shine upon both our eternal tombs.*

Henry closed the book with moist eyes and decided that those words about love would be the last words he would ever read. How appropriate, how privileged, how providential it all appeared to be for him in his final moments of life. He added to his thoughts, *Getting rid of those corrupt sons of bitches who bring misery and hardship, which destroys the hope of love for the people they swore to serve: This deed is my parting gift to the people.*

It was 7:45 pm, and the October sky in Richmond just started to darken as Henry entered the American Legion. In the hall, he observed about a hundred people (mostly seniors) who were already seated. Meanwhile several others who appeared to be in charge were shaking hands and directing activities near the door. Henry spotted an empty chair in the front row, and he sat down. He wasn't quite sure how it would work out, but he would seize any opportunity that presented itself to make his move. Since escape wasn't part of the plan, the only important thing was to make the hit. At 8:05, pm the program chairlady offered some partisan remarks and introduced the congressman.

Congressman Nobles spoke for about 30 minutes. He then fielded some questions from the audience and happily offered to greet his constituents for several minutes before parting. Henry knew this would be the only opportunity he would have to make his move, so he joined the line to shake the congressman's hand.

The congressman stepped down from the stage and took a post conveniently near an exit door to Henry's right. Henry was third in line to meet him. Henry extended his nondominant left hand for the handshake. Gripping the congressman's hand tightly and without releasing it, Henry shot him in the right temple with a 25-caliber palm pistol.

As Henry was executing the congressman he whispered, "You better hope God forgives you for the damage you have done to our country. The people will not."

As the congressman slumped to the ground, Henry ended his own life with a shot to his head.

Henry fell on top of the congressman, and their bloody bodies horrified the screaming ladies in the hall. Henry couldn't hear the screams, but his face bore a very peaceful expression.

CHAPTER THIRTY

I t was nearly 8 pm when Mike and Hank returned to their car. It had been difficult getting all of the names from that bastard Daniels. After waiting for several hours, Hank was so annoyed that he jokingly suggested going to the basement and giving him a little physical persuasion.

Mike and Hank walked into a crowded restaurant and found a cozy table in a corner, which had good lighting.

"This will do fine, Hank. We will be able to review the identities on the photo while we wait for our dinner."

"Great, only let's get something ordered fast. I'm starving."

"Me, too."

A waitress greeted them with menus and began reciting the specials.

"What is the quickest?" Mike interrupted.

"Everything listed as a special is quick."

They both ordered the tenderloin tips covered with onions, peppers, and mushrooms, smothered in gravy on a bed of wild rice.

"And drinks, gentlemen?"

It was a beer day for Hank, so he ordered a cold mug of draft

Rolling Rock. Mike was a martini mood, so he ordered a vodka martini. The order was placed, and as they were sipping on their drinks Mike rolled out the rectangular photo of the May 21, 1974, class of the Adamsburg Consistory graduates.

Alongside of the photo he had the list of names identifying the graduates. Front row from left to right they were identified as:

1. William Rodgers*
2. John Powell
3. Carl Duffy
4. Anthony George
5. Peter Fallow*
6. Kenneth Oakdale
7. Joseph Richards*
8. Keith Stockton
9. John Grubb
10. Lawrence Smith

SECOND ROW FROM LEFT TO RIGHT:
1. John Weatherly
2. George Stanton*
3. William Burger
4. Donald Wadsworth*
5. Thomas Shade
6. Dennis Monk
7. James Petri
8. Thomas Whitaker
9. Henry Lister *
10. Leonard Stank
11. Noel Jones

"My God, Hank. Look at this. The second row, second man in from the left is George Stanton—Congressman Buckle's assassin. And the fourth man from the left in the second row is none other than Donald Wadsworth, our mystery suicide man."

"You have me convinced, Mike. If not a conspiratorial connection, at the very least they definitely knew each other. Now we need to know the extent of their relationship."

"Okay, let's assume that Wadsworth was involved in the Jersey assassinations, and we know that Stanton was. Can we extrapolate further and theorize that others in this photo were also involved? Do we now have the organizational hub in this photo?"

The television program was interrupted for a special bulletin: "At 8:40 pm, Congressman Luther Nobles was assassinated in Richmond, Virginia. He had just finished addressing an audience of his constituents in the local American Legion hall. While shaking hands, he was shot by a senior citizen who then shot and killed himself."

The commentator went on to describe the pandemonium in the hall and explained that they hadn't yet identified the assassin.

"No. No. Hold on a moment. They now seem to know who the assassin was. Let's go to our crew outside the American Legion in Richmond. What do you have? What can you tell us?"

"Good evening, I'm Sarah Walters, reporting on the scene. It is confirmed that Virginia Congressman Luther Nobles was shot and killed in the Legion Hall directly behind me just minutes ago. After killing the congressman, the shooter took his own life. While no official statement has been made by the authorities, our source has identified him as Virginian Henry Lister, based upon an automobile that was located in a nearby parking garage. Inside the car, a suicide-type note was discovered. I will stand by with our crew until there is an official statement from the police."

Mike looked at Hank. Not speaking, he gestured his amazement by throwing both hands into the air. Hank was about to say something when the news was interrupted once again.

"We're going live to Richmond, Virginia, to hear an official report from Richmond Chief of Police Robert Stern."

"At this time, I can confirm that Congressman Luther Nobles was shot and killed during an appearance before his constituents in the American Legion Hall here in Richmond, Virginia," Commissioner

Stern said. "We identified the assassin as Henry Lister of Roanoke, who then took his own life. Both bodies have been transported to the city morgue where autopsies will be performed. I have nothing further to report at this time."

Reporters were screaming, "Is this part of the other assassinations, chief? And, "Is there a connection?"

"I have no comment, other than this will all be thoroughly investigated."

Mike and Henry grabbed the list of names and the photo and hurried out of the restaurant.

"Hank, first of all, Lister is on that list. I need to get back to DC to brief John and the President, but I also want to have Linda go to Richmond and participate in that autopsy."

"Mike, Do you really think she will?"

"Don't say it. I know what I did and what I said, but now the pieces are coming together, and I genuinely *do* need her help."

"Good luck, I hope you can convince her that you're sincere now."

"Let's gas up and get the fuck on the road. I'd like to be in Washington tonight so we can have a fresh start in the morning."

"Okay, boss. Let's roll."

CHAPTER THIRTY-ONE

I t was 8 am the next day when Mike called John Craig and stated, "There is a major development," before requesting a meeting of the principal investigators for 10 am.

John responded in the positive but reminded Mike that this better be something very important because he was going to cancel another meeting scheduled with the mayor.

"Do you feel that the mayor should be present?" John asked.

"No, not at this time. I wouldn't want this to become public just yet."

"Okay, see you at 10." John said

Mike hung up with John and immediately dialed Linda's number on his cell. He dialed the number frenetically, hoping she would pick up herself and not allow some secretary to run block for her. Linda answered on the third ring, and her voice caught Mike a little off guard.

"Hello?" Linda asked.

"Linda, is it you? Mike asked.

"Yes. This is Dr. Marshall."

"This is Mike Walters. Doctor, please give me a moment to explain our new development."

"Mike, you have my undivided attention. I can't wait to hear this."

"Did you hear the news last night about the Congressman who was assassinated in Virginia?"

"Yes, I did."

"Do you remember the Masonic group photo we found in Wadsworth's New Jersey apartment?"

"Yes, I remember that as well."

"Well, here it comes, using a court ordered federal warrant, Hank and I were able to gain the identities of the men in the photo. As it turns out George Stanton, the man you did the post on in Memphis who died after assassinating Congressman Buckles, was in the group photo. It gets better: Donald Wadsworth is also identified on the photo. And now for the most interesting of all: Henry Lister, who assassinated Congressman Luther Nobles last night in Richmond, Virginia. . ."

"Let me guess, he was also on the list?"

"Yes, Linda. He is in the photo. I'm calling to tell you all of this because I promised you nothing but the truth, and the truth is that I need you please to go to Richmond and take charge of the Henry Lister autopsy. Will you do it? Remember, you're still officially a member of this investigative team."

"Mike, of course I will. You're not the only dedicated patriot. I also care."

"Great, I'll make it up to you. I will particularly need to know what underlying diseases, if any, might have motivated his murder and suicide. Hank will make the arrangements in Richmond and take care of the travel. Do you mind if I have Hank meet you there and provide any support you may need?"

"Not at all, I'm very comfortable with Hank."

"Okay, you'll hear from Hank very soon. Good luck, and again, thank you. My sincere thanks."

It was nearly 8:30 am when Mike called Hank. Hank anticipated Mike and was already planning to go to Virginia and assist Linda.

"You're an alright guy, Hank."

"Yeah, I know I am. I should probably be thinking ahead about being a best man."

Mike laughed heartily and responded, "I really must keep my word with Linda and keep this thing professional."

"Okay. But remember, it's me you're talking to now."

"All the way professional, that's it, Hank."

"Okay, I'll be your parrot and repeat your words, if that makes you happy."

"Good, now get to work."

Hank sung in a gravelly voice "I'm on my way to Richmond, on a professional mission."

They both laughed and hung up their phones.

It was 10 am when John Craig opened his office door and motioned for Mike to enter.

"Well, Mike, what do you have?"

"I have the identities of the men on the 32nd degree Masonic photo I told you about—the one taken at the Adamsburg Consistory in Pennsylvania of the Scottish rite graduates on May 21, 1974. The one we found in Donald Wadsworth's New Jersey apartment."

"How did you manage to shake that info from the Masons?"

"Well, they first refused the info telling me that it was their policy. So, Hank and I went to a federal judge in Scranton, Pennsylvania, for a warrant. He wasn't easy to convince because of our lack of probable cause. But with some word tweaking, he authorized a limited warrant specifically for the names."

"Where's Hank? We're getting a little ahead here."

"Hank's off to Richmond. I'll explain that later. Here it is in a nutshell. George Stanton the assassinator of Congressman Buckles in

Memphis Tennessee is in this photo, too. Right here—I have his head highlighted for you."

"Jesus, Mike, you've really got something here."

"It gets better. That next highlighted man is Donald Wadsworth. And as for the next highlighted man on the photo, did you see last night's news, the man identified as Henry Lister who assassinated Congressman Luther Nobles in Richmond Virginia?

"Yes."

"Well, believe it or not that's Henry Lister."

John took the photo and examined it for several minutes. "Mike, this is so implicitly connected that it's almost too good to be true. My God, man, this is great work. What's your next move?"

"Okay, now let me share with you why I sent Hank to Richmond. I definitely believe that these men, particularly Stanton and Lister, were part of an organizational plot. It doesn't take a rocket scientist to figure out that at least part of the organizational membership consists of Masons. Now, Stanton dropped dead of a coronary following his kill of Buckles, and Lister took his own life after assassinating Nobles. Besides their Masonic acquaintance, Stanton's autopsy results showed he had very little time to live. And that is why Hank is on his way to Richmond. He will join Dr. Marshall, who is on her way to Richmond from Memphis as we speak. I'm hoping to identify motive: Why did Lister take his own life? Was he terminal, too? Meanwhile I need some support staff to help locate the other men on the photo and uncover brief biographies."

"Okay, Mike, I will arrange for our office staff to do those workups immediately. Very possibly we'll discover that some are deceased, though."

"That is fine, as long as they expired before all of these assassinations started," Mike said. "Now that you are briefed on all that's developed, I must update the President and the FBI. If we're correct, we're on a very hot trail. With a little luck, we can bring this to a quick end."

John laughed and said, "Yeah maybe the rest of the group will die of natural causes before they have a chance to take other people with them."

"Mike, watch your step with the politicos. They eat people up and spit them out daily without conscience. Also, remember the people we're looking for are acting out of disappointment in their government. And although we are duty bound to bring the assassins to justice, in the end we don't want to wonder if while achieving justice, right was sacrificed."

"I promised myself that I will stay focused on the law and that will be the extent of my duty. When this is all over, I hope to God that what I did was ethical and contributed to the safety and well-being of my countrymen. Throughout my career I was never political, especially not in the performance of my duties."

John rose from his chair behind the desk, walked over to Mike, embraced him with a bear hug, and said, "I've always known that, Mike."

"Now get the fuck out of here before we start sobbing and make fools of ourselves. Go get 'em."

"Okay, I'm out of here."

"Call me when you have those profiles."

CHAPTER THIRTY-TWO

Outside on the White House lawn, reporters from all over the world were anxiously awaiting the Presidents response to the latest assassination of a US Congressman.

Their wait was ended when the press secretary announced, "Ladies and gentlemen of the press, I am honored to present the President of the United States."

The early October sun was bright but more bronze than its summer yellowish gold. It felt good and foreboding at the same time, making one wonder if they should enjoy the moment or dread what was coming. A slight wind gently flapped the American flag, making a sound both eerie and uplifting. The ineffable mood within the gathering crowd of reporters cast a serious air of unease. It was about to change. Would the President offer a message of hope or would doom eclipse our traditional freedoms?

Silence fell over the crowd of reporters as the President approached the microphones. He was looking angry and older than he did a short while ago during the last press conference.

He opened his remarks with his usual greeting to all citizens of this great nation.

"My fellow Americans, last evening Congressman Luther Nobles was assassinated in Richmond, Virginia. He had just completed a town hall meeting when an elderly gunman shot and killed the congressman and then took his own life. We believe this latest assassination is part of an organizational plot to disrupt the operation of our government. We will not allow that to happen. I am once again directing all members of both houses of our government to continue to operate openly and conduct their duties without disruption. We will not run for cover. We will not cower because of these cowardly acts."

The press secretary announced, "The President will now take a few brief questions."

Mark Lewis of *Universal News* magazine, a former political science professor turned reporter, appeared on many political talk shows. He was a non-partisan reporter who prided himself with being a truthful, never embellishing the facts, which made him a favorite with both left- and right-wing talk show hosts.

"Mr. President," he said, "it's all well and good for you to take the high road and direct all congressmen to appear in the open. But with all due respect, sir, it's not you that they're shooting at. Would you comment please?"

"Mark, I say this not to appear undaunted by the threat that obviously exists for all members of Congress, but with regards to the oath of office we all take. Particularly the words, 'to protect and defend.' There is much more at stake here, and we must not allow these malcontents to get away with these acts. If a member of Congress feels that his/her life is in danger, then they must decide whether or not they want public service or private citizenship. They have the choice to stay or resign. I remind all of you that we are at war with a thing called terrorism—a war we're sending our young brave soldiers to fight against and die for. I proclaim that no less is expected of our elected officials."

George Steockel, of *Future USA News* asked, "Mr. President, the point you make with the military vis-à-vis elected officials is well taken, but what do you think of the difference that the military are armed to defend themselves and elected officials are not?"

"Well, George, that is a very good point. And the only way I can respond is by asserting that we have many layers of law enforcement all designed to protect our Houses. I'm not implying that there isn't risk. There of course is risk, and it's a risk we have chosen to take based upon our oath and allegiance to America."

Dorothy Cohn, of *Chicago Voice* asked, "Mr. President, since you used the war on terrorism as a metaphor, if you would have stayed the course in Afghanistan until you captured or killed Osama Bin Laden, wouldn't that have achieved the vindication for 9/11 Americans needed? And if so, wouldn't that, if achieved, remove your motivation to invade Iraq? Some sources believe that outsourcing the pursuit of Osama to Afghanistan tribes guaranteed that he would remain at large, thus allowing you to continue your goals into Iraq?"

Oh shit. Here it comes, the President thought, but he said, "That's nonsense. At all times I have been thoroughly advised by my Cabinet and military experts on how to prosecute this war on terrorism. I direct your attention to the fact that there have been no attacks in the United States since the Trade Towers. Do you think that is just a coincidence?"

The last question went to Pat Sherman of *Baltimore News.* "Mr. President, what if anything, has the investigative team achieved since you announced your appointment of Detective Michael Walters to serve as a special investigative commissioner?"

"Thank you, Pat. I have been notified by Commissioner Walters this morning that he and his team have uncovered some relative information regarding the assassinations and requested a meeting with me and my advisors. I will be attending that meeting today. Thank you all for coming, this press conference is over."

Some reporters were shouting to the exiting President, "Mr. President, why are the American people losing faith in their elected congressmen?"

"What motivates our seniors to resort to assassinating their elected government officials?"

The same chorus of questions was shouted at the departing back of the President. His backhanded wave was indicative of disgust and dismissal.

IT WAS 20 PAST TWELVE NOON WHEN HANK CALLED MIKE ON his cell phone, "Mike, I have the results on Lister's autopsy. Are you ready?"

"I'm on my way to the White House for a meeting. Give it to me fast."

"Lister was dying from cancer. He was treated with chemo and radiation in the past, but he was terminally ill with new metastasis. Linda indicated that he probably had only days of life remaining."

"How was Linda? Did she seem okay with my request to do the autopsy?"

"Yeah, Mike, I'm telling you she's quite a pro. She never flinched, she was businesslike and said to me, 'I hope this helps.' That's all she said, except that she would submit a complete written report. Mike."

"What?"

"Words aren't everything; I think she cares about you. If that's really what you wanted to know."

"Okay, Hank, good work. Get back to the office and make a report of your activities to date. When I get back, I'll review everything with you, and we'll take it from there. I want you to get some rest or get laid, whatever it takes to freshen your mind and body, because I think we're going to be busy as hell when I get back. So, my friend, it may be a while before any of us we are able to relax again."

"Good enough, Mike. I can manage to strengthen my spirits and take care of my own physical needs, but what about you?"

Mike laughed at that and said, "Hey, guy, I'll just have to live on memories."

"Forget the memory and work your imagination with Linda. Do you want me to give you some guided imagery?"

"Thank you very much, but I think I can handle the imagery all by myself. Goodbye."

"Goodbye yourself, and sweet dreams...."

Mike entered the White House and looked at his watch. It was now 12:40, and his meeting wasn't scheduled until 1 pm. He announced himself to the receptionist, who directed him to the room where the meeting was to be held. She explained that he could have a sandwich, soup, and a coffee brought in while waiting for the President and the others. He needed the nourishment and also the time to go over his notes for the meeting, so he was grateful for the opportunity. The room had no windows, although it was well furnished with a quality conference table and impressive wall hangings and sound-proofed, too. A large impressively framed copy of the "Bill of Rights" was hung on the east wall of the room. The room had an air of intellect and power about it, and Mike felt inspired to do his best. At exactly 1:10 pm the President entered the room, accompanied by George Prendergast of the FBI and Maximillian Bird, CIA Director.

After they were all seated and went through the usual greetings, the President said, "Mr. Walters, I understand you have some powerful developments concerning the assassinations to report. I certainly welcome anyone bearing positive news, so let's have it."

"Well, Mr. President and gentlemen, while acting on a hunch and accompanied by Dr. Linda Marshall and Detective Hank Craigle, I went to Wrightstown, New Jersey. There I arranged for Dr. Marshall to participate in the autopsy of Donald Wadsworth, a senior citizen who took his own life shortly following the funeral breakfast assassinations in Wrightstown. Although the autopsy offered nothing atypical, the surprise came when we conducted a warranted a search of his apartment. Among our discoveries, there was a group photograph of 21 graduates of the Scottish Rite 32nd degree Masons, dated May 21, 1974, and taken at the Adamsburg Consistory in Pennsylvania."

"Yes, yes, and what did that tell you?"

"Detective Craigle and I went to the consistory to conduct an inquiry about the members in the photograph. We obtained the names of the men in the photo. To my amazement, three of our suspects were in that photo: George Stanton, Donald Wadsworth, and Henry Lister. The entire group is now suspected as the mother organization behind the assassinations. These men at the very least knew each other and had a comfort level to plot and confide under the protection of their traditional oaths of secrecy."

Maximillian Bird inquired, "Do you have any reason to believe that it could involve other Masonic groups? Could it be more wide-spread and involve others outside the brotherhood? Actually, is it possible that this may only be a small fraction of 32nd degree Masons?"

"No sir I do not. It's entirely possible that it is just a few members on this photograph—and that some of the people in the organization aren't in the photo. For example, New Jersey waitress Marie Lemon can't be a Mason because women aren't allowed to become Masonic members. Right now, my team is researching the other members in the photo."

George Prendergast volunteered to use the resources of the FBI to accelerate the profile development of the others in the photo. Prendergast interlaced his fingers together when Mike noticed he was wearing a Masonic blue lodge ring on the middle finger of his right hand. Mike felt that an injection of diplomacy was now needed.

"Gentlemen, what I have shared with you here are the material facts. All of this speculation into the Masonic institutions could very well be limited to a handful of political activates acting on their own without any Masonic lodge knowledge or support. I hope that we can all be politically discreet and keep the Masonic auspices out of our public revelations, announcing only that we have some solid information leading us to the assassins. Mr. Prendergast, I noticed your ring and hope you are not offended by my report."

"Not at all, I am impressed with the material you presented, and I assure everyone in this room that my first loyalty is to the position of trust I hold in the law enforcement of the United States. You can count upon my discretion and appreciation for your achievement."

"Mike, I speak for all of us in this room and America," the President said. "You're doing a great job. I'm pleased with what you have shown us today, and I'm confident that you're on the right track. Once we've advanced the investigation more, I'll call the four of us together for another press conference. Mr. Walters, thank you for being here today. My schedule is demanding so I must bring this meeting to an end. Good luck with the hunt."

"George and Max, I'll see you in my office in ten," the President directed at the pair.

CHAPTER THIRTY-THREE

It was nearly 2:30 pm when Mike returned to his office. He sat at his desk and crossed his legs over the corner. His work section was next to a window, which he always kept half open. The busy street noises—car horns, shouts, screeching brakes, and sirens—complemented the strangeness of his life and made him feel alive.

Mike shook himself away from the thoughts he was rationalizing. The southern exposure of his office added the mid-afternoon warmth of the sun to his exhausted, middle-aged body. He could smell October through the window, and a quiet contentment pervaded his being.

Between the anticipation of falling in love with Linda coupled with a successful day with the investigation, he was feeling intoxicated with life. Mike closed his eyes and drifted off in thoughts about life and death. He was experiencing a moment of enlightenment with the growing realization man might understand life, but he knows nothing of death. Death is a dark, boxed-in void occupying all the bright borders of the living.

Mike concluded his daydreaming with the ultimate awakening, *It's important to live life while you're alive and forget dwelling upon the need for a life in the hereafter and wasting the only real thing you know about: the here and now.*

Mike mulled that point over when his thoughts shifted to the assassinated congressman and the dead assassins. *They're all dead,* Mike thought. *None of them have another chance at life. It's gone forever. Jesus died as a sacrifice for our sins; did these assassins do the same for our children's future? Who the hell was right: the elected congressman or the assassins who ended their lives? When does a man know he's on the right side of an issue? How does one know when the right side of an issue morphs into the wrong side? And if that happens, do you have the courage to do the right thing?*

Mike called out to the office secretary that he'd be dozing off for awhile and asked her to call him as soon as Hank arrives. Mike reclined in his chair and guided his imagination throughout his body trying to relax while waiting for that bridging moment between being awake and asleep.

That's an odd expression, he thought as he fell sleep. *How does one fall without hurting himself in the process?*

A mental image of Linda kept trying to appear, but her beautiful face and hair were blurred and kept changing form. *Why does that happen? I know she's beautiful, and I desperately want to be in love with her. I need to be in love with her, and I don't know how to make it happen?* With the thought of loving her, Mike fell asleep.

It was 4 pm when the telephone began angrily ringing off the hook, waking Mike from his deep nap.

Mike answered. "Yes, Doris?"

"Hank's here."

"Send him in. Thanks, Doris."

Hank entered Mike's office, looking a bit tired and said, "I don't care who gets shot today. I need some fucking sleep before my next assignment."

"Fair enough, old pal."

"First, give me all the details from Richmond, and then we'll arrange a break for your exhausted bag of 206 tired bones." Hank said.

"The autopsy revealed that Henry Lister was dying of cancer and had only months or even days to live," Mike reported. "He was treated for cancer twice, but his second round of chemo and radiation therapy failed."

"So, what that tells us is that he had nothing to lose by ending his life," Hank mused. "The autopsy confirms he was a 77-year-old male with a terminal disease."

"Right, and our theory fits. He was part of a secret organization of patriotic elderly assassins on a suicide mission, who are duty bound to end corruption in America. They cannot be brought to justice because they're already dead. But ironically, they *can* bring justice to America. Because death is the ultimate consequence for a homicide, in a sense they're prepaid."

"Well, Mike, I'm sold," Hank said. "Everything points that way, but since dead men don't talk, we're left with the voice of their environments."

"Did I mention that Lister had a daughter in California?" Mike asked.

"Yes."

"Okay, you go home and get some rest. I'll find out where his daughter lives in California. But first, I'm going to get some rest, too. Tomorrow, we'll plan a visit to California."

"Okay, see you in the morning."

Mike and Hank, both fresh from a good night's sleep, drove to the Ronald Reagan National airport in Arlington, Virginia. They boarded a 747 Boeing jumbo jet with round-trip tickets to LA. The lift-off view—with the morning sun bathing the Virginian and DC homes, buildings, and traffic—was breathtakingly beautiful. As they gained altitude, the Atlantic shoreline became visible.

Mike imagined the earth below growing smaller while his

universal perspective grew larger and larger. He needed this exhilaration once in a while, needed to contrast the power of the universe with the smallness of man. Meditating upon the wonders of galaxy upon galaxy, networking that power throughout his nervous system gave him a cerebral orgasm.

Mike felt alive, and very special. He knew this entire metaphor was really about his feelings for Linda. In his eyes, God created the ultimate work of beauty in Linda. His thoughts of her beauty as usual fluctuated between detailed beauty and blurring features. The thought of her long, reddish-blonde hair touching her midback excited him continually. In his mind, he wanted her to turn and look at him with her tantalizing, green eyes. In Mike's imagination, she wouldn't turn, she would continue walking, but she always remained in the same place. He ached to hold her, smell her essence, and kiss her closed eyes.

Hank wasn't crazy about flying. He looked over at Mike and wondered why the hell he had such a pleasurable look on his face.

"You look rather content, Mike."

"I am."

"Would you care to share some of that contentment with me?"

"Being up here in the air, I was just thinking how beautiful the world is and the wonders of creation."

"Well, it certainly put a smile on your face."

"I feel fortunate to be alive and to be a part of this great world, with all its wonders, beauty, and mystery."

"Tell me about it. I'm still trying to figure out how the hell the picture comes through a television. It's beyond my pay scale, Mike. I just accept what's in front of me. I don't need to know why I'm a consumer of oxygen. I don't question those things about life or death, especially at 33,000 feet above the ground. I don't want to know why God created me or when he decides to call me back. I don't want to think about going to hell because surely—based upon the Ten Commandments, that's my destiny."

Mike, still euphoric from his pleasurable visions of Linda, looked at Hank and said, "My dear friend, you are one of the most grounded, reliable men I have ever known. I envy you at times. Sometimes I feel emotionally dysfunctional, wondering *Ah, shit, what the hell is wrong with me? Why can't I have a normal life and enjoy things that normal people enjoy?* Here you are—uncomplicated, solid as a rock, reliable, never complaining."

"If I haven't told you this before, I'm telling you now: My career would have been seriously lacking without you as a partner," Mike continued. "So, by all means, don't concern yourself about the stars, or hell—that's not where you're going. Shit, man, just stay as you are."

"I'm not as solid as you think," Hank said. "I'm just not the type to analyze or discuss my feelings. Do you know why I became a cop?"

"No, Hank, I don't. But I really would like to hear about it."

"When I was a teenager and just turned 16, I loved everything about life, people, and animals. I was always taught to respect my elders, so I got along well with the older people in the neighborhood. I was very close with my grandparents, who lived across the street from my family."

"I spent a lot of time with my grandfather, Neil Craigle. He was a man's man, the type of guy everyone in the neighborhood liked. He was a retired plumber who had the tool for any job a neighbor would need. His tools, along with his advice, were all over the neighborhood. By the time he was in his seventies, he was not nearly as strong as he was during his heyday. His hands were twisted and deformed from arthritis. His back was humped from working in damp, low-ceiling cellars. Despite his aging infirmities, he was able to take care of the home and enjoy the days with Grandma Shirley. Together they were my anchors, and I loved them dearly.

"My grandfather was generous with his tools and talents, but as like many older people those days he was frugal. It was rumored that old Neil still had his confirmation money stashed with other cash under his mattress," Hank continued. "One summer night a teenage boy and girl broke into their house thinking they would rob them of all that mattress money. When they didn't find it, they beat my grandparents until they drowned in their own blood. That's how my grand-parents were repaid for their goodhearted generosity in the neighborhood. After an investigation, the culprits were caught and punished, both receiving life sentences.

"I wasn't satisfied with the sanctions they received," Hank said. "My need for justice was never satisfied. I did mellow in time and gained a more balanced sense of justice. Now I still miss them, but in a more mature way. That's what made me want to be in law enforce-ment. Here I am today, in 33,000 feet above sea level, talking to a lunatic about the wonders of the world. Just kidding."

Both men laughed as the stewardess came by to take their beverage orders.

"I understand how you feel, Hank. I haven't ever seen that side of your personality before," Mike said.

"That's because, as I worked through the academics of law, I gradually understood all of the social dynamics involved and was able to let it go," Hank explained

"My belated congratulations, pal."

Their coffees arrived and silence fell between them as they sipped. The vapory steam entered Mike's nostrils as he sighed with gastric satisfaction from the coffee's warmth. The sun was still bright, and the occasional cloud drifting by deepened his contentment. Mike felt strongly that Henry Lister's daughter would provide a significant break in their investigation, believing she would give them the link they needed to identify the assassins' leader.

"Great coffee."

"Better than I expected, Hank."

The flight so far was free of turbulence, and the quiet whispers of jet engines cradled Hank to sleep. Mike, still pleased with his thoughts, reviewed his investigation plans as Hank went into a rhythmic snore. He visualized the sequence of events as they would take place, admitting that he must be able to accept any unantici-pated distractions and stay on his pivot foot. Mike felt ready, prepared.

The time of anticipated arrival in Los Angeles was noon New York time, 9 am in Los Angeles. Mike glanced at his watch and made a mental note of the time, 11:20 am, when the pilot announced that they were on time and would be landing in 30 minutes, where the ground temperature was 79 degrees and sunny. The weather conditions were great, considering the airport in Los Angeles was usually socked in with fog at 8 am.

"Please bring your seats to an upright position and fasten your seatbelts. We hope you enjoyed the flight. Thank you for flying American Airlines," the flight attendant said.

On the ground, Mike and Hank navigated to the car rental pickup. Their Ford budget sedan was booked in advance and ready to go. Their two-hour drive to Bakersfield, a rural upscale private community near Oilspill, California, and home to Henry's daughter, was for the most part quiet. Both men were alone in their thoughts and the time passed by without notice.

Mike parked the sedan across the street from her home. Without speaking, Mike and Hank walked up the short path to the front door. Mike knocked, and when the door opened, a tall, gorgeous, hazel-eyed woman with dark black hair who appeared to be in her mid-forties answered the door.

"Good afternoon, madam. I'm Commissioner Walters, and this is detective Craigle." Mike said, showing his badge. "Are you Joan Marley?"

"Yes, I am," Joan replied, looking a little nervous. "What is it I can do for you gentlemen?"

"First, please accept our condolences," Mike said. "We're sorry for the loss of your father. We are investigating the assassination of Congressman Nobles, of which your father has been accused. We are hoping you can answer a few questions to aid our investigation."

"My father was a decent man," Joan sobbed, wiping tears from her eyes with the back of her hand. "I can't understand any of this. Why would he do this? He never hurt anyone in his life. Please forgive me. Come in." Joan took a few steps backward into her house, opening the front door to allow Mike and Hank to enter.

"When was the last time you spoke with your father?" Mike asked.

"Actually, I hadn't spoken with him, or in fact even seen him much since my mother's funeral. I checked in with him, of course, but I'm very busy out here, and my father became extremely distant since her death. It felt as if he had exclusive grief rights, and he didn't want to be distracted away from his grief by anyone else's. My parents were inseparable, and he managed to carry on with that togetherness in death. I'm sorry I didn't mean to be impertinent, officers.

"Clearly, my father wanted to be alone in his grief, so I gave up attempting to console him and share the grieving process with him," Joan continued. "I quit calling and writing. I really don't know much about his activities after my mother passed away."

"We're you aware that he was a Mason?"

"Oh, yes," Joan said. "He was very involved in his Masonic lodge."

"Please look at this photo," Mike said, pulling the photo out of his bag. "Can you identify your father here?"

"Yes, I recall that photo. My father had it hanging on the wall in his office. Is that his? That's him right there," Joan said, pointing to the man who had been identified as Henry. "My father was a Mason many years before he advanced his Masonic life to the Scottish rite."

"This photo belonged to another man, who is also pictured here," Mike said. "We discovered it in his apartment during a search. My guess is that each man in the photo had his own copy. Other than your father, can you tell us anything about the other men in the photograph?"

Joan took the photo from Mike, paused, then asked, "Would either of you like coffee or tea?"

"No, thank you," Mike replied.

Hank said, "Yes please. I'd like coffee if it's not a bother."

"Not at all."

Mike changed his mind and said, "Ok, coffee, sure, thanks."

While Mike and Hank sipped their coffee, Joan sat and looked at the photo.

"I remember this man," Joan said, pointing at man in the photo. "He visited our home a few times, and he talked with my dad about their lodge back in Pennsylvania."

"Do you recall his name?"

"Peter? My dad called him Pete."

"Do you recall his last name?"

"No, I'm not sure if I ever knew it."

"Do you remember anything about him?"

"All I remember is that he and my dad seemed to enjoy being Masons, and they talked about the lodge when we lived in Pennsylvania. My parents moved from Pennsylvania to Virginia when things got tough in the coal region. I was young. However, I know that this Pete did call my dad occasionally during the years."

"And that was it? After you moved from Pennsylvania, he would call your dad occasionally?"

"Yes, and now that I'm thinking back, I remember that he also came to visit my father one time. He had a friend with him, and they all went to my father's lodge together."

"Do you remember anything about the friend? His name? Take another look at the photo. Do you see the friend there?"

Joan looked again at the photograph and kept shaking her head.

"I am really sorry, gentlemen. I can't honestly say yes. This one man looks like he could be the friend, but it's been a long time and I can't really say for sure if that was the friend or not."

As Joan was pointing to the possible friend on the photograph. Mike looked over his list of names to see that the man she was pointing to was Joseph Richards. The first man she referred to as Pete was identified on his list as Peter Fallow.

"To the best of your recollection did your dad and his friends ever discuss politics when they were together or on the phone with each other?" Mike asked.

"I'm afraid that even if they did, I wouldn't have understood it or paid any attention as a kid," Joan said. "Children and wives weren't privy to much of what the Masons did or shared at lodge. As far as politics, I knew that my parents always voted, and they preached to me about the importance of voting. I also knew that my dad was a registered Republican."

"Thinking back now, through the years, was there anything that your father was passionate about—anything or anyone he particularly liked or disliked? Was there anything that angered him?"

"He was passionate about boating, and my mother shared that passion with him. He loved my mother above all else, then me, and then his lodge brothers. He enjoyed his business and always preached about honesty. He was a wonderful husband to my mother, and a wonderful father to me. I've been out of my mind trying to understand how my father could have done such a thing. It's contrary to anything I could have imagined."

"Joan, there are no easy answers, so I won't patronize you with platitudes," Mike said. "If you have nothing more that you can share with us, we won't trouble you any further."

"Just one moment, officers, I want to show you a letter I received after my father's death. Other than telling me that he was proud of me and loved me and where to find his financial papers, it doesn't explain why he did what he did."

"In those financial papers, did you see evidence of any recent, large cash deposits?" Mike asked.

"No, and I learned from his life insurance agency that since he committed suicide, he won't be eligible for the face value of his policy. My attorney is pursuing the equity he contributed through the years."

"May we have a copy of the letter?" Mike asked. "Better yet, let me have the original, and we'll make you a copy."

"I'll make a copy for myself now, and you can have the original," Joan said, taking the letter with her out of the room.

Mike looked at Hank and asked, "Is there anything you can think of that I should ask her?"

"Not at all, you covered everything," Hank replied.

Joan returned to the room and handed Mike the original letter.

"Joan, again I want express our sympathies for your loss. And thank you for cooperating with us. You've been very helpful," Mike said, extending his hand.

"I'm glad I was able to help," Joan said, shaking Mike's hand. "We need to heal as a nation. Whatever motivated my father to do this thing, I pray that some good eventually comes of it."

"Well, there is an old saying," offered Mike. "No ill wind blows that doesn't create a good somewhere. Let's hope that the good isn't too far away. Goodbye, Joan, and again thank you for the coffee and the help."

Mike and Hank returned to the rental car and sat in the car for a long moment, looking at one another in disbelief.

"I now know we're on the right trail." Mike said.

"I agree." added Hank.

CHAPTER THIRTY-FOUR

Peter had just finished eating breakfast when he dialed the number of his friend Joe Richards. A message from the phone company stated that this number was disconnected and was no longer in service.

What the hell do I do now? Peter thought. *Since I never met any of Joe's relatives and he didn't have any children, how the hell can I find out what's going on with Joe? Oh fuck.*

Frustrated, Peter sunk back in his chair and searched his mind for answers. Was Joe sick? Did he have another stroke? Did his cancer return? Jesus. Was he directly involved in the last assassination of Congressman Luther Nobles?

Peter's mind was racing with all the possibilities, and with all of the considerations he was hopeful that it wasn't the latter. If indeed he was caught, it would be the beginning of the end. He had to think carefully when making inquiries. Peter called information in Los Angeles, California, and got the phone numbers for major hospitals in the region. He took the most prominent and started making his inquiries.

The second hospital Peter contacted did have Joe listed as a former patient, but the woman on the information line noted that he had been transferred to a local, long-term skilled care facility.

"Whom may I say is inquiring?"

Pete was prepared for that one and said, "Frank Somers."

"Are you an immediate family member?"

"No, madam. I'm not. I'm an old friend. I just heard that he wasn't feeling well. Can you tell me how he's doing?"

The woman would not give any further information about his status or location. She informed him that by law she wasn't allowed to give out information without the written consent of the patient. She apologized and said, "I'm very sorry, sir. Good luck in finding your friend."

At least Pete now knew that Joe had been in the hospital, and it wasn't any matter with the law. Where the hell is he, what nursing home is he in? Pete began calling LA area nursing homes one at a time. Luckily, he found him in a skilled care facility about 20 miles east of Los Angeles. The nurse who answered the phone at Saint Anthony's nursing home was kind enough to at least tell him that Joe was indeed admitted to their facility yesterday on October 6th.

Because Peter wasn't an immediate family member, they also wouldn't give him specific information concerning Joe's health status. They were able however, able to give him their visitation schedule. The person he spoke with was very sweet and encouraged visitation for their patients.

Peter was hopeful that his friend was still lucid and able to verbally communicate with him. He really needed to know about his network, contact continuum, and if he ordered the moratorium on the hits the pair had discussed during his last visit. He rationalized that during their last visit he was able to speak clearly and appeared to have very little residual effect from the previous stroke. But what if this was something different and not just another slight stroke?

No question about it, he would have to stop speculating, get his ass out to California, and see what was going on with Joe.

A few days later, Peter's flight landed at LAX.

"I'm getting too old for this shit," Peter said aloud as he hoisted his rolling suitcase off of the baggage claim conveyer belt, instinctively looked around to see if anyone heard his muttering. That could be a sure sign to any on-lookers that he might be a little on the strange side of the column. Peter exited the airport, then hailed an airport taxi and directed the cabbie to get him to St. Anthony's nursing home.

"Which one?" the driver asked.

"There are two?" Peter asked. "What's the difference?"

"Well sir, the Saint Anthony's in the city is Saint Anthony's Holy Light Nursing Home, and the Saint Anthony's Skilled Care and Rehabilitation Center is about 10 minutes outside the city limits."

"That sounds like the place I'm looking for, please hurry."

The cab got Peter there expeditiously. When he entered the center, he noticed an immediate smell of Clorox, an institutional smell that always gave him the shivers. That scent always made Peter think that either it's a very clean place or one where they've been cleaning up a lot of body fluids. Peter knew more than most about nursing homes because a friend of his was a state inspector of those facilities.

The receptionist inside the door was very young and cheerful, with bright blue eyes and smooth olive skin. Peter's immediate assumption was that she was working her way through night school, completely innocent of the horrors of death and dying.

Yeah, that's what this place is all about, just another fucking warehouse for humans in exodus, Mike thought. *They soften the image and cover up the insensitivities associated with death by calling it a "rehabilitation center."* He found himself visualizing himself as a stroke victim in a place like this and wondered if suicide might be a better option. *Or better still, making your death a weapon in the war against the disappearing middle class and using it to kill a corrupt son of a bitch on the way out.*

"May I help you, sir?" asked the receptionist, pulling Peter out of his thoughts.

"I understand you have a Mr. Joseph Richards here."

"And your name is?"

"Frank Somers." Peter lied, immediately realizing his mistake. He couldn't change it now without her alerting the authorities.

"Please sign the visitors register."

Peter signed the register and was more than a little nervous about falsifying his name. *Shit, what if they ask for some form of identification? If they do, I'll say I changed my mind and that I'll come back some other time. Sure, that gets me off the hook now, but how will I ever get to visit Joe?*

"Please, sir, take a seat in the waiting room," the receptionist said, motioning toward the waiting room to her right.

Peter sat on a teal-colored overstuffed couch and waited several minutes before a well-groomed man came into the waiting room. He introduced himself as Mark Hanlon, the facility social worker.

"Mr. Somers what is your relationship with Mr. Richards?" Mark asked.

"I'm an old friend."

"Well, I'm afraid the news of your friend isn't good. He's been in a coma since yesterday, and the prognosis isn't good. He didn't list any next of kin on his paperwork. Do you know anyone we should contact?"

"I'm afraid that I can't help you in that area," Peter said. "Can I see him?"

"Yes, you may visit him. We're not sure how much he is able to hear or understand, so it's okay to speak to him in normal tones just as though he is still capable of hearing you."

"I understand. Thank you, sir," Peter said.

"I'll have a floor nurse escort you to his room," Mark said, waving Peter off.

Once in the room, Peter was alone with his friend, feeling miserable seeing him in this state.

"Joe, I know you can hear me," Peter said. "I want you to know that you're my best friend, and you always were. I need you to wake up and smile. I need you to be alive, so that I can be alive too. If you leave, Joe, I'm dead. I know I will soon follow, and I'm not ready, so wake the fuck up."

Peter had tears rolling down his cheek as he looked around the room. An intravenous line was hooked to Joe's left arm, an oxygen catheter was in his nose, and a beeping monitor kept a check on his heart rate and blood pressure. It was not a very pretty sight. Peter was getting spooked by the thought of himself in this situation.

As Peter continued projecting himself in this condition, he looked at his vegetating buddy and said, "This can't be the end. I won't let it end for me this way." Peter took Joe's hand in his and squeezed it with affection, "We'll talk again. Good-bye for now, old pal."

"Oh, Mr. Somers, the floor nurse called to him as he was leaving the floor. Would it be possible for you to act as a contact person for Mr. Richards?"

"Well, I guess that would be alright," Peter said. "I'll leave a number with your receptionist when I leave."

"Thank you."

Peter made a hurried exit from the center without giving a contact number to the receptionist as he said he would. He knew it was over; he would never see Joe alive again.

At least it was some consolation, Peter told himself, that Joe's role in Take Back America would remain a mystery forever. Joe alone knew who his operatives were, and that information would go to the grave with him. Beyond their planning together and forming the organization, Peter knew nothing.

Peter's planning mind now kicked into high gear. Despite his feeling for the loss of his friend, he knew he had to be careful not to leave any traces of his visit that would lead investigators back to Hazleton, Pennsylvania. Joseph would understand that his action wasn't about abandonment. There was nothing he could do that would bring him out of the coma. It was over, and Joe would do the same thing if the situation were reversed.

Saddened by Joe's terminal state, Peter made his way back to Hazleton. While traveling, he decided to face the inevitable solitude his life would now reflect without his old pal. He knew that living on opposite coasts had separated them for many years. Yet knowing Joe was only a phone call away was always comforting. A matter of seconds, the time it took to dial 10 numbers, was all that it took to hear his voice. That reality is gone forever, and the loss of Joe forced Peter to deal with his own mortality.

Joe's end ends a major part of my life as well, Peter thought. *I'm now a senior in waiting, a senior who'll never graduate from anything again. I'm an old man, who'll never marry, love, have children, or have the newness of anything ever again. I'm waiting, waiting alone like Joe for death. Like Joe will my death be sadder because it came before we were able to carry out our final acts of patriotism?*

Now Peter would live on the memories of the things that he and Joe accomplished together. He would live out the remainder of his life believing that he and Joe were true patriots and that their actions were necessary to help our nation return to a government of the people.

That's it. That's what we were all about. Peter though, renewing his vow to remove a corrupt elected official when he learns of his own pending death. And that target was still undetermined. He laughed to himself thinking, *There are so-many of those corrupt bastards out there, it's a shame I wouldn't have enough time to take a group out with one hit.*

Peter returned to his home on the Hazleton Heights. As he closed the door to his home, he looked long and hard at the neighborhood. A strange feeling of solitude and darkness came over him. Peter sat on his favorite chair, turned on a music channel, and poured himself a drink. In his grief depression, he couldn't allow himself any feelings of contentment. This grief process would be his unity with Joe. The music was softly playing, and Rod Stewart was singing, "There's always tomorrow. Don't be sad. Don't let the blues take you back. We'll be together again."

Those words were somewhat comforting, until he sang, "Words, we'll have a lifetime together again."

God forbid, Peter thought, choking on his tears and thinking of his dear friend.

CHAPTER THIRTY-FIVE

Martha Parker, Congressional chairlady, communicated to the US Attorney General that due to the urgent, serious threat to national security, her appearance to testify before the congressional review committee was scheduled for October 10 at 10 am.

Attorney General Robert Lewis notified the congressional justice committee that he would also be available on the date and time requested to address the committee's questions concerning the assassinations. Robert Lewis served in the federal Justice Department as a staff attorney for two other Presidents. Prior to his confirmation as the US Attorney General, he served as a federal district judge during two other Presidencies. During the lengthy Senate confirmation hearings, his youthful conservative essays on abortion, coupled with some of his decisions favoring corporate America had delayed his ultimate confirmation. Attorney Lewis knew he was in for a tough discourse with this Congress, but he didn't blink when requested to appear. He accepted it as his duty, and he would not shirk that responsibility.

. . .

CHAIRLADY PARKER BANGED HER GAVEL AT EXACTLY 10 AM, signaling the opening of the hearing. Following the third gavel call, silence came over the anxious crowd. The room was crowded with reporters from all over the world with brightly lit TV cameras occupying every position of advantage they could find. A single witness table was centrally located below and in the front of the Senate committee's half-moon arrangement. Attorney General Lewis and two of his key aides sat at the witness table. While shuffling papers with one hand, Lewis adjusted his microphone by repeatedly tapping along the side of the microphone with his other hand. He was ready.

Chairlady Parker declared the investigative hearing concerning the assassinations of the US Congressman was now officially open. She established that each of the nine committee-members would have an opening round of remarks for five minutes. The chairlady would then acknowledge the key witness, allowing him to offer an opening statement. Following the witness's opening statement; she would allow each member to engage the witness for five minutes.

"No disrespect to either the witness or this committee will be tolerated." she admonished the members.

Chairlady Parker offered the first opening statement. "Today, our nation, its people, friends, and the families of the assassinated members of Congress are in a state of mourning. We grieve together as a nation saddened by the tragic loss of 14 Congressman assassinated by dangerous people with the misguided notion that their cowardly acts will make our nation a better place to live. Although we are in mourning, our work as a nation must continue uninterrupted. These murderous acts must end, but they can't end until we uncover their organizational motives and personal identities. Our anger over these assassinations must be dealt with openly and sincerely. If we are to restore dignity and confidence to public service, we must understand the things that are broken and have the courage to fix them. I hope that this desperately needed process will begin today with this hearing. If America is to remain an open, free society, we must cherish and obey the laws that protect us."

The other members of the investigation committee followed the chairlady with their opening comments consuming the allotted five minutes. As they spoke, it was painfully obvious that they were all conveying the same demagogic sentiments without much nuance.

Chairlady Parker looked at the clock and declared, "Since it is now 11:25, we will adjourn for lunch and reconvene at 1 pm."

At one pm, Chairlady Parker banged her gavel and re-called the hearing to order.

"Attorney General Lewis, you have heard from each congressional member of this committee. Are you now prepared to offer your opening remarks?"

"I am, madam chairlady. I want to thank this committee for this opportunity to share with you and my countrymen the facts as such that is involved with this tragic moment in our national history. Before I begin, I want to express my sincere sympathy to the families, friends and constituents of the assassinated lawmakers. In as much as grief is far greater for those immediate family members and close friends, I can assure them that the impact of their loss is deeply felt by all Americans. I now submit myself to your inquiry."

Catherine Goldberg was the first member of the committee to question Attorney Lewis. "Mr. Attorney General, was the President's decision to add Mr. Walters to the investigation team based upon his lack of confidence in the directors of the FBI and the CIA?"

"No. The President was made aware of Mr. Walters's proactive part in the DC investigation where the first assassinations occurred. Based upon information he received regarding detective Walters's involvement, the President summoned Mr. Walters along with the heads of the FBI and the CIA to Washington for a briefing. The results of that meeting gave the President the belief that the three entities could work together with the investigation. Since the President announced his appointment of Mr. Walters to the investigation team, Walters has proven his value to the team. The heads of the other two organizations continue to have the President's confidence.

They are valuable resource enablers for the foot soldiers in the investigation."

"What resources are you talking about?"

"Files, warrants, things of that nature."

"Have any of the assassin's been identified?"

"Since it's part of the on-going investigation, aside from what's been reported in the press, I cannot answer that question."

"Investigators report that recent developments are promising, which gives the President reason to believe that the investigation will soon end. Is that correct, sir?"

"Again, you're asking me for specifics that if I were to provide would impede the on-going dynamics of this investigation. I'm sorry I cannot answer that question either."

"Is there anything you can tell us?"

"Absolutely not, everything I can reveal I have revealed."

"Then perhaps, Mr. Lewis, this is a waste of time?"

"With all due respect, this congressional investigative committee is a healthy process that helps to demonstrate to the American public that the oversight duties of their Congress are in play. It helps to reverse the growing lack of faith the American people have in their Congress. Because I'm the federal prosecutor who will represent the people versus the perpetrators in court, I cannot provide any details to the public during the on-going process of the investigation. Nevertheless, I commend this committee for showing up for duty."

The committee process continued throughout the afternoon with all members asking similar questions with some political nuances and receiving nothing different with the attorneys general's diplomatic responses.

It was 5:30 pm when Chairlady Parker gaveled the session for adjournment. "This committee session will adjourn and be reconvened at a date and time to be determined."

CHAPTER THIRTY-SIX

Mike and Hank returned to Washington. En route, they discussed Joan's identification of Peter Fallow and Joseph Richards. She had identified them both on the photos and established that a friendship existed between the three of them for many years, and that the friendship was based upon their Masonic life.

"Hank, the facts surrounding this group photo makes it clearer to me that we do have the mother lode," Mike said. "These guys entered into a conspiracy to assassinate corrupt United States congressman. It appears as though they pledged their life for the cause."

"It certainly looks that way, Mike. I'll be glad to get this thing wrapped up. From what I can see now, it won't be long."

"Alright we know what we must do next: locate Fallow and Richards. My guess is that they will connect more of the dots. If we're lucky, one of them will be the leader."

"Joan said that her father and those two started their Masonic careers in Pennsylvania. So that's where we'll begin our search. When we get back to the office, we search for info on these guys and take it from there."

"Mike, when we get back, I have a few things to catch up on. Do you mind if I take care of them first? I need at least a day to get them done."

"You got it. Meanwhile I'll brief John and the administration on our progress and set things up for our trip to Pennsylvania. You take the time you need and call me when you're ready."

"Okay, Mike. Thanks."

"No thanks are necessary, Hank. You earned your time."

CHAPTER THIRTY-SEVEN

James Petri sat slumped in the golf course locker room with his elbows on his knees and his head resting on his hands. He realized the end was near. Tears were rolling down his cheeks and along the sides of his fingers. He was embarrassed to be around the men in his foursome who just helped him into the locker room after he had fallen out of the cart near the fifth hole.

It wasn't the first time they had to help James on the course. He'd been stumbling and tripping with greater frequency during their recent games. None of the men in his foursome, who were all younger than him, would risk hurting his feelings by suggesting he give up golfing. They were playing as a foursome for many years.

James knew that his Parkinson's disease was progressing rapidly. The medicine he had been taking for years was losing its potency, and his symptoms were worsening. His gait and movements were becoming more agitated and disabling.

A proud man, James never wanted sympathy from anyone. All he ever wanted was to keep on doing the best he could with the things he liked, like golfing. He knew that today's episode would end his days of golfing. The men wouldn't ask it of him, but he knew. He would have to insist that they accept his withdrawal from the foursome.

James, Jimmie as he was always called by his family and friends, was born in the central coal regions of eastern Pennsylvania. Pine Hill was a small patch town in Luzerne County. Being one of the smallest boroughs in the commonwealth, Pine Hill was often jokingly referred to as the borough where every resident had a seat on the council. The town had one large coal breaker, which employed nearly every town resident. The entire town consisted of 20 houses, 10 on each side of the main, dirt road. The homes were dirty from the burning of coal. The street was always muddy after a rain.

That's the way Jimmy remembered his childhood. He always hated Mondays in Pine Hill because it was washday, when the women hung their laundry outside on clotheslines to dry. He felt that the sooty air made it wishful thinking that they would stay clean.

There was a bright side to Pine Hill. When the sun did shine, it was the brightest sun of Jimmie's entire life. His young heart always enjoyed the sun as he remembered it from his youth. He was born in house number three on November 8, 1924. His father, Herbert Petri, and his new bride, Anna, emigrated from Germany to the United States in 1921. Herbert went to work at the coal breaker that same year. His mother (as did all mothers) worked 20 hours a day doing housework and caring for their children. As a child, James attended all of the local schools. He was a good student and received good grades. He graduated from the West Hazleton High School in June of 1942. The United States was one year into World War II, and James being 18 years of age was immediately drafted into the Army. He said his goodbyes and never saw his mother or father again.

Jimmie was sent to England following his basic training and participated in several invasions without being scratched. In 1944, while waiting for a transfer assignment, he received notification from the American Red Cross that his mother and father had perished of coal gas poisoning during a cold December night. As it was common in those days their house wasn't properly ventilated. James returned to Pine Hill after the war but decided to settle in the growing city of Hazleton, rather than busing into the city every day.

Taking advantage of the GI bill, Jimmie enrolled in college and received a degree in engineering from Penn State. He was quickly hired as an electrical engineer by a local utility company. He soon discovered the advantages of those who were members of the secret "Ring Club," an inner circle of Masons who were first to be hired and first to be considered for promotions in the company. Prestige and promotion were the name of the game. Jimmie, being a likable man, was easily admitted into the brotherhood in September of 1958, and he became a master Mason that same year.

At the age of 34, Jimmie married his high school sweetheart, Loretta Miller. Since the time they first met, they were devoted to each other and never had other partners. During the first two years of their marriage, James built their home: a beautiful red brick Cape Cod on the East Diamond Avenue section of town. In 1960, they became the proud parents of identical twin girls. James and Loretta had the perfect marriage and prospered together in love and life.

In 1974, when Jimmie entered the Consistory of Adamsburg, Pennsylvania, to become a 32nd degree Scottish Rite Mason, he befriended another brother in his class, Peter Fallow. As fellow Hazletonians, they quickly bonded, discovering they were also members of the same Blue Lodge in Hazleton. Over the years, their friendship grew beyond the brotherhood as they enjoyed joint family dinners and even family vacations together. Once, they attended a Masonic convention together in Pittsburgh.

That's where Jimmie became reacquainted with Joseph Richards, who had also been in their Scottish Rite class of 1974. That convention gave birth to many annual get-togethers throughout the following years. The class of 74 morphed into a political booster club for their cherished U.S. Constitution, which the men believed must never be altered in any way. Any legislator who even hinted of amending the Constitution received a letter from the group expressing their opposition of the proposed amendment. That became a solid intractable pact of the group. The men felt proudly patriotic of their loyalty to the Constitution.

In 1989, Jimmie retired at age 65. His twin daughters had married well and been well established for years. With no concern for their needs, Jimmie and Loretta, still in good health, sold their East Diamond Avenue home and relocated to sunny Florida.

The years of retirement in Florida were good to them. Loretta joined a ladies' club and enjoyed all the socials, while Jimmie took up golfing. He became a good golfer and enjoyed the twice-weekly matches with his foursome. His contacts with the class of 74 became less frequent—until August 2003 when he received a coded message from Peter Fallow inviting him to attend a very important meeting on August 30th.

Jimmie, now age 79, considered the invitation and rationalized that his traveling days were limited since he developed Parkinson's disease two years before. However, his medication kept the tremors at bay, so he decided to attend, not so much out of curiosity of what the meeting was about but mostly to see his old pals.

Loretta decided to remain in Florida and allowed Jimmie to make the trip by himself. She encouraged him to have a good time visiting his old friends in Hazleton. Reluctantly Jimmie agreed, promising to call her every night.

Back in Hazleton, Jimmie sat in that dimly lit hall, waiting for his friend to appear with plenty of time to anticipate their reunion. *What was the meeting about?* he wondered. *How will Peter look?* Suddenly as if it were some mystical illusion, Peter appeared at the lectern, looking powerful, even Godlike, waiting for full attention. Jimmie thought Peter aged well, and his salt-and-pepper hair made him look distinguished.

"It's what we have in common—our love and devotion to our country. It's why we were chosen." Peter's words and magnetism were almost paralyzing. When he invited the uninspired to leave the room, Jimmie couldn't rise and leave. Looking back, Jimmie remembered, *As five other men departed, I entered that next room and bought into the plot. I was in.*

As Peter said, "Your final life's purpose will now be revealed," Jimmie thought, *My God, it's as if he was in charge of my destiny all along.*

Jimmie was not only was sold on his assigned destiny, he was inspired and grateful for the privilege of having a higher purpose. He was a man among men whose higher purpose was to right the wrongs and evil acts men had committed against their fellow man. In the end, he believed he could ascend to the open arms of God, bathed in the glory of leaving the world a better place.

After the meeting in Hazleton, Jimmie returned to Florida, feeling refreshed and eager to get his things in order. He was totally committed to his assigned mission. He felt clean and worthy of the trust his brothers had placed in him.

With a sigh, Jimmie returned his thoughts to the present-day. He picked up his head to look around the locker room for what he told himself was for the last time. He knew what he had to do, and he would do it—about quitting golf and about fulfilling his commitment to Peter Falllow's group.

Jimmie looked in the mirror and touched his wrinkled chin. Ah, yes, he remembered that proud day when he returned from Pennsylvania and how great he felt about his final purpose. Now he would proudly prove his trust position with the brotherhood. He had been reading the newspapers and watching the evening news about the assassinations, and he was proud. He wondered how his comrades felt as they achieved their final duty.

Jimmie greeted his foursome with a laugh and a handshake and said, "My good friends, the time has come for me to end what you will not. I must eliminate myself from this foursome and give you guys the opportunity to get someone else who won't be a drag on your game."

"Bullshit, Jimmie. We won't let you off the hook. We'll help you, won't we guys?" said Jimmie's long-term golfing buddy George.

In chorus the other two golfers agreed.

"Forget it, guys," Jimmie said. "I know you would help as much as possible, but I won't bring that upon you any longer. Thanks, but no thanks. You've all been more wonderful than you could imagine. But it's final. I'm out."

They men shook his hand and wished Jimmie well.

Funny, he thought as he walked away as his tremors seemed to ease.

When Jimmie was first diagnosed with Parkinson's disease, he had researched the disease and became as knowledgeable about it as the physicians attending him. He understood that he could go for years with progressively worsening tremors and a festinating gait, tripping and falling with more and more frequency (which is about where he presently was), until he would need care in a nursing home, where he could languish for years.

That's not for me, he thought. *I have a higher purpose for the final days of my life. It appears that my time has come. I must now honor my destiny.*

The next day, Jimmie made several attempts to contact Joseph Richards. Unsuccessful in reaching Joe, he decided to work up his own hit.

On October 8, 2005, in Saint Petersburg Florida, Congressman Raymond Shapiro quietly left his bedroom, not wanting to disturb his sleeping wife. He entered his bathroom and began his morning grooming. With a heavy schedule planned in his home district, he needed to be especially well groomed to meet his constituents.

Laughing to himself, he thought, *It's important to have that star quality, that thing that separates you from the average and subordinates them to you.*

After showering, Shapiro wiped the steam from the mirror and applied shaving cream to his 42-year-old face.

Not too bad, he thought. *I look pretty damn good for my age.*

In saying that, he stretched the skin on his left cheek and noticed that the creases in his forehead were deeper than he remembered. He looked intently at the deeper creases and wondered if he had been fooling himself, wondering, *Jesus, God forbid, do others see me as flawed?*

In seconds, his ego took over, and he dismissed the notion, reasoning that it made him look more distinguished.

I really am a sweet guy, but sweet guys don't cut it in politics, so my sweetness is a cover for my interests. Those silly little old people fall all over me when I write a letter praising their clubs or do a photo op with their group. But they are so fucking dumb about things. They never get wise to the fact that they're being used. Place your arm around the sweetest little old lady who heads the committee, and there's one in every group, and they'll defend you to the death. Like that group of assholes proposing to name a street after me, "Ray Shapiro Drive." I'll meet those idiots today and offer some laudable remarks about their dedication to the community. I'll thank them and tell them how important their work is and how volunteerism is the glue which binds a community together. I'll humble myself as their servant. Those fools will never know how much money I grabbed for myself with their project.

While slapping his favorite shaving lotion on his face, he heard his wife moving around in the bedroom. That was his signal to rush the process and get the hell out of the house before she could pin him down to any evening commitments. Shaving a bit faster, he nicked the skin near his left ear.

"Oh shit," he muffled, not wanting to disturb his wife any further while he was applying a septic pencil to stop the bleeding. It worked. He wanted out fast, when suddenly he heard his wife making her God-awful awakening noises. He shouted, "I'm in a rush, dear. I have some important meetings scheduled."

"Will you be home for dinner?" his wife, Shirley, asked.

"Not sure, sweetheart. I'll call you when things are clear. Okay, dear?"

"I've heard that before, Ray. What you really mean is 'don't count on it.'"

"I promise I'll call."

"Goodbye, Ray."

"Goodbye, Shirley."

While backing his car out of the garage, he placed his cell phone on speaker, dialed, and asked, "Laura, is that you?"

"Yes, Ray, it's me. Sorry if I sounded odd; I'm clearing my throat."

"I'll be in the office by 6. Can you be there a little early? I need you to do something special."

"Well, the earliest I can be there is about 6:30. Your first appointment isn't until 9 am, Ray. You should be fine. I'll try to be a little early. Okay?"

"Laura, I mean *really* special."

"Isn't it always?"

"Very."

A three-term congressman, Ray had always been active in politics. While in college, he was active in the local Republican party. As a political science major, he formed a young Republicans club in college. He held various leadership positions in the club until he graduated. During holidays and spring breaks, he worked in the district congressman's office and also volunteered to help get Republicans elected. He developed a firm grasp of grass root politics and mastered the 30-second sound bite. He realized at a young age that people are like sheep: All you need is a good dog to keep them in line. Ray regarded himself as that dog. While working on election committees, he developed a skill that he learned during the Nixon days called "rat fucking." The dirtiest tricks of all. When he thought about those things, he laughed, thinking how easy it is to turn people against each other.

Ray learned all of the deceptive tactics to achieve a political goal, but the one thing he never understood was honesty. He repressed the hell out of anything honest. Quite frankly honesty scared him because to him it meant telling the truth, not accepting gifts, or giving up paid vacations to exotic places. It meant not accepting bribes; it also meant running the risk of displeasing the leadership when presenting an opposite view and then being punished by the leadership. His mottos were "go along and get along" and "take the perks and fill your freezer with cold cash." All that was necessary was to bring home some occasional pork. To the extent of his knowledge, it was working for him.

Even as a student, Ray knew that eventually he would stop working to get others elected and would use his talents to get himself elected. In 2000, he was elected to his first term in Congress. His office was located in the business district of St Petersburg. It was a great location with just the right mix of traditional retail businesses, financial institutions, and new-age coffee shops. He loved the blending of the old and new. At 42, he felt comfortable in the middle and wasn't concerned about generational gaps. He was amused at that thought, rationalizing that there is no age limit for thieves or liars. *Jesus, is that why I'm comfortable?* he thought.

Located two shops down from his office was Murphy's Coffee and Donuts Shop. Ray was in the habit of stopping in for a quick read of the morning paper while sipping on his first hot coffee.

Shop owner Tom Murphy, a big Irishman with a sharp wit, stood in front of Ray, wiping his hands on his dirty, white apron.

I swear to God, thought Ray. *He keeps mustard and catsup on that fucking apron as a trademark. He's probably superstitious enough to believe if he washed it, it would wash away his success.*

"How is everything, Congressman?"

Well, you know how it is, Tom."

"No. How is it, Congressman?"

"It's just a little short of orgasmic." Ray said, chuckling. He knew he could talk to Tom like that. It made Tom feel like he was close to the congressman. Vulgar street talk is a useful tool when dealing with tough streetwise types.

Tom laughed heartily and said, "Enjoy your coffee."

Ray deliberately waited until 6:35 to enter his office. He knew that Laura would be waiting. As he entered, he locked the door behind him and while closing the blinds he felt his penis begin to swell. The anticipation of seeing her 21-year-old naked body and smelling her perfume was so exciting that he feared cumming in his pants before they even did anything. She drove him wild with the blonde highlights in her thick chestnut hair, and her mass of black pubic hair. Nothing in life equals that momentary physical pleasure and probably never will. Her ass was solid. Her body was a gourmet treasure to explore. She had soft, pouting lips and a sexy smile. When his cock was in her vagina, it fit so well and felt so good that pumping wasn't necessary. Without motion, they would keep cumming together with sweet, sweet orgasms.

When they were through fucking, her legs would fall wide apart, and he would slowly withdraw his pulsating cock, leaving a few drops of semen on her black pubic hair. While remaining on top of her, he would put his left hand on her vagina while caressing the lips of her mouth with his right fingers. She would just lie there with a look of satisfaction and shock at the same time. They would spend long moments caressing each other, not speaking.

In those climatic moments, he wasn't Ray the Congressman, and she wasn't Laura his secretary. These moments were the essence of life—a human reality reduced by social standards to shame and guilt, a natural thing labeled sinful that forced them into secrecy. They, believe it or not, were reality.

When it came to Laura, Ray knew he was out of control. She could manipulate him in any way and anytime that she wanted. But somehow, they managed to put on a stoical front for the public. Well, at least he thought they were a secret. Laura and Ray showered together and opened the office on time at 9 am. She sat at her desk, and he went through his files in the opposite room. His affair with his secretary didn't cause him any guilt or concern. He felt worthy of his wife's devotion and also deserving of his delicious sex with Laura.

Ray was grateful for both of the women in his life, but his view on relationships was that they were games to be played—games with winners and losers. Shapiro believed himself to be a winner. He would always have his wife, and he would always have his Laura. Love wouldn't enter the equation because he reasoned that love would only fuck things up. His wife and Laura were both valuable political tools he needed to service and maintain his politics. Because Shapiro fancied himself a master of the political arts, he believed he would not have to worry.

It was 9:15 when Laura announced his first office meeting.

"Mayor George Eddy of Port Daniels is here to see you, Congressman."

"Send him right in, Laura."

Ray stood tall behind his desk and extended his hand to greet the mayor. "Mayor, as usual it's great to see you. How can I help you today?"

The mayor had the council president with him and said, "You know, Ray, the last time we were here to see you, we explained that our mid-city fire department is in desperate need of new air packs. Have you located any funding for us?"

"Yes, as a matter of fact I have."

"If you recall, I explained that two other towns in my district are in need of updated equipment as well. I managed to accomplish funding for all three of the municipal town fire departments, including of course yours. My staff will forward the paperwork to your office within the next several days, and then we can take it from there. If you'd like, we could arrange for a press release, featuring a photo of you, some of the firemen, and me."

"That would be great, Congressman. Since we're both up for reelection, that would be helpful."

"Are you going to the fall rally?" Ray asked. "I expect to be there along with the governor and offer some remarks."

"I always attend, Ray, and I also plan to be one of the speakers," the mayor replied. "I'll have a table of 10, and I hope you will do some table hopping. I hope you won't be like the other shitheads who sit among themselves, ignoring the party workers."

"I notice the same thing, and others do as well," Ray said, nodding. "As their congressman I feel that I owe it to the nuts and bolts of the party workers to press their flesh. Those guys just sitting amongst themselves is wrong—and just plain stupid."

"Congressman, I'm sure you're aware—more so than we—there's a crisis of confidence with our elected officials in America. The disconnect between the Washington insiders and the American public is widening. The most egregious example is this illegal immigrant situation. The public gets it and the politicians don't. What is it that elected officials who take an oath to protect and defend the Constitution don't understand about the word 'illegal'?"

"Well, mayor, *I* get it. It's a bread-and-butter issue for the illegals who need jobs and for the middle class who are losing jobs, but most of all for the greedy corporations that hire the illegals."

"It doesn't take a rocket scientist, Congressman, to understand that arresting the companies and employers who hire and exploit these people would solve the problem," the mayor said. "Remove the magnet."

"I agree, mayor, but what do we do with the 13 million illegals already here and some who have children born in America? Do you honestly believe that we can just send them back over the border?"

"The short answer is yes. I do believe it could, and *should*, be done. That's a very graphic picture, I agree, but don't you think that removing the jobs they're taking would automatically dry up their reason for being here and motivate them to return to their own countries?"

"Well, mayor, it's a very complex problem, and we won't solve it today. Ah, let's get together soon, okay," Ray said, dismissively.

"There you go, Congressman. It isn't as complex as you pretend. That's where the disconnect comes in. The people get it, but you don't. The people understand the definition of illegal, but all you do is accommodate the greedy corporations, and then stonewall the problem by telling us of the complexities. The people know that elected officials lack the will to enforce the people's laws. They know that corporate America has bought and paid for Congress. And they know that as long as that fact is true, Congress will not do the work of the people."

"I'm going to remain open-minded about this," Ray said, placatingly. "Maybe I'll hold public hearings in my district, after the elections of course. Thank you for the input on the issue, and I'll have that paperwork for you in a few days. Thank you for seeing us today. I'll see you at the fall social."

Ray watched for the mayor and councilman to completely exit the office.

"Laura, get Art on the phone please?"

Arthur Mope was a great political consultant. He was expensive, but worth every penny.

"Ray. Art's on line two."

"Good morning, Art," Ray said. "I just had Mayor Eddy and his council president in my office. He laid it on pretty heavy about the illegal immigrant situation. He pretty much suggested that I am out of touch with the people on the issue. Is he right?"

"Calm down, Ray. On that issue, there does appear to be a growing divide. The people want our borders protected. That's the national security part of the problem, but there is the reality about the whole thing, and that is the fact that our middle class are feeling insecure. This issue is causing a lot of concern about job losses. For the first time in our progressive history, the working middle class is losing faith in its future. You can bet this will bite us all in the ass if we don't ease their fears."

"Art, I have one idea and, but I need your feedback. Should I start saying on the campaign trail that I intend to conduct hearings in my district?"

"Your strategy is *what*? We better get together as soon as possible to plan the whole thing out. Tactically, it could be a disaster if you don't have a viable end game. Let's discuss tomorrow over lunch. I have a meeting tomorrow morning, but I should be able to manage lunch with you by noon."

"That's fine, Art. Your office or mine?"

"Mine. See you then."

"Laura, what do you have scheduled for 10:30?" Ray called out to his secretary.

"The League of Women Voter's president, Barbara Brobst. Remember the little lady with the big stick? She is due soon."

"Is anyone out there now?"

"No, you should still have 15 minutes."

"I need you here for a moment."

Laura entered and stood by him at the desk. Ray reached up pulled her down to his side, giving her a sensual kiss while sliding his hand up the back of her legs and pressing her rock-solid ass checks. They held the kiss for several moments.

Ray said, "I needed that, Laura."

He stood up, looking into her ocean blue eyes, and kissed her again. Laura felt her legs weaken. She was in love. Without words, she returned to the other room to prepared for the next constituent.

Ray met briefly with Barbara, then having seen all of his scheduled constituents, he ended the morning meetings with a few minutes to spare before noon. He took Laura to lunch at Murphy's. He never had to remind her to make it look like business, so Laura took along her scheduling book. Murphy was busy as hell with the lunch crowd, and no one paid any attention to Laura and Ray sitting at a table in the rear of the dining area. Laura was so convincing in her role of dutiful secretary that even Ray wondered how the hell she could separate the functions.

"What do I have scheduled for tonight, Laura?"

"You have two meetings. The first one is for 7 with the Lions Club. That's an easy hour, so you should be clear for your next meeting at 8:30. This one you'll like: It's your massage at the club. Please be on time for the Lions Club meeting. It's an advertised event, and you don't want to screw it up."

"I promised my wife that I'd call her about dinner tonight. Would you call her when we get back to the office and help her understand the importance of my schedule tonight?"

"Okay, I can do that. Will I see you tonight?"

"I will be going home directly from the club."

"I'll miss you," she whispered out of the side of her mouth.

Ray felt a pang inside. Laura's side mouth whisper made her pouting lips so kissable, but tonight he would make the sacrifice and be without her.

THAT MORNING, JIMMIE HAD READ THE MORNING PAPER, searching for any news about his district congressman. There it was, on the centerfold page: "Congressman Raymond Shapiro will be the guest speaker for the St. Petersburg Lady Lions Club. The Supper Club will meet at the Hotel Sands Regal Room at 7 pm and will hear the congressman's plans for funding the Blind Association's new eligibility program. Members are encouraged to attend."

Jimmie never liked Congressman Shapiro. Not only was he a crook, but he even had a crooked smirk on his mouth when he spoke on TV to the people. Jimmie had observed that Shapiro was so full of self-importance that it shows when he answers media questions. Jimmie thought Shapiro was a "bought and paid for" legislators who takes the power of his incumbency for granted, owns the office, and will never lose his seat in Congress.

Okay, Raymond, Jimmie thought, *Ole Jimmie here has a plan to revoke your privileged existence.*

When James was in the military, he qualified as a weapons expert. He had vast knowledge of rifles and handguns, and he owned several rifles and pistols. He decided on using his 22-caliber long barrel pistol with a homemade silencer. Jimmie was familiar with the Hotel Sands, and he ascertained the pistol would be perfect for taking out the congressman in the lobby or in the Regal Room.

Whichever provides me with the best opportunity. Jimmie

thought. The hotel was a very busy place, and Jimmie knew as a senior citizen, he would blend in. A shot with the 22 to the temple near the anterior aspect of the congressman's ears would terminate— or at least make him a vegetable unable to hold office. To reduce his tremors and calm his aim, Jimmie would need to lower his anxiety levels, so he took a double dose of Ativan one hour prior to entering the hotel. He was ready.

Jimmie registered into the Hotel Sands at 2:20 pm. They gave him a room with a street view on the 8th floor. He called the hotel restaurant and made dinner reservations for 6 pm and asked for a reminder call at 5:30. He took off his shoes and stretched across the bed. For a long while he replayed his plan until he gradually dozed off.

Jimmie awoke around 5:20 with a splitting headache. While rubbing the back of his head, he recalled the dream that had just awoken him. Bits of the dream were emerging—with incomplete images of Peter Fallow and Joe Richards coming in and out of mental focus. He remembered Peter's declarations of our "final purpose." In the dream, Joe's face kept hovering above Peter's head, saying something that somehow Jimmie would fail in his attempt to assassinate the congressman and get caught in the hotel lobby. Then in the dream, the congressman was laughing while Jimmie was being wrestled to the floor and handcuffed. Now, he understood his headache.

The phone rang interrupting Jimmie's dream analysis. It was the desk clerk reminding him of his 5:30 wake up call. He went into the bathroom and soaked his face in a hot towel. It was so refreshing he shrugged off the haunting message of the dream. After all, he knew the potential consequences of his action, and he vowed to stay focused. He was about to shave when he realized that it was pointless and whiped the lather from his face. He did brush his teeth because he couldn't stand his own breath. But it really wouldn't matter who would be offended by his hygiene when he was dead.

"Dead, dead." What a reality. That would be it. For a few seconds, Jimmie tried to imagine being dead. But that feeling was as elusive as the memory of his dream. How can one understand being dead, a time when there is no more thought? He removed himself from the grips of rumination and vowed to stay focused.

Jimmie glanced at the digital clock on the TV, which displayed 5:42. Time now to start his Ativan plan of double dosing. He popped two and speculated if he still wasn't calm enough to steady his hand and aim, he would pop two more when it gets closer to target time.

Jimmie spent the next half hour getting dressed for dinner. He put on a sport jacket and tie, formal enough to blend in with the others who might be attending the congressman's guest appearance. He knew it was a ladies' organization, but he also understood that all their support men would be properly attired. His age and gentle demeanor would do the rest to make him blend in.

Next, Jimmie opened his suitcase and stared for a long moment at the beautiful wood-grain pistol case on top of a freshly laundered shirt. The large, engraved inscription on top of the case read "James Petri," and smaller lettering read "Colt 22-caliber limited edition." The gun had been a gift from Loretta after they were married when he took up the hobby of target shooting. He loved the pistol so much he frequently referred to it as "Doll Baby."

Reverently, Jimmie removed the case from the suitcase and caressed the lid several times before he opened it. Once opened, he gently removed the pearl-handled, chrome pistol and began the ritualistic practice of balancing the weapon. He had an exercise of tossing it from hand to hand until he became accustomed to its weight. Within moments, he had restored his familiarization with its balance features.

He then loaded the seven-shot cylinder with 22-magnum bullets and tossed the pistol once again from hand to hand to re-establish balance and control with the loaded weapon. It only took several moments. So far everything was going well with his ability to handle the weapon. And now Jimmie went into the final stage of his rehearsal.

He stepped in front of a full-length mirror and started aiming at himself and various other targets in the room. His hands held the weapon without drifting or canting so that once the Ativan fully kicked in, he would become steady and calm enough to prosecute his plan. Satisfied with his ability to control the weapon, he placed the pistol inside a pocket in the left chest area of his sport jacket, just slightly below his armpit. With the weapon comfortably placed and concealed, he donned his sport jacket and confirmed in the mirror that no bulge could be noticed.

Jimmie did a final check around the room. His thoughts were that if everything went well, there was no need to worry about what he was leaving behind. It wouldn't matter anyway. They would have his body, so no evidence would be required to find out that he did it. It was important that the message to the public would be a positive one, and that would be that. Another corrupt, greedy elected official would be out of office and power—the self-servitude of power and its corruption, which hurts the people and the nation. That was the most important thing about their final purpose, but unfortunately Jimmie knew he wouldn't be around to see the results. The point is future generations might.

Jimmie slowly lowered himself to his knees, placed his elbows on the bed, and folded his hands to pray his final prayer. "Dear heavenly Father, my life has been rich with your blessings, and for that I have loved you and all your creations. The warmth of the sun and the intoxicating oxygen with which you have filled my lungs have brightened my eyes with the beautiful things you have given me to witness. My life in love with Loretta and our two wonderful daughters are beyond explanation. Dear Lord, protect them from the retaliations of my deed. In as much as I have been blessed in this life as a free man in a free nation, I am and have always been saddened by the plight and pain of the less fortunate. For that reason, I have at times wondered how you allowed the suffering of so many. But I trusted that there would be some heavenly sense of balance to justify their suffering. While I had the best wines and plenty of food, warmth, and clothing, my awareness of those who have not been given enough attention worries me about my own worthiness to join your angels in heaven. This act that I am about to commit is an effort to prevent the greediest and most corrupt among us from destroying this beautiful, free nation that you have given to me and my fellow Americans. Oh God, my Father, I ask for your forgiveness of what I am about to do, and I also ask for your forgiveness of my colleagues who have preceded me with the assassinations of the greedy. I call upon you to cleanse our government of evil."

At dinner, Jimmie ordered the lightest fish entrée of fish, hoping the fish would be calming to his intestines. He remembered reading about it in a book *Vermont Folk Medicine*. This was no time to overload his intestines, which would make him sluggish. He finished eating and felt satisfied and calm. The Ativan and light dinner worked, and Jimmie was ready.

Jimmie went to the rest room, relieved himself of bladder pressure, and took a final look in the mirror. He still looked okay. But when he lifted his right arm and pointed it at the mirror to test his steadiness, he wasn't quite satisfied.

Time to pop two more Ativan, he thought. *That should do it.*

Jimmie returned to his table and used the water to take his final dose. At 6:57, he sat in the lobby, pretending to be interested in the area. But, that proved difficult to do while mentally rehearsing the hit and always with an added prayer. From where he was sitting, he had a good view of the Regal Room. He could see all the ladies chatting at their tables, and at the head table he was able to see that there was an empty seat, which he guessed was for the congressman.

Oh shit, he didn't show, Jimmie thought, his anxiety building. Looking harder at the head table, he could see that the dinner plate at the empty seat appeared as though someone had already dined there. *Jesus, did he already speak and leave?*

Suddenly, Jimmie saw the congressman making his way behind the people at the head table back to his seat. Jimmie regained his composure and felt his nerves calming again.

"Ladies and gentleman," announced a nearly bald, old lady at the head table, "your attention please."

The chairlady lead them through a brief business meeting and then said, "It's my great honor and pleasure to introduce the honorable Congressman Raymond Shapiro."

Congressman Shapiro spoke to the group for the best part of a half hour, which also included a question-and-answer period. The ladies loved him and lapped up every word he said. The congressman ended his talk and thanked the organization for giving him the opportunity to serve them in his district.

Knowing the congressman would soon make his exit, Jimmie got himself into the best position he could establish within the lobby. There was no other way out for the congressman; he must pass by Jimmie to exit the hotel. While waiting for the congressman to make his exit, Jimmie laughed, thinking, *No need to worry about anyone protecting the great congressman. With an overall approval rating of 26 percent, who cared? Very soon, his reign of power will end.*

Suddenly, a very obese lady stepped in front of the congressman, blocking Jimmie's view. She was engaged in a conversation with another lady, and they didn't appear eager to move. By looking around her, Jimmie could see that the congressman's body language showed he was about to depart. Jimmie was annoyed at that point. He knew he would need to get closer to his prey, which might mean a closer body contact hit. He would now have to move quickly and get closer to the Regal Room's entrance, but not too fast so as to attract any attention.

As Jimmie started toward the door, the woman started to move, which enabled Jimmie to slow his approach. He was now several yards from the Regal Room door when the congressman reached the doorway to the lobby. At that moment, no one was paying any attention to anything but their own missions. This was it; the opportunity was now.

Jimmie stepped up to the congressman and said, "Hello, Congressman."

With a surprised and egotistical reply Ray asked, "You are?"

"I'm an unhappy constituent," Jimmie replied, while introducing Doll Baby to Ray's neck and pulling the trigger.

When the congressman fell to the floor, there was no immediate reaction from anyone in the lobby. But after Jimmie put the gun in his mouth, shot himself, and fell on top of the bleeding congressman, he heard the screams start as he quickly, quietly faded from life.

Within 10 minutes, the paramedics and police were on the scene. Both men were discovered to have pulses and were rushed to the University Hospital. They arrived at the hospital at 8:50 am, where surgeons were preparing for emergency surgery. The emergency center staff immediately placed both men on life support systems, in separate areas and under heavy security. Off duty surgeons were being summoned to the hospital.

Outside the hospital, print and broadcast media reporters were hounding every official for statements. They were angry and full of questions about national security, to which they were told, "No comment."

Less than an hour later, a public relation representative of the hospital accompanied by the St. Petersburg chief of police appeared outside the hospital entrance and motioned that they would address the media and public in 10 minutes. Meanwhile, maintenance men quickly set up a sound system. The two officials appeared at the microphones and addressed the crowd.

The chief of police spoke first. "What we have here is another assassination attempt on a United States congressman. A senior citizen, who we believe acted alone, shot Congressman Shapiro as he was leaving the Regal Room of the Hotel Sands. After shooting the congressman, the man then shot himself in an attempted suicide. Beyond that there is no further information I can give to you now. We are awaiting the special investigator form Washington to arrive who will lead the investigation. The hotel is sealed off until the investigator completes his investigation."

The chief waved off questions and introduced the hospital spokesman, Dr. Joseph Billig, who explained the status of both men. "Congressman Shapiro was struck in the lower jaw by a yet undetermined caliber bullet. The bullet entered above his Adam's apple and traveled around his cerebellum and exited near the base of his occipital lobe. He is breathing but in a coma. He is currently undergoing surgery and fighting for his life. The shooter apparently attempted to commit suicide following his act by placing the gun in his mouth and discharging the weapon. He is also breathing and in a coma. A second surgical team is exploring his damage and prognosis. Both men are in critical condition."

The reporters fired questions at both spokesmen. The doctor apologized and stated, "That's all the information available for the public at this time. We will update you as things develop. Thank you."

While gathering their papers to leave the lectern, a staff member from the hospital tapped the doctor on the shoulder and handed him a note. The doctor read the note silently then turned to the expecting reporters.

"Ladies and gentleman of the press, I have just received word that the assassin has now been identified as James Petri, and he has expired. The time of his death is entered as October 8, 2005 at 8:47 pm. He succumbed to a self-inflicted bullet wound into his buccal cavity—in other words his mouth. A complete forensics report detailing a precise cause of death will be available to investigators following an autopsy. That is all for now."

Shouts kept coming from the crowd, "What's the congressman's status?"

"As far as we know, he is still in surgery. We'll share whatever information that is appropriate with you, as it develops."

In the waiting area, Shirley Shapiro sat with red eyes from crying. She was joined by Laura, whom Shirley only regarded as Ray's secretary. Shirley always liked Laura and felt a sense of gratitude for Shirley's time management with his heavy schedule. She had no clue that there was an affair going on between Laura and her husband. Or did she?

"Why, Laura? Why didn't he just come home tonight? Who could do something like this to my husband?" Shirley asked, sobbing.

Laura was in her own world of shock, thinking, *How could she not know how much we loved each other?* She was crying along with Shirley. They both loved the same man, but Laura's love would have to remain a secret forever. From the bits and pieces of information Laura received she wasn't optimistic about his recovery. She pondered all the options and understood that if he died, she would also be out of a job. Maybe if he lived with significant disability, she could have a continued role in his care. Shirley would have all the recognition as his wife, but Laura fantasized that she would be the heroine of his TLC. She would be at his side in the secret role of a devoted lover. If Shirley only knew how intensely they devoured each other's bodies.

How could she? Laura thought. *She just sits there, crying those empty tears, empty as her arms were when he was making love to me.* Laura slipped into a darker side of her nature and hosted a thought, *It's better if he doesn't survive. Then the mystery of how our relationship would have progressed would never be solved. It would end with me being the last person on earth to have had his love. I'll have no more haunting thoughts of whether or not he'll leave Shirley and marry me, nor will I ever again picture him falling in love with some other younger woman.*

Laura never trusted the long-term picture. She was savvy enough to know that if Ray could cheat on Shirley with her, he could just as easily do it to her with another woman. She thought laughingly, *If he had eventually done that, I might have killed him myself.*

Shirley looked over at Laura and asked, "Laura, are you alright?"

"Never mind me, Shirley. I'm still in shock. How are you holding up?"

It was 10 pm when a tall doctor walked toward Shirley with his surgical mask hanging from one ear and inquired, "Are you Mrs. Shapiro?"

Anticipating the worst, Shirley put her hand to her mouth to choke back what he was about to say. "Yes, doctor, I am Shirley Shapiro."

"Mrs. Shapiro, your husband survived the surgery, but he's in a coma."

"Will he be alright?"

"I must be candid with you, there was a lot of nerve damage and blood loss. We cleaned up the damaged areas as best we could, and surgically there is nothing more we could do for him at this time. If you are a spiritual lady, I suggest that you pray. As it stands now, it's in God's hands."

Laura took Shirley into her arms and hugged her and at the same moment held her from collapsing. Laura didn't speak; she just hugged Shirley and thought to herself, *How fast things change. Just three hours ago, a powerful, young congressman was full of life and virility, and now he's in a vegetative state. And it was by the lone act of an old man, who also had a life just three hours ago. How could he have hated my Ray so much to want him dead? Everybody loved Ray, didn't they?*

"This is too unbearable," Shirley said. She regained her composure and asked Laura, "Would you mind helping me with the office and things that need to be re-arranged politically?"

Ray's politics wasn't Shirley's strong suit. She needed Laura's help.

"Of course, I will. I'll handle everything that needs handling with the office," Laura said, but she thought, *How odd it is that in the end they both needed me.*

"Thank you, Laura."

The doctor interrupted and said, "Your husband is in the recovery room now. He will be moved to the ICU when he's stable enough for the move."

"Thank you for everything, doctor. Is he going to survive?"

"Hope exists as long as a heart is beating, but God will be an extremely important factor with the congressman. We have a chapel for your convenience. I recommend that you spend as much time there as you need."

The doctor departed and went back into surgery.

The next morning, the hospital spokesman and the chief of police greeted the anxious group of reporters. The microphones were on, so as the doctor tried to speak it made a loud screeching feedback noise.

"Wow. What the fu-" the doctor caught himself and didn't complete the profanity. A maintenance man rushed to correct the system and signaled that it was ready to go.

"Ladies and gentleman of the press, last evening at 10 pm Congressman Raymond Shapiro came out of the surgery. The team worked as best as they could to surgically repair the extensive damage the bullet cased as it tore its way up through the soft tissue of his upper neck and brain. Currently his status is listed as critical and guarded. He is in our intensive care unit and is being monitored closely.

The questions began flying when Dr. Billig, lifted and spread apart his both arms, signaling the crowd for silence. Finally, they quieted down and listened.

"I am very sorry that beyond what I have told you, there is nothing more that can be given at this time," the doctor continued. "Again as significant information develops, we will share it with you. Thank you."

Chief of police Adam Hunsinger took the microphone and said, "I informed you last evening that we were waiting for the team of investigators from Washington DC to come here and join us in this investigation. I received word earlier today that they will be arriving sometime this morning. Only work by the investigators of the assassinations will show if this assassination is part of the TBA organizations proclamation or an individual acting alone."

Questions were being shouted as the doctor and chief of police made their exit from the podium.

CHAPTER THIRTY-EIGHT

Mike, Hank, and Linda entered the chief's office in St. Petersburg, identified themselves, and requested to see the chief.

"Hello. I'm Chief Adam Hunsinger. I'm so glad you're here. It's been maddening."

Chief Hunsinger looked like the type of chief who had been promoted from the patrolman ranks—the ones who do the right things politically—like kiss ass. Although he had that appearance, he didn't appear stooge-like, and Mike liked him on sight.

Mike explained, "I read your report identifying the findings of fact in this case. Now chief, on behalf of our team, we wish to thank you and your department for everything you have done. We need the crime scene at the Hotel Sands to remain sealed until we have the chance to examine the scene."

"It is still sealed, and I will keep it sealed for as long as you wish," Adam said, sincerely.

"Good, now please contact the morgue and put a hold on the post until Dr. Marshall is able to preside over it."

"What if they object, stating that it's a local jurisdiction and county policy to proceed on their own?" Adam asked.

"Just remind them that this is a federal case, involving the attempted assassination of a United States congressman. They will understand. And chief, I would appreciate your company during my examinations of the scene and the autopsy."

"I'll be more than happy to work with you in any way possible."

"Linda, you and Hank get over to the morgue and get that detail over with. I'll join you later," Mike directed.

Linda and Hank wasted no time and asked the chief for an escort to the morgue. The chief signaled to the staff sergeant at the desk to comply, and they were off in minutes.

"Chief, I apologize for being so abrupt with you and your staff. Please don't be put off by our demeanor," Mike said. "We're under tremendous pressure to bring this investigation to an end."

"I understand, believe me, I do," Adam said, nodding. "This my first major encounter with the media on such a magnitude, and I'm not crazy about it. I can only imagine what it's been like for your team."

The chief seemed to relax with those words, and Mike felt empathy for him. "Chief, we'll get along just fine. I need to make several calls. Is there a private place I can use?"

"You can use the mayor's office. He's on vacation. I'll explain to his secretary and she'll set it up," Adam said.

"Okay, thank you."

Mike made his first call to the President and said, "Mr. President, I now have solid information that I believe will lead to a conclusion of our mission. I will contact Mr. Prendergast upon hanging up and request a quick assist service from his control. I wanted you to be the first one to understand that an operation will soon be under way."

"That's great news, Mike, good luck."

"Well thank you, Mr. President."

"Goodbye."

That went well, Mike thought, *now let's see how well I do with*

Prendergast. It took a while until Mike actually got Prendergast on the line.

"George, I'm here in St. Petersburg, and I believe the 21 members of that Scottish Rite class of 74 is the hub of the organization we seek. Several days ago, I gave you the list of names that are on the photo. Has your department found their locations?"

"Well, Mike, as a matter of fact, we have the locations of the living—and the dead," Prendergast laughed at his own humor.

"I have already spoken with number one. I need you to have your agents bring in all the living members who are on that photograph. I don't have to tell you that they will need to be sequestered. I'm confident your agents will tactfully handle the custody angle. When I wrap my investigation here, I'll join you in Washington to depose the subjects. I will then give you all of the details. You are aware by now that Mr. Petri was also in that photo?"

"Yes, I got that when the news broke. As long as you have enough material facts to justify this action, I will issue the order to bring in the subjects. They will be brought in for questioning and not led to believe that they are being arrested. That should meet the legalities."

"Thank you, I appreciate the help. It shouldn't take too long to finish up what I'm doing here. See you soon."

"Goodbye."

"Goodbye."

Mike went back into the chief's office and asked the chief if he would accompany him to the hospital.

"I'd like to have contact with the congressman to verify his current physical status. Would that be possible? Do you have the time?"

"I certainly do have the time for this. We can leave now. The hospital isn't far."

"Good, I'd like to do this while my team is at the autopsy."

It was 11:45 am when Mike and the chief were in the ICU at the bedside of Congressman Shapiro. His wife, Shirley, was sitting at his side, holding his motionless hand.

"Mrs. Shapiro, I'm Michael Walters, special commissioner appointed by the President to oversee this criminal attempt on your husband's life. First let me offer my sorrow to you that this terrible thing has happened. Although the man who shot your husband is dead and no mystery therefore exist about who did this, we have reason to believe that this act is part of a large-scale plot by an organization to assassinate many elected legislators in Congress. It will be helpful if you can give us any information about your husband's recent activity. I know this is a sad time for you, but if you recall anything, anything at all, it may help us save others from the same fate."

"Honestly, sir, I was by choice pretty much out of the politics. I never asked questions, and my husband never volunteered anything. It seemed to work for us, I took care of the household duties, and he paid the bills. Why would anyone have hurt him?" she sobbed. "He was a good man, my husband. He wanted to help everyone. Why would someone do this?"

"I wish I could answer that, ma'am. I'm afraid I can't be of any comfort to you on that question. There are no easy answers."

"If anyone would know the ins and outs of his agenda and routines, it would be his legislative aide and executive secretary, Laura. She has pretty much handled all of his scheduling and research. I believe she would be in the district office now."

"Thank you, Mrs. Shapiro."

Mike checked out the life support modalities that were keeping the congressman alive. Looking at the young congressman lying there in a coma was an eerie sight for Mike. It reminded him of why he wanted to retire soon. He knew that if he stayed in the department too long, the odds of getting killed or wounded and winding up a basket case like this were increasing. He started to think of a perfect life in retirement with Linda. He shut off the thought and said, "The chief and I will be going, but I want you to know that we will be doing everything in our power to stop this madness."

"Thank you, commissioner, you'll be in my prayers."

Mike and the chief were in the hall when he did a time check; it was 12:22 on the corridor clock. "I know it's lunchtime, but if it's not too much of an imposition, chief, I'd like to interview the congressman's secretary. Will you take me to his district office?"

"I don't mind, but wouldn't it be better after lunch? We could call her and let her know when we'd be arriving."

"I think it would be more advantageous to get there as soon as possible," Mike replied. "I don't want her preparing and rehearsing her possible responses. Anyway, I prefer doing it immediately. I want to wrap things up here quickly so I can get back to Washington. Things are breaking fast."

In route to the congressman's office, the chief pointed out some historic points of interest.

"How long have you been living in St. Petersburg, chief"?

"I was born here."

Mike decided it was a bad move to start asking personal questions. He knew that the next thing coming was to explain where he was born and all the usual crap. So, he distracted the chief and asked, "Do you know Laura? Have you had any political connections with the congressman?"

"No, not really. I met him at several public functions, but to say that I knew him would be a stretch."

"That's good, because it would make her more compliant during a Q and A without any connection to you. If she knew you on a personal basis, she would be looking for you to clue her."

"Well, Mike, there is no need to consider that possibility. I never had any dealings with her, and I'm sure she will be very cooperative and give you any information you request."

"Okay, here we are. There's his office," the chief said, waving his hand at the building.

It was 12:53 as they entered the office. Mike saw a woman sitting at a desk. Her eyes were reddened from crying.

"Are you Laura?" Mike asked.

"Yes, sir, I am. How can I help you?"

Mike showed her his badge and introduced himself along with Chief Hunsinger. "I have some general questions for you concerning your employer, Congressman Raymond Shapiro. This shouldn't take long. Are you okay to do this?"

"Yes, sir."

"Good. What is your title?"

Laura seemed slightly amused at the question. "I am his legislative aide/executive secretary/researcher and any other related duties. In short, I took care of his schedule and agenda. I also attended public hearings with him and made sure all of his papers were in order during any of his presentations."

"Is it fair to say that the congressman relied heavily upon you when dealing with his functions in the House and also in the district?"

"Yes, sir."

"Is there anything you want to tell us, anything you feel we should know that might help in our investigation?"

"Nothing, sir, this is a total shock to me. The congressman seemed to be liked by his constituents and his colleagues in Congress. He was polite and respectful to everyone. I can't imagine why anyone would do this to him."

"During the past several days, has he displayed any kind of odd behavior? Was there anything different in his mood or attitude?

"No, sir, he was in good spirits. He met with everyone who was scheduled. Nothing seemed odd or different with his activities."

"How did the congressman treat you as an employee?"

"If I live to be 100, I'll never have a better boss."

"Is that because you worked closely?"

"Yes, sir. Since I was the one who kept things in order and arranged his agenda, it was necessary to work closely with the congressman."

"Did anyone else in his employ work closely with him?"

"No, sir, the other staffers worked closely with me, and I more directly had access to the congressman. He had confidence enough in me to coordinate all the staff assignments."

"What are your plans now that it is unlikely the congressman will recover enough to return to work?"

Laura became unfrozen with that question, and she slipped into a grief-depressed state of a lover. She began to sob and hold her hands to her mouth. "I don't know what I'm going to do without him. He was my whole life. Now she will be with him at his side doing everything for him." Suddenly, she caught herself and realized what she was saying. "What I mean is, I'm used to taking care of his political agenda."

"Laura, you really liked the congressman, didn't you?"

"Of course, I did, he's a good congressman."

"No, Laura, I mean you really cared for him. He was your lover, wasn't he?"

Laura broke down and cried uncontrollably. "Yes, yes. We were deeply in love, and he was going to leave her after the next election. He promised that if he won, it wouldn't matter about public perception anymore, and if he lost it really would no longer be the public's business."

She continued crying and stood up, immediately collapsing. Mike grabbed her, breaking the fall. Mike held her in a comforting way and whispered in her ear, "It's alright, nothing of this is a factor in the attempted assassination. Your personal relationship with the congressman won't be revealed as a material fact in this crime."

"Thank you, thank you, sir. I'm going to miss him terribly."

"I know. The chief and I are going to leave you now. The only thing I ask of you at this time is if anything comes to your mind that could help us, something like maybe he received a phone call that seemed to upset him, please call me directly. Here is my card."

Mike and the chief left and returned to the police department.

On the way back, Mike said, "I'd appreciate it if you make no public comments regarding anything you heard during these interviews. If you're pressed by anyone, refer them to me. I don't have to tell you how important it is not to offer information during an investigation."

"Mike, I haven't survived as many years on the force as I did without understanding certain protocols."

"Thanks for all your help today," Mike said. "I had a good feeling about you right off. And that's why I asked you to come along. I don't expect to be here too much longer, and if things fall into place as I expect they will, we should be ending this ordeal very soon."

"Good luck, Mike, it's been great watching you at work. I know why the President gave you this mission: You're good."

"Thanks. I'm hoping that Hank and Linda are back from the autopsy."

Mike and the chief waited in his department office for Hank and Linda to return. It was 2:05 pm when they finally got back.

"Sorry, Mike, it took a little longer than we thought it would," Hank said. "The pathologist and Linda spent some preliminary time discussing their protocols, so we got started a little late."

"But it all worked out," Linda interjected, "Well, anyway everything worked out after I made the local pathologist understand my federal jurisdiction and any ramifications if he were to obstruct the law by trying to limit my participation in the post. He got the message, and we agreed to do a double post, mostly by concurrence of findings. We then conducted a joint signing of the report. The results of the autopsy weren't all that unusual. Mr. Petri had suffered for many years with Parkinson's disease, which worsened recently, restricting his mobility. Toxicology tests show that his blood was loaded with Ativan, an anti-depressant that helped to slow down the tremors he was probably experiencing and also allowed him to control the weapon. Upon review of his internal organs and chemistry, his arterial network showed vessel narrowing typical of his age, along with age-related deterioration of his organs and skin. I will have a complete detailed autopsy report as soon as it's processed, including some theories."

"Thanks, Linda, include whatever you feel is important," Mike said. "Thank you both for getting this done. I know it wasn't a devastating cause of death with some mysterious disease motivating the man, but it has all of the elements peculiar to the other assassins. I have the info that I need to take us to the next level. I believe we have all that's necessary to wind this thing up. Now, if there's nothing else any of you need here, I suggest that we pack up and head back to Washington. Linda, I feel that it would be best for you to come with us to DC instead of going back to Tennessee at this time."

"I intended on going to Washington with you, Mike, but now I'm interested in the reason you feel it's necessary."

"Well, mainly because I strongly feel that this is going to conclude soon, and I don't want to waste anymore of your time going back and forth. This way, you'll only have one trip home. As for the reason you're needed, you will be participating in the final report."

"Enough already," Linda said, "let's hit the skies."

"Chief, would you be kind enough to get us to the airport?"

"Consider it done."

CHAPTER THIRTY-NINE

It was 11 pm, October 9, 2005, when they arrived in Washington, DC. It was too late to get Linda set up in a motel, so Mike invited her to stay at his apartment. Linda, feeling exhausted from the long day accepted and didn't—to Mike's surprise—even bother to place any conditions on the arrangement.

Hank's car was also parked at the airport. In parting he asked, "What time do you want to get together in the morning?"

"I'll call you in the morning," Mike said.

Mike and Linda spoke very little while en route to his apartment. When they did speak, it was in one-word sentences.

"Are you tired?"

"Yes"

"It's been a long day, hasn't it?"

"Very."

"Well, it won't be very long now. I only live 20 minutes away," Mike said.

"Good."

"Are you okay?" Mike asked.

"I'm fine, just exhausted. I really need a good night's sleep, then I'll be fine."

"Do you need anything from the convenience store? There's one just a block ahead. I could stop and get whatever you want."

"No, thank you. I think I have everything I need."

"Okay, we're here," Mike said, pulling into the condo complex parking lot, where each owner member had their own assigned parking. He couldn't avoid noticing how beautiful Linda was in the soft amber light that lit up the parking area. The sight of her profile and scent of her hair were intoxicating. As Mike rounded the car to offer assistance with her bags, she already had her right leg on the ground. Her dress was pulled slightly above her knee, revealing just enough thigh.

Dear God, thought Mike as he did a visual scan of her calf. *Help me endure this night.*

Mike helped her with her luggage—one suitcase and an overnight bag. Inside, he gave her a brief tour of the unit. He intentionally avoided going into the bedroom with her but simply pointed at it and said, "That's the bedroom. You use it. It has a separate bathroom. I'll sleep in my office."

"That won't be necessary, Mike. I could sleep on the couch. You don't have to baby me. I'm used to roughing it at times."

"No really, it's fine. My office has a pull-out bed and a half bath. I'll be very comfortable. Actually, Linda, I very seldom sleep in the bed."

"Why is that? Why would you deprive yourself of a comfortable bed?"

"I'm a bachelor, remember? What difference does it make?"

"Bachelor or not, you still have to sleep."

"This may sound silly, but by not sleeping in the bed, I don't have to make it every day, and I don't have to change sheets either."

"I'm so sorry for you that you don't have to make up your bed every day and change the sheets," Linda said, jokingly.

"Maybe I'm not getting the concept through to you. I'm a cop. I work in a very demanding environment, and usually when I wake in the morning it's late and I have to get out in a hurry. Other times I'm responding to emergencies, so the fewer domestic duties I have, the better. Besides, don't you live alone? Who makes your bed?" Mike stopped and said, "Oh no, forget I asked that."

"Mike, you're too defensive. Yes, I'm single live alone. I guess, although I have a very responsible and a professional position, I do have more control of my time than someone with a family. I do understand the difference between your situation and mine, and I'm willing to concede that your reason for not sleeping in your bed makes some weird single-man sense. Anyway, screw the logic. I'm too tired to argue the merits between our differences. I'll use the friggin' bedroom, thank you," Linda said, then went into the bedroom and quietly closed the door.

Mike went into his computer room with shock coloring his thoughts. *Did I just hear that? Screw the logic and friggin' bedroom? Jesus Christ, she's not made of stone after all.*

Mike set up the bed in his office, undressed, and then slowly got into the pullout bed. Sinking slowly into its comfort, he knew it was going to be a very long night. He would think over and over about the investigation and his next move, and then shift to Linda. When thinking of Linda, everything would be wonderfully inarticulate. First her gorgeous body would try to appear, then her independence and her professionalism, and surprisingly now her ability to use street language. Her behavior tonight was the closest to allowing him to think he actually could melt her wall of stone.

Curiously, Mike drifted into the alternatives concerning the psychic dimensions surrounding her development. Why wasn't she married? Why didn't she have a boyfriend? The more he visualized her thigh and calf as she dismounted the car, the more aroused he became. He mentally undressed her and spread her legs wide apart. As she lay there naked, he imagined her pulling his head into her stomach while placing both of her hands on his shoulders pushing him into her pelvic area. When she started breathing heavily, he sensed she wanted him to enter his tongue into her waiting vagina. Her stone perfect, beautiful body was morphing and melting into a hot sex machine. Mike was so aroused that as he imagined getting her off with his tongue. He started masturbating to the rhythm of her ecstasy. He visualized her mouth and her pouting lips moving and groaning like an older virgin experiencing her first orgasm. He tried to muffle the sounds of his excitement so she wouldn't hear, but the fear of being caught caused him to lose the image and his penis would soften.

Scared and excited at the same time, Mike desperately tried bringing back the image. It was useless. There she was, only a few feet away in another room. The vivid images of her nudity were exciting, but the fear factor was so frustrating that he couldn't complete his masturbation. Feeling guilty, he pulled himself together and chastised himself for being a dirty, old man.

Yeah, I'm one of the good guys. A cop in his fifties trying to act like a viral young stud. And here I am betrayed by my own dick. I'm some fucking stallion. I can't even keep an erection, and I expect to be desired by that gorgeous woman just a few feet away. Mike sighed and almost sobbed. *I want her so bad. I never held her hand. I never touched her lips, and yet I'm hopelessly in love. Love her, yes. And now I fear her. She probably resents me and sees me as some pathetic slob she just got professionally involved with and can't wait to be rid of.*

Mike thought about tomorrow, and he realized how important it was going to be when he would be interrogating all those men in the photo. He would need to be at the top of his game. He had John Craig, the FBI, and the President of the United States to deal with. He couldn't appear amateurish. Mike got up and took a sedative, which he always had around for high energy days when he couldn't fall asleep. If ever there was a time for sleep aids, this was it.

Back in his bed, he started the routine of counting sheep backward from 100.

I wonder if she's asleep? Maybe she's just lying in there afraid to sleep. Maybe she heard my masturbation and is frightened that I might crash into her room and attack her. I must get that stinking thinking out of my head. She's a mature, professional. Hell, she's a doctor. Certainly, she understands human nature. Certainly she...sure she....

Mike fell asleep.

The next morning, while still in his pajamas and a white robe, Mike was fiddling around in the kitchen when Linda walked in.

"Good morning, Mike, did you sleep well?" she asked.

Mike, slightly embarrassed, gave her an indirect look and replied, "Yes, yes indeed. How did you sleep? Was my room comfortable enough for you?"

"I was very comfortable, and in fact it was actually a pleasant night. I rather like your room," Linda replied with a smile.

Mike felt relieved that she apparently hadn't been disturbed by his action, nor was she threatened by being in his apartment. Her smile allowed him to be more forward with her now, and he even felt a surge of manly humor.

"Would you like to have permanent occupancy in that room?"

Linda looked more beautiful in the morning light. She was wearing one of his dress shirts, which covered the lower part of her back and just enough of pelvic area in the front to hint of the delicious goodies below. Her hair was wild and everywhere.

"Why, Michael. Whatever do you mean?"

Mike didn't know how to respond, and he became aroused and boyishly silly. "Linda, here I am a man in his fifties. Middle fifties that is, a professional policeman at the top of his career. Ask me anything about the law. Give me a set of clues and circumstances and chances are I will provide a practical analysis of the case. That's been my life—everything structured and practiced predicable, reliable behavior. But being around you throws off my entire judgmental skills, and I feel exposed, vulnerable, and childish. I am a professional —good at what I do, but I also have feeling. I discovered my feeling the moment I laid eyes on you in Tennessee—an accomplished, professional lady with a brilliant mind and a drop-dead gorgeous body. You are in an unusual profession as a pathologist who can navigate her hands throughout a human corpse, examining the tissues and organs and telling the world what that person was and why. You're a very structured lady. But goddamn it, Linda, I see a woman. I'm so fucking in love with you. Do you have feelings for me?"

Linda looked at Mike for what seemed to him like forever. Her beautiful, bright eyes were moistened with tears. She turned away from Mike and while rubbing her eyes walked over to the window.

She spoke through a chain of sobs, "Mike, I do have feelings. As a child I was sexually abused by my father, but despite my education and medical training, I never really dealt with it. I suppressed it, hoping it could never interfere with my life. But I was wrong—very wrong. When you came into my life for that autopsy, at first, I did think you were an awkward oaf. I didn't think much of you. But gradually, after I realized that you were clumsy because you were off-track with your interest in me, I found myself thinking about you. And as hard as I would try to eliminate you from my thoughts, you would still keep coming back. After all those years of suppressing interest in men or sex, you started to break down any barriers I developed. You forced me to confront my feelings. I was accepting my feeling and about to remove my psychological shield and accept whatever would come. Then of course while we were in Wrightstown, you dropped that mea culpa bomb that threw me back into a protective state. My feelings about you were unsettling. I felt conflict between two possibilities: One that you were capable of dishonesty, and two that you were trying to be contrite and honest."

As Linda was speaking with her back to him, he moved slowly toward her. She turned to face him. But he was there, just an arm's length away. When he lifted his arms to reach out to her, she felt her heart miss a beat and turned reaching for Mike.

They embraced and held each other tightly. Their lips met as they kissed, moaned, and chewed each other's mouths hungrily. The agony of their long life of abject loneliness has come to an end. The passion beyond the ecstasy of their first kiss could only be heaven.

And now death is the only thing between them and heaven. Mike gently caressed and kissed her on the top of her beautiful head, and then her shoulders. Their lips would meet over and over again. The only thing she was wearing was his shirt, and he could feel her breasts against his love-starved body. Her voluptuous thighs forcing their way between his legs was a thrilling feeling. Lightning bolts charged through their bodies with each kiss. Mike thought, *I'm in heaven, and I'm not dead.*

He followed her into the bedroom, and without words they made love to each other in the purest way. It wasn't sex; it was love. Linda reached a climax before Mike, and Mike was so excited he followed in a wild explosive cry.

"I love you, Linda, I love you so much," Mike said.

Linda followed with, "I love and adore you," Linda replied.

When their love making was over and their heavy breathing was slowly returning to normal, they laid silently in each other's arms, feeling all the essence of God's ultimate gift to mankind. They were truly in love.

It was 9:35 am when the telephone rang.

"Mike, do you realize what time it is?" Hank said, breathlessly. "When are we going to get together? We have a lot to do."

Mike's voice was crackly as he was clearing his throat. "Sorry, let's meet at 10:30. I'll see you at headquarters. Before I get there, will you have staff schedule me to speak with Prendergast at FBI headquarters?"

"Good enough, I can do that. But why, my friend, are you so late? It's not like you?" Hank asked.

"Let's just say that I had the best night's sleep that I had in a long, long while."

"Don't bullshit a bull shitter. I'll see you later." Hank hung up, and Mike laid back down besides Linda. Her eyes were beautiful in the morning light. Mike rolled over and kissed her lovingly.

"Since you heard my conversation with Hank, you know that today's agenda will be full and long," Mike said.

"Yes, darling. I completely understand what comes today. I'm prepared to do what I can to help you make it a success. What would you like me to do?"

"I'm going to need you when the time comes for a summation of the posts you conducted on the assassins, but that won't be needed for now, actually not until a case is readied for court. Anyway, a federal prosecutor will need all that info to prepare his case long before going to any courts. So, I'm going to need you for reports and consultation for the duration of this investigation. The question is where to have you placed until this thing is over."

"Should I go back to Tennessee and get back to work? I don't know what's best at this point."

"My heart wants you here with me," Mike said. "Lord knows, I don't want you out of my reach, but I need to be practicable about all this. Our relationship and the investigation must be in the proper perspective, would you agree?"

"I certainly do agree," Linda said, pulling him down for a validating love kiss. They both laughed and knew they were in love, and it would be a forever thing.

"While I'm gone today, why don't you stay here and use my equipment to start on your summary report?" Mike suggested. "When I get back from doing my thing, we—I mean you—can decide what's best for you until this is over. Is that a plan?"

"For today, I agree that would be a good idea," Linda said, nodding. "I'll take advantage of the apartment and start my report. And if you are a good guy, you'll call me with some idea of when you'll be coming home I'll try my skills in the kitchen and prepare dinner."

"I don't want you to assume that you need to take care of me. I would rather take care of you," Mike said.

"Don't be silly. Let me do this for you," Linda said.

"Okay you do the things you want today— read, write, cook, listen to music—just feel my love as you navigate through it all," Mike said. "If you need anything, there's a market one block up the street.

I'll call you with a heads-up as soon as I have a plan of action, and I know what time I'll be back."

"Okay, I'll be fine here," Linda said. "I could use the peaceful time to settle my emotions. By the time you return, I'll have an idea of how to play this time element out. What I would like from you is a promise to have a special day."

"I promise to have a special day. How could I not, now with you in my life."

They agreed and once again embraced tightly and kissed with all the passion of new lovers.

It was 10:30 on the dot when Mike entered the office. John and Hank were anxiously waiting. Hank looked at his watch, shook his head, and said, "Okay, what gives? You're never this late. What the hell is that bright-eyed, cheerful attitude about? Oh. I get it. Where's Linda?"

"In a nutshell, you two burned-out, washed-up gum shoes, I'm in love," Mike replied with a smirk. "I'm retiring, and then I'm moving to the seashore to live happily ever after. Does that satisfy your curiosity? As for Linda, she's making arrangements for a preacher, and you two idiots aren't invited."

"Now hold on, Mike. Cut the shit," John said. "You can't just up and walk out on this investigation."

"I'm just kidding, guys," Mike said. "I have every intention of seeing this investigation through. But what I'm not kidding about is that Linda and I officially are now a couple, and I don't intend to give up any opportunity to keep her in my life. I do plan on retiring as soon as this investigation is concluded. But until those ducks are in order, I'll be here on the job. Let's get to work."

"You didn't mean that about not inviting us, did you?" Hank asked.

"No, Hank, I wouldn't be anything without my two best friends present."

Hank shook his hand saying, "I'm really happy about this, Mike. I knew she was the one for you."

John gave Mike his usual bear hug and wished him luck.

"I made a preliminary call to Prendergast this morning," Hank said. "He's standing by for your call. So, you should get on that immediately."

Prendergast answered on the first ring and asked, "How are you doing, Mike?"

"Couldn't be better, sir."

"Okay, this is where we are with the subjects on the photo. I have three field offices involved, and the special agents in charge in Cincinnati, Philadelphia, and Newark have brought in all the available subjects. I've instructed the SACs to withhold their own interrogations until you arrive and take charge. They understand. You'll need to make ETA arrangements with each office. The subjects can only be held for so long without formal charges being filed, and it's a fine line to question them without legal representation."

"I hear you," Mike said, nodding. "This means that I have to visit three field offices in three states within the next 24 hours. Shit, there goes dinner."

Mike contacted all the three FBI field offices and confirmed a time that he would be there. He planned to do Philadelphia and New Jersey before the day's end. He called Prendergast again and requested the use of a small plane.

"George, if I'm able to pull this thing off in 24 hours, I'll need that unrestricted resource."

"I'll take care of that immediately," George confirmed. "A plane will be ready within the hour. Just get to the airport and identify yourself. You'll have immediate escort to a waiting craft."

"Thank you, George."

"Good luck."

"Hank, don't ask any questions," Mike said, turning to his friend. "Just be ready because you're going with me. I must call Linda and let her know everything has changed for today."

Mike got Linda on the phone. He cupped his mouth and said, "Sweetheart, things here will require me to be in three states within the next 24 hours. I can make a case for needing you with me, but that would be selfish. I will leave it up to you. Do you want to come along, stay there and wait, or head for Tennessee?"

"Honey, I'll be packed and ready to go along with you," Linda said, excitedly.

"Fantastic. I'll have Hank pick you up in 30 minutes and bring you to the airport. Love you. You won't need any overnight things because we're going to hit all three locations and keep moving. We will rest on the plane between stops."

"I need to make some calls to Tennessee and let people know that I'll be away for an indefinite time," Linda said. "I'll be ready and waiting for Hank."

"Great. I'll see you then."

Mike hung up the phone and turned to John to ask, "There's no need to explain the what, when, and where's concerning the next 24 hours. Is there?"

"Well, all I can say is thank God we have you and Hank running this thing," John said, shaking his head. "I'm really pleased with you guys. You are an asset to this department. I'm God dammed proud of you. Now get the fuck out of here before I get too soft and lose my equanimity. I believe there's a plane out there waiting for you."

"Hank, please go for Linda. I'll meet both of you at the airport."

"I'm on my way."

Everything went smoothly at the airport. Linda was ready and waiting at the door for Hank when he arrived at Mike's apartment to pick her up. The pilot had the six-seat, twin-engine airplane preflight tested and ready to taxi onto the runway.

They were in the air by 1:00 pm. The flight to Newark was uneventful and lasted the better part of an hour. Mike decided to make the Newark interrogations first, then Philadelphia, and Cincinnati last.

A waiting car transported them to the field office. By 2 pm, Mike was extending his hand to special agent in charge Bruno Mathers.

"Good to meet you, sir," Bruno said.

"It's my pleasure as well, Mr. Walters."

Mike introduced Hank and Linda to agent Mathers. Then they got down to business.

"Regarding the subjects you requested for interviews, this is what we have," Bruno began. "We located Thomas Whitaker, who was living with his sister in Somerville, New Jersey. He seemed terribly confused and upset about being picked up. We also located Noel Jones, who was living in a group home in New Brunswick. There was no trouble with him at all. He seemed pleased to be getting out for a ride. Both Whitaker and Jones are sequestered in this building and ready to be questioned. The other man on our list, Leonard Stark, died from lung cancer in 2003."

"Thank you, Bruno."

Mike entered a room where a gray-haired, mild-appearing man who looked to be about 75 was waiting. The room had no windows, but Mike knew he could be viewed through a two-way mirror.

"Good afternoon, Mr. Whitaker. I'm Mike Walters, special investigator for the federal government." Mike reached over and shook Mr. Whitaker's hand.

"Hello, sir, I'm very pleased to meet you," Thomas said.

Mike turned on a recorder, looked at Mr. Whitaker, and said, "I'm going to record our conversation. Do you understand?"

"Yes, sir, I do."

Mike then announced into the recorder, "Today is October 12, 2005, and it's 3:10 pm. I'm in the FBI field office in Newark, New Jersey, and I'm about to interview Mr. Thomas Whitaker. Mr. Whitaker, I'm investigating the recent assassinations of 14 U.S. congressmen. Are you aware of the assassinations?"

"Yes, sir, I am. Only what I read about in the paper and see on TV."

"Are you a Mason, Mr. Whitaker?"

"Yes, sir I am, but I'm not active anymore. I can't get to lodge meetings. I don't drive anymore. They took away my license."

"What degree were you, Mr. Whitaker?"

"I was a 32nd degree Scottish Rite Mason," Thomas said proudly.

"Are you or have you ever been part of any group that has an anti-government agenda?" Mike asked.

"I don't know what you mean," Thomas said. "A 32nd degree Mason is an upstanding citizen. I supported all their charitable fundraisers. What are you getting at?"

"Mr. Whitaker, I have a photograph here I want you to look at," Mike said, pulling the photo out of his bag. ""Do you recognize this photo?"

"Yes of course, it's the graduate class of 1974." Thomas replied.

"Do you recognize any of the men?"

"Of course. I had this photo in my home. Everyone in the class received one. It was a one-month class, and as I recall, we only attended one or two days a week. Gee, that was a long time ago. I got friendly with most of the guys, but after the class was over, I seldom ever saw any of them. We all belonged to different blue lodges."

"Mr. Whitaker, are you telling me that you never met with or saw any of these men since 1974?"

"Once in a while, maybe at a Masonic convention or a lodge-sponsored trip, I would run into one of them," Thomas said. "Usually a guy would come up to me and ask if I remembered him from the class of '74. That was it."

Mike asked again, "Have you *ever* met with any of these guys since 1974?"

"Well, now that you mention it, back in 2003 I was invited to a meeting in Pennsylvania. The invitation was by telephone."

"Where in Pennsylvania?"

"It was in a place called Hazleton, some burned-out, rundown, old coal mining city," Thomas said.

"Did you attend that meeting?"

"Yes, I went and attended the meeting, which lasted only a few minutes. Some tall, gray-haired man spoke. I think his name was Peter. Let me see that photo again," Thomas said, his gaze shifting back to the photo on the table. He looked at the photo, pointed to Peter Fallow, and said, "That's him, there. He's much younger in the photo, but that's him."

"Okay. What was the meeting about?"

"Well, as I said it only lasted about 5 minutes."

"What was the subject? Why was the meeting called?" Mike asked.

I'm trying to recall what was said in those five minutes. I do remember it was the end of August, and I kept thinking at the time that I would like to spend some time in the Poconos, but that I wasn't really interested too much in any Masonic activities again. It's coming back to me now. This Peter guy was standing there telling us what we had in common—you know, loyalty, truth, and honor. Then he suggested we had a 'final duty' or words like that. Then, and this is strange, he asked those present if they wanted to continue on to enter into another room behind him. And for all others to just leave and forget that they were there."

"What did you do?"

"Well, like I said, I wasn't interested in anymore lodge work, so I left."

"Did you leave alone?" Mike asked.

"No, sir, others did as well."

"Besides you, how many others left?"

"As I recall, there were about five."

"Okay so you and about five others walked out of the room. How many went into the other room to continue on with lodge work?"

"My guess is about 15 or 16, maybe less? Hell, it's been three years, I don't know exactly."

"What did you do after you left?"

"It was getting late, and I wanted to get out of that depressing city, so I drove to the Poconos. I spent two days there then went home," Thomas said.

"And you don't know what was said in the other room?"

"No, sir, and like I said, I wasn't interested. I never thought about it again."

"I can understand that, Mr. Whitaker. But didn't you suspect anything funny about that final duty comment? Didn't that arouse your curiosity?"

"No, sir. In a Mason's blue lodge life, a lot of duty is required, participating in going through the Masonic chairs. I'm sorry, Mr. Walters, I can only tell you that I had no interest in anything, and as far as I was concerned I did my duty for God and country a long time ago. I'm an old man now, trying to enjoy what's left of my life."

"Mr. Whitaker, at this time I have nothing further to ask of you. Thank you for your cooperation here today."

Mike signaled for agent Mathers and said, "Agent, we're finished with Mr. Whitaker, so you may return this gentleman to his home. In a few moments, please bring in Mr. Jones."

Mike went to a desk and made some notes, conferred with Hank and Bruno briefly, and in a loving gesture touched Linda on her shoulders.

"Agent, how much of this are you getting through the intercom?"

"We're getting every single word," Bruno confirmed.

"Great. You may take me to Mr. Jones now. I don't expect this to take much longer. Hank while you're observing the interview, I'll give you a signal when I'm about to end the interview. When you get the signal, please contact the pilot and have him ready the airplane for Philadelphia. I'll brief you and Linda en route."

"I understand."

"Agent Mathers, after we depart, contact the SAC in Philadelphia and alert him of our ETA."

"Done. Anything else, Mike?"

"No. Let's get this Jones thing over with."

Mike entered the room where Mr. Noel Jones was waiting. He was an eager, little guy who had a broad smile on his face when Mike introduced himself. Noel eagerly reached over to shake Mike's hand.

"I very pleased to meet you, Mr. Walters," Noel said. "I saw you with the President on the news. A terrible thing— what's happening with all these assassinations is just terrible."

"Yes, Mr. Jones, it is a terrible thing, and that is what I want to discuss with you today," Mike said, sizing him up.

Mike repeated the entire routine of recording and gaining Mr. Jones compliance. He learned that Noel also attended the August 2003 meeting in Hazleton, and like Thomas, he also walked out when given the option to enter the next room. He, too, identified Peter Fallow as the man in charge of the meeting. Noel denied knowledge of what the next room meeting was about, but was also able to identify several of the other graduates in the group.

Noel quickly pointed to Donald Wadsworth and stated, "He was one of the guys I befriended during the classes. I liked him. He was a photographer and since I was an amateur photographer, I enjoyed discussing photography with him."

"Was Mr. Wadsworth also at the meeting in Pennsylvania?"

"Yes, he was," Noel said.

"Did he leave with you, or did he go into the other room?"

"He didn't leave with me or the others," Noel remembered. "But I don't know if he entered the other room because I couldn't see who entered the other room."

"But you know for sure that he didn't leave?"

"That's right; he didn't leave. I remember saying goodbye to him as I was leaving the room. Now that I'm remembering, Donald was listening very closely to what Pete was saying. He was a curious guy. Maybe it had something to do with a photographer's nature or something. Yes, I could see him wanting to know what was behind that door."

Having all of the information he needed from Noel, Mike signaled Hank to get the pilot ready. He thanked Noel for his time and waved him out the door. It was 4:03 pm. Mike thanked agent Mathers for the accommodations and reminded him to let the Philadelphia SAC know they just left the Newark office.

The flight from Newark to Philadelphia took 35 minutes. Mike and Linda sat next to each other while Hank played co-pilot, giving Mike and Linda a little quality time. Linda used Mike's shoulder for a pillow, and they quietly enjoyed their new feeling of belonging. The flight was serene.

While in flight to Philadelphia International, the crew and investigation team listened to the news. It was being announced that students at several colleges throughout the nation were demonstrating on their campuses. College bloggers were advocating a march on Washington DC to protest a "bought and paid for Congress."

The newscaster was edified, "This is reminiscent of the Bonnie and Clyde era when the people were rooting for the bandits. Are the assassins becoming heroes of the people?"

The pilot said, "You must admit: Some things are worth dying for. If killing some of those self-serving bastards brings honor back to Congress, then I guess that's worth dying for."

"Unfortunately, I don't have the luxury of expressing any opinions," Mike said. "It's my job to solve the crimes. I have the responsibility to get these guys and bring them into custody. That's where my job ends."

"Well, Mike that's true, but when do you become an American citizen who cares about the unpunished crimes these corrupt politicians are committing every day?" Hank asked.

"Hank, you know I care, but as long as I have this sworn duty, I must stay focused."

The pilot, growing more and more agitated by the notion of corrupt Congressmen, injected, "We all have sworn duties, but does that mean we surrendered our ability to think?"

Linda, in an attempt to distract the men from becoming angrier said, "Maybe this will end in a way that will restore some sanity to representative government. And just maybe, Mike will be able to retire, and we can give the next generation an honest world to live in."

"We all want a better life," Mike said. "We want to live freely in a great nation—for ourselves and more importantly for the future.

When I retire, I will become a good citizen. I have no idea where that may take me, but until that day I will perform my sworn duty."

"I'm with you, Mike," Hank said firmly. "We get the milk to market, but we let the people decide how much they need to drink."

Linda, Mike, and the pilot all gave Hank questionable eye rolls and laughed. Then, in chorus, they all mockingly sung, "Let's get the milk to market."

"That's good, Hank," Mike said. "Did you come up with the metaphor before or is it the altitude? Just kidding, we need less stress. With a little luck, this will end soon."

The pilot announced that he was in contact with Philadelphia International and was cleared for landing.

After a quick car ride from the airport, Mike and his team entered the Philadelphia field office and were greeted by special agent James Mullins, who reported, "Mr. Walters, this is the results of our roundup. The following men from the photo lived in the Commonwealth of Pennsylvania and all died in 2005: Henry Lister, James Petri, George Stanton, Donald Wadsworth, John Weatherly, Lawrence Smith, John Grubb, and Dennis Monk. Carl Duffy and Keith Stockton both reportedly committed suicide in September. William Rodgers expired in 2003. Joseph Richards, used to live in Pennsylvania but is currently in a coma on life support in a long-term care facility near Los Angeles.

"Peter Fallow of Hazleton, Pennsylvania, is alive and well and awaiting your questioning," James continued. "Anthony George and Kenneth Oakdale are also alive and awaiting your interrogation."

"Okay, please take me to Mr. Oakdale," Mike said.

Kenneth Oakdale was sitting in the interrogation room, which was constructed almost identical to the interrogation rooms in Newark. This room however, appeared to have a sunnier atmosphere. Maybe it was the color the room was painted, Mike thought.

Kenneth was a medium-built man, who seemed to be in fairly good health for a man in his mid-seventies. He stood and shook Mike's hand when Mike reached for it as he was introducing himself.

"Mr. Oakdale, I have some questions for you regarding your affiliation with the graduating class of Scottish Rite Masons in 1974," Mike said. "Before we begin, I will switch on this tape recorder, and our entire conversation will be recorded, do you understand? If you don't understand, we can arrange for someone to help you clarify the questions." Mike added this to his routine when it occurred to him that these older subjects could be a little slower with receptive hearing.

"No, sir, I understand you well, and I'm ready to answer your questions," Kenneth said.

"Mr. Oakdale, here is a picture of 21 men who graduated as 32nd degree Scottish Rite Masons in May of 1974. Do you recognize the photo? Can you point to yourself?"

"Yes, I do, and I have a copy of the same photo," Kenneth answered, pointing to himself on the photo. "I looked a lot younger then, didn't I?"

"Yes, sir, you did," Mike agreed. "You were a very handsome guy. Who else do you recognize?"

Pointing to Donald Wadsworth and Peter Fallow, he said, "I recognize these two guys because they always stood out during class interaction."

Then he pointed to Joseph Richards and said, "I sort of remember him, Joe Richards."

"Have you had any contact with any of the men in the photo since 1974?"

"Maybe at Masonic conventions through the years, but I can't say exactly."

"Did you ever attend any meetings since then? Perhaps in Pennsylvania?"

"Well, yes, I did attend a meeting in Hazleton," Kenneth said. "I think it was in the summer of 2003. It didn't last long. I was glad to get out of that depressing town."

"Who called the meeting and what was it about?"

"There, that guy," Kenneth said, pointing to Peter Fallow. "He was in charge. He was talking to us about final duties and our loyalty to each other, stuff like that. It only lasted a few minutes when he asked anyone who was interested in some sort of duty to enter another room or leave if we weren't interested. I left."

"Were you the only one to leave?"

"I was the first one out the door, so I don't know how many left. But I heard others walking behind me. I heard one man say, 'Fuck that loyalty shit. I'm enjoying retirement.' I remembered him saying that because I felt the same way."

"What else do you recall about that evening? How were you notified about the meeting?"

"I received a call, and I think it was that Richards guy."

"Recently a lot of congressmen were assassinated," Mike said. They were all over the news. Were you aware of these assassinations? Did you make any connection to your meeting that night in Hazleton, Pennsylvania?"

"No, my God, no. Is that what this is all about?"

"That's what we're investigating here, and I want to thank you for cooperating with this interview. If anything comes to your mind that could be helpful, please call," Mike said, handing Kenneth his card. "Agent Mullins will see to it that you are returned to your home."

Mike's interview with Anthony George was structured in the same format, and as Mike had predicted, he also attended the meeting in Pennsylvania. He also admitted to leaving the meeting after being invited into the next room for more detailed information. Anthony identified some of the other men in the photograph and pointed to Peter Fallow as the person in charge of the meeting. Mike also released him to be returned to his home.

Mike made several notes before calling the others into the room. He summarized his findings and expressed concern on how to proceed with his next subject: Peter Fallow. He knew that he was going to be key to ending the investigation, but he also had the Cincinnati interviews still to conduct.

"Hank, here's the problem," Mike said. "Knowing what I now

know about Peter Fallow, I don't want to rush this next interview. If he proves to be difficult to deal with, it could lead to him requesting legal counsel. I might need you to go to Cincinnati and get statements from the others. If it comes to that, will it be okay with you?"

"I completely understand what's at stake now, and of course I'll handle the Cincinnati thing," Hank said confidently.

"Good," Mike said, turning to Linda. "This might also lead to a lot longer mission than the 24 hours I predicted yesterday. You deserve the option at this point to hang around longer or head back to Tennessee. On the one hand, I want you near me every moment of the day, but on the other hand I'm not so sure that I can fully concentrate while you are near. It's up to you."

"Mike, I'm going to remain here with you until you know what you're doing," Linda said. "When we get back to your apartment, I'll decide based upon what we learn here today."

"Fair enough," Mike said, nodding. "Now we all have a contingency plan. Agent Mullins, I'm going to ask one favor of you. My team and I haven't had a thing to eat in hours. Could you have some sandwiches brought in? I think a little nourishment would be perfect before I tackle Mr. Fallow."

"You got it. Would you like anything in particular?"

Linda asked if there was any Chinese in the area, and if so she would enjoy an order of vegetables and tea. Mike and Hank both agreed and asked for the same.

"Someone check on the pilot," Mike said. "He needs to eat as well."

MIKE ENTERED THE INTERROGATION ROOM WHERE PETER Fallow was waiting.

"Mr. Fallow, I'm Mike Walters."

"Yes, I know who you are. I watch the news. I saw you standing with our idiot President when he was announcing your appointment."

"I gather you don't like our President. Do you think I'm an idiot because he appointed me to head up the investigation?"

"No. I really have no opinion of you, but, he's your President—not mine. He's an idiot, and so are those congressmen who gave him a free reign to prosecute this phony Iraq war."

"So, you dislike the President, and you dislike congress," Mike said. "What have you done as a citizen to help make changes?"

"I vote. I never miss an election. But it didn't matter, did it? They used the supreme courts to steal the last election. Pretty fucking sick, isn't it? Besides, Mr. Walters, you know as well as I do that we the people are irrelevant and routinely ignored by our elected members of Congress."

"Mr. Fallow, I'm going to start this recorder and ask you some questions, is that okay? Do you understand?"

"Mr. Walters, you're not going to ask me any questions—not one —until I'm represented by council. Do you understand?"

"Mr. Fallow, you're not being charged with anything. Why would you object to being questioned about something that we haven't explained yet?"

"It doesn't matter. I know my constitutional rights. I'm not playing your game."

"Well, Mr. Fallow, since you're unwilling to cooperate with this interview, we will now decide how to proceed. Are you sure you won't reconsider?"

Peter didn't respond. He just glared at Mike, using unmistakable body language that he was through. Mike signaled to his team that he was ready to terminate the interview. In the office, Mike explained to the team that it was now obvious that they had the right man in custody and instructed agent Mullins to hold him in custody and see to it that he was afforded counsel.

"I will also need a federal warrant to go through his house in Hazleton," Mike said. "Hank, I will continue on to Cincinnati with you. Linda, you may as well stick with us on the next leg of this mission. Is that okay with you?"

"No problem."

"Let's keep it moving," Hank said, "The pilot is ready to go as soon as we are."

It was exactly 7 pm when the team boarded the plane for Cincinnati. The flight was uneventful. Everyone reclined in their seats and took advantage of the opportunity to rest.

In the Cincinnati field office, Mike met with SAC Jack Spellman. Mike and Jack exchanged briefings. Agent Spellman identified the men he had for interviews as Keith Stockton and William Burger. Other men in the photo, Thomas Shade and John Powell expired in September. Powell committed suicide, and Shade died of lung cancer.

Mike conducted the interviews with Keith Stockton and William Burger, using the same formats as he used in Newark and Philadelphia. The results were pretty much the same. Keith attended the initial briefing and left when it was time to enter the second room. William didn't leave at first, but he entered the room, sat down, then got an eerie feeling about the whole thing and got up and left before the meeting got started. When asked if he could say how many were in the room waiting, he wasn't sure, but he thought there were about 15. The team was now able to determine that all 21 men on the photograph were accounted for.

Linda, making a victorious gesture, said "Okay then, this is a good thing. We have the problem solved?"

Mike and Hank looked at one another with concerned expressions. Mike said, "Not so fast. We can be certain about this class of Scottish Rite graduates, but what we don't know is if they were networked with other Scottish Rite classes. Until we can rule out any other groups, we aren't home free."

"Well, what's it going to take to consider this thing solved?"

"My guess is that we have the group responsible, but until we have a confession from Mr. Fallow, I won't rest comfortably with this case."

Hank stated, "We also could factor in if no more assassinations occur, then this organization was exclusive and has been dismantled."

All agreed that if that happened, they could assume it was over.

Mike looked over at Agent Spellman quizzically for a long moment and said, "Jack, could you arrange a conference call between agent Mathers, agent Mullins, and us? We need to be all on the same page."

"No problem. I'll have the desk set it up."

Once on the call, Mike announced, "Maintain all protocols, but by no means allow this to get out to the press. I will be returning to DC and bring the administration up to speed. When I have that and some personal things taken care of, I will return to Philadelphia. Agent Mullins, you and I will take it from there."

"Is there anything else you will need from me?" asked Mullins.

"No, nothing is more important than keeping things quiet for the moment. You may allow Fallow to contact his attorney. Is he comfortable?"

"Yes, he however isn't speaking to anyone."

"Okay you keep him safe. I don't need to tell you that this thing once it is known to the public it will no doubt bring out a bunch of celebrity seeking attorneys. Keep the lid on things until I get there."

"No problem, Mike."

The conference call ended. Mike thanked Agent Spellman. He looked at the clock, which was now showing 10:27 pm. "Call the pilot and have him ready for takeoff, Hank. We're out of here."

They were in the air heading back to DC when Mike did a time check It was just past midnight. *It's now a new day, October 13,* Mike thought.

Mike allowed the others to snooze while he mentally reviewed the events of the day. He thought of how much had happened since early this morning when he and Linda made love. What a day. He fell in love, rounded up all of the suspects, and was well on his way to concluding the investigation. In 17 hours, so much has happened—in his life and his future but also for our nation. Mike fell asleep to the rhythm of his own repeating words.

CHAPTER FORTY

The next morning, after a good night's sleep in Mike's apartment, before they had time to get up and greet the day, the phone was ringing angrily off the hook. At least that was Mike's perception. He believed that he could determine by the tone of a ring if the in-coming call was friendly or angry. This one was definitely angry.

It was John, who asked, "Did you see the goddamn papers this morning?"

"Jesus, John, I just got up. We were on the trail until late last night."

"Well, you'd better get in here and start your planning. The headlines aren't going to help matters.

Mike went to his porch to retrieve the paper. Shocked, he read: "Sources close to the administration reveal Masons involved in assassinations." And, "Could this have been a modern-day Boston Tea Party?"

"Mike, I don't like this," John said. "How did this leak to the media?"

"John, I agree. This sucks, big time. I didn't have the chance to brief you yet, nor the President. I assure you that the SACs in Newark, Philadelphia, and Cincinnati were all in a secure mode."

"Some fucking security."

"Okay, John, you try keeping the lid on things until I get there. Don't issue any statements to anyone. I absolutely have to contact the President and Prendergast. If any calls come from the White House, just say that I'm on my way in. Let them know that they will be the first contact I make, okay?"

"Okay, Mike. In the meantime, we'll pull up some more national papers. Damn, this isn't good."

"I think I know what may have happened," Mike said. "When I get there, I'll run it by you. Better have someone get the coffee and donuts ready."

Linda was sitting on the edge of the bed, waiting to hear what the call was all about, having heard Mike's voice and his responses were heightened.

"You won't believe this, honey. There were leaks to the press already."

"I'm sorry. I hope this doesn't screw things up with the case."

"Well, it may not have been a leak by anyone in the departments," Mike explained. "The Philadelphia field office needed to allow Fallow to acquire an attorney. This case could be a career maker for an opportunistic attorney."

"Well, Mike, what will you do if that is what happened?"

"We go into damage control."

"And what does that mean?"

"It means denial. No comment. Really, sweetheart, I will have to take it one step at a time. For now, Linda, I'll be spending a lot of time on this, and my guess is that the US attorney general will become totally involved from now on and requiring my reports. What would you like to do in the meantime?"

"I think I'll return to Tennessee," Linda said. "I can get a lot of my things in order and wait for you to get everything taken care of here. Nevertheless, I'll be thinking about you and missing you terribly."

"I agree. That would be the best thing for you to do at this time. I will miss you like crazy, but I'll be able to concentrate better and stay focused without your gorgeous presence distracting me."

Linda pressed her body against his. He held her face in both of his hands, and they kissed lovingly. Mike hugged her as tightly as he could.

"I have to go," Mike said, gazing into Linda's eyes.

"You do what you must, Mike, and call me as soon as you can. And don't worry about me."

Mike got dressed and headed out for what he knew was going to be one hell of a day in the office. While en route, he called Hank and said, "Better get in as soon as possible. Shit has happened."

At the department, John was waiting for Mike to brief him on the Newark, Philadelphia, and Cincinnati trip.

"I've given a lot of thought to your call this morning, John," Mike began. "My guess is that whatever happened, happened in Philadelphia. That's where we have Peter Fallow. Since Mr. Fallow shut down and wouldn't answer any questions, I had no choice but to have Mullins go through the Miranda process and allow him to acquire counsel. Now based upon my interviews with the men in the photo, it's safe to say that we have the leader of the organization in custody. The one unclear aspect of all of this is, was this group networking with other groups within the Scottish Rite to be participants in the 'final duty'?"

"How do you plan to investigate that?" John asked.

"I'll send Hank armed with a federal warrant to Hazleton, Pennsylvania, to search Peter Fallow's residence. Hank will also be looking at any other possible places that Mr. Fallow could have accessed storage. My first thing is to contact agent Mullins and find out what has been going on with Fallow. Then I will conference with the administration."

It was almost 9:30 when Hank entered the room, looking fresh from a good night's sleep.

"Good morning, John. Mike. What did I miss?"

"Nothing. I brought John up to speed on the interviews in Newark, Philadelphia, and Cincinnati."

"Well, it's all over the news this morning. All of the major papers are quoting sources close to the administration."

"Yeah, we certainly have provided the media with weeks of fuel," Mike said. "Okay, Hank, this is what I need from you. I'll get the warrant for a search of Fallow's property in Hazleton, and you'll conduct the searches. You'll be particularly interested in anything that could link Fallow's operation to other Scottish Rite groups or any other organizations that could have been involved. Meanwhile, I'm going to be on my pivot foot between the administration and Philadelphia and consulting with the US attorney general. I'm sure John will give you another detective to help you with the searches. Is that right, John?"

"Your choice, Hank. Anyone you want, as long as they aren't scheduled for court."

"Look, guys, I won't waste any time here. You have enough to do. I'll get cracking, and I'll call you as soon as I finish the search," Hank said with a thumbs up.

Mike went to his desk and called agent Mullins in Philadelphia.

"Good morning, James. How was your night?"

"Not bad, Mike. My kid had us up most of the night with a stomachache. But I'm good."

"Sorry about the kid, James. I'm sure you heard that the media is all over this thing already."

"Yes, what's new. The bastards have no sense of cooperation with the law."

"I hate to ask you this, but could anyone in your office be responsible for the leaks?"

"Mike, I'm sure that nobody in my discipline is directly responsible, but I'm also sure that indirectly we are. After you left, I had no choice: I couldn't hold Fallow without allowing him to have an attorney. I read him the Miranda and advised him of his right to counsel. I said he was being charged with accessory to capital murder. My feeling is that you can consult with the attorney general and he can come up with the specific charges."

"Did Fallow contact a lawyer?"

"Yes, he did. Don't ask me who he got because I haven't been contacted by any attorneys yet. Now here is the other problem: We can't hold him here in our field office, even on a temporary basis. We must transfer him to a federal jail today."

"Where will that be?"

"I'm thinking it might be Allenwood," James said. "When I know, I'll contact you immediately."

"Now, on the matter of his silence, is he engaging with any of your staff?" Mike asked.

"Mike, he's weird. He responds in single words, no matter what we ask."

"Did you have any problems feeding him?

"That's another problem," James said. "We don't have dietary facilities, so everything is ordered out. When we asked him what he wanted for dinner last night, he looked at me with an icy stare and said, 'I'm not hungry.' I told him that it would be a long time until breakfast. He just shrugged. I had a full platter with a beverage delivered to him, and only the beverage was gone when he was seen this morning. They tell me he requests water every few hours."

"How about breakfast?" Mike asked.

"I had eggs with bacon and orange juice sent to him at 7:30, but I haven't checked to see how that went."

"James, please confirm your staff is holding a very close suicide watch on him."

"Oh yes, we know about early incarceration watches."

"I'm very concerned about Fallow taking his own life by any

means available to him as well as going on a starvation diet. These guys are into some bizarre life's end pact. I think that's a major part of their Final Duty thing. And if I'm right, Fallow is our man. Unless there are more groups involved, he is the only viable link we have for solving this case. I hope you understand the importance of keeping this man alive."

"Yes, we'll make sure his every second with us is closely monitored."

"Great. Three other things. Number one, I think it would be wise to have a physician see him to prepare a report for any possible court needs. Number two, wherever you transfer him to, make damn sure that they are instructed as to the importance of keeping this man alive. And number three, he must be sequestered and have no contact with other prisoners."

"No problem, Mike, you can count on us," James said. "By the way, it's been a great pleasure working with you."

"Likewise, James. Thanks for all of your cooperation. I'll be so glad when all this is over."

After hanging up with Mullins, Mike looked at his watch, which was now showing the time as 9:03. He took a deep breath, knowing that his next call would be more than a quick update. This would be his biggest challenge yet. Slowly he punched in the numbers of the President's secretary.

"Good morning, this is Commissioner Michael Walters. May I speak with the President?" he asked when she answered.

"Hold the line, Mr. Walters. I'll see if he's available."

A few seconds passed when the secretary announced, "Okay, Mr. Walters, the President will take your call."

"Good morning, Mike," the President said when he got on the line. "I hope you have good news. I've had about as much bad news as I want already this morning. Those media sharks are hungry."

"Yes, Mr. President, the sharks are hungry and circling. The only thing we can do about that is give them as little food as possible."

The President laughed, "Yeah, right, maybe we could place some blood in the water further up the coast. So, what's the bottom line, Mike?"

"Everything leads to one man, Peter Fallow," Mike said. "We have him in FBI custody. We need to make sure that he didn't form a pact with other organizations. I have a man on that as we speak. If he didn't network with other groups, then it will be a matter of turning the prosecution over to the attorney general."

"So that's the good news."

"Yes, sir. Meanwhile it's critical for us to keep this man alive, and that may be difficult given the final duty thing, I suspect these men have. Also, he must be transferred to a federal jail some place and that's already in motion. In keeping with his constitutional rights we had to allow him to obtain legal counsel and I would bet that's how the media got hold of things."

"I'm impressed Michael, is there anything you need for me to do?"

"No sir, I just wanted you to be up to speed on the matter. Oh you should also know that George Prendergast has been a great help throughout our investigation. I couldn't have moved as fast without his resources."

"That's good to know, I'll pass on the Kudos. Thanks for doing this for our country Mike; I'm really pleased."

"And Mr. President— I will need to consult with the Attorney General at this time. He will need to see all of our material facts to determine the exact charges that are required to hold our man. Shall I call him directly or would it move faster through your office?"

"How soon do you need to see him?"

"He should be my next contact sir."

"Where are you this moment?"

"I'm in my office here in DC at 202-417- 0021."

"Hang up and standby."

"Thank you Mr. President."

Mike hung up the phone, stared at the silent phone on his desk for a long moment, and thought, *I can't believe I just spoke again with the President of the United States. My God, is it possible that I am becoming blasé about even that?" Does apathy grow in every relationship? Bullshit! that won't happen with Linda and me.*

Angry because he didn't have enough time before leaving his apartment this morning, he went to the men's room to relieve himself. While he was sitting on the commode, the intercom blasted, "Walters, line 2." Every few seconds, the message was repeated.

"This is just great," Mike said under his breath. "I can't even finish taking a crap in peace."

When Mike got back to his desk there, was a note that said, "Call Attorney General Robert Lewis." Mike quickly called on his cell.

"Mr. Walters, good morning," Robert answered, a bit too cheerfully. "What do you have for me? Have you heard about the picketers at the White House? They arrived about 30 minutes ago. You won't believe it."

"What's so strange about picketers?" Mike asked.

"Nothing ordinarily, but the signs say, FREE FALLOW: FIRE CONGRESS. Some have other statements, but that one caught my attention. Cameras are all over the place. Anyway, what do you have?"

"Sir, the FBI is holding Peter Fallow at Allenwood Federal Prison. We have solid evidence that he conducted a secret organizational meeting in August of 2003, and the participants in the meeting included James Petri, the known assassin of Congressman Raymond Shapiro; George Stanton, who assassinated Congressman, Edward Buckles of Tennessee, and Henry Lister, the assassin of Congressman, Luther Nobles of Virginia. Donald Wadsworth committed suicide in New Jersey, shortly after the funeral breakfast held for the New Jersey Congressman Todd Sherman, who was gunned down in the first round of assassinations. We suspect that Wadsworth had dressed as a female waitress named Marie Lemon and was one of the waitresses hired to serve the funeral breakfast. We believe Wadsworth posing as Marie Lemon poisoned Congressman Marcus

Hinkle of Pennsylvania and Congressman George Mitchell of Michigan."

"What material evidence do you have?"

"All of the assassins are in a group photograph with 21 Scottish Rite Masons at a Adamsburg, Pennsylvania, Consistory that was taken in May of 1974. The photo also includes Peter Fallow. We found the photo in Donald Wadsworth's New Jersey apartment."

"So, you think that all this ties them together in a conspiracy to eliminate corrupt congressman?"

"With all due respect, sir, I think that's a little more than circumstantial."

"Mike, I agree that these guys are guilty, but we need a confession. Is there anything else to help with the conspiracy meeting in August 2003?"

"We have pathology reports of the dead assassins that show signs of terminal states of health. We also know the speech Fallow gave in August 2003 imputed them to their 'Final Duty.'"

"I hear what you're saying, but in a court the words 'final duty' could mean anything."

"Okay, Robert, I know what you're saying, and I agree with you that we need a confession. We must keep Fallow alive and obtain that confession. There's one more thing: Upon questioning the subjects in Newark, Philadelphia, and Cincinnati, we learned that many of the men in the photo died in September, following the first round of assassinations. The five subjects who are still living had all walked out and didn't attend the secret second meeting held by Fallow. All of the other men in the group are dead. Isn't it peculiar that we have 15 dead members of that group and 15 dead congressmen?"

Lewis laughed on the other end of the line, then quickly apologized, "Mike, I'm not laughing at what you're saying. I'm laughing because your logic is so God-dammed right."

"Thanks," Mike said. "It will validate my theory if the assassinations stop with Fallow in custody and all 15 members who went into the secret meeting are dead."

"I'm betting they will," Robert said. "But keeping Fallow in custody might prove difficult. The pressure of the people and the media isn't going to make this a cakewalk."

"Well, sir, we'll have to get together so I can turn over all my reports and material evidence to your office. When would be a good time?"

"I'll be in my office until 6 pm," Robert said. "So come by anytime today."

"Thank you, Attorney General," Mike replied. "As soon as I get my papers in order and clear a few things here, I'll see you over there. Good-bye, sir."

CHAPTER FORTY-ONE

P eter sat in a special confinement area, which wasn't an actual jail cell but more like an efficiency room, a so-called "country club sentence." The chair he was sitting on was comfortable, made of leather and wooden trim. He had all of the comforts of home—except for a private landline. He had to schedule telephone privileges in a different area of the jail.

Peter was amazed that anyone would think of this as punishment. *The corrupt son-of-a-bitches in Congress, the bastards with their hands in the public "cookie jar" sure aren't taking any chances. They approved these country club jails just in case they got themselves caught. "White collar crimes," my ass. It's infuriating when a corrupt elected official or head of a corporation causes hardships or even the death of people, yet they are considered white collar criminals. If a hungry man uses a gun to get money that he needs to feed his family, he's tried by a whole different justice system and if convicted is sentenced to death. He's placed into the death row of a maximum custody prison. Yet, if a member of Congress votes for a piece of "health care legislation" from which he received millions of dollars from insurance companies for his reelection, and then that legislation with its cryptic language kills by deprivation and reduced coverage harms millions of men, women, and children, how is that not murder? What of the oil executive who orders home fuel increases during the worst cold snap of the winter by lying to the people about shortages that don't exist? His actions result in huge profits while young children and elderly citizens freeze to death. Is he not a criminal? What of the insurance executive who directs that all claims initially are to be denied and his actions go on to cause hardship and death to millions who never receive compensation for their losses? And the greedy prick's who kill with a silver tongue and a pen, they come here, while the hungry man with a gun is labeled a murderer and executed. The more people you kill, the less of a criminal you become. You are known as a politician or a public servant.*

Peter laughed to himself. He was unafraid. He knew that at his age there wouldn't be anything the government could deprive him of. He had nothing to fear. He would be housed, fed, clothed, medicated, and even recreated.

How else could they treat me? Even if they could convict me of murder, which they can't, who's going to risk the political uproar of executing a man suspected of trying to rid the U.S. Congress of corruption, thereby creating a martyr?

It was nearing 11 am when a corrections officer entered Peter's room.

"Mr. Fallow, an attorney, Frank Patton, will be arriving early this afternoon. He would like to speak with you concerning the charges being brought against you. You, of course, have the right to retain your own counsel, too."

"I'll be ready, thank you. Officer, could you do something for me today?"

"Well yes, if it's possible."

"I would like to get to the library. There's a book I'd like to read."

"What book is that?"

"*Born in Blood.*"

"I read that book several years ago."

"You read that book?"

"Yes, correction officers do read you know."

"I'm sorry, I didn't mean to imply that. Maybe if I get the book and read it, then we could discuss it?"

"Here's the thing, Mr. Fallow, I'll see what can be done about getting you to our library. I know without checking that it would have to be an isolation visit. If that isn't possible then we can process your request for the book and I'm sure it will be available for you."

"Thank you very much, officer."

Peter thought, *Shit, I guess I could add 'social opportunities' to the list of incarceration benefits.* He got up from the comfortable chair and walked around the room, and while he paced, he thought, *I miss him and wish he was able to share some of this with me. He was the only person who understood the extent of corruption our country faces. He could be dead now, for all I know.*

Peter continued to muse, now switching topics, *What will I say to this lawyer when he comes? Should I dismiss him without listening to his pitch? I must prepare myself — I must launch my defense either as a Not Guilty attitude or remain defenseless and give the public an impression of an elderly middle class man being persecuted by a bully government? I have no doubt that this Frank Patton is coming to my defense to acquire fame from the publicity this is going to produce. I must remember always during these coming days—to stay focused upon our pledged final duty. They deserve that from me; anything less would be betrayal.*

Later that morning, attorney Frank Patton was escorted to the room where he would have a private interview with Peter Fallow. As he waited, he took a legal note pad out of his briefcase and entered the date, time, and location. He pondered the essential questions he would ask Fallow, if indeed he could convince Fallow to accept him as counsel.

In the final anticipation, he settled on an attitude to take it one step at a time.

Then Fallow was brought into the secure room. As Frank looked

Peter over, he couldn't believe that this well-groomed, elderly gentleman could possibly be responsible for organizing a group of assassins. *He's a curious looking man,* Frank thought. *He doesn't look like a murderer.*

While extending his hand to Peter Frank said, "I'm attorney Frank Patton. Mr. Fallow, I would like to discuss your situation with you with the possibility that I can help."

Peter shook his hand cautiously and sat down, "Attorney Patton, when you parked your car in the visitor's parking lot, did you see a very big boat in front of this institution."

Frank looked at Peter quizzically, wondering, *Does he have dementia?* Frank said, "No, of course not. "

"I didn't just arrive on a banana boat," Peter said, amused at his own joke. "I damn well know that the publicity involved in my case will make you famous, and which means, I would actually be helping *you,* correct?"

Frank laughed briefly, stopped for a moment to gauge Peter's reaction, then broke out into a roaring laughter. "Mr. Fallow, I like your style."

"Attorney, what is my situation?"

"Well, sir, although your present confinement is comfortable, you *are* in a federal maximum security prison awaiting charges, which I'm sure will include the felony crimes of capital murder with conspiracy to commit murder. The United States attorney general will announce the charges."

"Do I look worried?"

"No, sir, you don't. And that puzzles me."

"My life is over, I have achieved most of my goals, and I accept the consequence of death. I fear nothing the government can do to harm or harass me anymore. Frank, if you wish to serve as my counsel, understand from this moment on I will have nothing to say to you, the press, the courts, or the government. I will speak of nothing other than my daily needs."

"With all due respect, Peter, how can I defend you if you don't give me any information?"

"If you want the fame, the rules of this game will be my silence. I know that they have nothing beyond circumstantial evidence even to hold me, and I'll be damned if I'll break my silence to aid them in my prosecution."

"Do you know that whatever you say to me must be held in strict confidence?" Frank asked. "The cannons of justice require attorney client privilege. I could be disbarred if I breached that confidence."

"You're human and subject to all human frailties, aren't you? Sure, you are, and that's where I understand the need for my strict silence. Let's say you elect at some future date, of your own volition, to betray our confidence, having weighed the consequences of disbarment against the windfall fortune you'd receive from a book and movie deal. Losing your right to practice law wouldn't seem so bad of a punishment then, would it?"

"That would never happen."

"You're correct because I won't *allow* it to happen. Frank, accept my vow of silence or be gone. There's no doubt in my mind that once you leave this room, I'll hear from many more lawyers who will want my case. What's your decision?"

"I accept."

"Good. Now if you'll excuse me, I must get back to my utopian room and see if that corrections officer arranged for me to get a book I requested."

Peter was escorted back in his room. As he waited to hear about the book, he thought, *This isn't so bad. The fear of being caught is over. I'm caught, and I like it. I'm safe here; I'm well taken care of. Hell. I have television, people to converse with, a certain celebrity status, and I have free affordable health care. What could be better at this time in my life?*

The corrections officer arrived and handed him a copy of *Born in*

Blood without a word. Peter shrugged, sat in that very comfortable chair, and begun reading.

Outside of the facility, members of the press were waiting for attorney Patton, who they knew was not camera or microphone shy. When Frank stepped up to the microphone, he was cheerfully greeted by the hungry mob of reporters. Slight variations of one question were barked out from the crowd of reporters in an almost harmonic sound, "Attorney Patton, are you representing Peter Fallow?"

"As a matter of fact, I am representing Mr. Fallow."

"Is he connected to the congressional assassinations?"

"Mr. Fallow has only agreed to allow me to represent him, and until the United States attorney general files specific charges against Mr. Fallow, the question of connection to anything is impossible to answer."

"Did he have anything to do with any of the assassinations?"

"All I can relate at this time is that I will be representing Mr. Fallow. We have no answers to any of your questions, but we will have plenty of questions for the attorney general. No further questions at this time."

Beyond the mob of reporters, another group of citizens were approaching the facility parking areas. Frank could see that they were carrying signs, so he waited long enough to read some of them. As they grew closer, he was able to read, "Free Fallow, Fire Congress." Another read, "Congress Auctioned Off the People, Now It's Time to Auction Off Congress."

Frank slowly drove away from Allenwood Prison and though, *This is going to be some battle. I like it already. How do I defend a man whose taken a vow of silence? What a position. On the positive side, even if I lose in the courts, I'll win in the court of public opinion. Fallow can't actually lose if he never speaks in his own defense. However, then the prosecution morphs into a persecution.*

Later that morning, Mike entered the office of the attorney general, surprised by the opulence and greed. The plush office suite was replete with rich, deep brown leather arm chairs and a very large, impeccably polished desk.

Mike thought, *There sits the most powerful prosecutor in the world, and I will feed him the evidence he needs to prosecute the most serious round of political assassinations in our constitutional history.*

Mike's amused attitude changed to professional focus as he extended his hand to Attorney Lewis, "Good to meet you in person, sir. I'm sorry it took so long to get here."

"No apologies required, Michael. You did one hell of a job with this investigation, and you have my respect."

"Thank you," Mike replied, handing the attorney general a folder. "In this folder are the material facts I developed throughout the course of this investigation. I hope it will be enough for you to prepare charges and win the case."

"I'll do my best, Michael. It won't be easy. The negative publicity is already starting out there. By now I assume you've seen the protestors. The media loves a good story. Couple that with an American public that loves underdogs, and we'll have one large mess to control. Anyway, from this point on the only thing for you to do is prepare yourself as my main witness in court. I will use the agency to do all the running around that I need."

Mike felt about 20 pounds lighter as he walked out of the office. He was comfortable with the idea of being a key witness in the prosecution; that would be easy. As he walked on, his thoughts turned to Linda. He couldn't wait to get to the office and finally have that long loving talk with her about their future.

As Mike left the building, he wasn't paying much attention to what was going on in the parking area, but in his satellite thoughts he was aware of a gang of protestors. At this point, he had accepted them without alarm or surprise. He continued toward the parking area without noticing a young man approaching him with a gun in his hand. In a flash, Mike understood he was about to be shot. He reached out to grab the man, and the gun went off, the bullet striking Mike in the right shoulder. By that time, Mike had knocked the young man off balance, landing him on his butt, but not before two more shots rang out. The first hit Mike in his right lower leg, and the second hit him in the right thigh.

Mike was lying on the ground, bleeding and seeing double vision from the loss of blood. Just before he passed out, he heard the security police subduing the attacker. In his semi-conscious state, he heard shouts of, "Fucking pigs."

Then he was out.

CHAPTER FORTY-TWO

Following four hours of surgery, Mike was placed in the surgical recovery intensive care unit. Fortunately, the two shots in his right leg caused only soft tissue damage. The shot to his shoulder broke his clavicle. The combined trauma, anesthesia, and surgery would keep him in a coma for an extended period. The surgery went well, and all of his vital signs were good. Mike was hooked up to an IV and a monitor, but he was breathing on his own. His prognosis was good.

Linda, Hank, and John were at Mike's bedside, watching him struggle to open is eyes. Mike came to consciousness, and as his vision cleared he was able to recognize them, but he was slow to remember what had happened to him. Linda bent over his head, kissed his closed eyes, and said, "I love you, and I'm never going to leave you alone again."

Hank and John joined in to say how happy they were to see him recovering well from the ordeal.

"I remember now," Mike whispered. "A young man was coming at me, and I knew I was going to be shot. Everything after that is a blank. What happened?"

John replied, "He was just a kid, a 22-twenty-two-year old fanatic. We have him in the municipal jail. The FBI ran a check on him, and he's clean. There's no possible link to the Fallow organization."

Hank reached over to touch Mike's hand and said, "Look, pal, there's only one thing for you to do now: Get well. The surgeon said everything went well. They expect you to have a full recovery."

Mike managed a smile as he looked at Linda. He asked Hank and John to get lost for awhile. Hank and John looked at one another, and John said, "I have a lot of catching up to do at the office, and, Hank, I'll need you for another assignment."

"That's me, always ready for another assignment," Hank said. "When will I be needed for a promotion, John?"

As Hank and John made their way out of the room, two nurses were entering with three large bouquets of flowers. Linda read the cards. The first card from the President of the United States said, "A grateful nation awaits your return to health, President Brazil." The second card was signed by the staff at headquarters. The third card said, 'I've waited long and searched hard for the right man to come into my life. That long-awaited man has finally arrived, and he's much more than I could have prayed for. Mike, I love you with all of my being, and I will never let you go. Forever, my love, Linda.'"

Linda looked over at Mike, who had tears rolling down both side of his face. "I can't move my shoulder, and I want to hold you so much," he said.

Linda leaned over, kissed the tears away from both sides of his face, and whispered, "I love you. I love you," as Mike also returned vows of love.

When Linda sat in the chair beside the bed, Mike promised to get well and that once recovered, he planned to look into retiring. Then he paused for a moment and said, "I'm getting ahead of myself here. Will you marry me?"

Now Linda had tears running down both sides of her face, "Yes. Yes, I will marry you, my love."

"Sorry I couldn't get on my knees for a traditional proposal, but you've just made me the happiest patient on earth. The ring will follow. I promise you. I'll have the speediest rehabilitation on record."

They both laughed and held a very, very long kiss. Linda explained that she would go to his apartment and see that it would be ready for his return. Then she'd go back to Tennessee and resign her position at the hospital. Following her resignation, she would close down her own apartment and place her things in storage.

"Will you be able to do all that by yourself, honey?" Mike asked. "Shouldn't you wait until I could help you?"

"My dear, Michael, you have just become engaged to one very efficient lady. I will handle everything without any help from up here. We also have moving professionals in Tennessee. I'll be fine. You just concentrate on your rehabilitation, okay?"

"Are you sure about giving up your position at the hospital?"

"I am toying with the idea of applying to the University of Pennsylvania, where I could teach as well as practice. Once you get out of here and settle on your retirement plans, we can decide where I'll practice. I don't plan on working many more years."

"You do what you have to do, Linda, and I'll take care of the rehabilitation end. Having you as my wife will be all the incentive that I need to heal."

Linda kissed him goodbye and left the room.

CHAPTER FORTY-THREE

I t was 10 am, when two black-suited FBI agents with regulation haircuts entered the Georgia office of CCN and asked to see Bernard Shade and flashed their badges to the receptionist.

"Wait over there, and I'll see if he's available," she said, motioning to a bank of chairs across the lobby.

The receptionist obviously had Mr. Shade on the other end of the telephone as she looked at the FBI agents, shook her head, and said, "I don't know."

The receptionist hung up the telephone and motioned for the men to come back to her desk. The agents complied and were instructed to take the elevator to the 10th floor, and then go to room 15A.

"Mr. Shade will be waiting."

The agents thanked the receptionist, and as they entered the elevator, they heard the receptionist calling to alert Bernard that they were on their way. Once at the 10th floor, Bernard's office was easy to spot, due to the large name on his door. The agents introduced themselves, flashed their badges, and shook hands.

"Agents, how may I help you?" Bernard asked.

"Sir, you met with a representative of the TBA on September 20th, is that correct?"

"Yes."

"What can you tell us regarding the man's demeanor?"

"Gentlemen, I'm in territory here that could be troublesome. Why do you ask"

"This is off the record: We have a man in custody who we believe is responsible for organizing these crimes. If you share any content of this interview, we will file obstruction of justice charges against you and this network. Do you understand?"

"Yes, I completely understand," Bernard said.

"What do you remember about the man you interviewed."

"Not much," Bernard replied apologetically. "I was hooded and led through a building to the outside, then taken for a long ride that had many, many turns, and then into another building. While I waited, they removed my hood. After waiting for several minutes, a man wearing a hooded jumpsuit entered and introduced himself as a TBA spokesperson."

"What could you tell us about his height, eye color, or race?"

"Not much. He obviously went to a great deal of trouble to conceal his identity. His shoes were wrapped in masking tape, he wore latex gloves, and he also had masking tape covering his wrists. His hood covered his neck, I couldn't see the color of his eyes."

"What about his height and weight? How about his voice, was there anything unusual about it?"

"I estimate his height to about 6'2" maybe and weight between 180 and 200 pounds."

"What about his voice?"

"Not a voice with a European or Asian accent. No, nothing like that. His voice was American, but not a Southern, Jersey, Philadelphia, or New York, accent could I detect."

"Do you think it could have been somewhat of a Middle American sound?"

"That's my guess. Ohio, Pennsylvania, or Michigan maybe."

"Bernard, will you come with us to the federal prison where Fallow is being held and possible identify his voice or any other physical things about him that seem to remind you of the man you interviewed."

"I suppose I could arrange that for the good of our nation."

"This will be an overnight trip, so we'll travel by an agency jet and return tomorrow."

"If that is the case, I'll have to make a good case for my absence. I suppose it's a doable thing."

"Well thank you but, here come some of the conditions. No one can know where or why you are leaving with us. Also, you can't share any of the material associated with the visit to the prison. There will be a proper time to release all of this, and you'll be released from these restrictions at that time. What you are doing would be expected from any decent citizen. Do you agree?"

"I do. What do I tell my people here about why I'm leaving the building? I have pressing duties along with my scheduled airtime."

"Tell them that you are leaving to assist the FBI in an investigation, which has nothing to do with you or anyone in this corporation. Ask them to provide a stand-in for your scheduled air times. Also inform them that they are not to mention anything about your absence or activity. Actually just use your good judgment to achieve our caveats."

"Couldn't we do this later, at a better time?"

"I'm sorry, Bernard. We can't delay this process. It must be taken care of now."

"Give me a few minutes with our station manager?"

"You have it. Please don't delay."

Bernard went to the manager's office, gave what he thought was a logical presentation, and left with his approval.

"Okay, gentlemen, we're good to go," Bernard said once he returned to his office where the FBI agents were waiting. Is there anything that I will need? I assume you'll do the driving and then return me to my office?"

"You need absolutely nothing, except for some toiletries and clothing to get you through the next 24 hours. If that's a problem, we have those things available for you. As for the driving, we'll take you and return you here or to your home, whichever you prefer."

The two agents left and waited outside the building for Bernard. In minutes, they were off to the airport. The agent driving the car noted the time of their departure as 11 am.

Meanwhile, the President stood at the podium, waiting for the crowd to become quiet. After several moments, the reporters stopped shouting, and President Brazil greeted them, "I have a brief statement to make and following that I will take a few questions. Special commissioner Mike Walters and the FBI have a man in federal custody who they believe is responsible for the assassinations of our congressmen. Attorney General Robert Lewis is making formal charges."

"Mr. President, are you going to tell us the man's name and where he's being held?" asked the reporter the President acknowledged first.

"For security purposes, I won't release that information until charges have been filled."

The President acknowledged another reporter who asked, "Mr. President, it appears that you're wearing a bulletproof vest. If the man you have in custody is responsible for the assassinations, why would you be worried enough to wear a vest?"

"Under the advice of the Secret Service, we are taking all precautions," the President replied.

"What happened to Mike Walters in the attorney general's parking lot?" a reporter asked.

"I will answer this final question," the President said. "Mike Walters was wounded by a picketer in the attorney general's parking lot. Fortunately, Commissioner Walters is doing well and is expected to make a full recovery. I am proud of Mike Walters and the lead role he has played in this investigation. As a nation, we owe him a debt of gratitude. Thank you and good day."

It was noon as the President strolled back into the White House. President Brazil entered the oval office and summoned his chief of staff, Leslie Sanders, "Please get me a staff vehicle. We're going over to the hospital to visit Mike Walters. Don't make a big deal out of this, I don't want to be hounded by the press."

"When do you want to go?"

"Immediately.

"What about the scheduled meeting with Ambassador Talibe?" Leslie asked

"Have a message sent to him informing him of a delay. You can give him the option of waiting until I return. Or, if that's inconvenient, reschedule."

All of the security protocols were put into immediate action, and the President was taken to the hospital by 12:45 pm.

Mike was just finishing his lunch when the President appeared unannounced at his bedside.

"Mr. President, I am honored that you came to see me," Mike said, surprised.

"Our nation would be nothing without brave men like you to protect us. I want you to know how much I personally appreciate what you have done to end this investigation. If there is anything you need during your recovery, I'll see to it immediately," the President said, reaching for Mike's hand.

"Sorry, sir," Mike said in a moment of confusion as he extended his injured left hand toward the President's right. "Thank you so much for coming to see me, Mr. President. It means a lot to me. When a busy man like the President of the United States can take the time to visit me and thank me, I will always know that my efforts were justified."

It was almost 1 pm when the President left Mike's room. Highly motivated from the President's visit Mike decided to get ready for his afternoon therapy. Now he couldn't wait for the gorilla-like physical therapist's manipulation of his right shoulder. Despite the pain the PT caused Mike trying to increase his range of motion, Mike was grateful that the therapist weren't giving him any special tender treatment.

After a painless flight, the two FBI agents and Bernard entered Allenwood Prison. Peter Fallow had been moved to an observation room so Bernard could study his voice and demeanor. The warden greeted them and explained Fallow's vow of silence. As the agents and Bernard watched, a social worker entered the room with Fallow to conduct a routine follow-up on his care, a ruse the agents hoped would trick Fallow into breaking his vow of silence.

Bernard was by Peter's appearance: a well-groomed, elderly man with sharp, toned features seemingly untouched by time's battle against gravity. He estimated Peter's height to be 6'2" and wondered, *Jesus, could this have been the man hooded, suited, and taped to conceal his identity? What a challenge this is going to be.*

"Mr. Fallow is your room comfortable?" the social worker asked.

"Yes, Peter replied.

"How is the food?"

"Actually, it's not bad. It's a lot better than cooking for myself."

Bernard watched the interaction intensely, thinking Peter could be the man he interviewed, but he couldn't say so positively.

The social worker continued, "I understand you requested a book to read. Did you receive it?"

"I did receive the book, thank you."

"What is the title of the book you asked for, Peter?"

"*Born in Blood.*"

"That's an interesting title. What's it about?"

"It deals in part with the history of the Knights Templar and the Knight Hospitaller during the peasants' uprising and the 100-year-war during the 11th and 12th centuries."

"Why does that interest you?"

"Well, as a Mason, there is some hint of our origin. I just started the book, and I will know more about that when I'm finished. I heard of the book years ago, but I never had the time to read it. But now it seems that I do."

"Do you know why you are here?"

Silence. Peter sensed where this was headed, so he just looked calmly at the social worker and used his body language to show that he wouldn't go there.

Bernard looked at the agents and said, "I don't know. He certainly has the clear, accentless voice, but I don't know for sure it's the man I interviewed."

They continued to listen and observe the social worker's process.

"I see you aren't answering my question. Aren't you concerned about being here?"

Peter evaluated this new aspect of the question, and he replied, "It's a nice place. When was it built?"

"I'm not sure, but we have a brochure in our library. I can have that sent to your room. Our physician's report of your examination when you arrived indicates that you have some heart muscle weakness, and he prescribed medication for you. Have you received that medication yet?"

"Yes, I have, thank you."

"Are you satisfied with the medical services you have received so far?"

"Yes, thank you very much. To think I didn't have to wait in a physician's office for hours, waiting to be seen. What more could I ask for?"

"You look a little tired. Are you sure you're okay?"

"Yes, I'm sure. I really do feel good, and I can't complain about the accommodations. But it would be nice to get outside for some fresh air. I've been indoors since my arrival."

"Well, I will be your counselor while you're with us and if there is anything you would like to tell me or anything you think you need, I'll do my best to see that it's provided. I'll see to it that you have an escorted outdoor period daily."

"Is this interview over?"

"Yes, I'll make notes of our conversation and schedule another session with you in a few days."

"Thank you. Iook forward to our next session."

"Just one more thing, Peter. It's strictly routine. You'll be scheduled for an interview with our staff psychiatrist before our next session."

"Oh, dear, that should be fun," Peter said sarcastically. "I guess I'll have to remember if I wanted to fuck my mother when I was a boy."

Peter laughed as the social worker gathered his papers and stood. He left the room and joined the agents and Bernard in the observation room.

One of the FBI agents looked at Bernard and asked, "What do you think?"

"As much as I'd like to say to you guys 'yes, this is the man I interviewed last month,' I can't do that. He has the height, approximate body weight, and tone of voice, but I can't say for sure."

The agent placed the 1974 group photo in front of Bernard and said, "This is a long shot, but take a long look at the men in this photo. Could it have been one of them?"

"Guys, how could I possibly recognize a man wearing a disguise in a 31-year-old photo?" Bernard exclaimed.

"I said it would be a long shot. It's a part of the process of elimination, and if we don't ask, some sharp lawyer will embarrass us in court with the same question, so please humor us by looking."

Bernie looked and then replied, "No, none of the men in this photograph appear to be the man I interviewed."

Prior to leaving, the agents returned to the warden's office to thank him and let him know they weren't likely to hear specific charges from the attorney general until they get some of these loose end facts back to him today.

The lead agent said, "I'll call the results of this session into the Bureau while we are en route back to Georgia. Thank you very much, Bernard, for your cooperation and accommodations. You're welcome to stay and have lunch with us.

"Thank you again, but we really must get under way.

By 11:55 am, they were in the air, returning to Georgia. Bernie relaxed and thought back over the past hours. He said, "What a ride it's been. Hey, guys, I know it's mid-day, but do you mind if I try to get some sleep? I know when I get back, I'll get no sympathy for my absence, and since I can't explain anything to them I better be awake and ready to hit the airways."

"Go ahead, Bernard, kick back," the lead agent said.

CHAPTER FORTY-FOUR

Attorney Frank Patton called a press conference October 16, 2005, at 10 a.m. in Philadelphia, where he announced, "Members of the press, I represent Peter Fallow of Hazleton, who was taken into custody by federal agents and is being held in Allenwood Federal Prison. Mr. Fallow has been held since the 12th of this month without being formally charged. This is a violation of his constitutional rights. We want this man released. I've contacted the attorney general's office daily, requesting clarification of his custody and the charges. I have not received a return contact from their office. I hope that public pressure through the media will now be brought to bear."

"Mr. Patton, is it true that your client is the organizer behind the recent assassinations of all these congressmen?"

"No evidence, other than circumstantial, links my client to the known assassins."

"Isn't it true that since his incarceration, there have been no more attempted assassinations?"

"That assumption isn't factual evidence to prove my client had anything to do with previous crimes."

"Do you think they're holding him under the National Security Act? Is it possible that he's being regarded as a terrorist and therefore comes under the President's discretion?"

"I don't know how to answer you because I haven't been given any answers. If any of this is true, let's have straight-forward response from the administration. If they have solid reason to detain this man, then let's have charges filed. Mr. Fallow is an American citizen who should be treated with all due constitutional regard. That is all I have to share with you at this time. I hope you will be more successful than I have been in forcing the administration to answer the people in this matter. I hope you'll carry all of these questions that I can't answer to the only people in our government who can answer them."

"Is it true that Mr. Fallow has taken a vow of silence and won't even speak with you?" a reporter called to Frank's turned back.

"Mr. Fallow has agreed to have me as counsel," Frank replied over his shoulder.

An official press release later announced that Attorney General Robert Lewis files the following charges against Peter Fallow in the District of Columbia federal court:

• Conspiracy to commit capital murder against members of the United States Congress

• Acts of terrorism against the government of the United States of America

• Conspiracy to overthrow the government of the United States of America

Specifics to the above charges:

Count One: Peter Fallow did so gather together in Hazleton, Pennsylvania, a group of Scottish Rite Masons on August 21, 1974. On that date, he did solicit 21 members to enter into a conspiracy to assassinate members of the United States Congress.

Specifics of Count Two: In an open statement to a member of the media, an agent of the organization then known as TBA "Take Back America" developed by Peter Fallow did publicly state intent to assassinate members of the United States Congress with a mission to overthrow Congress.

Specifics of Count Three: By virtue of count one and two of these charges a conspiracy to overthrow the government of the United States of America was and is intended by Peter Fallow.

At the ensuing press conference, Attorney General Lewis was beleaguered by members of the press, who were bombarding him with questions concerning the detention of Peter Fallow.

In the background a growing line of marchers and picketers chanted, "Free Fallow, Fire Congress."

Lewis answered the media's biggest question, "Why have I held Peter Fallow in custody this long without filing the charges? Mr. Fallow can be held at the discretion of the President of the United States for acts of terrorism under the National Homeland Security Act."

A chorus of angry questions followed, "Mr. Fallow is a United States citizen. How can you deny him his due process under the US Constitution?"

"Mr. Fallow has been charged in accordance with the laws of this nation and will be accorded all of the protections of our Constitution. As you know he is being afforded counsel."

"What are the charges?"

"I've just filed the charges, and the Freedom of Information Act gives the public the right to check it out. Therefore, I suggest that you check it out."

"What are you doing about the corruption of Congress? When will the people see indictments against corrupt congresspeople?"

"Congress has its own ethic committee looking into its members' conduct, and my staff is also looking into allegations of congressional misconduct."

"What conduct are you talking about?"

"We're particularly interested in special interests and government contract bidding."

"When will we hear something from your office on that?"

"Soon. Very soon."

"Will criminal charges be brought against members of Congress for their acts of fraud?"

"I'm committed to justice no—matter who is in violation of the law."

Each question brought more questions, so feeling satisfied he answered enough, Lewis brought the session to an end and said, "No more questions. Have a nice day."

CHAPTER FORTY-FIVE

ttorney General Lewis, upon returning to his office, directed
his assistant to have all of his prosecuting aides assembled here
for a meeting by 4 pm.

"As soon as you contact them, patch me through to the
President."

"Consider it done, sir," she replied.

Lewis and the President were on a private secure line by
2:10 pm.

"Mr. President, I filed charges on Peter Fallow this afternoon.
That's taken care; however, I feel that under our civil constitutional
laws and his rights as a citizen we are treading on very flimsy
grounds; everything is circumstantial. I grant you that they are strong
circumstantial grounds, but circumstantial just the same. I believe
that you will have to invoke the National Homeland Security Act.
That, too, is weak, but it's at least doable. Fifteen members of the U.S.
Congress assassinated in a month's time is domestic terrorism."

"Are you recommending that I use my office to make that public
statement?"

"Yes, sir. I am."

"Why can't you make that public statement with the explanation that you've made that recommendation to me based on provisions of the Homeland Security Act? After all, Bob, you're my legal counsel, aren't you?"

"You are correct, sir, but also I'm the people's U.S. Attorney, and based upon the law, I will herein make that recommendation to you."

"Good, Bob, put it in a formal written memo to me."

"Okay, sir. The memo will be in your hands shortly. After filing the charges, I announced to the press that you held Fallow for these past days without charges, under the Homeland Security Act."

"Well, it's a damn good thing you told me that before I acted ignorantly with the public. Get that damn memo to me now."

"It'll be in your hands by special courier within minutes," Robert continued. "I believe this is the best way to proceed. It's a good judgment call. Since 9-11, you're the only President to exercise this law, so until we have solid evidence to convict him under civil law there is no court established precedence to reverse your decision. Look sir, we know that we do have the main man in custody. The longer he's off the street and in custody and the further we are away from the assassinations, the whole thing will speak for itself."

"Listening to you, it sounds good, but remember I'm going this route based upon your interpretation of the Homeland Security Act, but I want you to know that I'm doing so with the understanding that you will be vigorously checking out the civil approach during the interim? Is that correct?"

"That is correct, sir. I promise you that I will give this 100 percent of my time."

"Good, now there's one other thing we must look into."

"What's that, sir?"

"All of this isn't without cause. An organization has assassinated 15 congressmen in a short period of time. Couple that with the anger and outrage the American people who hear daily about a corrupt Congress. Public demands will only intensify."

"What are you doing to indict some of those sons of bitches?"

"That's on my agenda for a meeting I'm having this afternoon with my prosecution staff. Remember, Bob, which party nominated you for attorney general."

"You don't have to mention it; you know I'm loyal."

"Thank you, Bob; I'll be alert for that memo."

Lewis hung up the phone and stared at the voiceless receiver thinking, *What a wimp. He wants to put the whole thing on me. He's the one who desperately wanted the Homeland Security Act passed to give him the power of detention he needed, and now he has it, but doesn't want any blame for the action. Oh well, I serve at his pleasure, and when his pleasure conflicts with my pleasure, I'll keep on keeping on, until he says otherwise. Fuck the Texas bastard.*

Lewis called out to his secretary and instructed her to deliver the written memo he just completed to the President by special courier —stat.

It was 4 pm when Lewis entered the conference room where seven assistant attorney generals waited—four men and three women. Lewis was proud of his entire staff, and he was confident that what he now needed would be delivered in spades.

"Gang," he affectionately barked, "gather around and hear this. I have a mandate from the President. He wants speedy action for completing the investigation of Peter Fallow. You all know he's incarcerated in Allenwood prison. I filed the charges today. The problem is there's marginal conflict between the civil aspects of his Constitutional rights and the Homeland Security Act. The President has accepted my recommendation to stand behind the Homeland Security Act to justify the several days of detention without formal charges. If we had justification to hold him under constitutional law, charges would have been required within a 24-hour period. That period having elapsed without charges required the only justification available, and that was the Homeland Security Act.

"The number of assassinated Congressmen in a month's time along with the TBA's admission and intent to proliferate the acts, make this domestic terrorism," Robert continued. As confident as I holding him under the Act, the President agrees, but he's too weak, and he wants a complete review of the matter. That's where you all come into the picture. I want all of you to evaluate all of the dynamics with this threefold mission.

"One: redo the search of Fallow's home and the prison with a Sherlock Holmes–focus. Two: a growing number of American people understand the in-your-face corruption by their congresspeople, and the President wants an indictment. Someone must be thrown to the wolves. I don't have to tell you that he'd like it even better if that someone is a fucking Democrat. Three: All your findings must be compatible with the homeland security aspects of his detention."

The assistants laughed while clearing their throats. One staff member asked, "Aren't we also becoming corrupt if we are investigating the corruption of one party?"

"Don't think of it that way—just prioritize. You should also understand the significance of time in this matter. The more time passes with no more assassinations, the greater the justification will be of the charges we filed. If the assassinations resume, we know our investigation is incomplete. So, let's get cracking."

"What about Walters? Could he be useful?"

"Mike Walters isn't available to us at this time. He's rehabilitating. Besides he opened all of the doors for us. Now all you have to do find something his team may have overlooked during their searches."

While agents Eileen Vans and Mark Vale went to the prison to conduct a search, two other agents went to Hazleton to search Fallow's home. The other three AAGs initiated an investigation into congressional corruption.

CHAPTER FORTY-SIX

Agents Vans and Vale introduced themselves to the warden at the prison and requested the removal of Peter Fallow from his area long enough for them to conduct a sweeping search of his room.

"This guy is meticulous," Vans said to Vale as they searched. "Look at how neatly he has all of his things."

"Well what does that tell you?" Vale asked.

"It tells me that he has obsessive compulsive disorder. He's rigid and can't tolerate things out of order. And I guess in some bizarre abstract way, it seems like he wanted his government neat and orderly. With the way things are going in America today, he must have been in agony."

Agent Vale laughed and said, "Let's be pricks and leave everything in chaos when we're finished with the search."

"Hey, that's not as funny as you think. This guy is in a vow of silence and disrupting his order could throw him into a rage. Let's just keep looking for that something that is missing from our case against him."

"Okay."

As Vans paged through Fallow's Masonic bible, a piece of paper fell to the floor. She picked up the paper and realized that the pyramid made of lines of small, circled letters had some significance. The base line had five circles. The second line had four, then three, two, and one at the top. Each circle had a capital letter with the letter "F" in the top circle. At the top of the paper was 5/21/03. Agent Vans shared the paper with her Vale, and since neither one of them had the whole body of evidence at their disposal they were unable to completely evaluate the importance of the paper, but they knew it was a valuable find.

Vans and Vale returned to meet with Attorney General Lewis in his office. Lewis looked at the sketch, recognizing the pyramid was of the organizational hierarchy, with the letter "F" in the top identifying Fallow as the leader. Lewis sent for the prosecution file and pulled the group photograph out.

Pointing to the photo then the paper, Lewis said, "Let's match the people in the photo with the letters on this pyramid."

"With all due respect, sir, there are 21 men on that photo and only 14 letters in the pyramid," Vans said. "What do we do with the surplus?"

"We know that at least five of the men in the photo didn't follow through to the next meeting that Fallow had. We aren't sure if all of the remaining 16 members actually went into the meeting. Once they were in the meeting, we don't know that one or two didn't get up and walk out, do we?"

"If no more assassinations occur, sir, wouldn't that tell us that we have the man we need in custody?" Vale asked.

"Unless we can establish without a doubt that the conspiracy was limited to the men in this group, even if no further assassinations take place, we will always worry that it had spread to other groups."

Lewis looked at his phone and noted for the record that it was now 9:45 am. "Okay, Vans and Vale, you have your assignment, so, let's not waste time."

CHAPTER FORTY-SEVEN

Mike was in physical therapy exercising his right upper arm.
"Mike, this looks good," the therapist said. "You're almost back to normal ranges of motion. Your gait is coming along well, and you're able to walk short distances without a cane. I wouldn't be surprised if the doctor releases you now to outpatient care."

"That good to hear, but do you really think I'm ready for the outside?"

"You are ready, believe me. However, I recommend using a cane until you've built up more endurance."

"What makes you think the doctor will think I'm ready?"

"Because, I will complete a report of your progress, and in it I will recommend your transfer to out-patient therapy. The physicians usually accept my recommendations."

"Well, "I'm ready to get out of here, and from what you're saying it shouldn't be very long."

"I'm going to complete this report and deliver it to the doctor this morning. Will that be soon enough?"

"You have no idea how soon enough it is. Thank you."

Mike returned to his room with thousands of converging thoughts going through his head. He'd call Linda first, let the department know, get his apartment ready, and make arrangements for outpatient therapy. It was noon, and yet the doctor hadn't been in to see him yet. *Where the fuck is he?* Mike thought. He wasn't a swearing man, but there were times when his impatience wasn't exactly concealed.

Come on, doc, come on! I know you're busy, but, shit who am I kidding, I'm no better than anyone else in this hospital, Mike told himself. By that time, a dietary aide entered his room with his lunch. He lifted the warming lid off of the tray and looked at the plain piece of chicken sitting on a bed of wild rice. The coffee was okay but definitely not Starbucks. For dessert, he had a small dish of fresh fruit. All in all, the food was decent, but Mike couldn't wait to have some good old-fashioned home cooking. He laughed at that last because it had been a long time since he experienced any home cooking. Mike relaxed and settled into eating his lunch. He thought that it would consume some of the time he needed while waiting for the doctor. He finished his lunch and went to the bathroom to empty his bladder when the doctor entered the room. As he heard the doctor, he shook the dribbles of urine off the end of his penis.

With great anxiety in his voice, Mike shouted. "Hey, doc, I'll be right there. Don't leave."

"Relax, Mike, I'm not leaving."

Mike re-entered the room and apologized, "I'm sorry, doc. I know you're a busy man, but I had to go."

"Bullshit. You deliberately went into the bathroom because you didn't want me to tell you you're going home," the doctor joked. "We know you like it here. You don't have to cook. Here, you have three warm meals a day in bed. Shit man, you love the attention."

"Very funny. I've waited to hear those words you're going home since I've been here, so don't joke."

"No jokes, Mike. I just spoke with the therapist, and he feels that you can be cared for on an outpatient basis, and I agree. So, you're going home."

"How soon can I get out of here?"

"You'll have to go through the formal discharge procedures, but as far as I'm concerned you can leave immediately. I'll leave some prescriptions for pain medication and outpatient therapy with the nurse. I want you to call my office and make an appointment to see me in two weeks." The doctor reached over to shake Mike's hand and said, "Good luck and thank you for everything; and I mean everything. Patients come and go all the time and as much as I pride myself with caring for all patients equally without bias, I usually don't remember much about them. But you, I'll never forget."

The doctor left the room at the same time a nurse entered and said, "Mr. Walters, I have these forms for you to read and sign. When you finish signing, you may get dressed and call whomever it is that you want to take you home."

Mike signed all of the papers, and then he encountered his first problem. The clothing he arrived with was torn and soiled with blood stains. Linda, who he thought would pick him up, was in Tennessee. Since his discharge wasn't anticipated this early, he hadn't arranged for her to come. Luckily Hank was still in the office.

"Hank, I need a favor?" Mike said once Hank picked up his cell.

"Anything, Mike, what is it?"

"I'm being discharged today, and I need somebody to pick me up and take me home. Could you help? But first I need you to go to my apartment and bring me some clothes, can you do that?"

"I can and I will, Mike, except how do you expect me to get into your apartment. I don't have a key."

"Hank, you didn't forget how to pick a lock, did you?"

"No. Very funny, Mike."

"Well you have my permission to pick the lock at my place and get me some clothes."

"Okay, Mike. I'll clear up a few calls that I have to make, and then I'll get right on it."

"Thanks, but please make it fast."

They hung up.

Mike couldn't think of anything else but getting out of the hospital. He had no complaints. Every staff person gave him royal treatment, especially following the President's visit. And he was grateful, but he wanted this all behind him. He had an overwhelming feeling that once he entered the outside, his new life would begin.

Around a half hour later, Hank pushed Mike from his room to the entrance of the hospital in a wheelchair, in accordance with hospital policy. Hank said, "Here you are, my friend. Breathe in this beautiful autumn day's oxygen."

"I have a lot to be thankful for, Hank. You have no idea just how grateful I am. Thank you for getting here so quickly."

"Are you freaking nuts? This is the least I could do for my good buddy."

Hank carried Mike's things into the apartment, with Mike was two steps behind.

"Just throw everything on the sofa, and I'll take care of it later," Mike directed. "Would you like me to get you some dinner or something from the deli?"

"I'll be fine. I think for now I just want to be alone and relax. It's been a long day."

"Would you like me to hang around and take care of a few things? Anything, anything at all. You just name it, and I'll take care of it for you."

"I'm feeling so many things at once that I think I need to be alone while I sort through my emotions," Mike said.

"I totally understand. I'll be out of here in a flash."

"Hank," Mike paused, looked at his friend for a long moment, and said, "among all of my life's blessings, I couldn't have wished for a better partner or a friend for life." Mike turned away to pretend he was looking out of the window while he wiped a single tear from his eye.

"Okay, before you have a meltdown, I'm out of here," Hank said, smiling.

Mike listened to the foot sounds Hank made as he left the building.

The clock above the refrigerator in the kitchen was showing 4:15. Nothing, but nothing could delay Mike's next move. His hand was trembling as he dialed the Tennessee numbers. Linda's phone rang and rang until finally after the 10th ring Mike hung up. Rationalizing that she was out taking care of business, he followed with the negative thought, *Maybe she changed her mind and doesn't want to spend the rest of her life with a burned-out policeman.*

Alternating positive and negative thoughts dominated Mike's mind for the next hour. It was too difficult for him to settle in and start the routine activities of being home. Glancing at the clock, which was now showing 5:20, Mike grabbed his phone and dialed her again. On the third ring, he heard her voice.

"Hello? Mike, It's so good to hear your voice."

"Linda, I'm home. I was discharged this afternoon."

"Oh, darling, that's such wonderful news. Is everything okay?"

Mike felt his heart grow calm, knowing that his love for her was again validated.

"Yes, sweetheart, they felt that my progress was ahead of schedule, and I can continue therapy as an outpatient."

"Oh, Mike, that's so wonderful. I'm so happy to hear that. What do you need?"

"I don't need anything but you. How are things going down there?"

"I turned in my resignation as soon as I got back, and it was accepted. I'm clear in that matter. My unit is on the market, and my Realtor feels that it will sell quickly, and I don't need to be here for that process. My Realtor can handle everything except for the closing. I would naturally have to be present for the transfer signing. So, I guess everything really is good to go."

"Great. Would I be too ahead of things to ask you to get up here as soon as possible, I need you— not to take care of me—I need for us to be together and take care of each other. I miss you so much. I love you, and I ache to hold you."

"I can't wait to see you and hold you, too. As soon as we hang up, I'll make travel arrangements. I think I'm going to garage my car fly up. That will get me there faster than driving. Do you agree?"

"Yes, I do, and believe me the next time I open my door; I want it to be you standing there. Sweetheart, put your car in a garage and get the first available flight up here. When you have everything arranged, call me and I'll ask Hank to pick you up at the airport. If you can't get a flight soon enough, we can always see how much influence we still have over at the headquarters."

"Okay, love, I'll call you as soon as I know what I'm doing."

"Linda, please don't worry too much about the car. We can go back to Tennessee together and take care of the loose ends."

"That would be wonderful, Mike. I think I would like that."

"I love you. Goodbye." "

I love you, and I adore you. Goodbye."

Mike was intoxicated with love for Linda. He wanted to hold her and protect her from all of life's harm. He walked over to the window and looked out at the day's end. It was almost 6 pm, and Mike could sense the fall season giving way to the winter's shorter days. No possible struggle could prevent the seasonal change from happening. Mike felt a compelling need to let go of his past and enter into this coming new season with open arms.

He understood more clearly the reason why he needed to retire. He had fought crime and corruption for more than 25 years. He had gained the respect of his department and community, but he had lost his chance at a family. More than all of that, he realized now that he carried with him a dead soul—a soul so vacant of feeling and trust that it became almost certain that he would never have happiness again. So, he served throughout his career fiercely focused on investigative results. He was a fact-based detective from the beginning of his day until logging off duty at night.

Walking back toward the chair, he knew that he would never do anything to lose Linda. Strangely he thought, *The silent phone now has an aura of contentment in the wake of its last call. That fucking phone must have been as lonely as I was, listening and waiting for happiness to enter its inanimate life.*

Mike couldn't wait for the rest of his life to begin.

CHAPTER FORTY-EIGHT

Peter Fallow just finished his breakfast when a correctional officer appeared and announced that he would be having a visitor at 10 am.

"Who is it this time?"

"It's a female reporter form the *Washington Chronicle* who wants to interview you. I informed her that you probably wouldn't have anything to say, but she said she'd take her chances anyway."

"I'm just getting to some interesting chapters in my book and looking forward to a peaceful morning, but okay I'll see her," Peter said.

Peter readied himself for his visitor and thought, *If she thinks she's going to do some star reporting, I can't wait to see her reaction and frustration when she realizes that she getting nothing.*

All of his life, Peter had been a man of order and true to form he spent most of his time organizing and reorganizing his thoughts. He needed to have everything in perspective. He always felt that the first 5 minutes of exposure to a person were the most important and powerful for gaining respect. If you fumble, you fail.

It was nearly 10 am when a correctional officer escorted Peter to a private visiting room. Before entering that room, he was stripped of his clothing and body searched. Upon completion of the search, he was provided with a new set of inmate clothing, which were especially used for visitations. When the entire process was complete, he was taken into a location where the reporter was waiting.

"Good morning, Mr. Fallow, I'm Sarah Ross, on assignment from the *Washington Chronicle.*"

Peter could see that she was trying very hard to afford him respect, so he said, "So, then, will I call you Sarah or do you prefer Ms. Ross?"

"I'm comfortable with Sarah."

"Okay, Sarah, what is it that I can do for you?"

"I am interested in doing a profile for the American public. What I would really like is to have your biography published. What you are being accused of is horrible, and I think the public needs to hear from you the details, the under belly, of the organization you created: the whys, whos, whats, and wheres."

"Sarah, there is an implied 'guilty' in your request. Don't you think that the traditional trial by a jury of my peers should come first?"

"I'm terribly sorry, Mr. Fallow, I didn't mean to imply that you're guilty. Perhaps I should've phrased it differently."

"Well, let's say that you made a beautiful textbook request for my cooperation to give you details of an alleged organizational plot. Why would I do that? How old are you, Sarah?"

"I'm 23," Sarah replied indignantly.

"What's your background?"

"I'm a graduate of the University of Maryland with a degree in journalism. I have been with the *Chronicle* for a year."

"I see, Sarah, and if you bring home an insightful article about me and the God awful injustice of the Homeland Security Act, you will become the darling of the press."

"That's a rather cynical view of my motivation. However, you're partly correct about me wanting to expose the Homeland Security Act. I have more fears about the potential for governmental abuse from that than I do about the so-called mushroom cloud."

"Sarah, would you please stand up for me?"

"Why?"

"Just do it. Humor me and stand."

Sarah slowly stood and looked searchingly at Peter, who extended his right arm and made a circular motion with his index finger for her to turn around. Sarah reluctantly made a full 360-degree rotation. Peter made a sexist gesture, nodded his approval, and said, "With that great body and lovely face, you'll do just fine on all of the talk shows."

Sarah quickly sat back down, clearly self-conscious, and said, "Enough of that. What can I say to gain your help with a story?"

"Well. Here's the situation. I'm committed to not making any comment regarding any of the charges against me. If in fact the government has any material facts sufficient to hold me in custody, they must do so without my help. I will not be my own prosecutor. So, Sarah, I'll answer questions limited to my personal history. If you can accept that format, you may proceed. But know I'll be questioning you as well."

"Fair enough," Sarah agreed. "First question: How do you feel about being in prison?"

"I'm not in prison; you are. If my government has imprisoned me using abusive covenants of a phony law, I'm not the only one losing freedom am I? Every American citizen is as well, and that includes you, my dear young journalist."

"Tell me about your childhood."

"Please, I have very little patience for Freudian over-simplifications of the Oedipus and Electra complexes. There is so much wrong and too little right within our New Age mis-informational form of government to waste precious time on dysfunctional families."

"I want to back up a moment," Sarah pivoted. "Are we clear about the fact that everything you're saying is for the record?"

"Absolutely, you may quote me unless I stop you."

"Then it's your feeling that discussions about your childhood are a waste of time?"

"It's not me alone that I'm thinking about. We're an entire nation of unwitted citizens being over indulgently distracted by such psycho-babble, while a lying corrupt government is gradually making us irrelevant."

"In what way do you feel that the government is making us irrelevant?"

"They don't care what you or I think. They don't care if you submit a view as an individual or if you submit a petition with 100,000 signatures. They'll return some euphemized, politically correct rhetorical answer and go right ahead with a positive vote in favor of some corporate lobbyist. In that regard, by not representing the true needs of the people, the people become irrelevant."

"Do you see this as isolated incidences by elected officials, or is it more widespread?"

"I believe the feelings of mistrust for public officials is at a critical level. The President of the United States lied to the American people about the reasons for America to invade Iraq. He and his Cabinet cronies said that the Iraq had weapons of mass destruction that placed our national security at risk. They frightened the American public by saying if we didn't attack them, they would attack us, and of course using the term 'mushroom cloud' was the icing on the cake. After the invasion, no proof of weapons of mass destruction was ever found. The truth that Iraq had no weapon of mass destruction. All of this happens while more than 3,000 American soldiers were killed and many more thousands wounded for life. That's not the worst part of this mess. Our beloved Congress offered no oversight. You ask if it's just isolated incidents? Do you really care about my relationship with my parents? Let me ask you some questions, and you give me just a yes or no answer."

"Okay."

"Do you, Sarah Ross, trust the President of the United States?"

"No."

"Do you trust the Congress?"

"No."

"Do you trust your local and state officials, sheriff, mayor, assembly-people, etcetera?"

"No."

"Maybe you belong in a jail. Sarah, do you understand that if you approach the average person and ask him or her those questions, you'd get the same answers. It's becoming so bad that elected officials will lie to you while knowing that you know they are lying and you know that they know you know that they're lying. Truth is a lie, and a lie is the truth."

"Mr. Fallow, doesn't trust require taking a chance?"

"The people took a chance when they believed the campaign rhetoric and elected the officials into office. What's happening more frequently in this once great nation is the people are becoming blasé about betrayal."

"What about our enemies? Don't we have to defend this country against those who threaten our national interest? Isn't it important to allow our commander-in-chief to prosecute our wars without interference?

"The Iranians, Iraqis, Chinese, Koreans, Republicans, or Democrats are not our enemies. Our enemies are right here in Washington—the corrupt, greedy elected officials who on a daily basis place money in front of all reason. The perpetuation of the great military industrial complex, with its growing appetite for the dollar, is becoming too bloated for our nation."

"Well, aren't we a free nation with the ability to throw them out of office if we're not satisfied with their performance?"

"That's another thing, incumbents have all of the advantages of the office. They use taxpayers' money to send out news releases. Because they have the power of the vote, they have immediate access to corporate resources, and for that reason get their support. They appear on network TV addressing current issues with sound bites that appear to be telling their constituents what they want to hear. What chance does a fresh new candidate have against the power of incumbency?"

"Well, Mr. Fallow, with all of your political insight what have you done to help bring about change?"

"I always vote. But that's cute, Sarah. I told you the rules of this interview, and I won't answer any more leading questions."

"You're in prison for what? Because you have no freedom?"

"I'm in this federal jail for reasons that you as a journalist will have to explore. You find the answers to that question. When you find it, look around and ask yourself, Am I free? As for me, I am free, freer than I've been in a long time. They can keep me here for all of eternity. I will have nothing to tell them and while I'm telling them nothing, they will be keeping me fed, housed, and clothed."

"Wouldn't it be better for the America you love and served to clear up questions about your part if any in these assassinations?"

"You're becoming a little more creative with your indirect questions concerning my involvement. Nice try. My service to my country will never end, nor should it. A man's worth is not only his convictions, but his willingness to die for them. That also extends to those who join with him in the cause. Betrayal is the name of the government's game. Loyalty is the master ingredient of my thing."

"I would still like to get back to your childhood if you don't mind. I know you don't want to get into the Freudian babble, but, perhaps you could share with me some things like when and where you were born, were you from a poor family or wealthy, things like that."

"I have no objection to that type of general questioning."

"Where and when were you born?"

"I was born the day after Christmas, December 26, 1930, in Hazleton, Pennsylvania, in the maternity ward of the Hazleton State General Hospital. Oh yes, Sarah, in a state hospital."

"What do you mean a state hospital?

"For all practicable purposes, we had socialized medicine back then. If you were able to pay, you paid, but if you were the working poor, you might pay as little as a dollar a week. If you had no means of paying, you contacted a local politician, who wiped your bill clean. Getting sick or needing to be hospitalized wasn't an economic disaster, like it is today."

"And in your mind that was socialized medicine?"

"Actually, Pennsylvania had 10 state hospitals during that time—all of them in the coal regions."

"Do you have any siblings?"

"I have a younger brother, Andrew. He's eight years younger than I am. He lives in Somerville, New Jersey. Also, I have a younger sister, Regina. She's five years younger than I am. I remember the day my mother brought her home from the hospital. I was five years old at the time."

"What about your mother and father?"

"Both my parents are deceased. My father was born in America. I think it was July of 1905. He was also born in Pennsylvania in a small town called Jeddo. He was a hard-working coal miner until he was in his forties when he went to work for the Lehigh Valley Railroad Company. He worked there until he retired at the age of 65. He died in 1975 at the age of seventy of black lung disease. My mother, Pearl, was a good woman, a typical home maker. She was born in New Jersey, in 1907. She was a calm lady with a strong sense of family and protective of her husband and her children. She would never buy herself new dresses or anything she felt was squandering hard-earned money. Everyone else came first, and she never changed even later in life when everyone was self-sufficient. She died two years after my father in June of 1977. I really miss her."

"Were you and your father close?

"My father was a quiet, stoical man. The only passion I remember him having was for baseball. He could tell you player's averages and things like that. He never showed affection for me or my brother or sister for that matter. But, he never laid a hand on any of us. Basically, he left the family issues to my mom."

"How was he about community matters? Did he vote?"

"He went to work every day, brought his pay home to my mother, and never got involved with politics. Only one time I recall him being political, and that was when Eisenhower was running for President. He liked Eisenhower."

"When did you start taking an interest in politics?

"What makes you think that I ever had an interest in politics?

"Please don't read anything into that question. I just assume that you, like most senior citizens I know, have an active interest in politics."

"Thank you for the clarification. Actually, I became interested in politics when I was in college, Political Science 101, as I recall. I had a good professor who made systems of political socialization very interesting. I registered to vote and never missed a general election since that time."

"In what party are you registered?"

I registered as a Democrat initially, was an Independent for a time, and when I became a Master Mason at the age of 30 or 31, I changed to a Republican and have been ever since."

"Do you miss your fellow Masons?"

"I miss the fellowship of those lodge nights."

"I'd like to change the subject now toward current events. Do you mind?"

"I don't mind as long as the questions don't jeopardize my incarceration."

"Okay, fair enough. Have you been reading in the newspapers and listening to the television news concerning the 15 assassinated United States congressmen?"

"Yes."

"Do you have any concerns for their loss?"

"You are asking me for my feelings concerning their deaths, correct?"

"Yes, that's part of it, but I am interested in whether or not you have any sympathy for their losses and for the terror it has caused in our country?"

"First of all, I believe they were assassinated by some citizens who felt that they were corrupt politicians. Are you, my dear Sarah, concerned about the assassins who sacrificed their lives and a corrupt misrepresentation? Is killing a representative of the people who steals the public's money, who votes in the interest of pharmaceutical companies for a law that ends up telling America it cannot bargain for drug costs not a good thing? Is killing a representative of the people who votes to make it mandatory for every citizen to have health insurance or auto insurance not a good thing?"

"How does that figure into a free nation?"

"Haven't you been at all shocked by the shameful conduct of Congressman Duke Cunningham, who is now sitting in federal prison? And, what about a congressman like Daniel Delune and his association with the Harrison scandal?"

"Then you believe that the assassins are the good guys?"

"Sarah, that's a question you must answer."

"Well, Peter, as a journalist I'm trying to bring truth and clarity to this matter. I am trying to see America through your eyes. I hope that whatever truth is out there will eventually surface, and it will end up being a good thing for our country."

"Bullshit, Sarah. Whether you know it or not, you're part of this new-age journalism that's more interested in manufacturing news than you are in reporting it. But I do appreciate that—but, I must tell you it's not my eyes you need to explore, it's the hearts of every suffering American being betrayed by our elected members of Congress. Go to the emergency rooms of every hospital and feel the hearts of mothers without insurance hearing for the first time that their child can't be admitted or that they themselves don't qualify for a mastectomy. Go to the drug store and watch the sorrow of people telling the pharmacists to fill only one-third of their prescription because they don't have enough money to pay for it all. Go to the home of an elderly person and feel her pain while the sheriff is issuing her a notice that her home is being taken for nonpayment of property taxes. Go into a home where the furnace has shut down from the lack of fuel, step into their agony as they shiver through cold nights. When you're finished, then visit our borders and watch the millions of illegal immigrants entering our country and taking jobs away from our existing labor force, jobs they say our citizens won't accept.

Bullshit. It's all about cheap labor, and big business is in bed with the national Chamber of Commerce. All of them are in bed with a United States Congress who is on the take in exchange for amnesty. Sarah, when and if you've entered into the hearts of these suffering millions, you come back and ask me again: Did those lying, stealing bastards have anything to do with the misery and suffering of our people? Ask me then if I'm concerned for their loss. After you've been in their hearts, you can open your eyes and visualize the hopelessness of their futures."

"You obviously have a bleak picture of our Democracy."

"Yes, I guess I do. I am among those with abject fear we are entering into a divisive class struggle in this country, which will become more and more uncivilized and result in a revolution. And then comes the end of this once great nation. Look, Sarah, you're 23 and still shedding narcissism. I've given you a tool to help you acquire some insight, aside from your own stereotypes about the America in which you live. I don't expect you to flip a page that fast. When you have felt the heartbeat of a sick, lonely man, woman, or child who's in abject poverty and have opened your eyes to see the hopeless downward slide of our democracy, then we'll have a useful dialogue."

"My God, Mr. Fallow, you make it sound so fatal, as if it's all coming to an end."

"I'm sorry, young lady, that I can't paint you a rosier picture of our future. The truth is that corruption is so entrenched in our government institutions that it's not a matter of if it will end. It's a matter of when."

"If what you're saying has merit, do you think that the recent assassinations were designed to delay the inevitable? Or do you believe they will prevent all of the doom you forecast?" Sarah asked, looking a little shell-shocked.

"Again, your question is an implication that I had something to do with the assassinations," Peter replied. "So again, let's be clear about that, I will not answer anything loaded with self-incriminations. Now theoretically I would say that the potential for reversal of tendencies to steal is possible. But if you leave the bad apples in the barrel certainly all of the apples will rot. On the other hand, if you pluck the rotten apples out of the barrel, it's a good bet that the other apples will not spoil."

"So, you're saying that the assassinations could change the corruption that's destroying our nation?"

"I did so as a theoretical response to your theoretical question."

"No. I am asking you these questions just as I would ask any man on the street the same thing."

"Okay, Sarah Ross," Peter stopped and looked at her as if he were seeing her for the first time. At 23, her eyes were ocean blue with a dangerous magnetism that could pull you right in. Peter turned away and said, "Thank you for your interest in my biography, but I must conclude this interview. I'm tired and want to rest."

"Mr. Fallow, I only have a few more questions. Could we go on for a few more minutes?"

"No, I have no desire to continue."

"Could we reschedule for another day?"

"Perhaps another time, but I'll let you know when, but not now." With that note of finality Peter signaled the officer to take him back to his area.

Sarah watched with interest as the likable old man was escorted away from the visiting area. Her mind was swimming with possible headlines and leadins foor her story about the man who may be behind the assassinations of 15 congressman. What balance was required to show the distrust people have for America's leadership versus the horrible murders which were committed? She knew that if she weighed the story too heavily in one direction, she would disclose her own bias. As she walked away, she wasn't certain of her personal feelings. What she did know is that she needed more from Peter—much more.

CHAPTER FORTY-NINE

Mike was singing in the shower when suddenly he heard his cell ring. He shut the water off and ran bare-ass naked to his phone. As he reached for it, he stumbled over a strip of carpeting on the floor, but when he landed he had the phone in his hand and breathlessly said, "Hello."

Linda said, "What's wrong? You sound out of breath."

"Nothing's wrong. I just tripped on the carpet when I was reaching for the phone."

"Oh God I thought something more drastic happened," Linda said, relieved. "I'm at the airport. Could you have Hank come get me?"

"Linda, I'll have the United States Army pick you up if necessary. Just kidding. I'll call Hank now."

It was 10:30 when she knocked on his door, Mike opened the door, and there she was—the most beautiful creature created by God standing and smiling with the most kissable lips in the universe. Mike hungrily pulled her into his arms and kissed her as his entire body trembled with excitement and a fear that if he stopped it would go away. When they ended their long embrace, they both walked toward the couch and sat down.

"How was your flight?"

"Fuck the flight," she reached out to him, and they started kissing and exploring each other with their hands. Linda began breathing heavily while her hand felt his cock. His cock was so hard he started panting and sighing with her, he felt his fingers enter into her moist vagina. Together they were ripping each other's cloths off as they moved toward the bedroom. When they landed on the bed, he felt his cock slide into her heavenly love canal. With her legs wrapped tightly around his waist, he forced his rock-hard cock as far into her vagina as it could go and he left it there pulsating against her vaginal walls. They stared lovingly into each other's eyes until they came together. She was moaning and sighing as Mike was coming into her with the semen of many lonely years that waited for love. As she was lying on her back, Mike was on his side caressing every line of her sensuous body, her green eyes sparkled like sea washed emeralds.

For several minutes, no words were spoken. They were in love, and every cell in their bodies exuded contentment.

Suddenly Linda raised herself up on her elbows and said, "I love you so much. Nothing in my life has ever made me this happy."

"I not only love you Linda, I adore you. I waited for you all of my life, and I'm never going to do anything to lose you."

"You'll never get rid of me. I'm here to stay."

"I lost one wife because I was too dedicated to my career; that's not going to happen to us; tomorrow morning the first thing on my agenda is to retire."

"Mike, we're going to make it work. I have no fear or regrets of giving up my career. I feel now that I won't even if I take a teaching position anywhere. I have enough money in a trust fund that I don't need to work. We'll retire together and enjoy life."

They sealed their understanding with a loving kiss, and Linda said, "The very next thing on the agenda is for you to find a preacher."

Mike smiled and asked, "Where's Hank? He brought you here from the airport, didn't he?"

Linda laughed, "I told him that I wanted to be alone with you and asked him to not be offended. I didn't even finish the sentence when he laughed and said he understood. He's a really nice man."

"I'm glad you think so because I plan on asking him to be my best man."

October 23 at 9:30 am, a correctional officer threw a newspaper into Peter's cell. "Better prepare yourself for the press; you're on the front page."

Peter picked up the folded paper and opened it slowly. The headline read: *Fallow Sees Democracy Coming to an End in America Peter.* The article began, *Fallow, who is being held at Allenwood Federal Prison in Pennsylvania, under alleged Homeland Security breaches, expressed his views that "It's not will it end; it's when." Fallow was responding to questions concerning the assassination of 15 United States congressmen. Although he was stoical about the deaths of the congressman, he showed passion for the assassins.*

Peter finished reading the article and walked over to his bunk, thinking that Sarah was fair about their interview. He then wondered what effect it would have on the people. Would the people begin to understand how their great free democracy was being systematically stolen from them by a corrupt Congress and corporate America? Could they see the piecemeal erosion of our middle class, the working class with lowering wages while seeing higher costs? Will they wake up and rebel against the so-called Homeland Security Act? Will they stand tall against advocates of gun control? The final stage of ending a free nation is to remove all the guns from its people. Will they understand when the people of any nation are disarmed and the police are the only ones armed, we then become a police state? If the people are unarmed, why do the police need to be armed? Peter began to see that he might be able to continue his fight against corruption from within his prison walls.

No longer sought as a fugitive, and now as a martyr, with the help of the press, he could still fight corruption and help enlighten the people enough to take back their nation. Peter called the officer and asked him to contact Sarah Ross and ask her to visit him for a follow-up interview. Peter was full of satisfaction as he realized the significance of that news article.

He wanted desperately to share the developments with Joe. He was saddened as he feared that would no longer be possible. He drifted into thoughts of spiritualism and wondered if he could have some kind of metaphysical connection with his old pal. *Maybe if I explore the world of spirits, he would appear to me in ghost like form and then I could share with him all that has happened. He would then be at peace with all that we have shared. Well maybe there are some books in the library on the subject. I must check that out later.*

Peter went to a desk in his room, which was part of the furnishing in upscale federal prisons. He sat down and drafted things he wanted to share with Sarah, things that he felt were crucial for the average citizen to understand. As he made notes he thought of an old platitude, "If you don't know where you're going, any road will get you there." It's true he thought most people don't know where the hell they're going and don't have enough sense to care. Maybe it's too hard for them to process the horribleness about things and what happens is we have an entire neurotic public suppressing the truth. But he continued thinking, *They are the same fucking assholes who know the batting averages of ball players. Through my imprisonment, I have a new opportunity to shed a light on the path of doom that the leaders of the United States are leading the public.*

He made his first note: Memo to self. 1. Insurance (explain how they're destroying the economy) 2. Oil Corporations; (explain) 3. The Military Industrial Complex. Peter leaned back in his chair to think about his approach and asked himself *Will they even care?* Fearing an abject relapse, he recoiled and went back to making notes for Sarah.

Just after Peter finished eating his breakfast, the correctional officer gave him a message from Sarah that said, "Peter, I will be happy to see you this afternoon around two o'clock and continue the interview."

Peter was really upbeat and began to feel a sense of worth, a feeling of spiritual reconnection with his Masonic brothers who fulfilled the promises of their final duty. If his new direction with the eager journalist helps shed a brighter light on corruption in America, he will have fulfilled his final duty as well.

The weather had been especially beautiful in fall up until this 24th day of October. Today it was pouring rain, and the forecast was for several more days of rain. Peter hated rainy days, which went back to his trucking days when the rain made the roads hazardous, especially at night when approaching headlights reflected off the wet roads turned every two headlights into four. *Funny,* he thought, *and interesting as well, how a man never becomes more than the things he's done for a living* The more he thought of it, the more confusing and less real it seemed.

After Peter finished preparing notes for his interview with Sarah, he went back to reading *Born in Blood*. It was difficult to read without constantly being interrupted by interfering thoughts. It took Peter awhile, but eventually he got back into what he was reading. It was 11:30 when the correctional officer entered Peter's cell with his lunch.

Peter, as a special prisoner under the Homeland Security Act, wasn't allowed to commingle with the general population. Instead, he dined in a private area. He didn't mind the separation from the mainstream prisoners because his private dinning afforded him a cleaner environment for eating. It also gave him a closer relationship with his guards.

The correctional officers would at times try to engage Peter in conversations concerning the assassinations, but Peter distracted them, moving the conversations toward academics.

At was exactly 1:15 pm, Peter was escorted to the conference room where Sarah was waiting. Although Sarah's hair was all frazzled from the pouring rain, she looked stunningly youthfully, and she greeted him cheerfully. He looked at her for a long moment and saw her fresh young beauty, as if he were seeing her for the first time. There she was, all wet and weather beaten, looking like a tantalizing little goddess. He lamented the curse of being an old man. He mused laughingly, the curse of an old man with 20/20 vision. What he wouldn't give to be young and handsome again. He would ravish her young, solid body.

"Mr. Fallow, are you okay?" Sarah asked.

"Certainly, I was just admiring your youth."

"Were you pleased with the article I wrote for the *Chronicle?*"

"More than you could ever know, young lady. Actually, I was inspired and read it several times to make sure there were no cryptic messages or secret codes hidden between the lines. Finally, I was convinced that it was pure journalism, and I want to thank you for that."

"You are very welcome. I was just doing my job, and I believe I did so without bias."

"I was not only inspired, I was also enlightened, realizing your pen is more lethal than any assassin's bullet," Peter said. "I hope that you'll continue to write about my incarceration. I believe you might inspire the sleeping public to wake up."

"Mr. Fallow, I'll continue with these interviews and report all relative facts in the *Chronicle,* as long as what you relate to me isn't fabrications or just confinement rhetoric."

"Would you mind indulging me an old platitude?"

"Not at all."

"If you don't know where you are going, any road will get you there. The general public doesn't know or understand where this corrupt administration and Congress of "ostriches" are leading our nation."

Sarah had her laptop perched on her lap, and she was taking notes when suddenly a different correctional officer entered the room and ordered her to leave.

"Are you sure officer?" she asked. "I understood that I could have as much time as I needed as long as it didn't interfere with scheduling."

"I'm very sorry, miss, but this isn't about anything you or Mr. Fallow did," the guard explained. "Mr. Fallow is being transferred. You must leave."

Sarah departed. It was exactly 1:30 pm. The officer took Peter by the arm and escorted him back to his cell.

The next day's *Washington Chronicle* headline read, "Peter Fallow's Mysterious Removal from Allenwood Prison Is Questioned," and the article began, "During a follow-up interview at the prison with Mr. Fallow yesterday, journalist Sarah Ross was ordered to terminate the interview and leave the facility. She learned that Mr. Fallow was being transferred to another undisclosed facility without notice or benefit of counsel."

Later, in Washington D.C., Attorney General Lewis held a brief press conference at 3 pm, where he stated, "Members of the media, under the advisement of our Homeland Security expert, the President of the United States was informed that some indications are that the recent assassinations of our Congressmen may have foreign connections. If the connections are verified, the assassinations are then classified as external acts of terrorism—not domestic capital crimes. Under provisions of the Homeland Security Act, until further notice, Peter Fallow will be detained in a protective venue until the investigation is complete. That concludes this conference."

The members of the press pool were angrily shouting questions at the attorney general, who simply responded, "I will answer no questions at this time."

"What are you hiding?" "Whose butt is the President covering?" the reporters called as the attorney general disappeared into the building, swallowing the man, who would never be seen again.

As the journalists departed, people were gathering in the street with shouts and signs reading "FREE FALLOW — FIRE CONGRESS." The public demonstrations obviously were about to increase—in number and in intensity.

CHAPTER FIFTY

November 1, 2005, at 2 pm, Linda Marshall, MD and Michael Walters stood before Justice Loretta Gonzales, who was about to unite them in marriage. Standing alongside them were Hank and John.

Justice Gonzales broke the silence, "We are gathered here together in the sight of God and this company to join together in holy matrimony this man and this woman. Is there anyone here who has cause to object to this union let them speak now or forever hold their peace."

Mike didn't even hear the words, they were just sounds coming from the woman's mouth as he felt happiness flowing through every cell of his body. Looking into Linda's eyes, he knew that she was feeling the same way. Suddenly the judge repeated, "Michael Walters, do you take this woman, Linda Marshall, to be your lawful wife, to have and to hold, through sickness and health until death do you part?"

As Mike was choking back his tears of joy, he replied, "I do."

It was Linda's turn; the judge repeated the dialogue and received her loud reply, "Yes. Yes, I do."

The judge declared, "You are now husband and wife. You may kiss the bride."

Mike and Linda kissed with the passion of teenagers on a first date. Hank and John looked at each other, then John tapped Mike on the shoulder and both he and Hank congratulated the newlywed couple.

"Just a moment, Mike, it's our turn to kiss the bride," Hank joked.

"Be my guest," Mike said, then John and Hank gave token kisses to the bride. Without the usual trappings, Mike and Linda drove away from the judges office and headed for Tennessee. It was a beautiful, sunny day. The leaves were into autumn's most gorgeous colors. It was nature's time for change, and theirs as well. They were now the happiest couple on earth.

Driving along, Linda looked at Michael and explained, "You know, Mike, all the while we were involved in the investigation, I couldn't help thinking that the assassins who were all senior citizens with terminal health conditions know something we don't." She continued while Michael remained silent, "When will it all end, all this inhumanity, corruption, and wars--and now a declared bogus war against terrorism?"

"I'm so happy at this moment in my life," Mike said. "I wish that every man in this entire world could have the same love and joy that I have with you. And yet, I know that can't be. As long as there is more than one opinion, and as long as men have opposing ideas, there will be war. So, I guess, the answer is it will never end."

They were heading west as the sunset was spreading its awesome crimson colors against a darkening sky. Mike breathed in all of the spectacular beauty, thinking it matched his feeling of love for Linda. He felt the whole spirit of the moment, the sun he knew would soon disappear beyond the horizon, and the complete darkness of night would host their contentment until tomorrow's light. He suppressed any emerging ideas of their happiness fading away with time. Mike finished trying to explain all this magic to his new bride without much success. He took a deep breath and acquiesced to the ineffable.

Linda moved closer to Mike and snuggled into his armpit. As he kissed the top of her head and thought of her beautiful hair and face, he suddenly understood why some species eat their lovers. As they drove, they didn't speak. They just enjoyed the feeling of being in love.

CHAPTER FIFTY-ONE

Sarah Ross was angered by the governmental dismissal she received at Allenwood Prison. Without concern for anyone's rights, they showed her the door. Perhaps it wasn't only the inconsideration they provided her, but the abrupt way they swept Peter Fallow away, without warning or benefit of counsel also concerned her. She was experiencing some conflict between the professional aspects of objective reporting and her growing feelings that something wasn't exactly right about the handling of Mr. Fallow's incarceration. Based upon her last brief session with him, she felt that he was expressing some populist views regarding a corrupt United States in the fatal stages of ruin. Sarah was more aroused than ever and now she somehow felt that he had transferred the ball over to her. My God.

Sarah pondered that thought for a moment and felt a combination of anxiety and outrage. She wondered, *Am I overreacting? Am I too cowardly to pick up the ball and carry it to the goal post? Why me?*

She picked up her phone and called her mentor, Mark Phillips, a communications professor at her college, who became her friend after she graduated. Mark answered on the second ring.

"Hi Mark, I need to review some things with you," Sarah said.

"Hey Sarah, it's good to hear your voice. I'm never too busy for you, what's up?"

"Have you read my articles about Peter Fallow in the *Chronicle*?" she asked.

When Mark answered yes, Sarah said, "Great, let's cut to the chase. Are these assassins actually in the right?"

"The assassins essentiallyare advocating that the America, "the republic for which it stands" may well be "A Republic Fascism." I read that progressive liberalism is rooted in fascism. Back in 2003, I read in *Free Inquiry* magazine about the 14 characteristics of Fascism. Check it out, it could be helpful."

Sarah thanked Mark and hung up. She Googled the article by Dr. Lawrence Britt with interest as it identified 14 characteristics of Fascism.

1.Powerful continuing nationalism

2.Disdain for any recognition of human rights (torture is now acceptable)

3.Creates enemy scapegoats as a unifying cause (Islamic fascism) (uses rally round the troops to gain support for their bogus cause)

4.Supremacy of the military (when domestic needs are growing —a disproportionate amount of the budget goes to the military)

5.Rampant sexism (almost never are there women in the hierarchy)

6.Obsession with national security

7.Controls the mass media

8.Religion and government are intertwined (use religion to gain control)

9.Corporation powers are protected (corporations provide the money for them to remain in power)

10.Labor power is suppressed

11.Disdain for intellectuals

12.Obsession with crime and punishment

13.Rampant cronyism and corruption

14. Fraudulent elections

Sarah had more than one self-loathing moment since she first met Peter. He had liked her first article, and she felt somewhat validated, and now she hoped that wherever he was incarcerated, he would be allowed to read her follow-up article. She felt that if he did, he would also feel that he achieved his goal of transference to her. Maybe he would see that the pen is finally arriving on the battlefield of corruption and awaken a sleeping people.

Sarah's article series on Peter had captured the nation's attention. For the next several weeks, she guested on most of the popular talk shows. Her article struck a blow to the sleeping public, who for the most part suppressed any suspicions they had about the government's abuse of power. While they were ignoring the signs, they would justify wrongful actions of the government with the thought that they are in charge and must have good reasons for their actions. Things that ordinary people weren't informed of.

And most certainly the government officials know what's best to protect its people. It's a convenient form of suppressing the ugly truth about corruption. As the calls were now coming into the host stations, Sarah and the hosts could see how the enlightenment was now growing. Comments were angry and incredulous.

Sarah was becoming more seasoned in her articles and answers to questions. She admonished for cooler heads to prevail and for concerned citizens to contact their elected officials and let them know that the people know what's going on with Congress. She imputed the people to challenge house bills that on the surface seem to be fair, but they should question the details of such bills for the hidden content.

Sarah received hundreds of e-mails and letters expressing outrage over the government's conduct. Most of them wanted specific information about the National Security Act and why our borders weren't being protected. Some of them encouraged her to run for Congress in the next election cycle. One person wanted to set up a fundraiser and a "Sarah Ross for Congress" website.

Sarah declined, but she expressed her gratitude. She felt was that she could better serve the people as a journalist loyal to the truth and impervious to bribes. That's the one thing that greedy people can't understand: People who won't accept payoff money or bribes. Sarah confessed that she was greatly affected by the imprisoned Peter Fallow; when she questioned him about his imprisonment, and he enlightened her about her loss of freedom.

Sarah thought, *I'm aware of the corruption going on with a bought-and-paid-for Congress, and if I ignore my awareness, it makes me an accomplice. I recall in one of my college law classes that if a person becomes aware of a violation of the law and doesn't act upon it, they become a party to it. In affect, they are just as damn guilty as the perpetrators. Since my readers have now become aware, they too have a duty.*

FINAL CHAPTER

Several weeks went by, and things begun to quiet down. The administration was busy lobbying Congress to increase the war budget. Lobbyists were busy meeting in congressional offices, and lawmakers were doing business openly. The weird thing about it is that so many of them were very hard to find during the assassinations. Every indication was that nothing was going to change.

One day, Congressman Rodger Samuels, a Republican from the state of Idaho, entered the dining room of the Hotel Madison in Boise and approached a table with two waiting men. Both men stood and greeted him. They shook hands and the three of them sat.

"It's good to see you again, Congressman," said Ralph Soda, who was representing the Civil Liberties Union. The other man was Congressman Richard Dickson from the state of Oregon.

Rodger said, "Shall we order first, gentlemen, or would you rather get on with business?"

"I've been waiting here for you for a while so if you don't mind I'd go for food first," Congressman Dickson said.

All three ordered very expensive entrees, and following the delightful meal and martini's they got down to business. Ralph opened the conversation by introducing a proposed House bill that Congressman Dickson was co-sponsoring and asked Rodger if he was aware of the bill and if he had any understanding of what it would mean if it were to be passed.

"I certainly am aware of the bill, and as it stands I'm leaning toward a yes vote." Dickson pointed out that although he is a co-sponsor of the Bill, he is doing so in the hopes that it would actually be defeated. He continued, "I'm up for re-election this year, and I needed to come out showing that I'm for strong defense of our borders as a solution to the growing demand by my constituents to stop illegal immigrantss from coming in by the thousands. And that's why you're here, Rodger. I'm hoping that you will change your thinking on the bill and help to defeat it. I thought that since you're not up for re-election this time around, perhaps you would reconsider."

The dialogue continued with Ralph observing the discussion between the two Congressmen. He knew he would eventually be the dealmaker.

"Is that what you thought, Richard? Why exactly did you think that I would change my vote, just like that?"

"Well, when you need a favor to help you out with your constituents, I'll be there for you."

"Okay, let's say I reverse my position at the risk of helping you and wind up losing favor with my people and then you're defeated? What then, Richard?"

"Well, there is another consideration, Rodger. That is a double quid-quo-pro, and that's why Ralph is here. The American Civil Liberties Union doesn't want this bill out of committee. He sits on the committee and could cooperate in sealing its doom, and if you were to do that, now if I'm out of line here let me know now and that will end this session."

"You may continue."

"Okay this is my one time offer. You help kill the bill and $100,000 will be placed into an untraceable Swiss Bank account."

Rodger looked over at Richard and asked, "How well do you know this guy and how reliable is he to deal with?"

"Very, Rodger, very."

"Is that from experience or hearsay?"

"Experience."

"Okay, I'm in."

The three men shook hands, and Rodger said, "I'm leaving shortly for Washington. D.C. Our legislative agenda is intense. How are you getting back? Do you have scheduled flight?"

"I have a private twin engine chartered that's leaving in one hour. Do you mind if I hop a ride with you?"

"Okay, Richard, we could get back to our legislative business together.

They were in the air, and the flight was silky smooth. Both men felt a sense of personal enrichment and were content. The pilot, a young dark-skinned man probably in his mid-twenties, wearing sunglasses, suddenly appeared to fix the plane's course on automatic pilot. He fiddled around in the cockpit a short while, then got up and walked to the rear of the plane. The two passengers watched the pilot open a hatch door, smiled, said, "Paybacks a bitch. Good-bye, you miserable mother fuckers," and bailed out, touching what the men quickly realized was the string of a parachute.

News of the two Congressmen killed in the plane crash created a new fear throughout the nation's congressmen. Great alarm was spreading and getting legs when the federal aviation inspection discovered that the pilot, who couldn't be found, was young, and possibly Muslim.

This immediately brought the theory of the 15 Scottish Rite Mason assassins acting alone into question. This young missing pilot suggested that the organization might be more widespread and culturally and generationally mixed.

The following day, Mike Walters received an urgent message from the White House requesting his immediate return to service.

Linda was reading the message over his shoulder when Mike turned to her and said, "Not today. Not ever again."

She kissed him on the back of head and said, "I agree."

Since their marriage, their loyalty and devotion were to one another and nothing beyond.

Mike sent a message back to the President of the United States and stated, "With all due respect, I suggest that you convene both houses of Congress and let them know that their failure to listen to and represent the people must end. Your Bully Pulpit must be employed now and without delay. Good luck, sir. I'm not returning."

*Post Novel observation: At the time this novel was written, the congressional approval rating was around 25 percent, today it's still polling in the basement.

YEARS LATER

One morning in 2021, George awoke sensing he was waking from a confusing dream. George swung his both legs from his bed. Both feet planted firmly on the floor as he ran his fingers through what was left of his receding hair.

Wobbling through the corridor to the bathroom, George posed for the antique mirror while bracing himself against the wall with one hand on the sink. He felt a little woozy and remembered that the night before he definitely had one drink too many.

In the image his clearing vision was beginning to see, his eyes were a little puffy, but otherwise he still wasn't showing his age. After a cold compress and a shave, he'd be ready to greet the day. Suddenly it came to him he had a luncheon meeting with the investors at noon. A quick glance at the clock showed it was almost 11 am.

George returned to the bedroom to find something appropriate to wear, and there was the evidence of a wild night on the bed and floor.

Half naked, lying on the other side of the bed, a woman smiled, smirking, and said, "Hi Fred."

"I'm sorry, who are? What? How did? Never mind, get up, and I'll take you wherever. We'll talk on the way," George said, beside himself half pissed and half embarrassed as he he handed her a pair panties he picked off the floor.

As they were both getting dressed, from an occasional glance he admired her long slender body. From what he could see, her hair was long and her breasts were tiny. "Cookies and raisins" is how he often referred to small breasts, which he usually preferred.

George wondered, *Was this a confusing dream? Did they make love? Why can't I remember? 'Fred?' How did that come about? I'm George Peters. At least I think I'm still George. Me, the guy with two first names. This is going to be one interesting fucking ride listening to her story.*

He drove through the late morning streets of Hazleton, Pennsylvania, and pulled up at the Wyoming street address she gave him. Not waiting, she opened her own door and thanked him for the interesting evening.

"Wait a moment," George asked. "What are you thanking me for?"

"You don't really know, do you Fred?" She answered. "I have your land-line number. I got it while you were sleeping. Maybe I'll give you a call and explain."

With a curious smile George watched her walk away, sexily dropping her left shoulder then the right, causing a rumba-like sway in her hips. Slowly he drove away and honked his horn.

George was almost a virgin. He remembered his first kiss with a girl he met in the 11th grade. They caught each other's eye while seated opposite one another in the lunch room. They finished their lunch and purposely approached each other with extended hands gesturing a "get to know you too demeanor." Dating after school was inevitable.

Sandra Miller and George soon became known as a couple on campus. It was on their second week of kissing and hugging when parked in a car he borrowed from his foster dad, John, the kissing turned to heavy passionate breathing when Sandra removed her blouse and bra exposing two bullet-like breasts she pushed into

George's waiting mouth. George's erection was so hard he couldn't believe what was happening when Sandra grabbed his penis and thrust it toward her pulsating vagina. Before entry, he exploded in an orgasmic relief. He entered her vagina, and in a frightened reactive second he withdrew fearing she would scream in pain - and he would be hurting her just like he heard his father would hurt his mother.

Sandra quickly got dressed and started to weep asking George through sobs, "What's wrong with me? I thought you loved me?"

"I didn't want to hurt you," George said.

George drove her home, and they never dated again. It was clear the trauma of his mothers cries were still with him. He wondered if he would he eventually have a normal sex life. Re-examining what just happened, he felt ecstatic pleasure, embarrassment about his climax, and confusion about his mothers painful cries while being raped by his father. Could it be she was experiencing ultra orgasms as his father was providing her with the pleasure she craved that later she would disguise as abuse? Would he ever know the truth? The excitement of the sex he just experienced was returning, and he decided "heaven exits between the legs of women. Sigmund, you have a new fan."

George's driving slowed as his thoughts drifted back to his early childhood days. The image of his mother was struggling for clarity. She was beautiful in an odd way. He remembered her dimpled smile and comforting, soft, angelic voice. He thought of her graceful, calm walk was as if she was being escorted by angels. George was in and out of his memory drift, when he soberly confirmed she was an angel.

Some asshole behind him was angrily beeping his horn, and George gave him the finger as he passed. His mother's image kept returning to his thoughts, and the truth was winning the battle over suppression. What he always denied was her weakness—her being an enabling accomplice for his drunken father's addiction.

George felt guilty for not intervening when hearing his mothers cries while being angrily raped by his father. He would pull the blanket over his head to mute the sound of her agony. As a result of the dreaded sounds of his helpless mother being raped, he thought that he was a coward and unworthy of praise or love. George was a troubled boy. He loved his mother but felt a conflicting hatred for her weakness, which caused his cowardice.

George's mother, Laura Ann Peters, died in 1987 from ovarian cancer when he was seven years old. His father was shot and killed in a barroom brawl in 1990. No one mourned his loss. Following his mother's death and the years until his father death, Adam Peters rarely interacted with his son. George now 10 years old was mostly on his own.

The children and youth agency placed him in foster care twice. The first time was a bad fit, and he ran away. After several days on the street, hungry and unwashed, he was spotted by the police and returned to the custody of children and youth.

They again placed him into Foster Care only this time it worked. His new foster parents were understanding and slowly helped George develop a feeling of worth. With their support, George got a high school diploma and eventually by working part time in a day care center he managed to get a bachelor's degree in Social Science. Throughout those early dark years of self loathing and doubt, he was able to survive and enter pubescence with the understanding embrace of his second foster care parents, Mary and John Colombo.

Mary was a home maker and unable to carry out a pregnancy, and with the cooperation of her husband, John, they became foster parents. John, a civil engineer, was employed by the county and worked closely with code enforcement and the planning commission. He had a good income, which enabled his wife to fulfill her maternal needs through foster parenting.

George was forever grateful for their kindness and love when he was a troubled boy. His social science studies helped him understand that his youthful experience of hearing his mothers cries weren't because he was unable to intervene, but in fact he was also a helpless victim of his father's abuse. The wisdom of his foster parents combined with his studies prevented him from becoming a debilitated victim of PTSD. Under Mary's foster care, George experienced his first angel. He forgave his mother's weakness, but he was unable to justify his father's cruelty. George, just out of college, a 20-year-old guy, six-feet-five-inches tall, sporting a handsome five o'clock shadow from an unshaved beard, with his confident glowing smile, had emerged as a charismatic adult man.

Mary and John Columbo beaming with pride sat in the front row watching their foster son accept his college diploma. Chest heaving sobs and proud tears fell from Mary's eyes , while John cradled her in his arms. It was a moment of triumph; their investment in the welfare of a troubled parentless boy was realized. It was the ultimate feeling of being the best part of a good thing that had to be done. Mary felt a nod of approval from her God, while fearing this may be her final duty as a woman. She wept joyous tears as she and George left the graduation ceremony.

In June 2000, George, eager to start a career thought joining the military would be an honorable way to both serve his country and improve his resume for civilian life. He remembered entering the army recruiting office in Wilkes- Barre, Pennsylvania. He approached a military looking desk where sitting behind it in an equally military looking chair sat a very serious female recruiting sergeant. The American flag and a missing-in-action flag asserted her authority.

Because George had a college degree he was offered a choice of OTS: Officer Candidate training School for approximately 17 weeks and receiving a second lieutenant commission upon completion or enlist, go directly into basic infantry training at Fort Dix , New Jersey, then start his military career as a private. Basic training seemed okay with him and he signed the papers. George passed the written and physical exams, received all the vaccinations, and was on his way.

In Basic Infantry training, George discovered that he was more gung-ho than he expected. Since he was a buff physically fit young man, he breezed through the obstacles courses and he enjoyed weapons training. The smell of gun powder that lingers after grenades explode and cannon are fired gradually becomes nostalgic.

Upon completion of basic training, George choose Combat Engineer as his next three-month phase of military training. Following a five day pass, which he spent with Mary and John, he arrived at Fort Leonard Wood, Missouri. There he learned to build temporary bridges that allowed troupes to cross and gain forward access positions along with other constructions under combat conditions. The first phase of Combat Engineer training was 14 weeks. George entered another twenty eight days to train as a Sapper (French for spade). As a Sapper, he learned to clear mine fields and to use explosives and implosives in demolitions. George was fortunate to complete his three years in the Army stateside. He was honorably separated from active duty and at the age of 23 armed with a college degree and special skill sets in demolition. He was ready to roll.

George bounced around working for different construction companies for several years, sometimes as a general laborer, a framer, roofer plumber. He did it all. George knew the experience was okay, a necessary part of his total knowledge in construction. He wanted to start his own company specializing in demolition. Using his savings he bought a pick-up truck and placed magnetic signs on both doors, reading GPDC - George Peters Demolition Company, and under the signs was a telephone number and an address. He was a crew of one. He was in business.

Since he had no local competition, his business took off quickly; he gradually hired a secretary and a crew. In his hiring he sought out veterans who served as Combat Engineers. His hiring policy proved to be successful his business flourished and at the age of 30 he was a millionaire. He joined the Chamber of Commerce and the Lions Club during the first several years of his business. Although he dated several girls during his social climbing years, he never married.

George wasn't a man of faith. He never thought of himself as a Christian, something about the hypocrisy he observed in the church goers who never seemed to practice what the bible taught troubled him. They seemed to be against any program that provided food, health care, or housing for the under privileged. They are against abortion but don't want to help a child when it's born. They simply never seem to care about their fellow man, unless it increases their financial bottom line.

Although George wasn't a church goer, he wasn't an atheist either. He felt a higher power certainly must exist. He believed the bio-mechanics of all living things are too perfectly engineered to ignore. So in his own way, his body and his work were his prayers, and he never criticized the value of other people's faith. He believed the third temple of God is in the church that resides inside your chest wall in your heart.

George was in a restaurant having a between contract negotiation with another businessman who brought up the subject of faith. Then the man paused and said, "I'm a Free Mason, and I belong to a local lodge. A person can't ask to become a Mason. You can only be sponsored by a member, and you must be a person of high moral character. The Masons have a program called 'Friend to Friend to recruit good men. You are a good man, well respected by me and in the community, and I'd consider it an honor to sponsor you if you're interested."

"Don't you have to be a Christian?" George asked.

"No," the man replied. "You must believe in God, but they don't tell what God to believe in." His friend went on to explain all of the good things Masons do and the charities they support like the Shiners Hospital. George was interested because he thought belonging to the Masons would be a way to fill that empty place in his soul. Although he as a successful businessman with a comfortable economic cushion, was ready to share his fruits with needy children. His friend did sponsor him, and he sailed through the home visitation.

It was a great enlightening experience as an Entered Apprentice, even more enlightening as a a second degree Fellow Craft Mason and the final third degree York right Master Degree Mason. He proudly walked among some of the greatest men in history, men such as George Washington, and Harry S. Truman. He later became a 32nd Scottish Rite Mason and a Noble Shiner. In that moment, a spiritual level of quiet contentment pervaded his being.

By the time George was in his late 30s, he was a well rounded, successful man. He enjoyed the respect of his friends and community. During all his growth years he never forgot his foster parents, and he visited them often and took them on some island cruises. He offered to buy them a new home, but they declined because they were comfortable in their humble home—the home where fate brought them all together.

The night before, George celebrated his 40th birthday, and some of his friends had a surprise party for him at the Pines bar and grill. The fog in his brain was clearing as he remembered downing Crown Royal shots to chug-a-lug shouts.

George was fully awake when he became aware of street life in Hazleton now picking up. He heard the sound delivery trucks make with their conveyor belts zinging cases of soda to a receiving man calling out their numbers and voices shouting to pedestrians waiting for a green light to cross the street. His thoughts turned to the meeting he would soon be attending. Do I really want to get involved was a replaying theme.

He was now in West Hazleton looking for the address when suddenly he was there. It was an office complex where all kinds of professionals had their private or corporate headquarters. He parked and started walking toward the entrance and then stopped. He couldn't decide if he should continue or just leave and forget the offer ever happened. Slowly, he moved forward and entered the building. On the wall was a directory. And there it was: Bevan's Development suite 10, third floor.

George felt the agony of a mysterious invitation to attend a land development proposal, which he assumed would be pitched to because of his demolition company. He entered the board room, which was well furnished with hand carved wooden chairs and expensive calf colored leather upholstery. His gaze went from the expensive furnishing to the three people sitting at the board table with their legal pads and pens in hand.

Two distinguished looking men had their faces pointed at him while a long haired woman with her back to him who was looking at a map on the wall, swung around and defiantly looked him in the eyes. It was none other than the woman from last night.

"George, I'm Sarah Ross," she began. "There is a project being considered to develop a large primary 100 hundred-acre piece of land into a modern community complete with recreational and commercial facilitation. Your company GDPC will be propositioned for the land preparation phase."

"My uncle Thomas is co-owner of Bevan's Development, and I asked him to help get me acquainted with you." Since he was already planning to invite your company into his development project he allowed me this opportunity.

"When I was 23 years old, working as a journalist on assignment for the *Washington Chronicle*, the big story at that time was about a series of congressmen who were assassinated. There was an organization known as TBA (Take Back America) allegedly led by Mr. Peter Fallow.

"Mr. Fallow was subsequently arrested and placed in Allenwood, a federal correctional facility in Pennsylvanian. I was assigned to go to Allenwood and interview Peter Fallow. Mr. Fallow was guarded and protective initially. However in dribbles he revealed some very interesting theories about wide spread corruption in our government. On my next scheduled visit with him, I was met by a member of the administration, who informed me there would be no more interviews with Mr. Fallow.

"It was all so mysterious and left me with an empty feeling. I could never understand why it all vanished. He simply disappeared, it was as though he never existed."

"Sarah, what does all of that have to do with me?" George asked.

"Have you ever heard of Michael Walters?" Sarah asked.

"No," George replied.

"All of the years since I was expelled from that prison interview, I've been driven to find out what happened to Mr. Fallow. Part of my research led to Ancestry.com, which gave the possibility of a match with you. Apparently you went into Ancestry one time to gain information about your own history. It turns out that Mr. Walters also researched his family history. The results are inconclusive, however the possibility exists that you may be a nephew.

"I propose you and I go to Tennessee and see if Mr. Walters, possibly your uncle could help me find out where Peter Fallow is."

"Sarah, why don't you just go by yourself," George asked. "Why do you need me?"

"Well, George, if he finds out that you might be his nephew it would become a more welcome visitation?"

The other two guys sitting at the conference table shook their heads in agreement and said, "George, the land development we have in mind when ready will still include an offer to your company.

George looked at Sarah for a long moment, keeping her in suspense then with a smile he said "hell yes."

They all stood up, shook hands, and thanked one another for the pleasure of their acquaintance. Sarah and George made plans to leave the following morning. They agreed to leave from his house at nine o'clock.

Right on time, Sarah Ross and George Peters were on the road heading for Knoxville, Michael Walter's last known address. George's curiosity was heightened since there was now a possible uncle in his life. Sarah's hope for an end to her seven-year mystery concerning Peter Fallow's disappearance was giving her a smug but orgasmic look on her face. George looked at her and smiled.

They made a pit stop in Columbus, Ohio, gassed up, had a hot dog and soup in the attached deli, and hit the road again. Their next stop was in Lexington, Kentucky, as they were having coffee in the service station they over heard someone mentioning Senator Mike McConner's name.

Sarah looked at George and George unable to control his emotion said "fuck that son-of-a bitch." The man in the booth who mentioned his name tapped on George's shoulder and said, "I agree."

They all laughed and continued on to Tennessee. The rest of the trip was scenic and peaceful, and on board were two crazy bastards in pursuit of hope.

It was closing in on noon when they arrived in Knoxville. They located the Walters' residence on Neyland Drive, on the North side of the Tennessee River. The house had great curb appeal—a white house with cobalt blue trim and a New Orleans feel to it upon our approach.

Answering their door knock was a very well preserved red haired female.

George nervously introduced himself and said, "There is a possibility that I may be your husband's nephew and I would very much like to meet him."

"Please come on in and sit," the woman said, pointing toward a leather upholstered coach. "By the way I'm Linda."

Linda left the room and appeared to be calling Michael from a stairway. A long minute passed when he finally appeared. He was a jaw dropping 68-year-old man who didn't look a day older than 50. He had a powerful looking muscular body absent the usual six pack, but he was still trim.

Mike charged toward George, extended his hand which he quickly retracted for an elbow bump, mindful that Covid variants were on the rise.

"Linda tells me that you believe you are my nephew?" Mike asked.

"Yes sir," George said. "Ancestry results indicate we could be a match."

"Honestly, George, my ancestry has been a mystery, but since my retirement I have more time to explore my heredity. In the interest of time, let's accept that we are related and go on from here as an uncle and nephew. Who's this lovely lady?"

"I'm Sarah Ross," Sarah said. "I was the journalist in 2005 who went to Allenwood prison to interview Peter Fallow who was incarcerated for the congressmen who were assassinated back then. My interviews were terminated and Mr. Fallow was mysteriously relocated to somewhere unknown. Anyway, since you were the lead investigator in the case, I hitched my wagon to George in the hopes of meeting you. I was hoping you might have some inside knowledge of where he is today and indeed if he is still alive? I'm saying that because if he's still alive I'm guessing his age to be around 91 or 92. If there is anything you know that could give me closure, I'd be ever so grateful."

"Ms. Ross I certainly understand your unfinished interview with Mr. Fallow in 2005, but I have absolutely no knowledge of where or what happened to Peter Fallow," Mike said. "When I resigned I was no longer privilege to any information. Linda and I have been enjoying our life together here in Tennessee, and have no regrets about our decision in 2005."

"I'm well aware that our country is suffering from the inept conduct of our former president and we are a deeply divided nation as a result of his pernicious untruths," Sarah said. "Mr. Walters, what is the difference with today's widespread corruption and that of 2005?"

"Sarah, in my opinion back then the TBA (Take Back America) was an organization comprised of disgusted hard-working Americans across the landscape: Democrat, Republican, Independents, Black, white, and every color in between. Their common concern was about the conspicuous in their face corruption of a sold out Congress.

"The obvious purchasers of our Democracy were the power grabbing Corporations," Mike continued. "Today's division is mainly raced based, with a vicious determination by White pseudo purists to take away all the minorities rights to vote. The US Constitution and our Democracy is in their way, and the only way to poison the history ignorant American people is when the elected political leaders systematically lie to the American people, and in that effort they are covertly aided by Russia. And through the use of social media are able to reach the unwitting susceptible idiots to swallow and perpetuate the lies.

"Back then, Sarah, I wasn't worried too much. I had confidence in our government. Today, I am worried, and you should be, too. Our Democracy is badly broken and in serious jeopardy. I'm sorry to let you down, Sarah. It saddens me that I can't be more helpful, and I do wish you well in your mission to locate Mr. Fallow. But now that you and George are here why not stay awhile. I'd like to get more acquainted with my nephew."

"Mr. Walters, will this mistrust of our government ever end?" Sarah asked.

"I hope so," Mike said. "But I think it will get worse long before it gets better. There are some 330 million Americans who are desperate for the tranquility of yesterdays unified United States. The division we are experiencing today makes it unlikely to see a unified America again. Well not in my lifetime, but maybe yours. The best advice I can offer is for you is to continue your search, use the contemporary social media tools, and motivate others of your generation to join your search."

Looking sheepishly at George, Sarah said, "If George agrees, I don't mind extending our visit, that is if we have separate rooms - for now- that is."

Linda lovingly moved toward her husband, wrapped her arms around his shoulders, and kissed him on the chin. "I don't know about the end of our Democracy or about the political corruption, but this I do know, my love for Michael will never end."

At that moment, a chime clock fell off the wall and broke into hundreds of pieces.

EPILOGUE

You're an unemployed parent with two children. You have no money, your family is hungry, and there's nothing to eat. You go into a grocery store and steal cheese and meat. You get caught, the police put you in jail, you're prosecuted as a thief and put in the county jail.

Or you point a gun at someone and take their money and credit cards. You're caught, taken into custody, and charged with armed robbery. You're found guilty and sent to state prison.

Or you plan to murder somebody and follow through. You're caught, charged with capital murder, convicted, and sent to prison for life.

The above men are convicted criminals and punished under the provisions of the law.

What about these scenarios?

You're a pharmaceutical corporation that buys a failing company's inexpensive drug for pennies, which has saved many lives. You rebrand the cheap drug and place it on the market, increasing the price by a thousandfold. People can't afford the drug, and as a result many die. Its euphemized murder, or at the very least fraud. The corporation makes millions, and instead of being called a criminal its executives enjoy the status of being a businessmen. If for some reason they are investigated and proven to be wrong, it's classified as "white collar crimes."

If you are an elected President or a member of Congress who votes for a phony war on a sovereign country without any evidence or just cause. And is conspicuously for the corrupted motivation of financial gain for war manufacturing corporations, and for the profit opportunity for private special military forces. And by their mercenary action millions of soldiers and unarmed citizens are killed, who are you who deceive and murder under the shield of our American flag? If you are a member of the house of representatives and accept cash or goods from a corporate lobbyist and exchange a yes or no vote on a bill, which is against the needs of the people you represent. In my opinion, you betrayed your oath of office and your constituents. Subsequently you leave the Congress and go to work for that same corporation's interest and then for big money you become their lobbyist. The people you fucked live in the ashes of your betrayal and you are never held accountable or prosecuted.

In America today, the common man who commits a crime with limited consequence on society, are quickly pounced upon by ambitious District Attorney's eager to make a name for themselves as being "tough on crime." Most often common people are unable to afford lawyers and have an adequate defense. On the other hand most of the corrupt politicians and Corporate leaders have armies of lawyers who are never prosecuted or held accountable for malfeasance. And they walk away and are rewarded with millions and sometimes billions of dollars in the bank.

Meanwhile the common people aware of the growing out of control irrelevance to the people are vulnerable and hungry for honest representation. But they are listening to the con men whose single ambition isn't to work hard every day for them to have a better quality of life, But instead they are systematically deceiving the people with untruths and blame others for all the social problems.

Ultimately they too become corrupted, and leave behind a trail of broken hearted citizens.

As Congressional replacements follow the same pattern of self enrichment, the suffering of the people becomes unbearable, and the lack of Congressional trust has become pernicious. And of course the bastards are never held accountable or prosecuted. As a result of a wide spread lethargic judicial system and the corruption in all our institutions of government - a government subservient to Corporate America are dedicated to their share holders; "we the people are being systematically deprived of the promise in our "pledge of allegiance - "liberty and justice for all," conspicuously is not happening. Voting rights and vote challenges are putting our Democracy in serious jeopardy. A woman's right to choose and voter rights have\s already been denied in some states. So how does a seriously divided people find a pathway back to a truthful unified nation and legally redress a failing democracy?

Allow me to introduce the social scientist John Locke, who in his treatise of government (parenthetically) related, "The people have a duty to obey their government when government acts in the best interest of the governed. However, when a government operates against the needs of its people, the people not only have a right to protest but a duty to civil disobedience."

With John Locke's theory in mind, let's remember our own Martin Luther King Jr and India's Gandhi's successful peaceful civil protests. Their Final Duty was by peaceful, civil protests, which today unfortunately is under attack by glorified racists who refuse to understand Section 1 of the 14th amendment. Peaceful demonstrators having no guns, clubs, firebombs, or stones. They're armed with the truth in peaceful, persistent protest demonstrations, honorable in the pursuit of their objectives.

Under the banner of truth, in victory everyone wins, and a people's Democracy is saved.